Hollywood Hookup

Also by Christy Swift

Celebrity Crush

Hollywood Hookup

CHRISTY SWIFT

FOREVER

New York   Boston

Copyright © 2026 by Christy Swift

Cover illustration by Cannaday Chapman
Cover design by Daniela Medina
Cover copyright © 2026 by Hachette Book Group, Inc.

Forever
Hachette Book Group
1290 Avenue of the Americas, New York, NY 10104
read-forever.com
@readforeverpub

First Trade Paperback Edition: February 2026

Forever is an imprint of Grand Central Publishing. The Forever name and logo are registered trademarks of Hachette Book Group, Inc.

The publisher is not responsible for websites (or their content) that are not owned by the publisher.

The Hachette Speakers Bureau provides a wide range of authors for speaking events. To find out more, go to hachettespeakersbureau.com or email HachetteSpeakers@hbgusa.com.

Forever books may be purchased in bulk for business, educational, or promotional use. For information, please contact your local bookseller or the Hachette Book Group Special Markets Department at special.markets@hbgusa.com.

Library of Congress Cataloging-in-Publication Data

Names: Swift, Christy author
Title: Hollywood hookup / Christy Swift.
Description: First trade paperback edition. | New York, NY : Forever, 2026.
Identifiers: LCCN 2025037757 | ISBN 9781538767788 trade paperback | ISBN 9781538767795 ebook
Subjects: LCGFT: Romance fiction | Novels | Fiction
Classification: LCC PS3619.W537 H65 2026
LC record available at https://lccn.loc.gov/2025037757

ISBNs: 9781538767788 (Trade paperback); 9781538767795 (Ebook)

Printed in the United States of America

CCR

10 9 8 7 6 5 4 3 2 1

To my BFF, Minna, who was the inspiration for Josie. Also to my friends in Spain and Mexico who shared their country, their culture, and their language with me.

Chapter 1

Nobody's looking at you.

Josie

IF I COULD have any superpower, it would be invisibility. Yes, I know flying is more fun, healing more practical, and controlling people with The Force more gratifying, but as I stride up the sidewalk to the gates of Sweet Spot Productions in Hollywood, I can't help wishing I could blend into the sun-bleached brick walls.

The security guard sees I have Peyton with me and waves us to the head of the line. Emmy told them I'd be bringing her, and while that's all I'm doing—dropping my best friend's daughter off to her at a studio—half of the nerve endings in my body are acting like I'm crossing into Dante's inferno.

Relax, Josie. Nobody's looking at you. And you'll be out of here before the taping even starts.

We duck out of the breezy October air and squeeze past the snake of studio audience participants waiting for permission to find their seats. My gaze skates across the sea of California-ready women, their hair: perfect; clothes: designer or as close to designer as they can manage; makeup: influencer-approved. Meanwhile, Peyton is the Gen Z poster child in a Bruh baseball cap and FBI shades, and I'm—what am I even wearing? Yoga pants and a Maná T-shirt I bought at a concert in Mexico City when I was seventeen, so it doesn't even fit anymore. My boobs look like they've been shrink-wrapped to my chest.

The shirt was a bad idea on several levels but mostly because it's a clue as to who I really am, and I don't need to be giving anyone any clues. I don't need any of this Hollywood crap—the cameras, the adrenaline, the "magic" of television. I forfeited a place in this world a long time ago and did a pretty good job avoiding it, but then Emmy got famous and kind of pulled me along in her wake.

Yeah, we'll just blame it on her.

As we *excuse me* our way through the excited crowd toward the stage, each glimpse of the hulking, heavy TV cameras sends my heart galloping. As a makeup artist for *Lost Star Dance Troupe Saves the Universe*, I work in a studio, but I know where all of our cameras are, and (spoiler alert) they're not in the makeup room. A few feet away, a grip shifts the spotlight, and my whole body flinches, but he's not turning it on me. He's highlighting a sign at the corner of the stage: *Date Your Celebrity Crush!*

Lord have all the mercies, the game show is a cringey gimmick, but it worked. Emmy says the contest featuring the four leading men from *Lost Star* has raised over two million dollars for the local children's hospital. If it had cost body parts instead of money, I expect we'd be seeing a lot of women hopping on one foot for a chance to go on a date with one of the hottest hunks in Hollywood. I would not be one of them.

"There's my mom!" Peyton shouts. I love this kid as if she were my own, but she is loud. If the *Quiet Place* aliens ever show up for real, Peyton and anyone within one hundred feet of her will be the first to go, which is too bad because otherwise, I'd easily be the grizzled old survivor with a rifle and a bunker full of pork and beans. I've been operating under the radar for so long, it's become second nature.

Emmy waves us out of the crowd, her highlighted curls pulled into a flirty pineapple ponytail, her dewy makeup making her look sun-kissed and shiny in her formfitting gold dress. She's cohosting the show today, and even though you can't tell she's pregnant from the back, it's her waddle that gives her away.

Until Emmy got pregnant, the only things I knew about pregnancy were what I learned when I fake-delivered a six-month-old on set during a taping of *Bajo el Mismo Paraguas* at my stepfather's studio down in Mexico. My Spanish was decent, but my character's wasn't, so there was a lot of me shouting a poorly conjugated *push!* over and over again. Now, however, I've got an insider peek at what two people in love making a brand-new person looks like. It's pretty amazing.

It's also pretty amazing seeing Emmy in her element like this—the star I always knew she'd become. "You look great," I tell her as she kisses her daughter's baseball cap before sending her off.

"Thanks." She hugs me and adds an extra squeeze. "Listen, I need a favor."

I freeze. I don't like the sound of that. Not here. Not now. On set, cameras everywhere.

"One of our contestants had to bow out. I need a replacement."

I glance around and spot the other Jason—the colossal Jason "Mount" Ramirez, not Emmy's husband, Jason Connor—skirting a corner. Through an open door, someone rises from a chair, his identity blurred by a swarm of hairspray particles. I think it's Zachary Tay.

I swallow hard. "Wow, you need a replacement contestant for a celebrity dating show? Wherever will you find one?"

Emmy's nostrils flare. "It can't just be some rando, Josie. What if she's a serial killer? Or a multilevel marketer? I can't subject the guys to that."

"Is that why your contestant had to 'bow out'? You found out she sells essential oils?"

"No! She had a heart attack. She's, like, eighty, and she's had transplants and I don't know what else, and she's got a super-huge crush on Sean O'Sullivan."

At the mention of his name, my traitorous heart leaps. There's no excuse for it. It's not like I've never met the guy. He's one of Jason Connor's closest friends, and I do work on the *Lost Star* set. I've gotten a hug from the fearless Captain Footwork, danced with him once, too. I'm still recovering from both of those things. But this is too big an ask.

"Emmy, I can't," I whisper.

"Why not?"

My voice box slams shut like she's asked me for the launch codes. I haven't told Emmy everything about my past. She knows I used to live in Mexico when I was a kid, long enough that I sometimes still think in Spanish, but I kind of left out my show-biz career and the dumpster fire that turned into. For example, she has no idea that, for six years, I starred in the highest-rated bilingual children's show in the country. My stepsister, Lupe, and I had a regular segment with her ventriloquist puppet about learning languages and cultural exchange and how not to be a total jerk to kids who were different from you, which is ironic because, off set and at home, we were often total jerks to one another.

Club Bilingüe was an instant hit. In fact, we were so popular that an educational firm in the States licensed our content for their ESOL and Spanish-language programs. Our smiling faces appeared in textbooks and classrooms from New York to LA. We were featured on *Sesame Street* three times. We even had a theme song: "Friends Para Siempre." Emmy has no idea that, for a lot of folks in Mexico and the U.S., this gringa is a household name.

Well, not *Josie Days*. They don't know me by that name. They know me by my real name—Savannah Bateman.

"You know how I feel about cameras," I say.

I don't remember exactly what excuse I gave Emmy the last time she tried to wrangle me into the spotlight. When you tell enough lies, they all start to run together, like watercolor paints. Not that I use watercolors. When I create art, I like it bolder: acrylic and gouache or thick, sticky oil pastels. Anyway, I think I told her something she could identify with—that the eye of the camera triggered me because it reminded me of the Eye of Sauron. Stupid, I know, but a lot of people were traumatized by *The Lord of the Rings* movies. That was a lot of orc. Mucho orco.

"Sometimes, in our heads, things can seem bigger than they are." Emmy's hazel eyes are determined. "I need you. A lot of people gave money to this. We've announced one hundred contestants, so we can't run the show with only ninety-nine. Contestants have to be vetted, and because I know you and I love you, you're automatically vetted."

"Whatever happened to backups?"

"We already used the backups. Apparently, there's this thing that happens to people called life."

I don't want to disappoint Emmy. She's my best friend, practically my family. She got me the makeup artist gig on *Lost Star* after I mortgaged my soul for F/X makeup classes, and I love getting to be a part of showbiz again, in a safe, hidden, backstage kind of way. But I can't be in front of the cameras ever again. It's just…not possible. If anyone finds out who I really am, it'll be another shit show.

It's amazing how something stupid you did when you were eighteen can haunt you for the rest of your life. But whatever. That's life, right? We screw up, we flee the country, we dye our hair and change our name, and we move on, hiding out with our estranged bio dad, getting him all excited that he's reconnecting with his kid, and then we find out he's really sick and take care of him until he's gone, and then we're alone, with a cosmetology certificate and just enough money to buy a trailer and plop it on a pad in a sweaty trailer park on the Gulf of Mexico. Maybe make a friend or two. Or just one.

But she's a good one, and those are hard to come by.

Maybe I'm overreacting. My rational brain tells me the world should have forgotten about me by now. They probably would have, too, if my stepsister's beloved puppet hadn't been ruined and gone missing along with me. There wouldn't be news stories and conspiracy theories and *Bring Back Chuy* memes. I haven't seen one of those for a while, thank goodness.

Still… "It's a hard *no*, Emmy. I'm sorry."

I hate the hurt look on her face. She doesn't take my shit as much anymore since she leveled up from bestselling novelist to bona fide celebrity, so I know I've got it coming.

"Anxiety is a liar, Josie, and I'm not going to let it make you miss out on a chance to go on a date with Sean O'Sullivan." My face heats, and she adds, "Uh-huh," as if I've just openly pledged my undying love to the man instead of having a completely uncontrolled physiological reaction.

"I don't want to date anyone famous. That lifestyle isn't for everyone," I complain, but she's already grabbed my hand and is navigating us through the staff-choked hallways like a couple of spies through a lasered security net.

"This wouldn't be *dating* him, it would be *a date*, just like it would be for poor Vera hooked up to her EKG right now. No strings attached. . . . just electrodes."

Emmy halts in front of a barely cracked door. The sign above it reads PRIVATE GREEN ROOM. Inside, five of the hottest men in Hollywood are sitting along the walls, sipping clear or dark liquid out of etched glasses, chatting, and looking at their phones. What they spent on shoes and haircuts alone could fund a small nation for a year. You wouldn't think a show called *Lost Star Dance Troupe Saves the Universe* would contain as much testosterone as it does, but hoo-boy. I think it's the choreography. Or maybe all that butt-hugging space-leather.

The scent of them wafts into the hallway—subtle, like a fragrance insert in a men's magazine—and I'm yanked back to the night I danced with Sean O'Sullivan at the Pershing Square ice skating rink. He was wearing a ridiculous stocking cap, and his coat smelled like this when I hid my face from the cameras in it. I held on tight as he led me, spinning and spinning, while the air throbbed with Wham!'s "Last Christmas," and the lights around us sparkled, and I got lost in time and space and the firm grip of Captain Footwork's arms just like his alien lover in that one episode that I secretly watched over and over and lied to Emmy about when she caught me.

"Josie?"

"Electrodes," I repeat to confirm I'm listening, not fantasizing. Also, electrodes sound pretty good right now. I could use something to zap my heart back into rhythm.

"I know you like him," she says. "It's written all over your face."

Accurate, if the going definition of *like* also describes the feeling I get when I see a perfect pudding parfait with its whipped cream in a flawless whirl like Ramona always manages to do with Captain Footwork's pompadour. I just want to shove my face into it and gobble it up without breathing. The parfait, not the pompadour.

"I work on the show," I argue. "That's got to disqualify me."

"Nope," Emmy chirps. "Our lawyers kept it wide-open on purpose. Even their moms can win it. Heck, their *dads* could win it!"

"Aren't I supposed to make a donation? I don't have any extra cash right now."

"I'll do it in your name. Come on, Josie. You deserve nice things, too."

A bud of guilt blossoms in my chest. Would she say that if she knew that I've been lying to her about who I really am? In six years of friendship, I've never had the guts to find out.

I'm scrambling for another excuse when the green room door pulls all the way open, the scent of cologne mushrooms our way, and suddenly there, standing in a rectangle of light, is my perfect Irish cream pudding parfait—Sean O'Sullivan.

Chapter 2

Why am I still here?

Josie

ALL SIX FEET one inch and one-hundred-ninety pounds of Sean O'Sullivan engulfs the doorway in an amethyst purple unstructured suit, eggplant scarf, and John Lennon glasses. I freeze as the proximity of this outrageously sexy Professor Plum living his best life in tweed overwhelms me. He smells like a dark room full of leather-spined books, maybe with a spinning door leading to a mysterious lair with a low bed covered in silk sheets. His fingers are adorned with rings of every flavor of precious metal: gold, platinum, vibranium, unobtainium—I'm not sure about those last two. Jewels, too. Emeralds, diamonds, a thick slice of amber.

God, why am I so attracted to him? It's not even fair.

"How's Vera?" he asks Emmy in a breathy whisper. His Van-dyke facial hair only serves to accentuate the natural pout of his extraordinary mouth. I've touched that mouth—twice, actually. For work.

"In surgery, but her prognosis is good."

Who are they talking about? Oh, right. Heart attack grandma. "You know her?" I blurt out, and when those emerald-green eyes fix on mine, something inside me lurches to life like a rickety carnival ride that's not safe to operate.

"No, but I'm her Number One."

"Her Number One?" Why am I asking so many questions? Why am I speaking? Why am I still here?

"I'm trying to talk Josie into taking her place," Emmy explains, "but she's being difficult."

Suddenly, I'm fully aware of how not-California I am right now. Yes, yoga pants are acceptable, but not these yoga pants, purchased in a three-pack from Costco. I'm a makeup artist, yet I sport a rush job—base and some tinted lip gloss and mascara compared with Emmy's popping eyes and Sean's pores-don't-exist cheeks. My beat-up Skechers with their toes pointing toward Sean's calfskin loafers embroidered in gold thread (probably by artisans in Spain) look like poor orphans asking *please, sir, can I have some more?* In my defense, I thought I was just dropping Peyton off!

"You'll do it, won't you?" he asks.

The question is delivered in a gentle, vulnerable, dare I say, pleading way. I've seen him deliver lines this way a million times, but I'm hypnotized and battle the urge to reply, *Yes, of course, anything you want, Sean.*

"Yes, of course, anything y—" I manage to cut myself off

there. Blurting has always been my toxic trait. "Anything for the children," I choke out.

"Excellent!" His pleading expression transforms into one of confident satisfaction. He follows it up with a soul-destroying wink and then smooths the dyed-yellow lock of hair on his wavy, dark head before turning and taking his place in the Seventh Circle of Hot Guy Heaven.

Emmy shoves a ticket into my hand and gives me a loud, smacking air-kiss. "Thank you! You're seat number sixty-three. There's a QR code on the back of that ticket. Use it to fill out the questionnaire in case you make it to the later rounds."

I mumble something unintelligible. A Colombian friend taught me a phrase for this cosmically horrible type of happenstance. Cagada marciana. *That shit fell from Mars.* I feel like that sums up my current situation quite nicely.

"Remember, you're just a butt in a chair." Emmy steers me through the backstage maze to the audience seats. "The math is in your favor—one hundred contestants and only five winners. If you tank the questions on that questionnaire, you'll have even less of a chance of getting picked."

"What if I don't answer the questions at all?"

"You have to."

"What if I don't?"

"Then I'll have Peyton answer them for you."

"Sold. Tell her to make them horrible."

"It'll make her day."

Emmy's co-emcee, Terica, appears at her shoulder in a bright blue wig, her halo eye impeccable. She flashes me a sheepish grin. "I need to take this mama away from you for a few minutes. There's been an incident with my cue cards."

"What incident?" Emmy whirls, the end of her curly pony-tail almost whipping me in the face as I lean back. But I don't wait to hear the rest because I have my own incident to deal with, and seat number sixty-three to get to, and a panic attack to head off at the Not-OK Corral. The audience is a restless, murmuring sea around me as I slink to the third row and find my designated place between Smiley Bohemian Lady and Emo Teen. My seat is far to stage right. That's good—less of a chance of the cameras finding me.

It'll be okay. I'm just an audience member, one of a hundred. There's no reason for anyone to single me out. I'll do whatever it takes to get eliminated early on, and this crisis will be averted. Note to self: drop Peyton at the gate next time. She'll be fine. We'll both be fine. Everything is fine.

My notifications ping. It's a message in Spanish from Miguel—the one friend from my past whom I've kept in touch with. We start chatting.

> **Miguel:** Did you watch the last episode of *Más Allá de las Estrellas*? It's the one I was telling you about! The one where I cry real tears!

> **Savannah:** Of course I watched it. But I don't believe for a minute those were real tears. Juan Ernesto was off camera flicking water at your face.

> **Miguel:** ¡No manches! That's my proudest moment.

> **Savannah:** Seriously, you were great. You're all great. It's the best show on TV.

It's true. Miguel is doing a fantastic job on this new sci-fi show my stepfather, Juan Ernesto, is producing. Everyone is, in fact, including my stepsister, Lupe, who plays the young, female captain. The writing is fantastic, the characters are nuanced, and the plot lines have surprised me at every turn. I'm happy for all of them. It's the first big hit Castillo Studios and its cast have had since I blew up *Club Bilingüe.*

I'm pretty sure that my recklessness cost my stepsister a couple of prominent telenovela roles over the next couple of years. Mom told me when she was auditioning for them and when she was turned down. I watched both of those shows after they came out. Lupe would've been a perfect fit, but the studios likely considered her a liability. How could audiences see her as anything else but that girl from the puppet scandal?

A scandal that could have been avoided if I'd made better choices.

Miguel: How's Florida?

I hesitate. I haven't told Miguel that I moved to California.

Savannah: I'm starting your fan club. I'm the president. Now I just need to find another member to make it official.

Miguel: Ha ha. By the way, your mom says hi.

I grimace. I haven't told my mom about the move, either. It's harder to stay hidden here in Hollywood than it was in sleepy little New Port Richey, Florida, and I can't take any chances. Besides, talking to my mom always ends in the same conversation—her trying to get me to come down there for a visit, which I can't do. And it's not like I never see her. After Dad died, we set up a yearly get-together. She flies into Orlando every spring, and we spend a nice weekend at one of the Disney resorts. Even that's been hard to pull off since I moved out to LA. I suppose I could tell her I'm in California now, but then there'd be questions, speculations, and whatnot. People could overhear. People could talk.

Savannah: You haven't told Juan Ernesto that we talk, right? Or Lupe?

Miguel: You ask me this every time.

Savannah: Is that a no?

Miguel: It's a no. Although, would it be such a bad thing?

Of course it would be a bad thing, and Miguel should know this! Savannah Bateman needs to stay buried and forgotten, like velociraptor DNA. She was a spoiled little diva whose temper tantrum on live TV ruined a show and a brand, not to mention a puppet beloved by children across North America. Well, they're all adults now, but whatever.

Just then, a woman with a headset steps onstage and begins to hype us up. I tell Miguel I need to go and add my reserved clapping to the hubbub. Wow, these women are positively rabid for their celebrities. That's good. If I somehow get picked, it'll be easy to do a handoff. In the midst of our cheering, Emmy and Terica take the stage. Our handler urges us to cheer even louder, if that's possible.

"Welcome, welcome!" Terica greets us.

"Thank you so much for being a part of this important event!" Emmy adds.

"Out of the thousands of entries in the *Date Your Celebrity Crush!* contest, you all were lucky enough to be chosen to be here today!"

"And no matter what happens, you're all going home with an amazing gift!"

The volume of cheering rises. I should have brought my noise-canceling headphones.

"But…" Emmy pauses until the decibel level dies down. "Only half of you are going to get to come up here with us onstage…"

"…when we bring out our five dreamy studs and really get this competition going!" Terica finishes.

A curtain at the back of the stage is whisked away, revealing several rows of empty chairs. "Look under your seats right now! See if you're one of the lucky fifty!" Emmy cries.

"That's it, right now! If there's something under there, hold it up!" Terica crows.

A rustling sound rips through the audience as a hundred contestants, mostly women, reach down under their seats. The only difference between them and me is that they are hoping to find something while I'm begging the universe to let the bottom of my chair be empty.

My palm smacks against the plastic underside of the seat. For a split second, I think I might be home free and able to slink out the emergency exit for a Starbucks on the way home. Then I feel it—the laminated corner of something taped to the bottom of the chair. I rip it free and stare at the yellow sign screaming WINNER in a chunky black sans serif font. My heart starts whipping like a sheet in a hurricane. I need to get rid of this. Like *now*.

"Here, take this!" I shout to Smiley Bohemian Lady, realizing a split second later that she's not paying attention to me because she's too busy screaming her head off over her own laminated winner sheet.

I pivot to Emo Teen, but she's got one, too. What the hellustrations? Am I sitting in Winner Row?

Apparently I am, because the first several rows of women are all on their feet, waving their yellow papers above their heads and jumping up and down like the studio has transformed into an adult bouncy house. The staff steps in, guiding us to move from our seats to the chairs onstage in an orderly fashion.

Oh, hell to the no. I can't do this—be onstage where anyone can see me. I didn't sign up for that. Still, I follow the crowd, brain firmly in lizard mode, eyes peeled for lit exit signs. I spot one and lurch in that direction only to be blocked by a team of grips toting an enormous cutout of Sean's head. I try to wait them out, but the line of women presses against me from behind. There's no way I'm strong enough to hold back the *Celebrity Crush* Sea! As I'm buoyed forward against my will, Peyton falls into step beside me, further blocking my access to freedom.

"I used an AI program to fill out your questionnaire." Her eyes shine with pride as she hands me a printed sheet of paper.

"Did you tell it to answer the questions like a sociopath?"

She giggles. "Of course not, Tía. Why would I do that?"

At this point, I'm squarely onstage, and if I bolt now, I'll call even more attention to myself. In a move born of pure, desperate self-preservation, I snatch the ball cap off Peyton's head and transfer her sunglasses to my own face. The only thing that's going to save me now is wardrobe.

"Gracias, querida," I say, giving her a heartfelt squeeze. Peyton and Emmy are always begging me to teach them Spanish, and I love doing it. It's a little piece of Mexico I've gotten to hold onto. And to share.

"De nada, Tía," she replies. "¡Suerte!"

I don't need good luck.

I need the opposite.

And just like that, I'm on-camera for the first time in twelve years.

Chapter 3

It's showtime, Cap'n!

Sean

I EASE BACK into my chair in the green room and take a sip from my tumbler of iced mineral water. I've got three more pounds to lose before my movie audition, so alcohol's on the no-go list for now. Besides, the studios never invest in anything nicer than Wild Turkey. A good Johnnie Walker Blue Label...now that's worth an extra one hundred sit-ups, not the watered-down dishwater in Jason Connor's glass.

I peek at my phone. Five minutes until the online auction wraps up. I'm still in the lead. Some jerk-off could swing in and snipe it from me at the last minute, but so far so good.

I swipe around to the main photo and have to bite back a huge grin from just looking at the item I'm bidding on: Christopher

Jackson's hat from his role as George Washington in the original Broadway production of *Hamilton*. The thing is epic. It's huge. It's iconic. It's got that weird little bow thing on the front right side. I gotta have it.

Four more minutes until the auction ends.

Jason leans over. "Whatcha doin'?" he asks.

"Nunya bidness." I slip my phone under my thigh.

"Do you always swipe with your ring finger? I've never noticed before."

"Don't you have anything better to do than bother me?"

"Nope!" He grins, and I know he's being honest. We're in a holding pattern here. "By the way, did you get everything taken care of?" he asks.

"What are you talking about?"

"The gaping hole in your dance card since Vera went to the hospital."

"Oh yeah, right." I peek at the phone. Shit! Someone's outbid me—@cosplayhero92. Well, we'll see who the real hero is. "Uh, Emmy's friend is filling in."

"Which one?"

I know her name, I do; I just can't think of it at the moment as my ring finger stabs in a higher bid. I could wait until the last second, but then I run the risk of bad Wi-Fi ruining it for me. "The pretty one who works on set. Alien makeup girl."

"Josie?"

I snap my fingers. "That's the one."

He cranes his neck at my phone. "What are you doing? Shopping for women's hats?"

What a pleb. "It's a men's Revolutionary War–era tricorn hat."

"Oh yeah," he replies. "Like the one that was stolen a few

weeks ago in New York City. It's all over the news." His eyes go wide. "Maybe it's that one!"

My stomach lurches. I didn't expect Snack to be versed in any current events that didn't involve American football. "That's a stupid thing to say. Do you think I shop on black market auction sites? What do I look like, a criminal? Besides, this is just for research."

A quick peek reveals that @cosplayhero92 has outbid me again! Who does this guy think he is? I up my bet to something outrageous, something that would make Christopher Jackson blush.

I do shop on black market auction sites—at least, I have been lately—but I'm not a criminal. I'll turn the hat in after I win it. I just want to see it up close. Touch it. Wear it. It's Christopher Jackson's hat, for crying out loud. From *Hamilton*.

"Research for what?"

God, is he still here? "Just something my agent found," I lie. "Soldier, secondary character, takes a bayonet in the chest."

"And you're interested in that?"

I roll my eyes. "Yes, I want to die on-screen, tragically. It's on my bucket list, right next to a sweaty, passionate night with you."

He grins and downs his drink. "I'm flattered, Sean. I didn't figure you were passionate about anything."

"Ha ha," I deadpan. I don't owe Jason any explanations, and besides, no matter how I try to explain it, it'll sound stupid. I know it's just a hat. A silly indulgence, unimportant in the grand scheme of things. Unimportant in the not-so-grand scheme of things, too. But it's important to me.

Christopher Jackson's original hat from *Hamilton* is one of a kind. It's special. Unique. Priceless. I love that show, and it would look great on me. I could wear it to the *Hamilton on the Roof* gig in Van Nuys before returning it. Of course, I alone would know it was me, Sean O'Sullivan, wearing Christopher Jackson's original hat to what amounts to *The Rocky Horror Picture Show* for Lin-Manuel Miranda fans, but that would be enough. I wouldn't even care if I didn't get reimbursed by insurance.

Everyone around me is standing up, setting their drinks down, and checking their looks on their phones. I confirm my bid and curse as @cosplayhero92 outbids me immediately. Who the hell is this guy? My costar Andrew Valentine steps across my lap to get by me, pausing with his chinos-clad package squarely in my face.

I lurch backward. "Do you mind?"

His shit-eating grin tells me it was on purpose. "It's showtime, Cap'n!"

"I need a minute."

"Minute's up."

Andrew's right. I'll look like a douchebag if I miss my entrance, but I can't let @cosplayhero92 get George Washington's hat! I shuffle into line with the others, still scrolling on my phone.

Two minutes until the auction ends.

I raise the upper ceiling of my bid to a new number. A shameless number. The floor should open up and plunge me straight into the fiery depths of rich people hell for this number. I count and recount the zeroes, because if I make a mistake, I'll be eating dinner at the Salvation Army tonight.

Now we're all lined up in the wings, a herd of well-dressed cattle radiating adrenaline and cologne.

"Hey, Sean, look at that." Jason points up into the rafters. When I glance up, he snatches the phone out of my hand. I should've seen that coming. Shit, and right when the auction's about to end, although there's no way I could bid any higher.

Jason scoffs. "This isn't research. It's an online auction. Jesus Christ, is that your bid?"

I snag the phone back, my heart in my throat as I check the results.

I won! Christopher Jackson's hat is mine. The victory tastes as sweet as Mam's trifle, and it feels like helium's been pumped into my veins. I don't even look at how much it cost me. Whatever it is, it's worth it.

"No, of course not." I pocket the phone, glancing past Jason, my face neutral. It's a power move I've learned—deflection, part of controlling the narrative. "That would be ridiculous. Now quit messing around. It's a fundraiser, after all."

I won the auction! The hat is mine. All mine. I wish I could shake @cosplayhero92's hand. He put up a good fight.

The grip waves us in, and I launch into a roundoff backflip across the stage to outrageous applause. It's the only way I can think of to burn off some of this pent-up energy. The audience is on their feet, screaming their heads off. I jump up, touch my toes in the air, and then take a bow before settling into my seat between Andrew and Jason Connor.

"Show-off," Andrew mutters.

"Eat your heart out, cowboy." I lean back in my chair, tuck my plum-colored scarf back into the neck of my shirt, and straighten the lapels of my lilac Comme des Garçons tweed jacket. The suit was surprisingly stretchy and accommodating during those stunts. I give my pompadour an exploratory pat. It doesn't feel like it suffered any casualties.

Well, that was fun, but now it's back to work. I force my face into nonchalance as I turn to the sea of women before me and await my fate.

Chapter 4

Is my dancing not bad enough?

Josie

IT'S EASY TO hide when the *Lost Star* guys come out. All I have to do is hunch my shoulders and take a teeny-weeny step backward, and suddenly I'm concealed by a wall of celebrity-induced insanity. Geez, ladies, they're just men. They have the same hardware as all the other guys you see on the street every day; it's just packaged differently.

I have to say they do look good. Emmy's gotten Jason away from those athleisure pants he loves so much and into jeans with a black silk vest over a charcoal, long-sleeved button down. The other Jason in the cast, Jason Ramirez, looks like his floral shirt has been painted onto his muscular torso, the dark teal background and cherry-red flowers complementing his brown skin.

Andrew's all in white. I think he's got a "good guy" complex, either that or he's planning on scooting out of here as soon as possible to jump on the next yacht to Monaco. Zachary Tay is so lovable it doesn't matter what he puts on. He could show up in a unicorn onesie, and the next day, unicorn onesie stock would go up ten points. Today he's got on a cream-colored crewneck sweater, dark jeans, and square-toed leather shoes.

The thing they all have in common is that they look halfway normal, unlike Mr. Grape Soda Bedroom Eyes Tilt-a-Whirl. I don't think Sean could call any more attention to himself if he tried. That purple avant-garde getup. The flips. All those rings up and down his fingers suggest he shook down the Elves and Dwarves and Men in a dark alley outside of Mordor. The One Ring probably threw itself at him, crying, *Take me, too! Please!* I know I would—he could wrap me around one of those fingers. Confidence is attractive.

Oops! We're sitting down again. I tug Peyton's cap farther down my forehead and press the sunglasses up the bridge of my nose. I'd better pay attention. Stay alert for my next opportunity out of this heinous trap. I swear, Emmy owes me big time.

Emmy and Terica banter with the celebrity crushes as the grips deal out lanyards with numbers on them to all of us contestants. Sean can't sit still. Does he have grasshoppers in those purple tweed pants?

"All right, contestants!" Emmy booms into the mic. "That last selection was based purely on luck, but you're gonna have to earn this next one."

The women around me exchange nervous glances. I'm just glad I'm going to have an opportunity to fail. Whatever it is, I'm ready to suck at it. Hard.

"Our next game is a dance-off!" Emmy trills.

"Out of your seats!" Terica shouts as Rihanna's "We Found Love" blasts across the speakers. "Come on, let's see your moves!"

We're herded to a dance floor in front of our chairs. I have to say, being a contestant is the life. All you have to do is show up, and people tell you exactly what to do from then on. I wish I had this kind of direction in my real life. And I have zero doubts about my ability to dance poorly. I mean, I can dance well, too, but nobody needs to know that.

As soon as I'm in place, I turn my back to the cameras and the audience. All of the celebrity crushes are watching us, each with a flip pad and a pen. Are they writing down our numbers if they like us? I hope so, since they can't even see mine. My neighbor on the right is doing the suburban-white-girl shuffle. My neighbor on the left has some skills, but I'm worried she might get whiplash. As for me, there are a few ways I could play this. In a nod to the fact that it's Halloween season, I go for a zombie-with-its-head-halfway-chopped-off-by-a-marginally-effective-axe-blow and hold out my arms in "Thriller" stance. My sneakers stay planted on the stage because I'm afraid of getting too close to Whiplash Girl—the human skull flung with enough velocity can act like a wrecking ball. Instead, I just do some knocky knees.

A grip marches my way, and my heart soars as I anticipate the inevitable tap on the shoulder that will signal that, *Awww, sorry, you're eliminated*. But she just takes my lanyard and whips it over my shoulder so the guys can see it. Fair enough.

But why am I still here? Is my dancing not bad enough?

My knees are getting tired, and my neck is getting sore. I peek at the men. They're all scribbling away on their notepads, taking this very seriously.

Dammit. I'd better up my game. Or perhaps less is more.

When I get tired of dancing TikToks with Peyton, I do this thing that drives her nuts. I just gaze up at the ceiling and turn in a slow circle. I call it "The Old Tired Adult move."

But when the music cuts out, I'm still here.

I take my seat, bewildered, as Emmy and Terica chat up the celebs.

"So, what were you guys looking for when you made your choices?" Terica asks.

"Was it how good their moves were?" Emmy offers.

"I don't know," Andrew says. "I was looking more for attitude. And energy."

"Everybody knows I'm no authority on this subject," Zachary adds, earning laughs. Apparently, his dancing was so bad in the short time he was on *Lost Star Dance Troupe Saves the Universe* that they had to write it into the script.

"What about you, Sean?" Terica prods.

"Well, Terica, I just looked for something interesting. Something different." His green eyes laser straight to me, and I feel all the blood vessels in my face go supernova.

Then I spot the eye of the camera and that nuanced little combination of movements that tells me it's zooming in.

Crap! I slink down into my seat. Why is this happening? Everything was good. Everything was fine. I was happy, quote unquote, for whatever that trite sentiment is worth. I should have stayed in Florida working at Tranquilidad Spa. It kept changing owners and names, but the tips were decent, and it gave me a chance to use my Spanish. But after Emmy and Peyton left, I was lonely.

That's it, isn't it? I overplayed my hand. Got too cocky. Forgot my place.

I adjust my hat and glasses. No more games. No more nuance. I'm getting kicked out of this competition if I have to get arrested to do it. The trick, however, is to fade into obscurity rather than attract attention. I need to be boring. Forgettable. The kind of woman Sean O'Sullivan would overlook. A beige lamp on an oak end table.

Challenge accepted.

Chapter 5

Since when do I make women wince?

Sean

"ALL RIGHT, ALL right, all right!" Emmy says in a not-terrible imitation of Matthew McConaughey. "Moving right along to the next competition. We're down to thirty contestants, and it's getting real."

"We know everybody made a donation to the Children's Hospital Fund in order to be here today." Terica pauses while the screen behind her jumps to life with information about the fundraising initiative. "But we also want to make sure our celebrities have fun. They're giving up their personal time, so the least we can do is make sure we match them with someone who's a good fit."

As she speaks, the dance contest winners are filed by us like cuts of steak in a restaurant. I have to admit it's nice that they're trying to fix us up with someone compatible, but it's not like any of us cares. It's not a date. It's work. Whoever I get is getting two hours of my time, tops.

Unless maybe it's that quirky makeup girl—Emmy's friend, Josie. What is up with her? It's almost like she doesn't want to win. Who wouldn't want to win a date with one of us?

Maybe she thinks she'll get Jason Connor. She's probably sick of him since he's married to Emmy and they hang out all the time at their nerdy game nights. But I'm her Number One pick, or at least, I was Vera's Number One pick, which is transferable. That means I'd most likely be the one she'd get matched with. If she doesn't want to go on a date with one of us, it's me she doesn't want to go on a date with.

Why wouldn't she want to go on a date with me?

The rest of the contestants are smiling and waving and blowing kisses to us as they take their seats. I'm feeling more and more like the steak in my analogy. But sometimes you just gotta own it, like Tay, who is spread across his chair like a tomcat, nodding and winking and aiming finger guns. Connor's smolder might burn the whole place down if he's not careful, and Ramirez is relying on his dimples, the cheat. Andrew isn't even paying attention—he's leaned way over, deep in conversation with Emmy with his hand over his mic, probably bragging about the great date he has planned for his winner. That dude always ruins the curve.

Next thing I know, the mysterious, purple-haired friend of Emmy's is headed my way, trailing the pack. I lower my Gucci teashades and set my sights on her. It's proven that people can sense when other people are staring at them, and she's gotta feel that burn. But she shuffles right past me, face forward and hidden under a ball cap and a pair of tinted Oakleys. I've seen

Emmy's daughter wearing both of those before. Did she lose a bet to Peyton or something?

That has to be it. She's doing it for a bet or on a dare, and she's embarrassed. That's adorable. I feel better already.

I thank the grip who slips me a paper with the numbers of the ladies who listed me as Number One or Two in their top choices and who are still alive in the competition. Then I'm ushered, along with the others, to my own private *Dating Game*-esque box with a computer screen nested in it. Upon closer inspection, I see the screen contains questions for us to ask the contestants along with the answers they provided on their applications. Ramirez is up first.

"Number Eleven, Nancy, what's the most adventurous thing you've ever done or would like to do?" he reads from the monitor, his voice deep and gravelly on purpose. He flexes his pecs for emphasis, and everyone laughs.

A thin, nervous-looking woman answers. "I've always wanted to drive a riding lawn mower."

Silence follows, because what do you say to that? She hurries to add, "I don't mean like a regular one, but the kind that spins around on one wheel. We have a big lawn, and they look so fun, and they do such a good job of mowing!"

"A zero-point mower," Emmy explains to a baffled Ramirez. He's probably never mowed a lawn in his life. I know I haven't. "And yes," she confirms, "they do do an excellent job."

Terica steps in. "Okay, Number Thirty, Soraya, why don't we have Sean ask you a question?"

I clear my throat and scan my touch screen. "Hello, Soraya," I say as I stall. "Thanks for being here today."

"My pleasure," she replies in a voice that's all velvet and unfiltered cigarettes. "And yours, if you'll let it be."

I don't respond to her blatant advance, instead focusing on picking a question from the list. "What's the most unique talent you have?" Oh boy, that was a mistake; I can tell already.

"I can put my legs all the way behind my head."

"Impressive." She wrote "acrobatics" on her application. I guess that tracks.

Terica and Emmy have moved on, so I have a few minutes before it's my turn again. I try to catch Josie's eye in the meantime. It's hard to tell with the cap and glasses, but it feels like she's avoiding my gaze. I'm not used to being avoided. I pull up her application on my screen so I can decide which question to ask her. When it's my turn again, I'm ready.

"Number Forty-Four. Josie," I say, delivering a thousand-watt smile reserved for special occasions only—I've melted pillars of ice with that smile. "What would be your perfect date?"

"Dinner and a movie," she clips.

I wait because, obviously, she's not done. That can't be her answer, can it? It's so unoriginal. "Your perfect date *with me*," I clarify.

"Dinner and one of *your* movies?"

Jason Connor guffaws.

I'm so confused. "That's not what it says on here." I tap the monitor in front of me. "It says here, *a romantic whale-watching tour.*"

She winces. Since when do I make women wince?

"Maybe you're reading someone else's," Emmy cuts in, and my gaze snaps from her wide, warning eyes to Josie's pinched mouth to Jason Connor's half-hearted attempt to channel his laughter into his fist. Have I crossed over into an alternate universe? According to the *Lost Star* writers, it's a thing.

"Andrew, your turn!"

Terica thinks she's closed the matter, but I'm a long way from done. I did *not* read someone else's entry. I have eyes and a brain, and I know what I saw. As Andrew takes his turn, I lean into my monitor and scour the rest of her responses like a police detective deciphering the clue to a murderer's whereabouts.

"She was a last-minute substitution, remember?" Jason Connor whispers. "Just go with it."

"But she's lying."

"What do you mean she's lying?"

"I mean, there's no way her answer to that last question was 'dinner and a movie.' Something's going on."

"It's a fundraiser. Play along, like you always do."

I loosen the scarf around my neck. Connor is right. So what if the answers don't match up? So what if Emmy's friend is lying? So what if she doesn't want to win the contest? None of it matters. It's a silly gimmick for a good cause, and that's it. I don't even care.

I catch Josie eyeing me before she looks away. She thinks she's being all clandestine about it, but I get stared at a lot. I recognize the subtleties.

If she likes me enough to secretly ogle me, then why is she lying? Or is she really as boring as her answer suggests? I've met her a couple of times. I don't think she's boring.

I mean, I didn't give her a lot of my attention, to be honest. She's Emmy's friend, and I'm not a skirt chaser. I don't have to be. But I noticed her.

When it's my turn again, I'm ready. I know I'm supposed to ask someone else a question, but they can't make me.

"Number Forty-Four, Josie. Let's try this again." I use my best Captain Footwork voice, the one that stops even the likes of Emmy and Terica in their tracks, evidenced by how they both open their mouths, hesitate, and then retract whatever objection was on their lips. "What's the most embarrassing thing that's ever happened to you?"

Josie's chest rises as she takes a breath, and I make a show of giving her my undivided attention.

"A waiter spilled wine on me once."

Womp, womp. "You can do better than that."

She swallows. "My skirt was tucked into the back of my pantyhose at church."

I emit a pained chuckle. "What is this, 1950? Try again." I'm being too pushy. I can tell by the way her nostrils flare, like a startled horse. "Come on, tell us the truth," I wheedle. "It's for a good cause."

She opens her mouth and lets it kind of hang there. It's a pretty mouth. Pink and heavier on the top, giving her an endearing almost-overbite.

"You can do it," I urge. "I know you can. Please?"

The words come out in a torrent. "I was on a bus in Mexico City, and I was using the bathroom at the back of the bus, but the door wouldn't lock, and the seat was dirty, so I hovered, as you do, but then the bus lurched right and I lurched left, and my shoulder hit the door, and it burst open, and I fell into the bus aisle with my panties around my ankles, and for the rest of the five-hour bus ride, the other passengers referred to me as Nalguitas, which means Little Butt or Little Butt Cheeks or just…Butt Girl."

Wow.

Seriously, *wow!* I want to congratulate her after that long, brave, run-on sentence of a confession, because this woman delivered, but no words come. All that comes out are semi-restrained puffs of laughter as my brain processes the scene she just described.

It's not just me, either. The entire stage and audience erupt into laughter. If Josie were a stand-up comic, it'd be the best day of her life. But she's not a stand-up comic. In fact, she's turned a deeper shade of purple than my scarf.

Now I feel bad. This is my fault. I should do something. I put my lips right up to my lapel mic to ensure my voice carries. "Yeah, that happened to me once, too. But they called me something else."

Anyone who was finally getting control of themselves loses it again, but at least now they're laughing at me, not her.

Sorry, I mouth at her in the hubbub.

I'm not sure if there's an "it's okay" in her tight-lipped smile or if it's more of an "a pox on your house." Either way, this gig just got way more interesting.

Chapter 6

Where are my fellow prudes?

Josie

ON THE *Lost Star* show, there's this transportation device that looks like a futuristic pen; you draw a doorway in the air with it and then walk through into a completely different place. What I wouldn't do for one of those things right now. I don't even care what's on the other side. A raging hurricane? A two-hundred-foot drop-off? A gas station men's room at the Yeehaw Junction? Whatever it is, I'll take it.

But because I'm living in this stupid, low-tech world and the universe hates me, I move on to the final round.

I just told the Mexican bus story on national TV. Why did I do that?

It's Sean's fault. He got me flustered. It was that mouth. Those "c'mere to me" eyes. Everything about him flusters.

The booths our celebrity crushes were sitting in are rolled away. Our chairs are taken, too. Why are they taking our chairs? I don't do well with uncertainty. There are big red dots on the floor I hadn't noticed before. We're supposed to stand on them. Oh, please, please, please let mine be a trap door that drops me into a pit of foam chunks.

No such luck.

I do my best to stand still instead of swaying from side to side like a human metronome. I don't want to give anyone a reason to look at me. I need to get kicked out of this contest *now*. Manifest failure, Josie. It's not that hard. You can do this. You're fine. Everything's fine.

Beside me, a fellow contestant chuckles at something on her phone as she waits out the reset period, and I instinctively glance at her screen. She's scrolling through memes on Instagram. It's a nice distraction—the dogs, the cats, the pithy captions. Just what I need to settle my nervous system.

Then, her thumb swipes upward, and my insides seize up like a pair of rusty scissors. Is that...?

No, it can't be. But it is—a video clip of a puppet that I know all too well.

Chuy was designed to look like a duende, one of those mythical so-ugly-they're-actually-kind-of-cute little house goblins that nibble off the toenails of little children at night. But he doesn't look very cute in this particular video as a teenage girl in pigtails and overalls snatches him off of another teenage girl's lap and hurls him onto a Day of the Dead altar, knocking over several candles and a bottle of aguardiente in the process. "You're the bitch!" she shouts. "I hate you! And your stupid puppet, too!"

As if on cue, everything flammable ignites, tongues of flame leaping up into the black sky. This particular version of the meme reads in all caps: *WHEN THE STARBUCKS BARISTA SPELLS YOUR NAME WRONG.*

Gulping down a bout of shame and nausea, I home in on the pigtailed girl's fury-twisted sneer flickering in the firelight. For the hundred-thousandth time, I tell myself that there's no way anyone would recognize her today. Her hair is no longer long and dark blond. She's not one hundred pounds soaking wet anymore. Her youthful features have sharpened with age and wisdom and regret. In fact, you'd probably need facial recognition software to confirm that that girl is me.

Please don't tell me this stupid meme is making a comeback! The last time I saw it was five years ago, but it was only circulating in Spanish. The media jumped all over it, though, reminding everyone that Chuy was not only "killed" that night, but that whatever was left of him had gone missing as well. When Chuy didn't show up in a dumpster or wood pile in the days that followed, everyone assumed I'd taken him with me when I ran away, and that I was either hiding him or had disposed of him somewhere outside of Mexico City. One well-known psychic suggested I'd used witchcraft to turn Chuy into a baby so I could raise him as my own (untrue). Another claimed he'd be found in a flat in England (unlikely). Occasionally, in the years that followed, there would be a Chuy "sighting." Most of those were fake, although one of them was an actual old photo of Chuy at Castillo Studios from before his accident. Nobody figured that out, or, if they did, nobody admitted it. I suppose it made better TV to keep the story alive.

And clearly, it's still alive.

The unhappy noise that escapes me must be louder than I

realize because the woman with the phone looks up and locks eyes with me. My heart makes one brief, swollen *thunk* inside my throat, the question hanging in the air like a caption: *Did she recognize me?*

No, Josie, of course she didn't. To her, the meme is just a meme, not a clue to an unsolved mystery, and I'm just a nosy fellow contestant, not a puppet-torching ex-diva on the lam. Although, she *is* the right age to have studied our materials in school.

I turtle my chin into the stretched-out neck of my T-shirt as I launch Instagram on my own phone. Maybe it's a fluke? Thumbing through my feed, I spot the stupid meme twice more in less than sixty seconds. Both captions are in English. Both are humiliating. I scroll to the comments.

> *Hey, aren't those the Bilingual Club girls from Spanish class?*

> *Yes! I totally forgot about them until now.*

> *OMG, look what she did to the puppet!*

> *So much for "friends para siempre."*

Well, there you have it, folks. The curse of Chuy the Puppet has pursued me across time and borders. Fan-freaking-tastic.

I glance up from my phone to find a grip coming at me with a blindfold. I can't do this right now—I just can't. I back off my dot.

"Take off the glasses," she says.

"They're prescription," I argue.

"Take them off."

"What'll you do if I don't?"

She snatches the glasses off my face with the reflexes of a pit viper. "You signed the waiver."

I didn't sign the waiver, actually. I believe my waiver was forged by either my best friend or her fifteen-year-old daughter, so I have no idea what rights I've ceded. One of them, however, is apparently the right to back out.

I mean, I could cut and run. It's not like this is *Squid Game*. But I don't want to make any more of a scene than I already have, especially now that my face is all over the internet…again. I take a begrudging step forward onto the red dot and let the grip stretch a *Date My Celebrity Crush!* sleep mask over my eyes, which she does with an unnecessary level of fervor.

Now I'm standing on set completely blind. Frankly, the darkness is comforting. Lonely, in a good way. I can pretend that I'm not here, exposed, my carefully curated replacement life hanging by a thread.

"All right, finalists, this is the moment you've all dreamed about!" Terica booms.

"There are ten of you left," Emmy continues, "and only five celebrity crushes to match you with, so from here on out, you've got a fifty-fifty chance."

Not gonna lie, the math gives me hope. I wouldn't go into surgery with those odds.

"You're going to be lined up opposite one of our hunky celebrity crushes," Terica explains.

"Next comes the fun part," Emmy says with a giggle. "You'll have to identify which sexy superstar is standing in front of you…"

"Wait for it," Terica teases. It's clear they've rehearsed.

"…by touch alone!"

I must have misheard Emmy. *By touch alone?* Did the guys really agree to this? Meanwhile, the entire place has exploded into cheers. Are you kidding me? Where are my fellow prudes?

"Rules!" Terica barks, and the madness quiets. "Hands only, and only above the waist. No talking. Don't move from your spot, but you can move the guys if you need to. The first name you speak will be taken as your answer, so no thinking out loud."

"Questions?" Emmy asks.

I have so very many, but I'm not calling any more attention to myself.

"If you feel a tap on your shoulder, you're group A, and you'll go first," Emmy says.

"Be polite!" Terica warns.

"But don't feel like you have to be too polite," Emmy adds. "After all, they signed up for this."

I brace myself for the tap on my shoulder, but nothing happens. That's a tender mercy, because I need a freaking minute to process this. Team A must be having a grand old time because the audience is shrieking with laughter, and Emmy and Terica are struggling to hold in their cackles. Fine. Let them have their fun. I'll be over here forming my losing game plan.

It's simple, really. I need to be one hundred percent sure who's in front of me and guess wrong on purpose. Can I do that? I've met all these guys before. I've even gotten to hug them all once, thanks to Emmy's unflinching loyalty. But the rules are hands only.

Still, how hard can it be? I remember what they are all wearing. I should be able to identify them by their collars alone.

Team A begins to shout out their answers. Pretty soon, all five have made their choices. I already know someone got it wrong because two people named Jason Connor, and that's impossible.

Rookies.

"Okay, Team B, you're up!" Emmy announces. "Get those manhandling mitts ready! You don't want to miss a nanosecond of this golden opportunity."

I stiffen as the shadows shift around me and the air changes. Without my eyesight, all my other senses sharpen. There's the clomp of expensive shoes on the wooden stage floor as the celebrities take their places. A flutter of air over my skin as someone passes nearby. The subtle mix of myriad colognes. A figure blocks a stage light, casting a shadow over my blindfold. I can't see the man who settles in front of me, but I can feel him. It's like being in a room with a ghost.

My engine is pistoning faster than usual, but I've got this, because I've realized something. I don't have to manhandle anyone. I don't have to make a spectacle of myself. And I don't even have to remember what they were all wearing. My solution is binary. If the man in front of me is wearing a scarf, I'll know it's Sean, and I'll shout out someone else's name. If he isn't wearing a scarf, I'll know it's not Sean, and I'll shout out his name.

It's genius. I'll take my Nobel Prize now.

"Ready," Emmy cries. "Set. Go!"

With all the confidence of a sturdy handshake, I reach out in front of me, chest level, prepared for my fingers to meet either silky scarf material or something else—maybe the silk-lined V neck of a vest or thick, high-thread-count dress shirt cotton. What I don't expect is for them to meet skin. Warm skin. And . . . is that chest hair?

Holiest of holy shits, whoever this is, he's shirtless!

I snatch my hand back as if the guy is made of lava. He's not, but I think my face is. I was not prepared for this—a half naked, fully hot mystery man waiting to be groped. All around me, the other contestants giggle and squeal and have fun with it. Meanwhile, I'm paralyzed.

I can't just stand here. Nothing will be more noticeable than that. Besides, I need to figure out who this is in front of me, and I need to do it fast.

I reach out with a cupped hand, this time higher, and make contact with a cheek. There's facial hair there. Sean has a Vandyke right now. I got a really close look at it when he leaned in and asked, *You'll do it, won't you?*

Something liquefies inside me as I think about that husky voice and those pouty lips while my thumb trails itself across the jaw in front of me. Madre de Dios, I'm getting turned on. That's not allowed. Not here. Not now.

Besides, this might not even be Sean. Who else is growing facial hair at the moment? I can't remember!

Panic revs its engines, but not today, Satan. Maybe I can tell who this is by the hair on his head.

I go for a blitz, two-handed, but my detective work is thwarted by hairspray. I'm not sure what I'm feeling, but it's sticky and stiff. I run my fingers along the hairline behind his ears. No curls. It's not Jason Connor. That's good. I didn't accidentally get turned on by my best friend's husband.

Oh God, I'm overthinking this. I need to focus.

Oh God, now I'm frozen.

Oh God, now I can't even think. Think!

Emmy and Terica are poking fun at the fact that I'm standing like a statue with one hand barely touching the short hairs behind some extremely hot movie star's ear. I'm sure I look ridiculous. I feel ridiculous. Tomorrow, I'm going to be all over the gossip columns. Win or lose, I've blown it.

Then a warm hand closes over mine. With my vision taken away from me, I'm acutely aware of the mild calluses against my fingers. I catch a whiff of spicy cologne as he brings my hand to his mouth. His breath is hot on my fingertips, and all the frozen parts of me melt because somewhere in my subconscious brain I know who this is even before his lips press ever so slightly to plant a kiss against the pads of my fingers.

Oh my God, those lips! That mouth that haunts my dreams just kissed my fingers! And the sensation is so soft and intimate that I almost forget I'm blindfolded on a stage in front of who knows how many viewers, imagining instead that we're in a room all alone, curtains drawn, shadows thick, blood running hot and fast, the bomb inside me ticking down the seconds.

Should I take advantage of this? I mean, this is Sean O'Sullivan standing shirtless in front of me saying, *Grope me; I'm famous.* And I want to, so badly, even though he's the worst possible guy for me to have a celebrity crush on. I can't afford to be in the limelight, and he bathes in the limelight. Swims in it. Luxuriates in it.

Now I'm imagining a shirtless Sean O'Sullivan luxuriating. Oh no, am I breathing? Great. I've forgotten how to breathe.

"Are you okay?" The words vibrate against my fingers, and suddenly, I have a terrible realization. That wasn't a kiss at all. He was just moving his lips to talk to me, you know, because I'm in the middle of a crisis, and the rules say we're not supposed to talk, but I obviously need an intervention.

It wasn't a kiss at all. It was *pity.*

Prickles break out across my skin. This is way worse than the Mexican bus story. I'm certain Sean can see the effect he's having on me. My whole body is on fire with desire and mortification and prickling. In fact, my neurons seem as confused as I am. They're all running around asking the other neurons *What just happened?*

I don't know, neurons! I don't know what just happened!

But you know what I do know? I know that the man standing in front of me is Sean O'Sullivan. And that's all I need to know.

I open my mouth and say a name.

Chapter 7

Folks, we have a winner!

Sean

"ZACHARY TAY!" JOSIE shouts. At the same time, her hand retracts from my face, and she grabs it with her other hand and holds onto it, like it might scurry off if not properly restrained.

Now it's my turn to freeze.

Did she just say *Zachary Tay*? That can't be right. She knows it's me. She heard my voice. Does she not know my voice?

Did she think I was Zach? Was she hoping I was Zach?

The contestants are given the green light to take off their blindfolds, and I wait to see if I can read anything in her face, but she won't look at me. Two red spots bloom high on her cheeks.

She knew who I was. She liked it. But she threw the game anyway. She doesn't want to win.

I shrug my shirt and jacket back on. Good luck getting my scarf tied properly without a mirror. That's a statistical impossibility, so I stuff it into my back pocket. I rescue my glasses from my lapel and pop them back on.

Why the hell would she throw the game?

Whatever. Stay blasé, man. If she's not interested in winning a date with me, that's her business. I just find it interesting, that's all.

I take my seat between Jason Connor and Andrew Valentine and wait to find out which of the beaming fanwomen I'll be beholden to for two hours, tops. Andrew, all toothy smile, reaches over to give me a donkey bite on the thigh, but I block him with a forearm.

"Okay, well, here's the thing," Emmy says to the ten finalists, all standing in a line wringing their hands like Miss America hopefuls. (To be fair, we do have one Mr. America hopeful on Ramirez's roster.) She bites her lip. "None of you got it right."

The contestants erupt into gasps.

"I guess we're more reliant on our sense of sight than we realize," Terica remarks. "We hope you had fun, anyway."

The women and the dude all look like they had fun anyway, all except Josie. She looks like she's just been on a tour of the Amityville Horror House.

Meanwhile, Emmy and Terica are giving each other strange looks. Finally, Terica says, "I'm gonna be straight with you all. We didn't expect it to go this way. We thought you would be able to guess who these fellas were by touch alone, but you didn't!"

"And we now have to find a fair way to choose the winners," Emmy confesses.

I watch Josie take a couple of tiny shuffles backward, allowing the two women on either side of her to inadvertently fill the gap. She's got those glasses on again, and she's tugging the short ends of her hair forward, as if to cover her face. I really don't get it. I've seen her around with Jason and Emmy a lot. She's a beautiful woman—tall with an artsy-glamorous sensuality. Choppy haircut. Big, coffee-brown eyes.

That's what she looks like normally. Right now, she looks like a cartoon character.

Emmy and Terica have called a break and are conferring like a couple of *Lost Star* engineers when the Groove Drive is down. I check my watch. I'm ready for this to be over. I want to look at my George Washington hat again. Confirm the automatic payment went through and that it wasn't flagged by Interpol. There must be something I can do to speed this party along.

"Why don't you just have us pick numbers?" I suggest.

Their heads pop up. "What was that?"

"We'll all pick a number. First one to guess it wins."

The guys all murmur their approval. Apparently, they're ready for this to be over, too.

"That could work," Emmy says. She's always been good at reading a room.

"Why complicate things?" Terica agrees.

When they get the cameras rolling again, I offer to go first. If I can set the tone here, we can wrap this thing up.

"We'll start with your Number Ones," Emmy explains. "They're the ones who ranked you at the top of their list to go on a date with. Number Sixteen, come on up here."

A redhead in a teal mermaid dress steps forward, hardly able to contain her excitement. I smile politely.

"Pick a number from one to ten," Emmy says.

She wriggles around nervously, hopefully. "Six!"

I make a sympathetic frowny face. "Sorry. Next!"

Terica checks her papers. "Number Forty-Nine."

A middle-aged woman in a floral shirt and khaki capris steps forward. She looks like she might send me home with Ziploc baggies full of pot roast and potatoes. Normally, I wouldn't say no to that, but I'm on a strict diet these days. I'm up against Robert Downey, Jr. for a superhero movie role, and there's no room for weakness.

"Two?" she guesses.

"Better luck next time."

"Number Forty-Four, you're up," Emmy says.

Josie scooches forward with all the enthusiasm of a dehydrated snail. She's still gripping the hand I held to my mouth.

See, she liked it. I know she did. So why doesn't she want to go on a date with me?

I blink a few times at her and lift my chin. "Your number?"

"Six."

You've got to be kidding! What the hell is her deal? But I control my face and remind her, "That one's already taken."

Her face twists as if she's in pain. "Eigggggght?" she squeaks out.

Eight. That's a great number. A fantastic number. I don't see how it could possibly not be *the* number.

A grin spreads across my face. "Folks, we have a winner."

Chapter 8

El Cuento de los Butt Cheeks

CELEBRITY STRAIGHT TALK, OCTOBER 1

AMIL: Hello, beautiful people, and thank you for tuning in to Celebrity Straight Talk. I'm Amil Nair, your host, along with the devastatingly beautiful and talented Isla Wallace.

ISLA: Hi-la, it's Isla!

AMIL: Today we're talking about the *Date Your Celebrity Crush!* winners. Isla, can you please hold my hand? I feel like I might be hyperventilating. All the oxygen in the room has been replaced with envy.

ISLA: Amil, it's going to be okay. Here's my hand. Also, I think I have a paper bag in my car.

AMIL: Now I know I shouldn't be jealous. These nice people made a sizable donation to a worthy cause for the opportunity to go on a date with one of the five hottest hotties in Hollywood. But what's been haunting me for the last hour is the finalist round.

ISLA: All that flesh, Amil!

AMIL: Indeed! And how about the unforgettable moment when a shirtless Sean O'Sullivan pressed the hand of a contestant against that devastating mouth of his? Oh dear, it's happening again. [gasps] Did you say you had a paper bag?

ISLA: In the car, but I'm parked really far away. And yes, I did see that. That woman's name is Josie Days, and she's a makeup artist and the best friend of Emmy Connor. We've seen her around before. Here's a partial shot of her hiding behind some flowers at Emmy and Jason's wedding. And here's the back of her head at a gala event.

AMIL: Nepotism alert! Call my lawyer!

ISLA: I would, Amil, if Ms. Days had shown any indication of enjoying herself on the *Date Your Celebrity Crush!* show. Look at that face. She doesn't look like a contest winner. She looks like a hostage.

AMIL: She hardly even touched Sean during that skin-tillating finalist round. What is wrong with this woman?

ISLA: Maybe she's Ace.

AMIL: She's not Ace. Did you see her reaction when he did *the thing*?

ISLA: The thing?

AMIL: The thing with the hand! The hand thing! Her hand against his mouth—argh! Are you really going to make me relive it? You monster!

ISLA: Sorry, Amil.

AMIL: If Sean O'Sullivan had done that to me, my reaction would've been biblical.

ISLA: I don't doubt it.

AMIL: The roof would have come down. Angels would have blown their trumpets. People would have exploded into pillars of salt.

ISLA: So . . . where do you think Sean will take this Josie person on their date?

AMIL: Maybe a museum. She'd be right at home in the sculpture room, standing stock-still, staring into space.

ISLA: Agreed. What did you think of her most embarrassing moment?

AMIL: El Cuento De Los Butt Cheeks? Eh, I'd give it a solid seven out of ten on the embarrassment scale. But what was she doing riding a bus in Mexico?

ISLA: Getting from one place to another without a car?

AMIL: Yes, but was she on vacation? Most tourists don't take public transportation. They get shuttled around by their resort.

ISLA: Or they take a taxi or rideshare.

AMIL: Right? Buses are for locals.

ISLA: There seems to be a lot of mystery surrounding Sean O'Sullivan's *Celebrity Crush* date. I can't wait to learn more.

Chapter 9

Schrödinger's life.

Josie

MY CONVERSE SLAP the film lot's concrete as the sky slits one orange eye to the day. I'm part of the so-called "early shift," which includes mostly makeup artists and the actors we're turning into aliens. Sean won't be here, so that's a relief. Still, a low-grade dread grips me.

Freaking Sean! He picked me on purpose. I mean, *Yay, I got chosen by a superhot movie star.* That's how a normal person would react.

I avoided looking at any entertainment news last night or this morning because, well…Schrödinger's cat. As long as I don't open the box and see the carnage, good things are still possible. For me, it's also Schrödinger's name. Schrödinger's career. Schrödinger's *life*.

The only thing I allowed myself to do was compare the photo of Sean and me on the *Date Your Celebrity Crush!* website with my old headshot. The woman with the short purple hair, glasses, hat, and scowl looked very little like the blond, smiling teen. I hope it's enough.

Am I overreacting? Maybe. I mean, how many celebrities have done stupid shit, especially when they were young, and we all forgave and forgot? Although, for a lot of young fans, Chuy was an icon. There were lunchboxes with his face on them. T-shirts, too. We needed security to protect us from the swarms of children that would descend upon us when we appeared with him in live venues. So, yeah. I basically killed Mexican Elmo. And then hid his body.

Body? Is that the right word? What do you call something dead that was never alive to begin with?

I should have just apologized in the moment. Faced the consequences. But that's older me talking. I did consider making an official statement on social media a few months after I ran away, but every time I tried, these little bullets of fear ripped through my chest. What did I expect to get out of waking a sleeping dragon? Did I really want to reopen that wound? Plus, I was a little bit scared of the conspiracy theorists out there searching for Chuy. There's a fervor there.

Truthfully, though, I was more scared of facing my stepfamily. Mom told me to just talk to Juan Ernesto, that he wasn't mad, not anymore, just deeply hurt and disappointed. If that was supposed to be convincing, it wasn't. And Lupe? Well, apparently, she wasn't banging down my door to kiss and make up, so that was settled.

I'd had a chance at a family, and I'd blown it. Now, too much time has passed. If I ever had a chance to redeem myself, it's long gone. Too little, too late.

Besides, my secret little life isn't so bad. I found a place to belong with Emmy and Peyton, and now Jason and their new little baby on the way. Yes, I'm on the outside, but Emmy never makes me feel that way. The universe has given me one more chance. I won't overstep again, I promise.

I stare at the EMPLOYEES ONLY sign on the side entrance to Studio 11. I can't afford to stall any longer. I push open the door.

My client, Chelsea, is already in the chair, grande mocha skim no whip in hand. She's chatting with Howie, who relaxes in Li Jing's chair as they stretch a bald cap over his slicked-down afro with practiced, tattoo-covered hands. When I enter the room, all conversation halts.

"What?" I say, all nonchalant. "Am I late?" But inside I'm bracing for it.

Why didn't you tell us you were a child actress?

It says on the news your real name is Savannah Bateman.

I think we studied you in school. Friends Para Siempre, right?

Whatever did you have against that puppet? Where is it, any-way? Under your bed?

Instead, Chelsea holds out her fist for a bump. "Sean O'Sullivan, eh? Impressive."

I brush my knuckles over hers. "It was a dumpster fire. You don't have to pretend."

"You get stage fright?" Li Jing asks, their facial piercings shifting in sympathy.

I stuff my tote into my designated cabinet. "Something like that."

"It was the blurting that did you in," Chelsea says. "It's always the blurting."

"Yeah." Howie snickers. "Butt Cheek Girl."

"Look." I interrupt their laughter. "Some people are in-front-of-the-camera people, and some people are behind-the-camera people." I twist Chelsea's hair into a knot and clip it to her head. "I'm the latter."

They hum in understanding. At least we all know our place.

Relief begins to overshadow dread as I pull out my brushes and tray. If all they have to talk about is how weird I acted on the show, that means I'm in pretty good shape. But despite the resurgence of the Flaming Chuy meme and the possibility that I taught one or more of them how to ask for directions in Spanish back in high school, these guys aren't the audience I'm most concerned about. If I really want to know if I've been recognized, I need to tune in to *Hollywood, De Repente* with Hugo Valencia during my break. That dude has been reporting Latinx entertainment news since before I was born. He's Mexican-American, and he was one of a handful of media personalities who never stopped searching for Chuy's carcass (corpse?). Whatever. He never stopped searching for him. If anyone is going to recognize me, it's him.

"Where are you going?" Chelsea asks as I brush a cotton ball with witch hazel over her skin.

"Does it look like I'm going somewhere?"

"I meant on the date you won with Mr. O'Sullivan."

It weirds me out that she calls him Mr. O'Sullivan. I should probably refer to him that way, too, but Emmy introduced him to me as Sean. "I'm supposed to get a call from someone to set something up."

"That's romantic," Howie deadpans.

"You're just jealous," I reply. "You wish you had your own fake celebrity charity date."

"They're gonna have cameras in your face the whole time, you know," Chelsea says, and a fresh wave of anxiety lights me up.

"People are gonna know her name better than ours," Howie complains to her. "I should've applied to that contest."

"We'll get our day, Howie." Chelsea shifts in the chair and frowns as I continue prepping her to become a green-skinned Heltaroth. "It's coming."

"Well, next time you're in front of the camera, just act like a complete imbecile. That seemed to work for me," I say.

"Howie's already tried that," Li Jing quips.

"Ooo, burn!" Chelsea replies.

Howie shrugs. "All publicity is good publicity."

Not true, but I'm not about to broach that subject now. "You know what?" I squeeze green makeup onto my tray. "I don't want to go on that date. One of you can have it—whoever wants to buy me lunch for a week."

"I'll buy you lunch for a week!" Chelsea and Howie cry at the same time.

"It appears we have a bidding war. I'll accept your best offers in the break room at noon."

We work in relative silence for the next couple of hours until the rattle of a service cart breaks through our noise-canceling AirPods and Yesenia pokes her head into the room.

"Breakfast?" she asks with a big smile.

We mutter a bunch of affirmative replies, and she begins to hand out tacos de papa and red enchiladas and something she calls "breakfast tamales" although, even with my deep and long-standing relationship with the tamal, I can't for the life of me figure out what makes them different from lunch or dinner tamales.

"¿Quieres salsa verde?" she asks me. Yesenia is like everyone's mom around here, and she knows I love the spicy sauce in the squeeze bottle peeking out of her catering bag.

"¡Claro que sí!" I dress my mayo-slathered potato taco with a long, wiggly squirt. Yesenia's potato tacos are the best—the outside golden and crispy, the inside soft and savory. Broken in two with each half stuffed into a warm corn tortilla, they remind me so much of the ones I used to get in Mexico.

She and I chat a few minutes in Spanish. She didn't see the show last night, apparently, and I don't mention it. Yesenia has never shown any sign of recognizing me, and I plan on keeping it that way.

Yesenia repacks her things and is just about to push the service cart out of the room when a man in shiny black leather swoops into the doorway. He grips the doorframe and studies the room as if he's been sent to extract a high-value target. The potato taco in my stomach does a flip-flop.

It's Sean O'Sullivan.

Chapter 10

That was meant to stay in my head.

Josie

"hi," sean says to the room. His gaze cuts sideways to where Yesenia is blanching in the doorway. "Hi," he tells her. "Love those boxty tacos. Never stop." Then he zeroes in on me. "Can we talk for a minute?"

"I'll finish Chelsea up," Li Jing offers since Howie's transition is complete—he looks like a bona fide bald, blue-headed Zentharian in a slim-fit dress shirt.

Against my better judgment, I accept Li Jing's offer and trail Sean out of the makeup room. The set is busy with activity now as everyone gears up for taping. It looks like the first scene will be filmed in front of the green screen, so the "ship" itself is quiet. Sean leans against a doorway with the sprawling crescent-shaped bridge behind him, ever the fearless leader. He could probably play Captain Amadeus Footwork in his sleep.

"So," he says, "what do you like to do? What do you like to eat? Steak? Sushi?"

"No seafood," I blurt. "And listen, this isn't necessary. I'm giving my date away. Donating it."

A pair of androids pass us stiffly, forcing me into the glorious inner radius of Sean's expensive cologne. Just smelling him feels like foreplay.

"You're donating our date? Why would you do that?" His eyes are so wide and questioning that I actually feel bad for this guy who has everything he could ever want.

"It's for your own safety." It's not a lie. If I get discovered and canceled again, anyone close to me will be sucked in, too.

"How is going on a date with you dangerous?"

God, are we really doing this? Why can't he just take no for an answer? "I have a terrible infectious disease," I deadpan.

Sean mimes propping his chin on his hand in delighted curiosity. "Do tell."

Dammit. "It's too painful to talk about."

"Is it leprosy?"

"Yes." There's no point in wasting brain cells on cleverness. "A rare, incurable form of leprosy. I'm going to die a horrible death."

"I'll wear a mask."

There's commotion over by the main entrance, a boisterous voice with an accent. I catch a glimpse of a large man in a patch-elbowed sport coat heralding the way for a skinny dude with a camera on his shoulder.

That's odd. Why would someone bring a camera here? We have all the cameras we need. It's a TV studio. Then I hear a jovial expletive in Spanish, and my brain shoots off a warning flare.

This isn't just any guy with a cameraman! It's Hugo Valencia, the host of *Hollywood, De Repente*, and there's only one explanation for why he would be here—me!

With a whine of terror, I shove past Sean onto the bridge. That's it. Game over, man. Hugo must know who I am, and he's here to shake me down for puppet bones or at least an exclusive. I scan the set for a hiding place.

"What's wrong?" Sean asks, trailing me through doorways to the ready room, the med lab, the dance deck because, yes, the *Lost Star* ship has a whole deck that's solely used for dancing. "Is your incurable leprosy flaring up?"

There's nowhere to hide on the *Starlight Serenade*. However, there *is* a janitorial closet that doubles as prop storage in the hall. I whip open the door and squeeze myself beside the Dyson vacuum. Sean stops the door before I can close it.

"Don't you think this is a little over-the-top?" he asks. "And that's coming from me."

Over his shoulder, I spot Hugo heading our way. I fight with Sean over the door and win, yanking it shut. I stand in dark dustiness with the smell of vacuum cleaner and latex all around me. For a moment, here in the dark quiet, I can tell myself a lie that everything might turn out okay.

"You know I'm just going to stand out here and talk to you through the door," Sean says.

Why does he have to be so persistent? I crack the door and hiss, "You need a flat iron, stat, or your pompadour's not going to make it."

"My pompadour's had worse."

Through the cracked door, I spot Hugo peeking into doorways, first the bridge, and then the makeup room where we just were. Meanwhile, Sean is peering at me with interest. I feel like an unlucky sandwich that's captured the attention of a handsome seagull. Any minute now, Hugo will reach this part of the hallway. He'll probably ask Sean where I am, and he'll have no reason to lie.

Dammit!

I shove the closet door all the way open, grab Sean by his shiny leather space jacket, and yank him inside.

The door *thunks* shut, and now it smells like vacuum cleaner, latex, and musk. It's a tight fit in here. Too tight. My chest is pressed against Sean's chest. He isn't as tall as some of the other *Lost Star* guys, and I'm five ten, so we're literally face-to-face, my chin only a couple of inches below his. He's the perfect height for a cheek-to-cheek slow dance. But then I already knew that.

"What are we do—" he starts to say.

"Shh!"

"I'm just ask—" he starts again.

This time I shush him with a finger to his lips—those pouty, world-renowned lips. I can't believe I'm touching them. Again. Too bad I can't enjoy it because I'm wound up tight as a dollar store toy while I strain to hear Hugo Valencia's chatter as he passes by the closet door. I listen for my name—my old one or my new one—but the only name I hear is *Jason*.

Jason?

My gears whir. Oh! He's talking about Jason *Ramirez*. He got matched with the slim, mustachioed dude named Javier—that makes sense. Calm down, Josie, it's not all about you. Thankfully.

I take a breath, and the tightness unspools from my body. My senses are awakening, like bioluminescence in moonlight. One of my hands still grips Sean's uniform while the other has a finger pressed to his lips. He's holding my elbows. Our torsos have not a centimeter of space between them due to the Dyson vacuum shoving at my back. Even our knees are brushing.

I take my finger away, and now his lips are right next to my lips. I can barely see them in the dim light, but I stare at them. I can't stop.

This is absurd. There's no need for this if Hugo isn't looking for me. But when I start to shift, Sean's grip tightens on my elbows.

"Why don't you want to go on a date with me?" he asks.

"Why *do* you want to go on a date with *me*?" I counter.

"There'll be cameras everywhere, in case you think I'm dangerous."

"I don't think you're dangerous," I say. The word *dangerous* comes out of me so breathy it makes that whole sentence contradict itself. We're playing a game that I'm losing because that mouth is too close. He smells too good. He *is* dangerous. *This* is dangerous.

"So what is it then?" he replies in a matching whisper.

Oh God, this is bad. I'm not supposed to want Sean O'Sullivan. I mean, of course I want him, but it was never supposed to be a real, actual possibility. It was supposed to be a celebrity crush. It was supposed to be safe. And as long as we both stayed in our designated lanes, it was. But I'm being hunted by my past, and Sean is the bait.

"I don't date celebrities," I say. "I like my privacy."

"I like my privacy, too." He caresses my elbows so subtly it might be unintentional. That touch ratchets my DEFCON level up even further, though, and pieces inside me shift, clicking into places they're not supposed to. Unauthorized places. The freaking missile is in the freaking launch bay.

"You weren't supposed to pick me," I blurt, because someone needs to step in and turn this heavy elbow petting session back into an argument. "Couldn't you tell I was trying not to get picked?"

"I didn't pick you. You guessed my number."

He's a liar. I know this because it takes one to know one. "Why are you chasing me?"

He blinks a few times. "I'm not chasing you. I don't chase."

Every word he says, every movement of that devastating mouth, carves a piece out of my resolve. But I have to remind myself what's at stake. I can't be found out. I can't go through that again. The humiliation, the judgment, the shame.

You two are going to make the world a better place, Juan Ernesto had told Lupe and me the day he signed the licensing agreement for us to appear in schools across Mexico and the U.S. *You're going to be a bridge between cultures, between languages, between people. You two and this guy*—he'd patted Chuy on his bulbous head—*are going to make life better for immigrant kids everywhere.*

Our eyes met at that moment, like he knew I knew what he meant, which I did. Juan Ernesto wasn't the warmest, fuzziest guy on the block, but we were both kids raised outside of our birth culture—Juan Ernesto in New York and me in Mexico City. We both knew what it was like to never really be able to fit in. To have your accent made fun of. To be on the outside. To struggle to belong.

Maybe that's why Juan Ernesto worked so hard to get me into showbiz. He wanted to give me something, knowing what I was losing. He wanted to give the world something, too— something good.

I was all-in. I wanted to be that bridge he always talked about. To do something that mattered. To help people. It worked, too. The show was a hit, the educational materials were a hit, and everything we touched turned to gold. Juan Ernesto looked so proud in the promo photos with an arm around each of us, daughter and stepdaughter, Chuy perched on Lupe's knee. As for me, I felt like I was the biggest winner of all. I'd gotten a dad out of it. A real, honest-to-goodness family.

At least I'd had that for a minute.

The truth is that Sean O'Sullivan isn't dangerous. I'm the dangerous one. I can't be trusted. I've already torpedoed one person's life's work, already lost one family. If I hurt my found family, too, if I lost Emmy and Peyton, I couldn't take it. I'd shatter.

"What if I let you catch me right now?" I breathe. "Would you leave me alone then?"

I tilt my chin sideways, lining up my lips with the work of art that is Sean O'Sullivan's mouth. In the dimness of the closet, his green eyes are the color of the ocean depths. They flutter closed for just a second, as if he's imagining what I mean by that. And what *do* I mean by that? Are we going to go at it right here in the janitorial closet fifteen minutes before he's supposed to be on set? That pompadour wouldn't stand a chance.

His lips part, just barely. An invitation. Does that mouth live up to the hype? I think I'm about to find out. I close my eyes and lean in.

He squeezes my elbows, but this time it's different. Quick, as if in warning. He draws back as much as the cramped closet space will allow.

"Look, Josie." His tone is a curtain coming down. "I don't want to pressure you. That's not what I'm about. If you really don't want to go on a date with me, just say so, and I promise I'll never say another word about it. I won't even look at you again."

A war breaks out inside me. If this is a game, he has just

delivered a devastating blow. He's giving me what I want, what I asked for. But the idea of Sean O'Sullivan never looking at me again the way he is right now has another part of me screaming at myself, *No, no, no what are you doing, you idiota?*

"I'm giving you an out," Sean reiterates since I haven't replied.

A section of his pompadour is mussed. I reach up and let my fingers caress a soft, perfectly conditioned, dyed-yellow lock of movie star hair that will soon be styled into something that has its own Instagram account. I've never been a fangirl like Emmy. I was a celebrity myself for a time, and I know that good lighting, a great line, and a merciless personal trainer are all just that. That ninety percent of what we see is a persona, nothing more. But that doesn't mean I'm totally immune. Sean O'Sullivan is my celebrity crush, has been for a long time.

It's tempting. *So* tempting.

I press my palms into the firm muscles of his chest, noting how he flexes them under my touch. Not fair, but I asked for it. I should get that on a T-shirt. His hands shift from my elbows to my waist—a test. I don't pull away and am rewarded when his thumbs find the strip of skin under the hem of my shirt and trace along my waistline, a shivery, light touch. An offer rather than a demand. I lean in, pressing even closer against him. Why? Maybe because I'm stupid and reckless even when I'm doing the right thing.

I should get that on a T-shirt, too.

"I'm taking your out," I murmur into his mouth. God, this man's mouth is surely a portal to sexy Narnia. "But before I do, there's something I want to know."

"Ask aw—"

I press my lips to his. Our mouths fit together like two soft, pliant puzzle pieces, and with a zing of rapture, the rest of my body concedes that if it gets hit by a bus tomorrow, there won't be any hard feelings. My fingers walk themselves to his face and linger in the fine, trimmed hairs of his sideburns as we draw the kiss out, soft and restrained, like pulled taffy or a long, languid yoga stretch. I try not to taste his tongue, I really do—it's overkill for my purposes, which is to have this one nice thing just this once. But I can't help myself, and he responds with hungry enthusiasm, igniting a vortex of desire in my belly where the soundtrack is an endless loop of how that pouty, soft, sinful mouth is destroying me right now with a kiss and what the hell else it might be capable of.

I brace myself against the door and the wall and throw my head back as Sean's O'Sullivan's impossible mouth makes its way down my neck. It's exquisite. Matchless. I'm ruined forever, and I don't effing care.

"Tu boca me tortura," I murmur. That was meant to stay in my head, but whatever.

His tongue flicks the hollow at my throat, and I gasp, my hip striking the inside latch and jostling it just enough that my braced hand shoves the door open, exposing a surprised Hugo Valencia and his equally surprised cameraman heading back to the main entrance after their interview.

"Well, well, well." Hugo's face breaks into a crocodile grin. "What have we here?"

Chapter 11

You were a nun?

Transcript. *Hollywood, De Repente* with Hugo Valencia.
October 2. *[partially translated from Spanish]*

HUGO: *[in Spanish]* What a treat we have for you today, ladies and gentlemen. My crew and I came to the set of *Lost Star Dance Troupe Saves the Universe* for a chat with Jason Ramirez and his *Celebrity Crush* date, and look what we stumbled upon.

[video clip plays]

HUGO: Well, well, well, what have we here? *[in Spanish]* Keep that camera rolling, Guillermo. For our viewers at home, it seems like we've been focusing our efforts in the wrong place. The real story is with Sean O'Sullivan and his date. What's your name again, darling?

JOSIE: No hablo español.

[Guillermo mumbles something to Hugo]

HUGO: Her name is Josie Days? Great. Come now, Josie. You've spent time in Mexico, by your own admission. You must know *some* Spanish. Come on out of that closet and tell us about yourself. Everyone is curious. What took you to Mexico? Were you a student? A tourist? Do you have family there?

[the conversation switches to English]

JOSIE: I told you, I don't speak Spanish.

SEAN: Josie, don't be modest. You said something in Spanish a minute ago, and you sounded great.

HUGO: Oh, really? What did she say?

JOSIE: Nothing! She said nothing!

SEAN: I heard…tortura.

HUGO: Torture?

SEAN: Boca tortura…

HUGO: Torture mouth?

JOSIE: Okay, Sean, stop! Please stop helping me.

[the conversation switches to Spanish]

JOSIE: Hugo, don't listen to him. I'll talk.

HUGO: So you do speak Spanish. With conjugated verbs and everything.

JOSIE: Yeah. Sorry. That was … my other personality. Her Spanish isn't very good.

HUGO: Right. And *this* personality? Care to tell us what she was doing in Mexico?

JOSIE: *[pauses]* She was a nun.

HUGO: A nun?

JOSIE: A very bad nun with … urges.

HUGO: You were a nun?

JOSIE: She fell in love with a seminarian, but she didn't want to destroy his career and break his grandmother's heart, so she renounced her vows and got on that bus.

HUGO: And ended up here with Mr. Torture Mouth.

JOSIE: *[pauses]* Yep.

HUGO: What part of Mexico?

JOSIE: The D.F.

HUGO: The Distrito Federal, eh? Most Americans would call it Mexico City. Interesting. You know, you seem very familiar. There's something about you…

JOSIE: Nope! No, there isn't. I'm just your average, run-of-the-mill runaway nun with multiple personality disorder.

HUGO: Can you move your hair out of your face, darling? Let us get a better look at you.

JOSIE: The nun personality was also hideously disfigured… in a bullfight.

HUGO: Now, now. You're a beautiful young woman, Josie. There's no reason to be shy. And your accent is very good. I look forward to hearing how your date with Mr. O'Sullivan goes.

SEAN: *[in English]* I heard my name.

JOSIE: We won't be going on a date. I'm giving it away to charity.

HUGO: *[chuckles]* Now, that's the least believable thing you've said today, and that's saying a lot.

SEAN: *[in English]* Excuse me. I'm just going to squeeze out of here. They're calling me on set. Bye, Josie. *[holds a hand out to Hugo]* Sean O'Sullivan. Good to meet you.

HUGO: *[shakes Sean's hand]* Hugo Valencia.

[Sean leaves]

HUGO: *[to Josie]* He's gone now. You can tell me everything.

JOSIE: There's nothing to tell. I'm a very private person, Mr. Valencia. I don't like being in the spotlight.

HUGO: Well, Beautiful, I hate to break it to you, but that's no longer an option. And I don't know why you seem so familiar to me, but you'd better believe I'm going to find out. Here, take my card, in case you want to talk.

JOSIE: I don't want to talk. I'm never going to want to talk.

HUGO: *[mimes a phone and grins]* Talk soon.

Chapter 12

It's a constant battle to ward off my smoldering appeal.

Sean

I TUG ON the lambskin lapels of the navy-blue Continental Army coat draped over the mannequin in front of me. Did I get those first few buttons lined up just right? I step back and frown. The third one down on the left doesn't look quite right. But I measured!

"Mr. O'Sullivan, call for you, sir."

I glare at my butler as he loiters in the doorway, averting his gaze since I'm in just my bikini briefs. Or maybe he can't stand to look at the cluttered mess that is my cosplay room. "It's after hours, Rory. You shouldn't even be here."

"It's Mrs. Connor. She says she's been trying to reach you on your personal phone, but you're not answering."

I tap my phone to bump down the volume on my sewing playlist. "And did you maybe think there was a reason for that?"

"She was quite insistent. I don't feel good about upsetting a woman that close to her due date."

"You old softy."

I squeeze around racks of clothes, including one that holds the original Han Solo vest worn by Mr. Harrison Ford himself, the best Iron Man getup I've seen that didn't weigh a hundred pounds, and an authentic *Firefly* browncoat. Then there are my period pieces. I've got a restored (by me) Union uniform in the Civil War section along with a sick-as-all-get-out King George III costume. Not to mention my Wild West and steampunk stuff that includes Val Kilmer's original Doc Holliday costume from *Tombstone*. And did I mention the vampire stuff? Who's the owner of both Lestat's frilly blouse *and* Kiefer Sutherland's *Lost Boys* trench coat? Yours truly.

I swipe the phone out of Rory's hand and put it to my ear. "Emmy! Is it time for me to come deliver that baby?"

"For the last time, Sean, I'll catch it myself before I let you down there."

"Can I at least cut the cord?"

"Gross. Besides, you know Jason is looking forward to that part. He didn't get to cut the cord at Mattie's birth, and there's no way he's missing out this time. Anyway, stop talking about my placenta. I'm calling about Josie. What did you do to her?"

I hit SPEAKER and balance the phone on top of a tackle box full of notions so I can focus back on my George Washington coat. I might have been judging it too harshly. Those buttons are lined up perfectly.

"Are you talking about our closet tryst?" I smile at the memory. "I was just a passenger. She did the driving."

"She's giving up her date with you! Our lawyers are having conniptions."

I thread a needle through the last gold shank button. "I tried to convince her not to."

"So who should I give the date to?"

"This is your thing, remember? I just agreed to show up."

She sighs. "Well, there are three others who had you as their first, and I don't know how to make a fair choice. I think you should do it."

I loop the needle back and forth through the material. "Fine. Label them Options A, B, and C in your head."

"Okay," she says.

"Option C wins."

She pauses. "All righty, then. Thanks, Sean. You made that easier than it could've been."

"You know I'm easy. Like Sunday morning." I bite the thread off. Our business is done, but a tiny, nagging question rumbles in my chest. "So, um, did Josie tell you why she doesn't want to go out with me?" I slip the coat off its mannequin and slide into it carefully. Christopher Jackson's hat is going to be perfect with it. It's currently in transit from New York to a guy I know in Ojai with a reputation for discretion.

"It's not you, Sean. She doesn't want the publicity. She's a private person."

I check one profile and then the other in the mirrored wall. "You'd think she'd make an exception, especially after she kissed me and all." I rotate my shoulders in and flex, testing the shoulder and back seams. "I'm feeling a little used, to tell the truth."

"She said it was a moment of weakness."

I strike a general's pose in front of the mirror even though I have no pants on. "So, it's a constant battle to ward off my smoldering appeal? I'll take that."

"Wait a minute. Sean, do you *like* Josie?"

I flash myself in the mirror and then drop down to the floor and pop off a round of push-ups so I can meet my two-hundred-a-day goal. "I kissed her back, didn't I? Also, did she say anything about it? The kiss?"

"Sir." Rory knocks on the open door and gives me a concerned look from the doorway. "Your sister's here."

Dammit. I mute the phone. "Stall her! And I thought you were going home!"

But it's too late. Siobhan glides into the room with a smirk. "Playing dress-up again, I see."

"I'm not answering that," Emmy's voice says from the phone. "Do you want us to set up the date with Option C for you, or do you want to plan something more personal?"

I hit UNMUTE. "You can take care of it." I mouth *I'm busy!* to Siobhan and then murmur into the phone, "So, she liked it, huh?"

"Okay, your date with Option C will be Friday at six at the Shirley Brasserie. I'll email the calendar invite to your assistant."

"Friday?" I do some quick calendar calculations in my head as my sister peruses my collection like a thrift store.

"Yes, Friday. Is there a problem?"

"Nope." No problem. No problem at all. That's the evening I'm meeting my guy to pick up the hat, but there will be plenty of time for dinner beforehand. I peg a thimble at Siobhan. She retaliates with a poisonous glare, running her oily human hands down the front of Loki's pristine clover-green vest.

I will kill you, I mouth at her.

"All right. You're all set. Thanks again for doing this, Sean.

And for what it's worth, it's probably better that you and Josie don't take things any further."

My attention leaps back to the call. "What? Why's that?"

"She's my best friend, and when things ended, it'd be awkward."

When things ended? It's true my relationship stats aren't the best, but ouch. "Wow, Emmy, that's not harsh at all."

"Which plant on your windowsill grows, Sean?"

"What are you talking abou—"

"The one you water."

She can't hear my aggressive eye roll, so I add a scoff. "I… water things."

"Goodbye, Sean."

"Wait, wait!" I stop her. "How's Vera?"

"Still in ICU."

"Is she going to be okay?"

"I don't know. But I can keep you posted."

"Yes, please. I was thinking it might be nice for me to take her out on a date, too. She got a raw deal."

There's a long pause. "Wow, there's hope for you yet, Sean O'Sullivan."

I put on a cartoon voice. "And maybe one day, I'll be a real boy!"

We hang up, and Siobhan raises an eyebrow at me. "It's getting crowded in here. How many of these things do you buy a week?"

"Zero, on average. A half of one maybe," I lie.

"Da would sprout a second head if he saw this, you know." She flicks a Polaroid snapshot of me flexing and roaring in a reproduction of that little loincloth thing Sting wore in the original *Dune*. The photo is pinned on a corkboard next to about one hundred of its brothers and sisters, all of me cosplaying.

"Right?" I force a chuckle. Da used to get on me when he'd find me in Mam's sewing room. He didn't want either of his boys being a costumer like her. Said it was women's work. But I loved watching my mother create and restore wardrobe items—all those rich materials, the sparkle, the bling. And when she'd regale me with tales of where they'd been used, what films they'd been in, and who'd worn them, it was like finding buried treasure.

Now I have over a thousand costumes and accessories of my own. If anyone outside of my innerest inner circle—my sister and my butler, that is—saw it, they'd think I had a problem. And if Siobhan and Rory knew I'd started shopping on black market sites for even more exclusive stuff, they'd start to worry, too.

Not that they have to worry. I'm Sean O'Sullivan. A bit eccentric, yes, but it's a polished eccentricity. I'm king of my domain.

"Mam would love it, though," Siobhan goes on, musing. "Although I think sometimes she wonders if she indulged you too much, yeah?"

Siobhan's accent comes out when she's nostalgic or emotional. It happens to all three of us, even though I was so young when Da got his big break and we left Ireland for the States. And while Da's booming acting career shaped our lives and my childhood, Mam continued to work in theater. Maybe that's why I love this room so much. It's a lot like the sprawling, drafty backstages where I'd spend my after-school hours, Mam quizzing me on spelling words around pins pinched between her lips.

I roll onto my chaise and stretch out. "We can speculate on the various flavors of our parents' disapproval, or you can tell me why you're really here."

Siobhan shoves my legs out of the way to make room for herself and blows out a sigh that sends her ginger bangs fluttering. "Da's calling a family meeting."

I bury my face in my hands and reply with a muffled "About what?"

"Seamus is coming home."

I shoot up. "What? Why?"

"He ran Uncle's dinner theater into the ground. Uncle's kicked him out. Says he's been drinking and gambling."

"Ah, Seamus." I shake my head. "Was it the casino? Poker night?"

"Bingo."

"Ach, God."

"You know it's going to be a shitshow when the media gets a hold of this."

"Right." My brain whirs remembering that whole debacle four years ago that got Seamus sent to Ireland by Da in the first place. Suddenly, I see my cosplay room through my father's eyes, and a lump rises in my throat. I should tidy it up, get rid of some of the stuff I don't care as much about or at least cut back on the new acquisitions. But even as I think it, I know that I won't. O'Sullivans hold tight to the things they love.

"What're you drinking?" Siobhan reaches across to the workbench where my tumbler sits. She tastes it, grimacing in disappointment. "God, I hate your trainer."

"It's just till my audition." I split the George Washington coat to reveal my cut abs. "Almost there."

She rears a hand back and smacks my stomach with a flat palm. It stings like a mofo.

"Ow! What was that for?"

"To humble you." She snuggles against me, my ginger cat of

an older sister, and sighs. "He can't stay with me. I'll tell you that right now."

I swallow hard. "He can stay here."

"You don't have to do that. You don't have to be the hero."

I shrug off her half-hearted attack. "I have the room."

"He's going to need more than a roof over his head. You realize that, don't you?"

"Yeah, of course." I don't know what exactly she's getting at, but I don't want to fight with her. "I'll get him a therapist, too."

"A therapist?"

"What? Does he need a therapy dog, too? A therapy parrot?"

"This is going to be harder than you think, Sean. I don't know what you're telling yourself this is, but I promise you, it's bigger. Seamus is…"

Something akin to guilt washes over me—Seamus getting fired was what got me my big break. "I know what Seamus is," I interrupt her. "*Who* Seamus is. I'll figure it out."

Her mouth clamps shut. "Fine. Whatever. Get him a set of towels and a therapist. I'm sure everything will go smashingly." She grabs her bag and stands up. "I'll see you at the family meeting."

I loll my head on the back of the chaise. "Bye, sis! Love you!"

She points the purse at me like a weapon on her way to the door. "Scandals are like quicksand, Seanny Bear. Get too close, and suddenly you're up to your neck. I know he's our brother but…" Her final words echo from the hallway. "Don't get sucked in."

Chapter 13

Pink is out and sauce colors are in.

Josie

I LIFT AN eighteen-month-sized brown corduroy skirt romper over a golden-yellow onesie from the mountain of baby clothes on the guest bed. The color combination is hideous.

"Híjole," I cry. "Someone must think you're a terrible mother to gift you this. Why would someone ever put this on their child?"

From across the bed, Emmy gives me a stricken look. "I bought that!"

"Why? Because pink is out and sauce colors are in?"

"You're out of touch. These days, it's gentle parenting and non-gender-specific colors."

"There's nothing gentle about this outfit. It's a barrage of meatballs and mustard." I fold it and put it in its appropriate pile. "Hopefully, the baby will be a boy so he won't have to wear that."

Emmy folds another tiny outfit on her big belly. "Jason is hoping for a girl."

"No second opinions on the ultrasound pics?"

She massages her bump. "Nope. And since we opted out of genetic testing, we'll have to wait until the next ultrasound."

I hold up an adorable yellow sleeper with navy blue stripes and am surprised by a stab of longing. "If I had a baby, I'd only dress it in stripes. Babies look so cute in stripes."

"I would love your striped baby," Emmy says without missing a beat. "You could even name it Stripe."

"Stripe Days. Wow, that sounds like a band."

"Or would it be Stripe *O'Sullivan?*" she teases.

"Really?" I drop the outfit into its appropriate pile. "What are you, twelve?" I don't tell her that the chances of there ever being a Stripe *Anything* are close to nil. I can't imagine having a baby with someone when I can't even tell them my real name.

"Sean and Josie, sittin' in a closet," Emmy sings. "K-I-S-S-I-N..." She thinks hard for a rhyme. "Sausage!"

"Not even close." I chuckle. Then the ghost of kisses past ripples through me. "Actually, it came closer to sausage than I expected," I admit.

"'Closer to Sausage.' Isn't that an Indigo Girls song?"

"Ha ha, not even going there, but that's a good one."

In the living room, peals of laughter ring out as Jason, Peyton, and Mattie play on the VR. It's such a happy sound. So comfortable. Moving out here wasn't the easiest decision, but I don't regret it. Emmy's trailer is nicer than mine, and we found the perfect spot for it on their property until I can save up enough money to afford my own place. My trailer sold for just enough to fund my semi-new start in California. They've even loaned me a car to drive—a white MINI Cooper that will eventually go to Peyton when she gets her license but for now, helps me avoid a car payment and insurance.

Yes, being out here in LA is risky, but Emmy and Peyton are everything to me. I know I'm not officially family, but this is as close as I'm going to get. I just have to not blow it all up.

That means no more fantasizing about Sean O'Sullivan's mouth and all of its lucky charms. I need to make a plan. Letting Hugo Valencia catch us in the closet was a big setback. He's seen my face. He's heard me speak Spanish. He knows I spent time in Mexico City, and I wouldn't be surprised if he's still got that crime board of Chuy's disappearance on the wall of his office. Even if he can't put all the pieces together on his own, all he has to do is show my photo around until someone eventually says, *Hey, isn't that Savannah Bateman with a dye job?* But if I disappear out of the public eye, for example, by staying as far away from Sean as possible, Hugo will have no reason to show my picture around. At least I hope not.

The doorbell rings. It's A-list actor Margarita Ayala coming to pick up Mattie, her son with Jason. Emmy and I eavesdrop on their greetings as Margarita blusters her way into the house. I have to say I'm impressed with the way these guys have been able to co-parent for the past couple of years. I know it hasn't been easy.

Usually, Margarita just picks Mattie up and goes, so it surprises me when she appears in the doorway with her toddler, Eva, on her hip. Her gaze shoots straight to me, but she doesn't say anything. Emmy and I exchange confused looks.

"Hello, Margarita. It's lovely to be stared at by you," I say.

"Hugo Valencia is right." She narrows her perfect, smoky eyes. "You do look familiar."

My pulse shudders. Shit. Margarita is from Miami. She probably grew up watching *Club Bilingüe* on cable!

"I just have one of those faces," I mutter, lifting the blanket I'm folding between us.

This isn't going to go away on its own. I need to call Hugo and nip this in the bud. Get him to cease and desist. Beg him. Bribe him. Threaten him. Whatever. Everybody has a price. "Excuse me. I have to make a phone call."

Margarita spins to continue staring at me like a camera-headed robot as I grab my purse and head for the patio. Digging out Hugo's card, I close the French doors behind me. I'm not sure how I'm going to play this, but I have to protect the people closest to me. Juan Ernesto, Lupe, and Miguel are making a name for themselves with their new sci-fi show. Emmy is living the dream she's worked so hard for. None of them needs the Savannah Bateman scandal coming out of the woodwork to ruin it for them. Knowing Emmy and Miguel, they'd try to stand up for me and go down, too. My family…Well, it would just be another blow for them, and I don't think I could bear to let them down a second time.

Hugo answers on the second ring. "Bueno."

"Mr. Valencia, it's Josie Days."

His satisfied laugh is reminiscent of Jabba the Hutt's, but more *he he he* than *ho ho ho*. "What can I do for you this fine evening, Ms. Days?"

I wander to the far end of the patio and peer out at the sunset over the dark water, my heart hammering in my throat. "I was never a nun," I blurt. "But I do have very compelling reasons for keeping my identity private. Personal reasons that are no business of anyone else's." *And have nothing to do with a certain puppet.*

"I see."

"I'm calling you to find out what it's going to take for you to back off of anything at all to do with me. I just want to fade back into the wallpaper."

The Jabba chuckle again. I hope he doesn't ask for money. I don't have a lot of that to give. I hope he doesn't ask for sex. I have a lot of that to give, but alas, it's intricately tied in with my self-respect.

"Listen," I bluster, "it'll be really easy for you to let me go. I've given up my date with Sean. There's nothing between us. That thing you saw was just…a moment. So, what'll it take, Hugo? What do I have to do to make you forget I exist?"

I'm babbling. Too much. I need to get it together. I don't have a lot of leverage here, and I don't know if a cry for pity is the best tactic. Hugo Valencia isn't a guy who's easily moved by tears.

But to his credit, he says, "All right, Ms. Days. I don't want to put you in any kind of danger."

I exhale in relief. I must've given off witness protection vibes. That was unintentionally clever of me. I may pull this off after all.

"But I'm also not a man who gives away something for nothing. If you want my silence, it's going to cost you."

"Name your price." I squeeze my eyes shut and pray it doesn't include me in a skimpy gold bikini.

"You're going to go on that date with Sean, and you're going to give me an exclusive."

I hesitate in confusion. "I told you I already canceled that."

"Then you're going to un-cancel it."

"It's this Friday."

"That's the deal, Ms. Days. You go on that date with Sean, and you give me an exclusive."

I stare at the fingernail of sun on the hungry horizon. "But I don't want my face on TV. I thought I was clear about that."

"You can wear a disguise if you want. The important thing is that I won't take the story in the direction of *Who is this mysterious woman and what's her deal?* We'll leave your past in the past. We'll focus on the present. The future, too, if there is one."

The last bit of light is sucked into the sea, and suddenly, the patio is darker, cooler, haunted by shadows. "One date. One interview. And we're done?"

"One interview, and then you can fade into the wallpaper, as you put it, if that's what you choose."

The French doors open, and Jason is there, waggling a glass of red wine at me. Cocktail hour has officially started in the Connor household. I cross the patio to accept it and watch him close the doors, giving me back the space.

"Do I have to do anything special on this date?"

"Just have fun, and tell me about it, on my show, at least a week before you talk to anyone else. That's the deal. I need a ratings boost, and you, my dear, are it."

It sounds too good to be true, but I'd be a fool to say no. I'd actually really love to go on a date with Sean O'Sullivan. Maybe Emmy's right. Maybe I do deserve to have nice things.

I take a sip of wine, swishing it around in my mouth. It's quality, not the grocery store stuff we used to buy. I let the flavor linger on my tongue before swallowing.

One date. One interview. One final hurrah for Josie Days before she gets buried in the credits. "Okay, Hugo. You've got a deal."

Chapter 14

You're a bad influence.

Sean

I ARRIVE AT the Shirley Brasserie right on time for my date in my Maison Margiela black-and-white checkered suit and my point-tipped Santonis with the side buckle. The lights are low, glinting off the Spanish Colonial Revival architecture and the dark-wood-and-mirrored decor. I've done a few photo shoots here. It was a great choice on Emmy's part—sophisticated, yet relaxed. Glamorous, yet charming. A place where, most of the time, people like me can enjoy a fantastic meal out in peace.

Most of the time. When it's not the site of a celebrity dating show.

I spot Mount Ramirez and his contest winner at their table,

surrounded by cameras. Seems like the fun has started without me.

"Ramirez!" I swoop over to where they both sit like two pieces of petrified wood holding glasses of expensive wine. Clapping my friend's shoulders from behind, I press my cheek to his and give a hammy smile to the camera. "Ooh!" I toss a knowing look to his date. "Smooth as a baby's butt!"

"Get off me, dude!" Ramirez complains, pushing me away with a laugh. His date is chuckling, too. See, everyone's loosened up already. My work here is done.

I settle into a chair at the table they have waiting for me and check my watch. This is good. I'll spend an hour here and then head to the EV charging station in Ojai to meet the person-of-discretion who received my parcel. I open up the auction on my phone for another peek at my prize. Every time I do this, a spotlight comes to life inside me. That hat! It's so perfect, so full of all that good *Hamilton* energy. I can't wait to hold it in my hands.

I tuck the phone away and swallow my excitement. I don't even know which of the women on the show I'm meeting today. I didn't think to ask Emmy. Whoever she is, I hope she gets here soon.

Jason Momoa and Channing Tatum are having dinner a few tables over. I should go say hi. Katee Sackhoff and Tricia Helfer seem to be having a friends night out, too—that's a lot of beautiful, badass *Battlestar Galactica* in one place.

Just as I'm reaching for my water, a commotion breaks out at the door. Is there a fight in the foyer? That doesn't usually happen at the Shirley Brasserie. Actually, I think it's my date arriving. Option C is certainly attracting a crowd. I fight for a glimpse of her through the writhing mass of camerapeople and spot…blue.

That can't be right.

Except it is. My date is *blue*, like literally blue. She's got on dark jeans and kitten heels and a loose, gray plaid vest over a white tee, but her head is bald and blue with little bits of prosthetics glued to it to make her cheeks and chin more pronounced. My date is a Zentharian.

I chuckle to myself. This isn't Option C. It's Josie.

My chair scrapes the floor as I get to my feet to greet her. I go in for the cheek kiss, but her body language says "whoa there, step back, partner," so instead, I wrangle my grin into nonchalance as I pull out the chair for her. "Hello. Good to see you again."

"My rideshare was late. Sorry."

"No worries. He was probably a little surprised when he saw you. Maybe circled the block a couple of times."

"Yes, you human males can be easily spooked."

She's in character, no less. I don't even know what to say. Our server appears and asks Josie what she'll have to drink without a flicker of hesitation. I'll tip her extra just for that.

"I'll have a pinot noir, and fill it right up to the brim," Josie says.

"Cordero San Giorgio, 2020," I clarify, and the server nods and rotates away on a heel. Meanwhile, the cameras are all up in our faces, filming and snapping. I pinch my chin and go for an iconic "we're in the middle of a very serious conversation" look. Josie tolerates the intrusion for a good ten seconds and then hisses at them in true Zentharian form. Actually *hisses*.

I scrunch my nose at the camerapeople. "Can you give us some space?"

They back off, but not far. Meanwhile, Josie makes a fuss of hanging her purse on the back of her chair, smoothing her napkin, and moving her water glass to a different location. The alien getup accentuates certain details of her face: her deep-set dark eyes, the full upper lip. The kiss she gave me in the closet comes racing back to me, which reminds me…

"I thought you were taking my out," I say.

Her gaze finally meets mine. "I tried to."

"Was it another moment of weakness?"

"Nope," she says. "Something else entirely."

So much for my smoldering appeal hypothesis. Our server interrupts the conversation to give us our menus and Josie's wine.

"Shall we start with something from the raw bar?" I suggest.

"I don't do shellfish, remember?"

"Allergy?"

"More like an aversion."

"Charcuterie instead?"

"Sure." She peruses the menu some more. "And I'll have the wild mushroom and truffle risotto."

"The lobster with green beans." I hand my menu back to the server. "Oh, and throw some mushrooms on there, too. Why not?" I wink. "It's a special occasion."

Our server tries to take Josie's menu, but she stuffs it under the table and shows her teeth. Once the girl leaves, she raises it against her cheek, shielding her face.

"You really don't like being on camera, do you?"

"Is it that obvious?"

At the next table, Jason Ramirez and his date are getting a photo op with Orbit, the mascot from *Lost Star*, while Kai, his puppeteer, looks on.

"You getting ready for a role?" Josie asks, eyeing my water glass.

"Audition." I finger the rim. "For the role of a sexy seminarian who was wooed away from Mother Church by a naughty nun."

She smirks.

"She kisses me in the confessional, then whisks me onto the next bus to El Paso—"

"Okay, okay."

"—where we have a whirlwind romance involving ranches and horses and some guy named Pancho."

"Land the plane, Sean."

Our charcuterie board arrives. It's a work of art on a maple plank—meats and cheeses and crackers and olive tapenade. I devour a salami and Gruyère roll in two bites.

"So, what changed your mind about coming?" I ask.

She reaches for a sesame cracker. "Oh, you know."

She's being intentionally vague. No worries. I love a good mystery. "Mm. Yum. You should try this." I roll a piece of prosciutto around a sliver of Asiago and raise it to her lips. I expect her to pluck it from my fingers, but instead, she holds my gaze and takes it into her mouth with deliberately slow sensuality, regardless of the fact that she's got a big, blue alien head.

The smile creeps across my lips, unbidden. This woman is like one of those crazy indie flicks. The plot is all over the place, and you can't look away or you might miss a guy with a pornstache lurking in an alcove or a random flock of symbolic flamingos. You don't understand what's going on, but you feel it…whatever the something is you're supposed to feel.

Unfortunately, at this moment, I glance over to the bar and lock eyes with Kelly Kennerman, one of the *Lost Star* producers, who immediately excuses herself and makes her way over to our table. Kelly and I dated awhile back. It didn't end well.

Who am I kidding? None of them ever did. But what does she want with me now?

"You're supposed to leave work at work," she says, eyeing Josie's blue makeup. "That includes work resources."

I don't want Kelly taking out any hard feelings about me on Josie. "It's my fault, Kelly. I asked Josie to try the Zentharian makeup on herself to make sure it wasn't too uncomfortable. How does it feel?"

She lifts her wine glass in a toast. "Like I'm in my own skin."

Kelly frowns. "As proactive as that sounds, it's a waste. We're going to be phasing the Zentharians out."

What? "But they're our greatest allies in the quadrant."

"They're outdated," Kelly replies. "Viewers want something new and exciting. We've also gotten feedback that the show lacks diversity. We want to respond to that."

"By getting rid of a whole race of aliens?" I ask.

"We're still brainstorming ideas."

"You could do something like in *Más Allá de Las Estrellas*," Josie pipes up.

"I beg your pardon?" Kelly couldn't possibly sound more condescending, but Josie doesn't react as she spreads pepper jelly on another cracker.

"It's a Mexican sci-fi show on LatinXtremo. They've got this alternate history thing happening in another solar system, like time got twisted up into a knot. In this world, the indigenous people beat back the imperialists. The planet ends up being a sentient character of its own, too. I can't explain it; you'd have to see it."

I fix us both another prosciutto wrap and hand Josie hers. "Fascinating," I say. "I'd love to hear more about that."

Our server is hanging back with our main courses, but I wave her in so that our uninvited guest is forced to step aside. "Mm, this looks delicious." I point to Josie's wine glass, and our server nods her understanding.

"Well, I'll let you two get back to your dinner," Kelly finally says.

I waggle my fingers in dismissal. "See you, space cowboy." I set the little dish of melted butter aside and dig into my lobster. It's cooked to perfection. I hold a forkful toward Josie, but she scrunches up her nose.

"No shellfish, remember?"

"Oh yeah." I retract my fork. "Why's that again?"

"It tried to kill me."

"I thought you weren't allergic?"

"It was food poisoning."

I shove another forkful in my mouth. "According to that logic, I should never eat shellfish again, either. Or frozen yogurt. Or anything at a buffet. How's the risotto?"

"Trufflicious."

She offers me a bite. Holding her gaze, I take it into my mouth just like she did to me. I have to admit that it's weird flirting with her in all that makeup. The blue has rubbed off her lips from eating, and I zero in on them and relive the moment where she kissed me in the closet. She didn't even ask, just went for it. Although, let's be real. It was clear that I was not going to say no.

The risotto is heavenly. I let my eyelids flutter in a moment of ecstasy before I imagine Jamie, my trainer, bursting through the door with a war cry and an exercise band.

"I'm not supposed to be eating this stuff. I've gotta be ripped for this superhero audition," I admit.

Her eyebrows go up as she scoops another forkful and holds it out for me.

I narrow my gaze at her. "You're a bad influence."

She pulls it away at the last second and pops it into her own mouth with a smirk. "Am I?"

Before I can reply, the camera crew swarms our table. A still camera snaps, and the spotlight blinds me for a moment before Kai, our big, smiling puppeteer, appears and shoves Orbit between us, like a third diner at our tiny table.

Right. Back to work.

Chapter 15

I gotta dance.

Josie

I ALMOST LAUNCH myself away from the dining table when that awful, furry, blue thing appears next to me. Puppet Traumatic Stress Disorder isn't in any of the medical books, but it should be.

"Yum! That look good!" the puppeteer says in Orbit's squeaky-yet-throaty voice. "Let's take picture together."

I feel my face scrunch into a grimace. "Er—"

But Sean has already dragged his chair closer to mine and is giving his signature Captain Footwork smile for the still camera. The intrepid captain is typically very serious, having to run a ship full of dancing fools and all, but once in a while, he does this goofy Tom-from-*Parks-and-Rec* grin. Sean's got it down.

Of course he does—he *is* Captain Footwork. Meanwhile,

the risotto is swimming in my stomach, but I don't want to call attention to my puppet phobia by running away screaming.

"You give taste?" the puppet asks me—or, more accurately, the puppeteer asks me. Frankly, I'd rather spoon-feed the hand creature from the *Alien* movie, but I hold my fork steady as Orbit pretends to eat.

"Here, you can cuddle him," the puppeteer says in his normal voice, lowering Orbit into my lap before I can say *Sure* or *No thanks* or *For the love of God, take that cursed thing away from me!* It's as heavy as a baby, what with all of the animatronics. Not at all like Chuy, who was wood and cloth and oh-so-flammable.

Orbit's head swivels on his neck until he's looking up at me with his oversize, oval-shaped black eyes, twin pools of shiny doom. In a moment of sheer irrationality, I wonder if all puppets know one another, if they have a collective puppet consciousness, and how loyal they are to one another. For example, would they all band together for a singular puppet purpose, like vengeance?

A camera snaps, immortalizing the look of horror on my face. The puppeteer lifts Orbit from my lap before he can bare his puppet teeth and go for my jugular. At the same moment, the alarm on Sean's watch goes off, and I actually cry out.

"You okay?" Sean is looking at me, his grin gone.

I push back my chair. "I gotta go do something."

"What?"

There's a piano player in the other direction playing lounge music, kind of jazzy. A saucer of open floor space around him beckons.

I grab Sean's ringed hand. "I gotta dance."

I tug him over to the polished wood floor, which looks like parquet with a million dollars' worth of polish, and swivel into his arms. Again, he's the perfect height for me. I hold him close, more like a body shield than a dance partner. Our footwork is awkward and wrong, but it's not our fault. This isn't the kind of music you dance to.

"Are we hiding from the cameras again?" Sean murmurs as the pianist reads the room and switches up his song to accommodate us. Now he's playing "It Don't Mean a Thing (If It Ain't Got That Swing)." Sean reacts like he's been programmed.

"No. I just hate puppets."

"I hate puppets, too. Horrible little scene-stealers."

We dance, and the only way I can think to describe it is with the Spanish word fluidez. There are no sharp corners to him, no jerks or starts. He moves me around him like a planet around the sun, and we are in a galaxy of our own even though there are people and cameras everywhere.

"I've danced with you before," he says, as if just remembering.

"Have you?" I say with matching nonchalance.

The pianist switches it up again, to "Cotton Eye Joe." Line dancing, really? But, again, I guess the dude is psychic because it's perfect. I fall into the steps, and Sean improvises around me with some Irish dance moves, riling up the crowd. He's definitely in his element. This used to be my element, too, and the reminder tugs at a place just below my breastbone, like the ribbon on a gift tied too tight.

I'm breathless by the time the pianist changes to a slow song. I hope I'm not sweating off my blue makeup as my arms find their way around Sean's neck, and he stops showing off and just holds me close. My body lights up, and I can't look at his mouth because it'll be too much, so I rest my cheek against his and just relish the sensation of being in his arms. The bergamot in his cologne makes this feel even more intimate. I'd swear it even dims the lights a notch.

Sean's watch alarm beeps again.

"Do you have somewhere to be?" I whisper against his side-burn, both disappointed and hopeful at the same time.

"Yes." But he doesn't stop dancing, doesn't pull away from me, doesn't break our rhythm in any way, and the man has rhythm. His jaw moves against my cheek. "You know, if I'd known it was you, I would have planned something more."

A zing of excitement vibrates all the way to my toes. It's stupid of me not to let the topic die right there, but somehow, here in Sean's arms, dancing to an overachieving pianist's version of "My Heart Will Go On," stupid feels right. "What would you have planned?"

He hesitates, and something about the fact that he does makes this whole affair seem sweet. Innocent, even, like we're clueless teenagers drowning in insecurity and not thirty-something adults who know what the hell we want.

"I don't know," he admits. "That's why I came to find you at work. To ask you what you would like to do with me."

And it's at that moment that I realize how much I like Sean O'Sullivan—*this* Sean O'Sullivan—the man, not the persona, and I shouldn't, for a lot of reasons. Firstly, he's a celebrity, and I'm not anymore. He lives in a five-million-dollar mansion, and I live in someone else's trailer on someone else's property. Most importantly, he thrives in the spotlight while my entire world relies on me staying in the shadows. This moment isn't fair, isn't real, shouldn't even be happening. It's a weird little anomaly in the mind-blowingly huge expanse of space and time—a tiny bone tossed to me by a careless universe, so minuscule, so improbable, so negligible that it might as well not be happening at all.

But I don't want to let it go.

Sean's pulled back and is watching me, waiting for me to tell him what I'd like to do with him. I grasp for something to say. All the words in both the languages I have mastered seem to have fled. But I need to say something. It's time to end this…whatever this is. This dangerous game. These dangerous feelings.

God, I need to stop looking at his mouth. I also need to stop looking at his eyes, green as emeralds with the thinnest ring of golden brown around the pupils. When he finally gives up and tears his gaze away, I swear it takes a piece of me with it.

"I've got to go," he says.

"Where?"

"Ojai."

"What are you doing in Ojai?"

He hesitates. "I have to pick up a package."

"Is it a bomb?"

"No."

"A bioweapon?"

"No."

"A once-extinct creature from the Mesozoic Era?"

"Okay, now I'm starting to think you're messing with me."

He's already disengaging, leading me back to our table, pulling my chair out so I can sit but not sitting down himself.

I've blown it. Been too weird. Turned him off. He's going to say goodbye now. Walk away and leave me here alone. I guess that's good. I mean, that was the plan, right?

But he freezes. "Would you…like to come with?"

He did *not* just say that. Even after the dinosaur comment? "Are you serious?"

"Why wouldn't I be serious?"

I do want to come with. I want to get the hell out of this amazing restaurant even though we haven't had dessert yet. I want to slide into the passenger seat of his car, probably something low and leather, and watch his hand with all those rings work the gear shift like a king with a scepter.

But that's the impulsive part of me talking. The Josie who doesn't think things through, who reacts based on emotion and makes everyone around her suffer the consequences.

I don't even know why he's asking me to do this. I have an alien head, for crying out loud! He could throw a rock and hit three other women who would love to go with him—prettier women, happier women, easier women. Well, maybe not easier *that* way. I mean women who are easier to get along with. Easier to have a conversation with because they don't just keep making crap up to hide the truth.

He's standing at the edge of the table, looking at me. Our dancing has disheveled him in a good way. The shock of blond hair is awry on his forehead. Blue makeup mars his cheek and his white collar. There's a shiny layer of sweat on his neck, and everything else is a sinewy reminder of how this man can move.

Fluidez. Fluidity? Fluidness? Maybe the word is simply *smooth*.

"I really do have to leave, so if you want to come…"

It's the second time he's invited me to go with him. If I don't control my mouth, it will automatically say, *Of course, Sean, anything you want*, and the rest of me will follow him somewhere, anywhere, everywhere, but that's what got me into this mess in the first place.

"I can't," I say. "I'm sorry." *You have no idea how sorry.*

"O-*kay*." He draws the word out. His bottom lip protrudes in a forced frown, hands digging into his pockets. He waits a beat, giving me time to change my mind. When I don't, he says, "I guess I'll see you at work then. Goodbye, Josie," and spins on one expensive heel.

It's too abrupt, this ending. Awkward, strange, tragic, a crying shame. I start to say, *You, too* or *Thanks for dinner* or something equally lame to try and salvage it, but he's already headed for the door.

He doesn't look back.

Chapter 16

That must have been some pimple.

Transcript. *Hollywood, De Repente* **with Hugo Valencia.**
October 7. *[translated from Spanish]*

HUGO: Welcome, ladies and gentlemen, to our exclusive interview with Ms. Josie Days, the winner of a date with Sean O'Sullivan and a former resident of the beautiful country of Mexico, my homeland. She's promised us an exclusive first look at the date she had with Captain Footwork himself. Welcome, Ms. Days. You're not dressed as an alien today, but I must say it's odd to be talking to the back of your head.

JOSIE: I got the idea from Sia.

HUGO: Okay, before we share some photos and video, let's catch the viewers up on a little bit of your background. Josie is a cosmetologist from Florida who now works on the *Lost Star* set. She learned her Spanish in school and while at an unnamed nunnery, apparently. But we're all more interested in how your date went. Tell us a little bit about the conversation.

JOSIE: We didn't get to talk much. There were a lot of cameras.

HUGO: Ah yes! Look at that marvelous photo of you and Sean with Orbit. God, I love that little guy. So cute, isn't he?

JOSIE: Er—

HUGO: I suppose you also didn't get to talk a lot because of all the dancing.

JOSIE: There was some dancing.

HUGO: Look at these two punishing the tile! You have great rhythm together. I think I saw some sparks flying there. How about you, ladies and gentlemen?

[studio audience hoots and whistles]

JOSIE: There was nothing to see. It was a contest. The date was the prize. We had dinner. We danced. I can't help it if Sean likes to show off.

HUGO: Well, you like to show off, too, no? With your blue
head, all painted up.

JOSIE: I...had a pimple.

HUGO: That must have been some pimple.

JOSIE: Enormous.

HUGO: But aren't you a makeup artist? Couldn't you cover
it up?

JOSIE: I did. With lots of blue makeup. That we weren't
going to focus on during our chat.

HUGO: Right. But come on, Josie. We all saw you kissing
Sean in the closet last week. If it was just a contest, explain
that.

JOSIE: Um...explain what?

HUGO: The kiss?

JOSIE: Er...*[clears throat]* Right.

[long pause]

HUGO: It's not much of an interview if you don't speak, Ms.
Days.

[another long pause]

HUGO: Ms. Da—

JOSIE: *[interrupts]* Have you ever made a mistake before, Hugo? One you saw coming from a mile away, but you did it anyway? You knew better, you did. You knew there were going to be consequences, but the promise of pleasure and satisfaction from doing that thing was too great to deny yourself? Has that ever happened to you before, Hugo? Because that's what that kiss was. A mistake I couldn't walk away from. An opportunity to engage in sheer, intoxicating stupidity with Sean O'Sullivan's mouth. And I took it. Judge me if you must.

HUGO: Wow.

JOSIE: So, yes, that's done. I kissed him. We ate dinner. We danced. And now I can go back to living my normal life.

HUGO: I see. Except I think we're all asking the same thing.

JOSIE: And what's that?

HUGO: Why does it have to be over? He seems to like you, too. Who knows? You might be very happy together.

JOSIE: Happiness is a trite, impossible notion.

HUGO: That's a little dark, don't you think?

JOSIE: Is it? Well, then I'll tell you another reason Sean and I could never be together.

HUGO: And what is that?

JOSIE: I'm in love with someone else.

HUGO: You are?

JOSIE: Yes.

HUGO: Who is this person?

JOSIE: I can't tell you that. But he's very sexy, even sexier than Sean O'Sullivan. If Sean is an eleven on the sexy scale, this guy is a seventeen.

HUGO: I see. Is he another actor?

JOSIE: Oh no. You don't know him. He's a very private person with a very private profession. Perfect for someone like me.

HUGO: What does he do?

JOSIE: He's a . . . *[gulps]* spy.

HUGO: Like James Bond?

JOSIE: Yes. I probably shouldn't have told you that. But since you'll never meet him, it doesn't matter.

HUGO: Can we get a first name?

JOSIE: And blow his cover? What kind of girlfriend would I be?

HUGO: Can you tell us anything at all about him?

JOSIE: He's great. He's normal. He's the perfect, super-handsome but totally normal spy man. For example, he has a dog. A golden retriever. Everybody likes those, right? *Right?*

[audience cheers]

HUGO: So, does Sean know that the kiss was a mistake?

JOSIE: We don't speak of it.

HUGO: Why not?

JOSIE: I broke his heart. Sean told me he never wanted to see me again. That it was too painful. Oh, look, I think your staff is waving to us.

HUGO: You broke Sean O'Sullivan's heart? He hasn't said anyth—

JOSIE: Sorry, Hugo. I believe my time is up.

HUGO: So it is. Thank you, Josie Days, for speaking with us today. It's been…illuminating.

JOSIE: Where's the exit?

HARPER ROSE TALKS HOLLYWOOD, OCTOBER 8

HARPER: Welcome, welcome everyone. Thanks for tuning in to *Harper Rose Talks Hollywood*. Well, the mystery of the day is this strange interview Sean O'Sullivan's *Date Your Celebrity Crush!* winner Josie Days had with a Mexican gossip columnist and why none of the rest of us can get her to talk to us. Confused yet? I know I am. This girl is as gringa as her BFF, Emmy Connor, but somehow, she speaks another language. How is that even possible? Is she European?

Anyway, I've got a printout of the translation of that interview, and even reading it in English, I can't figure out what's going on. She's a nun, and now she's in love with a spy? What kind of spy has a golden retriever? You can't just grab a go bag and hop on a plane when you have a golden retriever waiting for you at home. Frankly, I think she's making all this stuff up. And why would she do that? I'll tell you why. Because she has a secret. That's right; you heard it here first. Josie Days, Sister Butt Cheek Bus Flasher, is hiding something. I think our debonair starship captain is smart to stay far, far away from her. That kind of crazy might be contagious, and he's already got a few cards in his hand from that particular deck. *[clears throat]* In case you don't remember, his brother, disgraced actor Seamus O'Sullivan and the original Captain Footwork, was fired for stalking a stuntwoman. Shocking and tragic, yes, but if Brother Number One hadn't turned out to be an obsessive, creepy weirdo, we wouldn't have our dashing Sean in the captain's chair, guiding us through the steps of the interstellar mambo, now would we? One door closes, people.

But I will admit that this Josie person did say one thing that didn't sound like a big, fat lie or the ramblings of a lunatic. She said kissing Sean O'Sullivan was the kind of mistake you know you're about to make but can't stop yourself from making. I felt that deep in my soul. If I were in a closet with Sean O'Sullivan, I don't think I could stop myself from kissing him, either. If someone told me the world was going to end if my lips touched his, I'd be like, *Sorry world, you're on your own. [sighs]* I'm not alone in that, am I? Let me know in the comments.

This is Harper Rose. Don't forget to stop and listen to the Rose!

Chapter 17

I'm a gosh darn hero.

Sean

THE DRIVE TO Ojai and back was uneventful. It's probably a good thing Josie didn't come with me. Putting aside the unethicalness of bringing an innocent to a clandestine exchange of illegal cosplay accessories, I don't think I would've been able to contain my excitement, and then she would've really thought I was a weirdo.

Still, I wish she'd at least *wanted* to come. She showed up at the restaurant, so why didn't she want to come with me on the drive? Was it something I said? Something I did? I thought about pulling her aside at work this week to ask but didn't want it to look like I cared that much, especially after I saw the translation of her interview with Hugo Valencia. I know by now that Josie makes crap up pretty much on a minute-by-minute basis, but it felt pretty personal when she said she'd ditched me for a guy she liked better. Truth or lie, the overall sentiment is the same: she's not interested.

And if she's not interested, I'm not interested.

The house is quiet. Rory's gone home for the evening. I punch in the code on the lock to my cosplay room and step inside, letting the glory of this place wash over me. I set my phone to shuffle the *Hamilton* soundtrack. There. The stage is set.

The hatbox awaits me. With gentle fingertips, I remove the lid and relocate my treasure to the workbench. God, it's gorgeous. I click on a gooseneck lamp, stifling a sneeze at the smell of dust particles burning on the incandescent bulb as I inspect the hat and pick off a microscopic shred of lint. It's perfect.

More than perfect. It's *epic*.

I place it on my head and turn to the mirrored wall, straightening my spine and assuming my most presidential stance. Christopher Jackson wore this hat for a whole year, and I get to wear it on my head. *My* head! The feeling is indescribable. Like time traveling. Like crossing the Delaware into paradise. Like falling in love.

I know I shouldn't have bid on it. It was reckless and dumb and dangerous. I should've just let it disappear into the seedy underbelly of the performing arts theft world forever.

Oh, but then what kind of a monster would I be?

My phone dings with a message. It's Siobhan giving me the time and place for the family meeting with two agenda items—number one, Seamus, and number two, Da's sixty-fifth birthday party.

I remove the hat and set it onto an empty wig head. It doesn't feel right to have something so special closed up in a box. Frankly, as good as it makes me feel to have it here in my collection, I need to turn it over to the authorities before they discover I have it—there was a news story about the ongoing search just this morning.

Of course, I'm not the one who stole it, just the unfortunate buyer. If Seamus knew about the hat, would he turn me in? I'd like to think blood is thicker than water, but who knows? He was pretty mad about me taking over the role of Captain Footwork. And that's not the first time I've stolen his spotlight. In high school, he had the lead role in *Oklahoma!*—Curly—but he came down with the flu on closing night. I was his understudy, so I stepped in. Brought down the house.

That was the first time I realized how good I was at the acting thing. And Da, well, he was so proud. He'd never responded that way to one of Seamus's performances. It felt good but also…wrong. Seamus was the elder brother. He was supposed to be better than me.

My brother punished me mercilessly for months after that show. Anytime I celebrated my success, he shut me down. He went out of his way to belittle and humiliate me. *Stupid, crybaby, weirdo, wanker.* It wasn't that different from Da's complaints about me—that I was too sensitive, that I needed to control my feelings. "Man up, Seanny Boy," Da said when our cat died. "It's not that funny," he'd scold me when I'd get in a giggling fit over something that caught my fancy. "Settle down."

"Seamus will get over it," Mam had soothed as we sewed together, me in tears because the brother I loved so much had turned on me.

I still wonder if my auditioning for Captain Footwork after Seamus got let go was an act of revenge. An unbottling of the anger that somehow got inside me without me knowing it. But it must be some weird kind of anger because I never felt angry. I still don't.

Truth is, I don't know what I feel.

I sigh. The hat's probably not worth the risk. Besides, I've already gotten to enjoy it for a week. Took a bunch of photos. I haven't had a chance to cosplay it in public yet—damn shame, that—but life is full of disappointments. There's a nonemergency police line. I'll look it up and call right now.

I reach for my phone, gaze still locked on my prize, but for some reason, my hand stops in midair, does a one-eighty, and retracts, smoothing the facial hair around my mouth instead.

You know what? Fear is a terrible motivator for decision-making. This room has a lock. All I have to do is use it. Besides, I saved this hat from disappearing forever. I'm a gosh darn hero. Soon, it'll be back where it belongs, in a storage unit in New York City, unseen and unappreciated.

Soon. Just not right away.

My phone dings again. I get ready to swipe the notification of Siobhan's text away and see instead that it's Jason Connor inviting me to their game night. I always say no, but this time my ring finger hesitates over the reply field.

If I go, I might get to see Josie. I'm pretty sure she attends those nerdfests.

My heart does a little flip-flop remembering the feel of her in my arms as we danced. The George Washington hat with its jaunty bow and five-star-general energy seems to be urging me on.

"Should I do it?" I ask the hat. It doesn't reply, so I answer for it. "Of course you should."

I type *yes* but stop before hitting SEND. What am I doing? I've let the excitement of the moment rule the day. I can't go to game night with Josie. I like her too much. I thought about her the whole drive to Ojai. I sang my entire playlist to her, pretending she was there in the car with me. That's not normal.

Settle down, Seanny Boy.

If I go to game night to see her when she doesn't want to see me, it's akin to stalking her, and that would make me as bad as Seamus.

I swipe a quick, rude reply telling Jason I don't want to go to his dorky game night. He replies back immediately.

Jason: Dude, please come. I have something really important to ask you.

Sean: Then ask me right now.

Jason: It's too important to ask over text. Plus, it would mean a lot to Emmy.

I groan. But at least it gives me an excuse. If Josie asks me why I'm there, I can truthfully say that Snack begged me to come. It's not my fault he's a needy little chump.

Sean: Fine, I'll come.

Jason: Great. See you at seven.

I stare at the screen. Then I start a text asking Jason if he thinks Josie will be there. I erase it and try again. Each attempt feels more forced and pushy than the last. Finally, I shove the phone away. Either she'll be there or she won't.

And why should I care either way?

Chapter 18

Do the math.

Josie

I SLAM THE door to the trailer, throw my purse onto the couch, and change into my purple-and-black Halloween pajamas and my super-fluffy pink sherbet robe. In my RV-sized fridge, there are two Coronas that have been astral projecting themselves into my brain ever since I left the studio. I plop down on the couch with one of them and enjoy an ice-cold sip.

Taking a deep breath, I open a browser tab on my phone. Here we go.

My thumbs tap the words *Josie Days* into the search bar. "Please, please, please, nothing new," I whisper, squeezing my eyes shut as I hit ENTER. It's been a week since my date with Sean. Six days since my interview with Hugo. Yes, I expected chatter in the aftermath of all that, but it should have died down by now. I mean, there's nothing left to say. Nothing new has happened. The main cast has been filming on location all week, and when Sean *was* in the studio, I either avoided him or made myself too busy to talk. Not that he came looking for me. All that adds up to *surely everyone has shut up about me by now.* Unless they've figured out who I really am, which, of course, is the doomsday scenario.

I grit my teeth and pop open one eye. There's a ridiculously long list of results—again. Dammit. And…wait. Is that Emmy's vlog? Tell me she did not.

I tap the link.

VLOG, RANDOM YOGA POSES, OCTOBER 13

EMMY: Good morning, everyone! It's time for *Random Yoga Poses* with me, Emmy Connor. As you can see, I'm getting further and further along in this pregnancy, and the poses I'm presenting are getting less and less random and more and more targeted to what a person with a watermelon inside her can do without losing her balance. And there's a lot, don't get me wrong! Yoga is great for pregnant women. Just check with your doctor or midwife first.

Oh, we've got a comment already. All righty, let me just waddle over here to the phone to see who it is. DestinyK says, "Hi, Emmy. Is your friend Josie still dating Sean O'Sullivan? And if so, has she been in his private jet yet? I've heard there's an Austin Powers love nest inside there."

Wow, DestinyK. So, unfortunately none of that has to do with yoga, except maybe a stretch between crow pose and a love nest. Ha ha, stretch! Get it? I was accidentally funny there for a second. It's hard to be funny at all when you're staring down the birth barrel at thirty-five weeks, especially when you've done this before and know what's coming, am I right, moms?

Anyhoo, let's keep it simple today, shall we? Tadasana. Mountain pose. That's the one where we just stand here. God, even that's hard. Did I tell you we're having a home birth? My midwife says second babies often come so fast it's safer to just have them at home. Isn't that comforting?

Oh, another comment! Wow, you guys are chatty today. HeyCheyenne says, "Hi, Emmy. Can you please tell your friend Josie that she and Sean make a great couple? Also, what's her favorite beauty tip?"

Yeah, I'll tell her that, no problem, Cheyenne. And I have no idea what her favorite beauty tip is, but her eyeshadow skills would make a grown man cry. Anyway, back to Tadasana. Let's connect through all the parts of our feet. Really grounding ourselves because, if we don't, we might just scream *Why, why, why did I do this again?* And the universe will respond, *Because your husband is smokin' hot.* And we'll scream back, *Yes, but contraception exists for a reason!* And that's on us, so now we shut up.

Okay, hands in prayer position at the breastbone. Plead to whatever god you worship or just beg for mercy from an ambivalent universe. What? Another comment? It'll have to wait, like every woman out there in her third trimester. Okay, fine, you know what? I'll read the comment. It's getting a bit existential in here anyway, and Kafka gives me heartburn. Or maybe it's the foot in my diaphragm.

Jojo1611 says . . . oh, hells no. Sorry, Jojo. Not another

message for Josie. Listen, people, we're here for yoga, okay? Yoga! Not gossip about Josie and Sean O'Sullivan and love nests and blah, blah, blah. That's not what we come to the mat for! Understood?

[sighs] I'm sorry I yelled. Is that another comment? I hope it's you guys forgiving me. Namaste4ever says, "I have another question about Josie and Sean O'Sullivan." Gah! You guys! We talked about this! But you know what? You win. Let's forget about yoga. I'm exhausted, and even standing in one place is too much. So, yeah, let's sit down on the mat, and I'll answer all your questions about Josie and Sean. Send 'em at me. Let's go.

I stop the video there. I'm going to kill Emmy! Except I can't kill her because she's my best friend and currently being held hostage by fatigue and hormones. And it's not like she's the only one. The Josie Days hashtag is all over the place. Why do people still care about me? I don't understand it. Hugo's popularity has skyrocketed from my exclusive interview, too, so kudos to him on a successful blackmailing campaign.

He's been true to his word, though. None of the chatter is about Mexico or what I was doing there, and no one, including Hugo, has shown any signs of recognizing me. All anyone seems to care about is whether or not I'm sleeping in Sean O'Sullivan's bed and my hottest beauty tips as a makeup artist.

But it feels weird leaving things the way we did at the restaurant, like dropping a coin into a well and never hearing the splash. I told Hugo I broke Sean's heart, and as far as I know, Sean hasn't disputed it. I probably should have run that by him, but if he doesn't care, I suppose I shouldn't, either.

A message pops up on my phone.

Mom: Hi, honey. Are you around?

My pulse spikes, like it does every time I get a message from her.

Savannah: Yes. Is everything ok?

Mom: Everything's fine. I just wanted to catch up. We haven't talked in a while. How are things?

Guilt immediately floods in. We haven't talked much because I have too many secrets. I search for something I can tell her that's at least partly honest.

Savannah: Work is good. I've been dating a new guy.

Mom: Oh? What's his name?

Savannah: Shane.

Close enough.

Mom: What does he do for a living?

Savannah: He's a homeless bum.

Mom: Come on, Savannah. I don't see you enough for jokes like that to be funny.

Savannah: Sorry. He's a captain.

Mom: Military? What branch?

Savannah: Space Force.

Mom: He's an astronaut?

Savannah: More or less.

Why did I pick this topic? I should have led with the weather.

Savannah: Hey, so the new sci-fi show is really popular, I hear.

Mom: Yes, it's up for an award. Juan Ernesto is really proud of it.

Savannah: Lupe makes a great captain.

Mom: I'll tell her you said so. Or you can do it yourself.

Savannah: You can tell her.

My heart is thumping like I'm in fight-or-flight mode. I wish someone would tell it that there's no saber-toothed tiger. It's just my family.

Mom: The awards are going to be announced next week. It'd be great if you could come. Juan Ernesto would love to see you.

Savannah: Mom, you know he wouldn't.

Mom: He's mellowed out over the years. And Lupe has changed a lot, too.

Savannah: Let them enjoy their success. I don't want to ruin it for them.

Mom: Oh, come on, Savannah. That was so long ago. I'm sure everyone's forgotten about the whole Chuy thing by now.

Savannah: Nope. That meme is back.

Mom: I haven't been on social media much. But it makes sense since TV Azteca just did a tribute. The montage was touching. Aunt Eulalia cried.

Savannah: Mom! You just said you were sure everyone had forgotten about Chuy by now.

Mom: There was hardly a mention of you, I promise.

Savannah: What do you mean by "hardly a mention"?

Mom: Well, there are still those conspiracy theories about you kidnapping him and holding him hostage.

Savannah: I'm not sure an inanimate object can be kidnapped. Or held hostage.

Mom: Maybe I'm translating it wrong.

Savannah: Right. And you still think it's a good idea for me to come for a visit?

Mom: Don't be silly. Of course it is. We miss you terribly.

And cue the guilt. My stomach feels like a wet cloth being wrung out. I know my mother misses me, but I don't believe for a minute that Juan Ernesto and Lupe do. I destroyed everything my stepfather built, and my last words to my sister were to call her a bitch on national TV. I'm glad their careers have both recovered, but it took a long time, so I doubt they're ready to forgive and forget. And it's not like they didn't try to do damage control. Juan Ernesto had a replacement puppet commissioned shortly after Chuy's demise (departure? forced retirement?). Anyway, Replacement Chuy went over like flat soda. So did Replacement Savannah Bateman, for that matter—I think her name was Caroline something-or-other. Whatever magic Lupe, Chuy, and I had created was not repeatable. The educational licenses were never renewed. *Club Bilingüe* closed out its final season a few months later. I learned all of this from Castillo Studios's lawyers via email.

I learned about the financial problems from my mom. They almost lost the house over the scandal. They didn't, thank goodness. But they could have.

No, Savannah Bateman making an appearance in Mexico is out of the question. It would be like digging up nuclear waste—the radiation poisons everyone and everything around it. Haven't I done enough damage?

Savannah: I miss you, too, Mom. And I'll be crossing my fingers for them. Gotta go. Love u.

I send a kissy face emoji her way and then switch over to my ongoing text chain with Miguel.

Savannah: Órale.

Miguel: Órale, wey.

Savannah: I heard you were nominated for an award. Congratulations! I'm really happy for you.

Miguel: Thanks! How are things going with that Shane guy?

Oh, yeah. I mentioned that to him, too, didn't I?

Savannah: I'm probably going to break up with him. He's too high profile.

Miguel: I thought you liked him?

Savannah: I do. But some things are more important.

Miguel: Like what?

Savannah: Like your award! The last thing Castillo Studios needs is an old scandal resurfacing.

Miguel: Listen to me, Sheet. You've got to stop punishing yourself. Go out with this guy again, if you like him. Nobody's going to take away our award over something that happened twelve years ago.

Miguel calling me by my old nickname (*sábana* sounds like *Savannah* and means "sheet" in Spanish) gives me a flash of nostalgia so sharp it hurts. Juan Ernesto and Lupe used to call me that, too.

Savannah: It's just better not to risk it. I couldn't live with myself if I screwed things up for you guys again. And Juan Ernesto would have a stroke.

Miguel: Your mom has him on a low-salt diet, so he'd probably be okay. But it's true, our parents aren't getting any younger. Go, girl, and be happy. We all want that for you.

I don't ask how Miguel knows about Juan Ernesto's diet. Maybe because he's been complaining about it at work. But something else in Miguel's message hits me harder. My parents aren't getting any younger, that's true. Are we going to go on the rest of our lives like this? Surface-level chats with my mom. No contact between Juan Ernesto and Lupe and me. What do I do if something happens to one of them?

I tell Miguel I have to go and then take another couple of swigs of beer to help my nervous system cycle down. That's when I notice the lump under the blanket beside me.

It's too small to be a person and too big to be a book. I live here alone, so there shouldn't be any mysterious lumps. The fact that Netflix has been plying me with horror movies all week doesn't help, either.

I pinch the edge of the blanket between my fingers, my beer bottle brandished at the ready. If it's a basketball-sized spider or a reanimated severed head under there, they're about to get a rude awakening. I throw off the blanket and stifle a scream.

It's a doll. A horrible, plastic doll with dead eyes and a broken mouth and a smudged face from years of love from Jason's son, who never did figure out how terrifying she is.

I'd almost prefer the spider. Or the severed head.

I consider putting Mattie's doll in time-out the way Jason does, but a terrible thought occurs to me: What if dolls are part of the collective puppet consciousness, too? If that's the case, the charred remains of Chuy are probably whispering to her right now. Any minute now, her plastic arms will take on flesh. Her face will stretch into a hateful grimace. Her freakishly strong baby hands will lunge for my throat. Every second it doesn't happen makes it seem more likely to happen the next, especially since it's Friday the thirteenth. In October.

I might have to trek over to Emmy and Jason's after all. I'm already on edge from my conversation with my mom, and there's no way I can relax with this thing in here. Call me superstitious or downright chickenshit, but Possessed Baby's gotta go. I can quickly drop her off and come back home. No sweat.

I stuff my socked feet into a pair of Crocs and begin the short walk up the manicured lawn to Emmy and Jason's house. Golden light in the windows gives the house a warm, friendly glow. In the driveway, I spot Amanda from *Lost Star*'s red BMW convertible and Sean's glistening black electric Fiat.

I halt in my tracks. Sean's here?

When did they start inviting him to game night? Or have they always been inviting him, and he turned them down until now? If so, why did he change his mind? Was it because of me? Was he expecting me to be there?

My swirling thoughts are stupid, every stupid one of them. Sean doesn't need to come to game night if he wants to talk to me. We work together. Yes, I avoided him on purpose, but he's

Sean O'Sullivan—he's only avoidable if he wants to be. Not to mention, maybe it's not even his car. There's more than one black electric Fiat in Santa Monica. Do the math, Josie.

Then Sean's silhouette crosses the dining room window, and my heart lodges in my esophagus so deeply that I have to swallow twice to get it back down. So much for my multiple Fiats theory. I glance down at Possessed Baby, seriously pondering whether I can make it one night with her in the trailer. The crack in her mouth has surprisingly sharp edges—perfect for gnawing off my fingers in my sleep.

"Guess what?" I tell the doll. "You're getting a new home. It's called the garbage can." But, of course, I'm not going to break a little boy's heart because of my own cowardice. With a resigned sigh, I trudge up to the front door and ring the bell.

"Josie, you changed your mind!" Emmy seizes me in a hug, dragging me inside at the same time.

I stumble over the threshold. "I'm just here to return Mattie's doll."

"Hmm. I wonder how that got out there?" Emmy muses, shutting the door behind me.

The pieces are falling into place. "You put her out there on purpose."

"Tía!" Peyton rounds the corner from the kitchen. The house is warm and smells like bacon-wrapped somethings.

"I'm really glad you're here. Jason and I have something important to ask you," Emmy says with a grin.

"Can't it wait?"

"No," she chirps.

Peyton folds herself into my arms. "Plus, we're playing Firefly."

I rock her in a hug. "I thought that was a TV show."

"It is, but it's also a board game," Emmy explains. "Nathan Fillion gave them out as Christmas gifts last year."

In the next room, Sean says something that makes Amanda laugh, and my gaze automatically flicks in their direction. "I can't stay. I left an open beer in the trailer. And I'm in my pajamas."

"I got you, girl." Jason appears with a Corona in hand, a sliver of lime bobbing inside the bottle. What is he, my personal bartender? "And when have pajamas ever stopped you from coming over?"

I'm about to make up another excuse for why I need to beat a floppy Crocs retreat back to my trailer when Emmy hooks my arm and Oompa Loompas me over to the dining room without my consent. Amanda pauses setting up the game to greet me. Sean reclines at the table, dressed like it's the 1940s with a white button-down shirt, suspenders, and an Irish tweed driving cap. I saw him wearing this exact outfit in a Giorgio Armani ad.

His emerald gaze cascades over my attire. "Is it bedtime?"

"It could be," I reply.

We exchange a clandestine smirk. It *is* fun to flirt with him, I'll concede that.

"Josie and Sean can play as a team," Emmy announces.

"Uh-uh," Jason objects. "Putting Sean O'Sullivan and Josie Days too close together might create a sarcasm singularity."

"That'll suck all your whining into it," Sean adds.

Emmy ignores them. "Peyton and I will be a team. Amanda and Jason, you're on your own."

"That's right! Fear me!" Amanda growls. I'd heard she could be competitive.

The Firefly game takes up almost an entire ten-seat dining

room table with a board that rolls out like a yoga mat, little colored ships, and many stacks of playing cards.

"Filming a sci-fi TV show eight hours a day isn't enough nerdiness for you?" I tease.

"I know, right?" Sean jumps in. "They forced me to come here. Nerds! Weirdos!"

"It's not weird. It's really fun," Peyton says. She flips through a deck of cards and pulls one out with a picture of Adam Baldwin wearing a knitted hat. "Look! It's Jayne's cunning hat from the show. It counts as influence."

"I have that!" Sean waggles his finger at the card. "I have that exact hat!" When we all stare at him, his face shifts. "I mean, I have a knitted hat that looks surprisingly similar."

"Awesome," I reply.

Sean's phone buzzes, and he gives it a quick look before tucking it away.

"Seamus?" Jason asks.

"That's probably what Siobhan's calling about," Sean says, with a sad, "We-Don't-Talk-About-Bruno" kind of vibe. "But it can wait."

Despite Sean being my celebrity crush, I've never dug up information on his family—I wouldn't have wanted fans doing that to me. I do know that he has a sister and a brother, though. I wonder what's up, and if there's anything I can do to help, but I don't want to be intrusive.

Jason slaps a player board in front of us. He and Emmy explain the rules as we settle in for an evening in Joss Whedon's fictional Wild West galaxy. Sean and I do okay as partners, mostly because Jason and Emmy tell us what to do. It's fun, I have to admit. Nathan Fillion is a good gift giver.

"So, did you pick up your package in Ojai?" I ask Sean while we wait for Emmy and Peyton to take a particularly long turn.

"I did," he replies.

"Was there a time machine in it?"

He looks confused until I reach out and pluck one of his suspenders. It snaps back against his pec, and he feigns pain. "It's newsboy chic. You know you like it."

"I do like it. It brings back fond memories of my grandpa."

"He must've been a right sexy bastard."

"He was a funeral director. But he turned a widow's head or two."

"I knew it."

"Seriously, though"—I reach out and flip cards for Amanda on her turn—"what did you drive all the way to Ojai for?"

"You guessed it back at the restaurant. Bioweapon. I sold it to that spy you dumped me for for a billion trillion dollars."

I bite my lip. So he did care. "Sorry about that."

He puts a hand over his heart. "I'll never heal."

"It's your turn," Emmy interrupts us. "Do you two aim to misbehave again?"

"Yes!" we cry in unison. Through a combination of skill and luck, we manage to pull off a heist for an interstellar crime boss and collect a bunch of oversize fake bills.

"You two are way too lucky," Amanda complains as we fist bump.

"Sean's not lucky. He's just good. He's good at everything," Peyton says, and then blushes when we all look at her.

Oh, snap. Does Peyton have a crush on Sean?

"That's right, kiddo," he says with a wink. "You tell 'em."

"Speaking of being good at everything..." Emmy's eyes are

shining as she looks between Sean and me. She glances at Jason, who's beaming, too. "Sean and Josie, Jason and I were wondering if—"

Sean's face breaks into a huge grin, and he jumps to his feet. "Yes! Yes, I'll deliver your baby! Thank you so much for this opportunity."

"—if you two would plan our gender reveal!" Emmy finishes.

Sean sits down and pretends to look disappointed. "That makes a lot more sense."

"Will you do it?" Emmy asks. She's grinning like a fool.

"Of course we will!" I say, thrilled.

"Yeah, man, absolutely!" Sean agrees.

"If it's a girl, we're going to name her Boba Tea," Peyton says. "And if it's a boy, Chai."

"Very cosmopolitan," Sean says.

Emmy tells me she'll give the radiologist my email, and from there, it's up to us to plan the reveal. When the game is over (Amanda won, so maybe she's not all talk), it's late. I'm about to excuse myself to head back to my trailer when Sean stops me with a touch on my elbow.

"Want to take a ride?"

Chapter 19

I'm not chasing you.

Sean

"IT'S LATE," JOSIE says. "I should go home."

Why is it *no* at every turn with this woman? "Come on. Just a short drive up the coast, so we can talk about the gender reveal," I cajole. "Don't worry. The paparazzi are all in bed by midnight."

She gives me a wary look before agreeing. Talk about pulling teeth.

The night air is fresh with a bite of chill. In the car, I crank up the seat warmers. How anyone survived in this cruel world before heated seats, I have no clue, but luckily, we don't have to. The electric engine whines as I head west to State Route 1.

"Have you ever done a gender reveal?" she asks.

"Can't say that I have."

"Me, either." She taps around on her phone. "There are a lot of ways to do it. Pink or blue cake. Balloons. Smoke bomb on a drone. Incorporate the siblings."

"Let's do them all."

"Do them all?"

I shrug. "Yeah. It's a big deal. Let's do it right."

"Agreed."

We make a plan for when the ultrasound results come in. Josie will take charge of the cake and T-shirts for Peyton and Mattie. I'll handle the smoke bomb with the drone and secure a bunch of balloons. She sends a text to my phone so we can communicate. Now I have her number.

"You cold?" I ask when she shivers. She's just in her pajamas—must have forgotten her robe at the house. I reach into the back seat and drop a black hoodie in her lap before she can reply. She lifts it up to study the golden star and the silhouette of a man with fist raised. "*Hamilton*," she muses before slipping it on and pulling the hood up over her head.

"You a fan?" I ask.

"Of course."

I knew I liked her.

My phone rings. It's Siobhan again. I swipe it away because I can't deal with that right now and launch my music app instead. The heart-wrenching notes of Ray LaMontagne cut through the night. I expected our gender reveal planning to take longer, but now that we've found ourselves with a chunk of time and a fantastic playlist, my ulterior motive gets to come out and play.

"So, Josie, what's your deal, if you don't mind my asking?"

"My deal?"

"Why are you so hot and cold with me?"

She hesitates but only for a beat. "Maybe because you keep chasing me."

I cough-chuckle. What a ridiculous thing to say. "I'm not chasing you."

She deepens her voice. "I'm Sean O'Sullivan! Come on a date with me! Drive to Ojai with me. Don't leave! We need to talk about the gender reveal!"

"Uh-uh." I hold up a ringed forefinger. "*You* kissed *me*, remember? I gave you an out, and *you* showed up at the restaurant anyway. And *you're* the one who crashed game night."

"You only came to game night because you knew I'd be there!"

She's right, but she doesn't need to know that. I'm controlling this narrative. "Listen, Josie, we're too old for games. There's chemistry between us. I know you feel it, too." She doesn't answer, which is as good as a yes. "Don't you think I deserve to know why you made me look like a schmuck to Hugo Valencia? What is the big deal with telling the truth? That, yeah, we're spending time together. That we enjoy each other's company."

I glance over to where she looks so small and forlorn peering out from the nest of my hoodie, and suddenly I'm acutely aware of the power differential between us. I'm a star on a show where she does the makeup. I'm part-owner of the studio that employs her. I might even be her celebrity crush. It feels almost predatory, pressing her like this.

God, that's a horrible thought. My stomach sloshes. My hands tighten on the wheel. "You know what? Forget I asked. You don't owe me any explanations. I'll take you home."

I pull off at a bluff and start to make a three-point turn to head back down the coast. As I shift into reverse, she gives a sharp "No."

I freeze with the car facing the black ocean and wait. She lowers her hood and brushes her hair away from her face.

"Hugo and I had a deal. He said he'd leave me alone if I went on the *Celebrity Crush* date with you and gave him the exclusive."

I bristle. "What do you mean by 'leave you alone'? Was he hitting on you?"

"It's not like that. I've got a skeleton in my closet, and I don't want anyone dredging it up. Hugo promised not to dig into my past, and for the most part, he's held up his end of the bargain. I told him I was dating someone else so people would stop taking an interest in me, but it didn't work." A sigh billows out of her. "Every day, there's more talk about Josie Days and Sean O'Sullivan."

"So, you only went out with me because you were blackmailed?" My phone rings. It's Siobhan again. I swipe the call away.

"You should take it," Josie says. "It must be important if she keeps calling this late."

"It's important all right. It's just..." I trail off, unsure how to finish the thought. I could just tell her. Why the hell not? She's being honest with me. "My brother, Seamus, you know about him, right? That big scandal with one of the *Lost Star* stuntwomen?"

She shakes her head.

"He got obsessed with her, followed her home, built this weirdo shrine to her and everything. Yeah, well, my da, he…Aw, never mind. You don't want to hear all this." I probably sound like a blathering idiot.

"Your dad did what?" she prompts me.

I study her quiet expression and find myself wanting to tell her, wanting to talk about this with someone. Besides, I've already started. In for a penny, right? I take a deep breath.

"After the scandal, Da sent Seamus to Ireland to help my uncle with this dinner theater he runs in County Cork. My uncle, hoping to retire, turned the operations over to my brother, and what does he do but bankrupt the place. Turns out, he was using the profits from the theater to feed a gambling addiction. He fudged all the books so my uncle didn't realize what was going on until it was too late. Of course, we're going to make it right financially, but now Seamus is getting shipped back to us. I don't know what's going to happen with him. My da almost blew a gasket at our last family meeting. Mam tried to keep a stiff upper lip, but I caught her crying afterward. Siobhan's all but written him off. I'm the only one…" I'm not sure how to finish the sentence. I've never had to say it out loud before. "I'm the only one he can really turn to."

There are hardly any lights on this slice of highway, and the stars are like confetti strewn across the night. With the electric car at rest, there's almost no sound either, except for the ocean and the howl of a single coyote. The moon glares at me, full and bright, like a warning signal saying, *What are you doing, sharing all your dirty laundry with this woman?*

"What'll happen when he gets here?" she asks.

I rub the faux gearshift with my thumb. It's so silly putting these things in electric cars, but it does make driving them more fun. "I'll have to take him in. I mean, he's my brother."

Josie's hand surprises mine on the gearshift, fingers tracing over my knuckles and the rings between them. We both look at my hand as she caresses it.

"You two are close?" she asks.

"We were, yeah." I open my fingers, and she lets them trap hers, a little game of touch. "Seamus was always a little strange, even when we were young. I didn't realize it at the time, of course. I looked up to him. We did everything together—" I cut myself off here. I don't want to give Josie the wrong impression of me—that I'm anything like Seamus. "He was the first Captain Footwork, you know. After Da broke into Hollywood, it paved the way for the rest of us O'Sullivan entertainers. Seamus was the golden boy and got all the big roles…"

I clear my throat. The words feel stuck there.

"You don't have to tell me if you don't want to."

A warmth spreads inside my solar plexus like a spilled cup of coffee. It makes me want to keep going. "When *Lost Star* fired him, I was offered a chance to audition for the part, and I took it. I don't think my brother's ever forgiven me for it. Although I suppose I'll find out when he comes to live with me. Fun times, eh?" I squeeze her fingers with mine and give a weak smile.

The night is so still, it's like the world has stopped turning. She's looking at me in a strange way that suggests anything might happen. She might kiss me. She might cuss me out. She might gift me all her secrets. She might close up even tighter. I have no idea. She's a hard oyster to crack, so why do I keep trying? Is it because I know there's a pearl inside? Or is it because, like my brother, I don't know how to take no for an answer?

I open my fingers to release hers and clear my throat again. "Thanks for listening." My lips twitch in an apologetic smile. "Ready to go?"

"I did live in Mexico, but I was born in Florida."

I freeze. Her eyes are luminous and shadowed in the moonlight—a ghost girl's eyes.

"My dad wasn't the most reliable guy, so that marriage ended early on. Eventually, my mom met my stepfather, Juan Ernesto. We moved to Mexico with him; I was eleven at the time. My stepdad was this big shot in the entertainment industry down in

Mexico City. He had his own studio and produced a lot of children's entertainment—kid shows, telenovelas for teens, that sort of thing. He thought I had an aptitude for acting, so he encouraged me to audition for parts, and I ended up getting them."

"You were a child actress?" I muse. "Wow."

"Not just an actress. A star."

Holy hell. How many layers does this woman have? Or is she just punking me again?

She sucks in a sharp breath. "Listen, nobody can know any of this." Her gaze flicks around the car's interior. "That's why I made all that crap up."

I don't get it. "What's so bad about the fact that you were a child star in Mexico?"

"Because I screwed up, Sean."

"Hasn't everyone?"

"Look, you're just gonna have to take my word for it. In my family, I'm the Seamus."

"You stalked a stuntperson?"

"No! Never mind. It's late, and I'm tired." She flops abruptly to face the dash. "I'm ready to head back."

"I think I missed something."

"Right now, please!"

I snap into action, shoving the stick into gear and whipping the car the rest of the way around to head south. The ocean is on her side now, the moon chasing rather than leading us.

In my family, I'm the Seamus? What could she have done?

It's a silent drive except for the music until we turn off State Route 1 toward Jason and Emmy's place.

"You won't say anything, will you, about what I told you?" she asks as we wind through the quiet streets lined with mansions.

"No, of course not."

"Nothing about my stepdad. Nothing about my time as an actress."

"No, nothing."

"As far as you know, I was a nun. Or a student. I don't care. Either one of those will work. I think Hugo went with the nun story."

"You were a nun," I confirm as we pull into Jason and Emmy's driveway. The car sighs and goes quiet.

"This is important, Sean," she says, eyes wild. "People can't find out who I am."

I feel all squirrelly and unhinged. I wish she'd just tell me what the heck is going on. "What did you do, Josie?"

"Don't ask me that. I'll just lie to you."

"I promise I won't judge you—"

"I joined a cult."

I didn't think it was possible for me to be more shaken. "You did *what*?"

"Robbed a bank, too."

Seriously?

"I ran naked through a grocery store, knocking all the cereal to the floor yelling, 'Down with sugar!'"

I knew she was messing with me. I groan in disgust. "Josie, what the hell?"

"I told you if you kept asking me, I'd lie to you." She tugs my sweatshirt off and tosses it into the backseat before I can tell her to keep it. Her hand goes to the car door handle. "Promise me you won't tell anyone."

"I already promised."

But she makes me do it twice more until she seems convinced that I'm not going to run around LA spilling the deep dark secret that once, a long time ago, she did some acting in Mexico.

What is she so afraid of? Whatever it is, it's what's driving a wedge between us. If she doesn't want to tell me, that's fine. It's none of my business, and I'm not gonna badger her, but I hate how it's eating away at her. She shouldn't have to feel that way. And I don't like the way this night ended. Again.

As she trudges up the driveway, arms crossed against the chill, I lower the passenger side window.

"Hey!" I call.

She turns around, eyebrows raised.

"I had fun misbehaving with you tonight."

Her head bobs. "I did, too." She pivots away.

"You want some advice on how to handle Hugo and the rest of them?"

She pivots back. "I'm listening."

"Control the narrative."

"How?"

"Instead of reacting to what everyone says about you, seed the field. Give them stuff to talk about so they don't have to go looking. For example, if you come with me to my da's sixty-fifth birthday party, they'll be talking about that instead of where you're from and what skeletons you might have in your closet."

Josie twists up her features, feigning deep thought, and now I'm seeing the actress in her. I don't know how I missed it before. "Nice try," she says.

Right. I'm not going to chase her. I'm not. "Well, good night."

I expect her to turn abruptly and disappear around the corner to where her trailer is, but she doesn't move. "How about we make a deal?"

My heart flutters against my will. "I'm listening."

"If, by next week, the masses have lost interest in me, I'll go with you to your dad's party."

"Deal!" I say before she can change her mind. I plunge my hand toward the open window, and she meanders forward at a reluctant pace to shake on it. I lower my voice. "Shall we seal it with a kiss?"

She lets go. "Another nice try."

It was worth a shot. But I don't want to end on that, either.

"You know," I say, "if you ever want to talk, you have my number. Kissing optional." I place my handshake hand on my heart. "Truly."

She turns to go with a whisper of a smile. "See you Monday, Sean."

"Bye, Josie."

I watch her walk away until I can't see her anymore. I can't believe I'm waiting in the wings for this woman to come around, but I kind of like the ache. Like Mam always told us kids when we complained about supper being late: *It's good to be hungry.*

Chapter 20

Do I look like a botanist?

CELEBRITY STRAIGHT TALK, OCTOBER 16

AMIL: Hello, everyone! It's *Celebrity Straight Talk* comin' atcha with Amil Nair and Isla Wallace.

ISLA: Hi-la!

AMIL: Listen, before you all start clamoring at the door like a bunch of proverbial zombies, I'll have you know, we have what you want—photos of Sean O'Sullivan and his edgy new girlfriend, Josie Days!

ISLA: Yay! It hasn't been easy. Josie hasn't made an official

appearance since she gave an exclusive interview to
Hollywood Days Repent.

AMIL: Uh, that's not how you say it, Isla.

ISLA: *Hollywood Day Repent. Days Repentay?* *[groan]* I
don't know how to say it.

AMIL: You have to roll your Rs. *Hollywood, De Repente.*
Like that.

ISLA: Anyway, that's the last we've heard from her, but not
the last we've seen of her. A little bit of expert investigative
reporting has revealed the following.

AMIL: Drumroll, please! One photo of Josie Days and
Sean O'Sullivan gazing lovingly into one another's
eyes. This was a social media post by Emmy's teenage
daughter.

ISLA: What the heck were they doing? Are they in a war
room? What are all those funny little things on the table in
front of them?

AMIL: An excellent question, Isla. I, too, was as confused
as a cat in a bag. But apparently, it was board game night
at the Connors', and according to Peyton (quote) These
two are going down. It's too early to misbehave (unquote).
Well, in my book, where Sean O'Sullivan is involved, it's
never too early to misbehave.

ISLA: It's the first time we're getting a really good look at Josie's face, isn't it?

AMIL: We found a video of her on Peyton's TikTok page as well.

ISLA: Um, I don't know how I feel about this, Amil. Isn't it kind of unethical to stalk celebrities' kids' social media accounts?

AMIL: It's fine, Isla! Don't be such a Debbie Downer! Here's Josie singing a lullaby to Jason's little boy. The video is about a year old, when Jason and Emmy first got married. I really had to scroll deep into Peyton's page. Almost drowned in Taylor Swift posts, actually.

ISLA: Oh God, that feels so wrong. But Josie does have a lovely voice. Oh, she noticed Peyton filming her. She's not happy about it. Oh my! We should've bleeped that.

AMIL: She's a feisty one, all right.

ISLA: I gotta say, I like her, Amil. Teenagers need a firm hand. And so does Sean O'Sullivan.

AMIL: I like her, too. She's got this je ne sais quoi, doesn't she? She's like Everywoman, but less pathetic.

ISLA: I'd say she's more like Anythingwoman. She'll say anything. Do anything. Dress like an alien. Hiss at the camera. Lie shamelessly about her past. There's a real nobility in that. Well, maybe not the lying part.

AMIL: Yeah, but I don't even care about that, Isla, and you know why? Because she's not lying about the important things. Like the kiss in the closet. I think we all felt that. And like this moment right here, with Jason's little boy. That's really sweet and authentic.

ISLA: And have you seen how Sean looks at her? I don't think I've ever seen him look at anyone that way before.

AMIL: That's a good point, Isla. The girls on his arm usually look like houseplants—like he's carrying a rhododendron to the sink to be watered.

ISLA: The rhododendron is an outdoor shrub, Amil.

AMIL: Do I look like a botanist?

ISLA: I think you meant philodendron.

AMIL: Rhododendron, philodendron, who can keep all those dendrons straight? Anyway, my point is, with the dendrons, he always looked so bored. But with this Josie Days person, he just…

ISLA: Lights up.

AMIL: Yes! *[sighs]* Fearless Josie Days, mystery woman

who we all want to be...please take good care of our smokin' hot bowl of Irish stew for us.

ISLA: And please tell us more about that mouth.

AMIL: Oh God, yes. That too.

JOSIE DAYS'S PERSONAL REEL

JOSIE: Hey everyone, it's Josie Days. I opened this account so I could talk to you all directly. Apparently, some of you out there like me, or think I'm interesting, and want to know more about me. That's why I'm recording this video. It's called Ten Things to Hate About Me. I'm hoping, after enough people see it, you'll all stop talking about me or cancel me or do whatever it is you have to do. Bottom line, you'll forget I ever existed. Let's jump right in, shall we?

One. I hate dogs. Yes, I said it. They're slobbery and high maintenance. All you dog people can start writing that hate mail now. Rest assured I'll delete it without reading it.

Two. I'm judgmental. Your hair, your makeup, your face. I'm judging it. Always.

Three. I ate horsemeat once. I knew it, too. Didn't even flinch.

Four. Halloween is overrated. Day of the Dead is way cooler.

Five. That goes for Christmas, too. In fact, I bear a curse where, if I hear a Christmas song before the day after Thanksgiving, an angel loses its wings. Plucked right off!

Six. I wasn't ever a nun. Yes, I lied. I'm a liar.

Seven. *[takes deep breath]* Get ready for this one…I never watched *Game of Thrones.*

Eight. I don't put things back where I got them. If I pull a book off the shelf at the library, I just stuff it back in anywhere. And, if you lend me something, just know that you'll never see it again.

Nine. I hate pumpkin spice. It's the symbol of the oligarchy.

Ten. Sean O'Sullivan and I are officially not together. There will be no more kissing. No more closets. I'm never talking about his mouth again. So, forget your FOMO. You're not missing out on anything. Lose my name, lose my hashtag, and go on with your lives. I don't owe you anything! *[shoots gang signs as she moves off camera, and then quickly comes back on camera]*

Oh, wait, I almost forgot. Some of you were asking about my artwork. Yes, it's available for sale on Etsy. The link is in my bio. I take all forms of digital payment. Please allow one week for shipping. Thank you.

MY EVERYDAY PAPARAZZI MOBILE PODCAST

WOMAN: We're out and about in Beverly Hills, and look who we've spotted—Sean O'Sullivan! Sean! Sean! Do you have a minute?

SEAN: Always.

WOMAN: Josie Days says it's over between the two of you. Do you have anything to say about that?

SEAN: Those Zentharians are cold as ice.

WOMAN: Was the breakup amicable?

SEAN: Have you asked her that question?

WOMAN: She won't do interviews. All we've seen since the *Date Your Celebrity Crush!* debrief is her Ten Things to Hate About Me reel.

SEAN: Her what?

WOMAN: You haven't seen it?

SEAN: I have not.

WOMAN: So you didn't know she hates dogs?

SEAN: No. But a lot of people don't like dogs. What else did she say?

WOMAN: She ate a horse once.

SEAN: Stop.

WOMAN: I'm serious.

SEAN: Well, I'm sure the horse deserved it.

WOMAN: She's against Christmas music before
Thanksgiving.

SEAN: Aren't we all?

WOMAN: She might be a communist. She said pumpkin
spice was a symbol of the oligarchy.

SEAN: She's definitely not a communist. She has an Etsy
store.

WOMAN: Well, never mind. We all still love her! And, by
the way, almost all of her Sean-osie art has sold out of
that Etsy store you mentioned. I tried to buy the last one
yesterday, but someone swiped it before I could complete
the payment.

SEAN: Sean-osie art?

WOMAN: Oh yes! She's got several originals and some
prints, too.

SEAN: Is it…suitable for work?

WOMAN: Mm, most of the time. So, do you think—?

SEAN: Could you excuse me? I need to…look at my phone
for a sec.

Chapter 21

The escape hatch is this way.

Josie

IT'S WEDNESDAY BEFORE I see Sean again. He's been off filming action scenes in the green screen studio, but today, the main cast is back, there are no aliens needed, and I have the rare pleasure of having him on my makeup schedule.

Jason Connor slides into Li Jing's chair. "You ready, Mr. Connor?" they ask.

"Yes, thank you."

"Good morning, Mr. O'Sullivan," I say, attempting to imitate their polite demeanor.

Sean side-eyes me as he takes his seat. "That's so weird. Promise me you'll never do that again."

"Yes, because professionalism is so early 2000s."

"Calling me Sean is still professional. You just can't use my sexy names. Seanilicious. Captain Underpants. Mayor Satisfaction of Lovetown."

"There are other people in the room!" Jason calls from his seat.

"Sit still, Mr. Mayor," I say, "and stop moving your mouth, if that's possible."

I sweep the blond lock of hair off his forehead and secure it with a clip. He closes his eyes as I brush a cotton ball with micellar water across his cheeks.

"How is controlling the narrative going?" he murmurs.

"I guess not moving your mouth *isn't* possible."

"I bought three of your Sean-osie paintings, by the way." One eye pops open. "Guess which ones."

Oh no! He knows I've been painting us. And some of that art is steamy. "I don't think I want to."

"I thought you wanted people to forget about you. Did you change your mind?"

It's a fair question. "More like pivoted. No matter how hard I tried to get people to hate me, they just…wouldn't. But they were happy to buy my art. And they asked for paintings of you and me, so I gave them what they wanted." It's the truth. I've been painting like a madwoman this past week, and my Etsy store is hopping, my bank account along with it.

"Capitalism for the win, I guess."

"Don't judge. If people see me as an artist, they aren't tempted to see me as anything else. In that way, I'm controlling the narrative."

Eyes closed, he holds a fist out for a bump. "I'm proud of you."

I bump it. "Thanks."

"Does that mean you're coming to Da's party with me tomorrow night?"

I hesitate. I've thought about this—a lot. "I can't, Sean. Things are going really well, but I'm sure a big part of that is because we haven't been seen together for a week, and Emmy's been policing Peyton's social media."

He squints at me. "So, you're reneging on our deal?"

"The deal was that people had to forget about me. They haven't."

"Only because you're turning them into customers!"

"I'm sorry, Sean. I took your advice, and this is the way it unfolded. If things quiet down, I'll go with you, pinkie promise. Now hold still so I can do your makeup."

I can tell he's not happy by the way he's got a frown on even when he's supposedly relaxing his facial muscles. I feel bad. I do. I would love to attend a swanky party in Vegas with him. I'd love to be on his arm, have him catch my eye and smile, let our hands touch like they did that night in his car, and give him that kiss he keeps asking for. Maybe more. But we can't always get what we what.

I squirt a moisturizing primer onto my bare fingertips and begin to massage it into his skin. His eyes are closed, so it's easy for me to study all the details. He has a strong brow with just a few subtle worry lines, but they give him the look of a leader. His nose has the tiniest hook shape—captainly. His skin is the skin of a person who takes care of it. His facial hair is perfectly trimmed, the shave around it close with just the faintest bit of razor burn at the neckline, but I'll cover that up. His lips naturally pucker, even when at rest, like he's in a perpetual state of having just bitten into a peach, sucking the juice to keep it from running down his chin.

I adjust the angle of his head. He lets me do it. Doesn't fight, doesn't try to help, just lets me do whatever I want. It's more arousing than it should be.

I dip my sponge into the foundation and dab it onto the tip of his nose, his cheeks and chin, and across his forehead. Then I blend. As I do, my traitorous brain imagines it's my lips working their way across these places instead of my sponge, and he's just lying here, eyes closed, letting me do it. When I get to his mouth, I hesitate. He doesn't need base on his lips, but for the purposes of this fantasy, I brush the sponge across them. His eyelids flutter, and I feel myself suck in a breath.

For the love of God, Josie, be professional! Is it really that hard?

I turn to my tools. Nice, safe, unsexy tools.

"Can I get your help with something?" Sean asks.

"Of course." My voice comes out way too husky. It's a wonder the whole room can't smell the pheromones I'm giving off.

"Kennerman reached out to that studio with the Mexican sci-fi show, and now I have to learn some lines in Spanish."

"His Spanish is terrible," Jason calls from Li Jing's chair. "Help him. Please!"

A tiny thrill sparks inside me. They took my advice and called Juan Ernesto! His show is getting noticed by Hollywood. "Don't they give you a coach for that?" I ask, keeping my voice level.

"Yeah, but—"

"Yeah, but he sucks so bad the language coach isn't enough," Jason answers.

"Shut up, Hard-On," Sean grumbles.

"I'd be happy to help you." I check my sketches. He's getting a white star on his face today. Very ABBA. "Any news on Seamus?"

"He gets in tomorrow."

"The day of your dad's party?"

"Yep."

"Are you taking him?"

"He's not invited."

"Híjole," I say.

"What?"

"Híjole. It's like saying *whoa* or *wow* in Mexico. So, he's just going to stay at your place while the rest of your family is celebrating your dad's birthday in Vegas?"

"I feel terrible about it, but my da doesn't want him there." Sean shrugs in his seat in a way that doesn't make his head move. "They don't even want him to know it's happening."

I'm gentle with the black eyeliner around his eyes, but he's used to this and doesn't flinch or squint. "Are you worried about him being alone in your house?"

"Rory will be there to keep an eye on him most of the time."

I start lining the gems around the perimeter of the star. I don't know how Sean manages to make this look manly, but somehow, he does.

"Mm, your breath smells like mint," he says.

"I ate a tube of toothpaste for breakfast."

As if on cue, Yesenia pops her head in. "Breakfast, anybody?"

I smile at her in greeting. "Dos tacos de papa, por favor, m'amiga." I look at Sean. "You want anything?"

He repeats my order in a clunky accent, but Yesenia smiles. "I'll do his the way you like yours," she tells me in Spanish.

"What did she say?" Sean asks.

"She said she's going to give you brain tacos instead."

"That's not a thing," Sean says.

"It's a thing," Jason and Li Jing reply in unison.

He shakes his head. "Would it kill you to give me a straight answer?"

I suppress a smile. Teasing him is so fun. "Hey, you're in luck," I say, changing the subject. "You have a native Spanish speaker right here who might be willing to give you an opinion on your accent." I look to Yesenia, and she nods her approval. "Why don't you go ahead and read her one of your lines?"

Sean dutifully lifts his script in front of his face where he can read it without looking down. "La escotilla de escape está por aquí."

Yesenia giggles and shrugs. "It's okay."

But she's just being polite. He butchered it. I repeat the sentence correctly for him and explain, "It's *escotilla* like *tortilla*, not *escotilla* like *Godzilla*."

"I knew that."

"And you pronounce all the *es* in escape. Es-CA-pay."

His shoulders rise as he blinks hard and gets into character. His green eyes burn at Yesenia from inside the copious amount of black eyeliner I just applied. "¡La escotilla de escape está por aquí!"

"¡Órale, capitán!" Yesenia replies.

Now it's my turn to laugh. "Well done. I think she's gonna safely make it to the escape hatch."

I wink at Yesenia, who bites her lip to stanch a big grin. Just then Jason Ramirez appears behind her like a mountain rising out of the sea. Startled, she shrieks, jumps, and practically crumples to the ground. Ramirez catches her, apologizing profusely in Spanish. When she finally gets to her feet again, she's beet red. I guess we all know who her celebrity crush is now.

"Almost ready in here?" Ramirez asks. "Hair is waiting."

"Ready." I whip the hair clip off Sean.

"Ready," Li Jing echoes.

Sean and Jason launch from their chairs, and I can't help but smile. With these three superhunks bustling for the door, it does kind of feel like we're hapless space travelers about to be saved by raw sex appeal and dance moves. As he clears the door, Sean shouts, "¡La escotilla de escape está por aquí!" He botches it again, but not as badly.

My phone chimes. It's a message from Miguel.

Miguel: Hey, guess what? Juan Ernesto got a phone call from some Hollywood bigwigs about *Más Allá de las Estrellas*. I can't say anything yet, but things are happening, and they're good!

Warmth spreads across my chest. First, Sean mentioned a collaboration and now Miguel has confirmed it. If I could have a hand in helping my stepdad's studio and my friends' careers, it'll be a tiny bit of recompense for blowing everything up twelve years ago. I type a quick reply.

Savannah: That's great news! Keep me posted, will you? I don't want to miss a thing.

Chapter 22

Sean O'Sullivan, Good Time Guy.

Sean

I'M EXCITED DESPITE myself as Milo pulls up the car. Seamus is slow to come out of the back seat. He looks terrible: puffy eyes, sunken cheeks, bad skin. His hair has grown into greasy, dark spikes. His dress pants, shirt, and vest hang off of him.

I step forward with wide arms. "Brother."

His hug is stiff. Short, too. I don't know what I expected. I lead the way into the house. "I put you in the west wing. You've got the whole thing to yourself."

"I could use a drink first." He leaves his bag in the middle of the foyer and wastes no time locating the bar. His hands shake as he grabs a tumbler and the lone bottle of Viski Irish Cut. "Want one?" he asks.

"Nah, I'm good. How was the flight?"

"It was a flight."

After watching him put down two fingers in less than a minute, I trail him to the patio with his refilled glass. He scouts out the remote for the wall-mounted TV, settles on a news channel, and plops down to watch, although he's more glaring at the TV than watching it.

I give up the slow roll and lower myself to one of the chaises. "I found a therapist for you. Best in the Valley."

He lifts his glass as if it's the one meant to reply. "Not interested." Well, that's a promising start. His red-rimmed eyes cut to me. "Where're Mam and Da? They coming later?"

I shift on my seat. "Maybe tomorrow." It's a lie. My parents have no intention of coming to see Seamus tomorrow. They have the intention of staying in Vegas for three days.

"And Siobhan?"

I can't lie about Siobhan. He'd never believe me. "Probably not."

"Right." Seamus pounds the rest of his whiskey and clucks his tongue. "Nice place you got here." He scans the wide patio, where I host most of my parties. The pool deck. The outdoor grand piano. I have an indoor grand piano, too.

"Look, I know you're gonna need a little time to acclimate, and that's fine. I'm here for you, brother. But there are some rules." I sound so stupid. So precarious. This must be what substitute teachers feel like.

He chuckles. "Go on, then, Seanny Boy. Tell me your *rules*." He does air quotes around the word.

I reach for my Captain Footwork persona, the fearless leader, the one everyone respects and counts on. "No gambling. You clean up after yourself, treat the staff well, and go to therapy."

He tries to get more out of his glass but it's empty. "That all?"

"Don't talk to the press. Don't do anything stupid when you're out and about."

"Aye, aye, cap'n." He gives me a loose salute from the eyebrow. "You gonna give me something to drive?"

No way I'm giving Seamus a car. "Milo will drive you."

He snorts. "Is that geebag supposed to be my babysitter?"

"Milo's my driver. He drives me places, and he'll drive you places, too. Or you can use a rideshare."

"My phone doesn't work here."

"We'll get you a new one."

Seamus rubs his forehead. "Listen, can I just watch TV? I just want to sit and watch TV. Is that allowed?" His eyes are glassy from all the whiskey.

"Sure," I say. "Watch all the TV you want. I have to go anyway."

I leave Seamus engrossed in the show and meet up with Rory in the kitchen.

"He stays in his rooms and the common areas," I say under my breath. "I don't want him in my rooms or in my costume collection. Keep those locked."

"Yes, sir. Shall I stay the night?"

I'd feel terrible keeping Rory away from his family overnight. "No need. He'll probably pass out early anyway." I clap him on the shoulder. "If anything bad happens, call me. Don't hesitate. You hear me?"

"Yes, sir."

"And see if you can get him to eat a vegetable or something. He looks like garbage."

"Yes, sir."

It feels like I've left something important out, but I don't know what. I just know I feel jittery and untethered. Like I've invited a serial killer into the house.

What is wrong with me? Seamus isn't dangerous. He's just... angry.

Up in my rooms, I peruse my closet. I was going to wear my rhinestone and brocade suit tonight, but I reach for my black tux instead. I don't need the extra attention. Luckily, I'll get to blow off some steam at *Hamilton on the Roof* next Thursday. I'll go as the Big GW, of course, with a wig and powdered face and all so I'm not recognized. I'll wear the hat, too, just this once. Belt out the songs at the top of my lungs. Let loose without anyone knowing who I am. No expectations. No role to play, except the one I choose.

But tonight, I'll be Sean O'Sullivan, Good Time Guy, at my da's party. Smiles and charm and elegance galore. How's your brother? Don't ask me. I just work here.

I reread the last flurry of texts between Josie and me.

Sean: So, what did you decide about Vegas?

Josie: It's a no-go. For some reason, people are still interested in me.

Sean: The gala's a private event, mostly friends of my parents. I doubt you'll get accosted by your new fandom.

Josie: Maybe next time.

I sigh. It'd be nice not to have to go to this thing alone. I mean, I don't have to go alone. There are a number of women who'd be happy to be my plus-one, but I don't want to go with any of them. I want my manic pixie dream girl by my side. Josie.

I drop another text. Cheerful. Not pushy.

Sean: Last chance! I'm headed for the airport. Private jet leaves in an hour.

Josie: Have fun.

She follows the two words with a string of emojis: confetti and devils and balloons and heart-eyed faces. Is there a secret code in there? Maybe I could call her and ask. Then I see my brother in my mind's eye, slamming back whiskeys.

No.

I'm not going to chase her. That's what *Seamus* O'Sullivan would do, not Sean.

I toss my phone onto the bed and start to get dressed.

Chapter 23

This is no time to become a rule follower.

Josie

I SET DOWN my phone and am just about to turn my attention back to yet another piece of Sean-inspired art—the man is a cash cow—when Emmy bangs on the trailer door. Once inside, she appraises my appearance with disdain: paint-stained oversize tee, ravaged jeans, and flecks of color all over my hands.

"I thought you were going to Las Vegas with Sean."

"I can't. It'll just fuel more talk about us. And it's partly your fault. You need to stop talking about me on your yoga vlog."

She groans. "I'm sorry. Your fans are relentless."

"I don't want fans! I just want collectors."

Emmy studies my canvas. It's a couple on the beach backed

by a sunset on the water, but muted, like an old California post-card. "I like that," she says. "It's not full of rage."

I scoff. "I'm not full of rage."

"Not lately."

I point my brush at her. "I haven't changed at all. It's your hormones."

"¡No!" she shouts in Spanish. "¡No es cierto!"

Wow, her Spanish is getting good. "It *is* true," I bark back. "And have you been practicing with Margarita?"

"Don't change the subject. And don't make this about me. You, Josie Days, have been different since you and Sean started...whatever it is you're doing." She plops down on the sofa and rubs her lower back. "I have to admit, I was worried at first. Sean isn't the easiest guy to get close to. He's got all these facades and trapdoors and clowns jumping out. But somehow, you've managed to get behind all that stuff. And he's gotten behind your defenses, too. Don't deny it."

I turn back to my painting. "I don't need somebody like Sean getting behind my defenses."

"Like hell you don't."

I add some more light glinting off the water. "I'm not like you, Emmy. I don't want the glamour and glitz."

"Well, I hate to break it to you, but the glamour and glitz wants you. Specifically, it wants to take you to Vegas tonight, and I think you should let it."

"Um, no."

"Why not? Because you're afraid some paparazzi might take a picture of you two together? So what? I don't understand this aversion you have to being on camera. You're beautiful, you're poised, you're not a vampire, so you'll definitely show up on the negative."

My brush hesitates just above the canvas. I could tell Emmy the truth, right here, right now. She's my best friend. She should know. "I just—"

"You just what?"

Chicken out, that's what I just do. "I choose not to."

Her features harden. "Fine. You asked for it. I'm going Josie on you."

A flash of fear zings through me. "Don't do that, please."

She bats her eyelashes. "Aw, Josie, precious flower," she wheedles, "don't challenge yourself at all, *ever*. Wilt away in the free plastic vase that some loser gave you on Valentine's Day when he was trying to get into your pants."

"For the record, Sean O'Sullivan would be happy to get into my pants, too."

She raises her voice. "Ignore the fifty-pound Swarovski crystal trumpet vase with two-hundred dollars' worth of roses being offered to you."

I plop my brush into the water glass. "You want me to be a gold digger? Is that it?"

"The metaphor isn't about money, you dolt. It's about quality! Sean is into you, and for more than what's inside your pants. I've never seen him like this before. One of the reasons the public is so obsessed with you is because they see that you're good for him! You make him happy."

"Sean isn't happy. He's, like, the most blasé guy I've ever met."

"Uh-uh." She wags a finger. "I know Sean, and he definitely has feelings for you. And he's not the only one. No matter what ridiculous things you say, what getup you put on, no matter how hard you try to hide who you are, people see past it to the real you, and they love you. Just like I do."

A butterfly flutters in my chest. People love me? That's not something I thought would ever happen again for Savannah Bateman. But maybe Josie Days is someone else entirely.

"I think Sean's falling in love with you," Emmy murmurs.

I shoot her a glare. "Boy, you just throw that 'l' word around like it's confetti, don't you?"

"It has a lot of different meanings, and you know it." Her expression softens. "But none of them are anything to be afraid of."

And here it is again…another opening from the universe to tell Emmy the truth about my past. But once the story is out there, I can't take it back. The more people in Josie Days's life who know about Savannah Bateman, the more danger it spells. Yes, this new life has been a quiet, shadowed one, but it hasn't been bad. I got to get to know my real dad before he passed. I saw that while, yeah, he had problems, he did love me in the way someone with those kinds of demons can. Emmy's right—there are a lot of different kinds of love.

But there are a lot of different kinds of hate, too. Just the thought of it makes my body go into fight-or-flight. I can't bear to get canceled again—I mean the real me, not this dating-Sean version of Josie Days I've created. I can't have my screwup resurrected and paraded about, my family forced to relive the scandal, my stepdad's studio disrespected again just when it's finally gaining the recognition it deserves, my friends embarrassed for me and of me. Dead things should stay buried—like burned-up puppets.

But my presence has been all over the entertainment world for weeks now, along with that horrible meme, and nobody has dropped even a hint that I'm really Savannah Bateman. Hugo Valencia was as big a part of the *Bring Back Chuy* movement as anyone, and he hasn't said squat. Sean's advice about controlling the narrative was good, too—giving people something to talk about in the present keeps them from getting too curious about the past. Castillo Studios is thriving. My castmates' careers are, too. Maybe everything has been set right. Maybe I've done my penance. Maybe the storm is over, and it's safe to come out.

"Go to Vegas with Sean tonight," Emmy prompts me. "You deserve to be happy, and so does Sean. Besides, I feel like he could use a friend right now."

Emmy is right. Sean cracked the door to his problems. In fact, he was supposed to pick Seamus up earlier today. I wonder how that went—he didn't mention it in his texts.

"Fine!" I groan. "I'll go."

"Excellent!" She claps her hands together. "Because Val is already picking out your outfit. Come on! Grab a razor and some underwear. You can shower in the house. I even got champagne."

"You hired Val to get me ready for a date?"

"Shut up. I'm nine months pregnant—I do what I want."

If I ever get to be pregnant, I'm totally using that line.

Inside the house, I luxuriate in the sinfully high water pressure of Emmy and Jason's shower while Val and Emmy mutter over the outfits he's brought for me. When I come out toweling my hair dry, they are brandishing their choice: a white, sequined jumpsuit straight out of the seventies with a wide-open back and halter neckline.

"I guess no bras are invited to this party?"

"Ah, sweet summer child," Val chuckles, a pair of silver platform heels dangling from his long fingers. "I got you covered. Literally."

"Don't ask how," Emmy cuts in, handing me a flute of champagne. "Just submit."

I down the champagne like a shot. I guess I'm about to get

loved, Emmy and Val style. I hold out my glass for a refill. "She submits."

"She submits!" they crow together.

When they're done with me, I look like the Disco Queen of the Universe. To aid my anonymity, Val produces a pair of lightly tinted sunglasses. Unfortunately, or possibly fortunately, they're purple and rectangular and futuristic. So, I guess I'm the Disco Queen of the Universe, Time Travel Edition.

Not gonna lie—I love it.

Jason stops drinking his protein shake in the kitchen long enough to mime how I look so good it about kills him. "Break his heart, Josie!" he calls as we hurry out the door. "Don't worry! I'll be here to pick up the pieces!"

Emmy speeds to the airport and the hangar where Sean's private jet is kept. "Oh crap, the plane's already leaving!" she cries, squealing into a RESERVED space. "Didn't you tell him you were coming?"

I'll admit, I was kind of in the moment, getting pampered and all. "No, and I don't think you're supposed to park here," I warn her.

"This is no time to become a rule follower!" She clicks the locks open on the luxury SUV. "Get out! Go get on that plane!"

She's practically shoving me out the door as I wrangle my purse and lightweight-but-warm Kate Spade wrap. I hurry to the tarmac in my platforms (it's not easy) and scan the multiple private aircraft—some sitting dormant, some being loaded, others taxiing toward the runway. How am I supposed to know which one is Sean's?

I turn back to Emmy and give an exaggerated shrug. That's when she gets out of the car and hoofs her pregnant self in my direction. It's a sight to behold. I can't help but feel guilty watching my favorite little Willy Wonka factory worker working up to those kinds of speeds.

"Dammit," she cries, and I follow her gaze to a sleek black jet with a green shamrock painted on the side taxiing away from us. "We missed him."

I don't want to acknowledge the disappointment flooding through me. I shouldn't care. This wasn't even my idea.

"I'm sorry." I pull off my purple glasses. "You and Val worked really hard to make this happen."

Emmy gives a defeated sigh. "It's okay. I'm just sorry for you, hon."

I *pshaw* at her. "It's fine. I don't need to go."

She chuckles. "Oh, you're going." I follow her hardened gaze to the glowing LAX pylons across the private landing strip. "I'm just sorry you're going to have to go coach."

Chapter 24

Don't upset your mother.

Sean

I STAB AN extra sliver of lime on a toothpick and drop it into my LaCroix on the rocks. Da's party is hopping, and it's huge. I've been here for twenty minutes, and I still haven't seen my parents or Siobhan.

Our tuxes and ball gowns fill up four connected event rooms at the Wynn Hotel. I make my way onto the terrace to lean on the railing and gaze out at the Vegas skyline. The neon lights against the black desert make it look more like a fictional realm from *Lost Star* than a real-life city. Not far away is the Sphere. I haven't even been there yet.

It feels weird being here all alone, drinking sparkling water no less. What have I become?

"Hello, Sean." The woman is wearing red silk and enough diamonds to blind an attacker.

"Heidi." I touch my cheek to hers.

"You're looking subdued tonight."

I nod as her gaze peels the tux off me piece by piece. "When a man turns sixty-five, another man shouldn't show up at his party and steal his thunder. It's rude."

"The classics suit you." She bites her red bottom lip.

"Have you seen my da?" I glance at the next room and point in its direction. "I think he went that way. He's been looking for me. Nice to see you again, Heidi."

I duck into the melee, past where Bono is warming up the crowd (he owed me a favor), and find my parents at the back of the room. Da is clapping hard with a big grin on his face. Mam is practically swooning, although can you blame her? It's Bono, after all. When she spots me, she throws her arms around me and gives me a noisy kiss.

"My boy!" she says, smooching me some more. "My handsome boy!"

"I love you, too, Mam," I say, patting her back.

Da wraps me in a wiry hug. "Good to see you, son."

"You're both acting like I just got back from the war," I joke. But I know why they're being overly affectionate. It's Seamus. Anytime he's in the picture, Mam and Da both get weird. They cling to me like they're afraid that if they don't love me enough, I might go off the rails, too.

"Seamus got in all right," I report, to spare them having to ask.

Da makes a noise of disgust. "I don't want to hear it!" But the relief is clear on his face.

"I put him in the west wing. There's plenty of food in the house."

"I said, I don't want to hear it!" Da puts his two pinkies in the corners of his mouth and whistles as the guitarist strums the intro to "Sunday Bloody Sunday." "This is a party. We're supposed to be happy. Don't upset your mother."

Mam nods, her lips turned down in a frown like a marionette. I don't want to upset my mother, but Seamus is back, and he's part of this family. I think we should at least talk about it.

Siobhan swoops in at that moment like a bird of prey, kissing both our parents on the cheeks. "You got Bono! Well done! Cheers, Mam! Happy birthday, Da. A word, Seanny Bear?" I don't even get the chance to properly greet my two nephews before she hooks her arm in mine and whisks me off to the buffet.

"You had to bring him up first thing, did you?" Siobhan pins me with a glare as she bites a shrimp in half with a vicious snap of her teeth.

"He should be here, don't you think? It feels wrong leaving him home."

"Seamus made his bed, and he can damn well lie in it. He doesn't belong here, anyway."

I look around at the ballroom full of powerful, beautiful, influential people. "You mean at this party or in our lives?"

"Ach!" She smacks my shoulder. "Don't be so dramatic. And I still think you were stupid to take him in. What are you gonna do when he fecks up again and you're the one in the blast zone?" Her accent is coming out stronger now.

"I don't think he wants that."

"I don't think he can help it. Something in him is . . . broken. He's always been strange—"

"Don't say that," I cut her off. A mix of feelings gush into my stomach like they're coming from a fire hose—nostalgia and sadness and I don't know what else. "I don't remember him like you do."

"I know." Siobhan's green eyes flash under her halo of ginger hair. "And I used to worry he was rubbing off on you too much. Mam and Da did, too."

The fear bucks inside me like a horse. I wonder if my parents know about the escapades Seamus dragged me along on. Spying on Siobhan with her boyfriends. Climbing the fence of his pretty young musical theater teacher's house. I didn't feel good about any of it, but I didn't back out, either, did I? "What do you mean by that?"

"You're eccentric, Seanny Bear, but in a good way. A likable way. Seamus..." She shakes her head, her lips pulling into a scowl. "He's different."

I do my power move—look over all the heads of the room like I own the place. My collar feels too tight. Beads of sweat have broken out on my forehead. When one of Siobhan's friends greets her, I take advantage of the distraction to slip out into the hallway.

Siobhan is wrong. I'm more like Seamus than any of them knows. I just hide it better. My brother swaps out obsessions: women, gambling, booze. Meanwhile, I've held onto the same one, my costume collection. It keeps getting bigger, the stuff that catches my eye, rarer and harder to get. And now I'm buying stolen goods, for crying out loud. That's not normal.

Then there's Josie, whom I can't seem to get off my mind. I've been so careful to keep women at arm's length, so how did I let my guard down with her?

I breathe against the wall as the waitstaff make their way past me, not looking my way, as they've been trained to do. Somebody like me losing his shit needs to be invisible if you want to keep your job.

It's fine. I just need a minute.

My phone chimes with a text. It's from Josie. What? Were her ears burning? I tap it open.

Josie: Stop what you're doing right now and do exactly what I say.

I take a couple of gulping breaths, and my heart rate downshifts. I wipe the sweat from my brow with my handkerchief and reply.

Sean: I'm listening.

Josie: Go to the bar. Get two glasses of the finest champagne available. None of that cheap stuff.

The corner of my mouth flicks, and I text back.

Sean: I'm not drinking right now, remember?

Josie: It's not for you. Just do as I say. No questions! No comments! No monologues! Just tell me when you've done it.

All righty, then. I head to the closest bar and order up two Dom Perignons.

Sean: I've got your hooch.

Josie: Now pour one of them into a to-go coffee cup.

I have zero hypotheses as to where this is going, but I don't ask or comment or monologue about it. Instead, I head for the elevators and down to the restaurant level to scout out a coffee shop. Is there a chance she's meeting me there? But no, that's ridiculous. If she'd wanted to come, she would've come with me. And it's a five-hour drive.

"Can I get a to-go cup?" I ask the skinny kid behind the counter. His face lights up when he sees me.

"Captain Footwork! Aw, man! Maddie, look! It's Sean O'Sullivan! Can you believe it? Hey, can we get a selfie?"

I put an arm around them both and grin for a photo taken by a woman waiting for her chai latte. Then I do the same for the woman and her husband. Ten minutes later, I have a coffee to-go cup full of champagne and a flute in hand. I find a quiet corner in the casino area and text Josie back.

Sean: Mission accomplished.

Josie: You could've been slower.

Sean: Delayed by fans.

Josie: Fine, you get a pass. Now head out to the pool area.

The pool area? I scout out some signage and cross the casino full of noisy slot machines. When the patio's automatic doors slide shut behind me, it's like the world has been severed into two parts, leaving the bustle inside and enveloping me in cool quietness.

Sean: I'm at the pool.

Josie: Do you see anyone?

There's movement by an oversize planter. For a moment, my heart thrills, but it's just a worker wiping down the pool's handrails.

Sean: A member of the cleaning staff.

Josie: Give her the coffee cup and let her take you to a second location.

I shake my head. This is a fun game, but I wonder if it's going too far.

"Excuse me," I say, approaching the cleaning lady. I expect her to look concerned at being approached like this in darkness, but her face lights up. She takes the to-go cup from my hand, a playful glint in her eye, and waves for me to follow her. "Sígame."

When we reach the far end of the pool, she stops, raises her coffee cup in an air toast, and disappears behind another enormous planter. My eye falls on a double lounger shadowed by a whispering palm. A woman reclines on it, but all I can see outside of the shadows are a pair of platform shoes and white bell bottoms.

The legs slide off the edge of the lounger and suddenly Josie stands before me dressed like 1973. Her white, sequined jumpsuit hugs every curve. Her platforms make her as tall as me. Her hair is styled away from her face, showing off a pair of futuristic glasses. I feel my mouth fall open as she takes the champagne flute from my hand and sips it with a sultry smile. Then she leans in close and whispers, "Surprise."

Chapter 25

I'm Not in Love.

Josie

"I THOUGHT YOU weren't coming," Sean says with his standard nonchalance.

"I changed my mind, but too late, so I had to fly Spirit."

His face crumples in horror. "I'm so sorry!"

"Eh." I shrug and take another swig of warm but expensive champagne. "I'm resilient."

His green eyes almost glow in the yellow outdoor lighting as they meander over me. "You look . . . astonishing."

"And you look like a startled waiter. No purple today? No cravat? No wainscot? What gives?"

"I think you mean *waistcoat*. And you're just being mean; I'm ravishing in a tux." He strikes a pose, hands burrowing into the pockets of his perfectly pressed pants, chin dipping, gaze darkening.

"That you are."

I finish off the champagne and slink forward. That pouting mouth tempts me, lips slightly parted, the bottom one full and heavy and dangerous. I wonder if he'll come in for a kiss, but he doesn't move, although a familiar hunger burns in his eyes. He's leaving it up to me, and no wonder. I've been giving him mixed signals from the beginning. He's waiting to see what I'll do next. Chaotic Josie. It makes me feel kind of powerful, not gonna lie.

I turn my cheek to the side, touching it to his for one of those air kisses I normally despise. With one final weighted glance at his lips, I thread my arm in his and angle my face away. "Aren't you supposed to be taking me to a swanky party? What are we doing by this dumb, boring pool?"

He tucks my arm tightly against his torso. You'd think it *was* a kiss the way my body reacts—wax under a flame.

"You could've just called, you know," he says, leading me across the empty pool deck to the casino doors. "Your serial killer scavenger hunt was not necessary."

"You loved every minute of it."

"I did," he replies without hesitation.

We cross the noisy casino, and I watch Sean's demeanor change as the elevator doors close with us inside. He adjusts his tuxedo jacket, flings back the blond swath of hair, and takes an extra-deep breath. He flicks me a wink and takes my hand as the elevator dings. His persona has officially switched on.

The doors open, and the live music greets us like a swelling tide. It takes a minute for me to register what I'm hearing. My heart stutters.

"Is that…Bono?"

"The one and only."

I look at him like it's a joke, but it's not a joke. Are you kidding me? I want to run down the hall screaming Bono's name—maybe even tackle him and then scream his name into his face—but instead I hold tight to Sean's hand as we follow the wide hotel hallway to a room where oh-my-freaking-hell it's honest-to-God Bono standing there singing in a room, and everyone around us is acting like it's normal.

"You've never seen him perform before?" Sean asks me.

"Well, yeah, but not like this." I'm practically frozen in place. "Do me a favor?"

"Sure," he says.

"If I look like I'm about to do something asinine, stop me."

"You're clearly on the verge," he says. "Come on. The buffet will keep you out of trouble."

He tows me by the hand to another room split in two by an ostentatious table piled high with food. My stomach rumbles at the sight of it. We grab a couple of plates, and I start loading mine up with anything that looks good. I don't recognize most of it, but who cares? At a party like this, it's got to be good. And I have to admit—I miss these kinds of parties. Of course, the ones I went to weren't this next-level, but Juan Ernesto's cronies could throw a pretty swanky fiesta.

Sean serves himself some protein and vegetables, and we eat standing up.

"How is it?" he asks me, and it's only then that I realize I've stuffed my mouth so full of some kind of savory puff pastry that I can't answer him for a full ten seconds. I also realize I have no idea what I just ate.

I swallow hard and put on the snobbiest British accent I can muster. "The truffle, goat cheese, caviar tartlet was a celebration for the taste buds."

"Wow," he deadpans. "You really don't know how to act around tourtière bourguignon."

I pick up the next piece of food-slash-artwork with my fingers and shove the whole thing into my mouth. Immediately, my eyelids flutter in ecstasy.

"And that one?" Sean feigns serious interest.

I swallow. "The stuffed pangolin scales sprinkled with flecks of forty-five karat gold was a gustatory delight!"

His face stretches in faux amazement. "That's impressive considering gold only goes up to twenty-four karats."

"What is that?" I stab my toothpick at a meat platter. "Is that prosciutto?"

"Iberico ham," he corrects me as I slide a thin rolled-up slice onto my tongue. My mouth literally comes alive.

"No, no, no." I point my toothpick at him as I chew in ecstasy. "It's zebra. Raised in a field of flowers and fed on the nectar of fairies."

He aims a melon ball on a toothpick toward my lips. "And this melon was watered solely with the tears of baby koalas."

"Yum," I say. "I can taste their koala-y sorrow." There's a bowl of smooth white nuts on the table. "Are those macadamia nuts?" I ask.

"The most expensive nut in the world," he confirms.

I grab a handful and shove them into my mouth. "How many Rolls Royces can I buy with what's in my mouth?" I warble.

"You could probably get a Kia."

As I reach for a crab salad stuffed pastry, Sean stops me with two hands out like a traffic cop in a school zone. "Whoa. That one's got shellfish in it."

· "I know." I pick it up and squint at it. It looks so good, but then again, looks can be deceiving when it comes to seafood. "It's complicated."

Bono launches into "With or Without You," and I shove the hors d'oeuvre into Sean's mouth and head for the stage area.

He trails me, still chewing. "I'm going to have to do fifty extra push-ups to make up for eating that, you know!"

For the next hour, I drink champagne and get introduced to a lot of actors I grew up watching alongside Keefe O'Sullivan. I can still feel my hand sandwiched between Liam Neeson's warm palms as he greeted me with enthusiasm. Mark Hamill's eyes are just as blue as they were in the original Star Wars. I almost aspirated my drink when Samuel L. Jackson recited the *Go the F**k to Sleep* book at my request. I think Jamie Lee Curtis may have unofficially adopted me, and I even got a chance to speak Spanish with Salma Hayek.

Eventually, it's time to meet the guest of honor. When Sean leads me over to his dad, I'm more nervous than I should be—it's not like we're a couple or anything.

"Congratulations on another year closer to the sweet release of death," I blurt, then try to make up for my morbid joke with a fun disco move.

"Thank you," Sean's dad says, raising an eyebrow. I'll be regretting that interaction for decades.

Sean's mother, Sorcha, is tall and slim with a classic beauty and Siobhan's ginger hair. I bob my head in her direction. "I won't even try to be clever with you, ma'am."

She pastes on a practiced smile. "How lovely."

At the end of his set, Bono announces that it's time for the birthday festivities to begin. We all join him in singing "Happy

Birthday" to Sean's dad, who smiles graciously all the way through before accepting the mic.

"Oh, g'wan, thanks for that," he says in his clipped accent. "Now that I've turned sixty-five, I guess that means I can retire!" Everyone laughs.

"He'll never retire," Sean whispers to me. "He loves acting too much, and everyone here knows it."

"It's not the number that matters, though, is it?" his dad goes on. "It's about the people you have around you. It's about friends. Thank you all so much for being here." He spreads an open palm wide, revolving on a heel to acknowledge the crowd as we all applaud. "And it's about family." His tender gaze falls on his wife, children, and grandchildren. "Come on up here and show these nice people how lucky I am!"

The sea of bodies parts for Sean and his sister and mother to make their way to the low stage along with Siobhan's husband and their two ginger boys, who appear to be about five and seven years old. Keefe O'Sullivan gathers them all in a messy, festive hug amid the applause. He brings the mic to his lips again. "I'm so proud of my wife, Sorcha, my daughter, Siobhan, and my son, Sean. My son-in-law, my grandsons. They're everything to me. Everything. Thank you all for the birthday wishes! Enjoy the party!"

I clap along with the crowd. Wow, Seamus wasn't even mentioned. I wonder how Sean feels about that.

Sean is leaning in toward Bono, saying something into his ear before aiming a smile directly at me. You'd never know there was turmoil underneath that polished shell. The fact that he shared his worries with me at game night makes me feel special. Favored.

"I've got one more song in me tonight," Bono says, the mic carrying his voice across all the rooms. "And I want to invite Josie Days to come up here and sing it with me."

My stomach falls out of me. Either that or it's teleported away using some futuristic tech one of these superrich people has access to.

"Come on up here, Josie. Sean says you've got a lovely voice. Let's hear it."

Next thing I know, I'm onstage standing beside Bono himself, and Sean has dropped down to audience level, grinning at me like a trickster in a tux. Bono cups the mic as he hands it to me. "What would you like to sing?"

Some noises come out of my mouth, but they aren't words, and they certainly don't represent any version of a "lovely voice."

"You pick," I finally manage to say, the mic heavy in my hand.

"A love song, I'm guessing."

"Oh!" I bluster. "I'm not in love."

He nods at his band. "Perfect."

The guitarist strums the opening notes of the 70s song by 10cc, and Bono sings the first line. I jump in just in time to catch the end of it. The crowd grows quiet around us as we harmonize on the anti-love ballad, a song where the singer doth protest too much. Sean stands motionless, hands deep in his pockets, a hint of a smile playing on his lips. I sing the title line right at him. I don't care that the harder I sing it, the more it looks like I, too, doth protest too much. Sean plays his part with a lot of shrugs and a venti order of charismatic nonchalance. We are actors acting, except, at the same time, tapping into the real thing, too. Isn't that what acting is?

It's strange to be up here onstage. This is something I was sure I'd given up forever, and I'd made peace with that. The purple tint of my glasses makes it even more surreal, like this parallel universe I've found myself in bends light differently.

I see Sean differently in this place, too. Instead of looking up at him, the lights winking off his pedestal, I'm the one on top. He blends into the crowd below, another macadamia nut in a bowl overflowing with them. But from this vantage point, little things begin to stand out. Not just that devastating mouth, but the grinding of his jaw alongside it. Not just the piercing green of his eyes, but the nervous way they watch the room. Not just the impressed look he rewards me with as I sing, but the flicker of wistfulness clinging to it. Spotting all these things should make me want him less. I mean, this is Sean O'Sullivan. He's supposed to be larger than life. No one wants to see his weaknesses. But somehow, the cracks in his shield only make me want him more.

It's like with art. When you first look at a piece, all you get is an impression. A feeling. Good or bad. Excited or disgusted. Energized or bored. But once you learn about technique, about color, composition, medium, or about the artist themself, you begin to look at the same piece in a different way. Something that made you sad before might move you to tears. A piece you love might bring ecstasy. One you originally hated might make you realize that you hate it because it reminds you of something you hate about yourself.

As I gaze down at Sean O'Sullivan, singing the heartless lyrics that are really a cover for the songwriter's authentic fear, I see something similar in him. He's protesting too much. Everything about him is protesting too much.

You deserve to be happy, and so does Sean.

It's a stupid, trite word—happy—but I have to admit, it's got appeal. Emmy thinks Sean and I could make each other happy. Is she right or just hanging ten on an oxytocin wave?

Regardless, if I came here to be a friend to Sean, the least I can do is be an actual friend to Sean. Get him alone. Ask him how Seamus's homecoming went. Let him talk. Really listen.

When we finish the song, I thank Bono for the duet and step off the stage, where Sean hands me a fresh flute of champagne.

"Well, well, well, you're full of surprises, Josie Days."

"Why? Because I can sing?"

"Because you can *perform*."

A part of me inside stiffens with fear. Did I just let too much Savannah Bateman out? Will people see it? Recognize it?

"Hey," I whisper, "you want to get out of here?"

He lowers his voice. "Where do you want to go?"

I raise my glass. "I'm tired of this top shelf crap. I want some watered-down, stay-up-all-night proletariat champagne. I want champagne to burn the Bastille for!" I pretend to throw the empty flute onto the floor but then place it on a passing waiter's tray instead.

Sean glances once over his shoulder at the rest of the party before his fingers thread themselves through mine. "Well, I do love a good revolution."

Chapter 26

Heckling won't stop the inevitable.

Sean

WE SLIP OUT of the party.

"Wait," Josie says, halting in front of the gift shop so suddenly that I boomerang into her. "Let's go in here first."

"You want a souvenir?" I ask.

"A disguise. We're going out among the masses, after all."

"Your *Quantum Leap* glasses aren't enough?"

"Hardly." She tows me through the shop, nose forward like a bloodhound until we find the small seasonal section. There are a couple of bins full of Halloween masks, fake beards, eye patches, and the like. She grabs a clown nose with a rubber band and shoves it at me.

"We're going to need to cover up that lock of hair, too." She rips a Las Vegas branded knit hat off a display.

While I would never for the life of me purchase a kitschy tourist hat like this one, I comply. She dons a fake beard. There's a little mirror mounted on the gift shop wall, and we admire our quick work. I look like a homeless clown somebody took in and cleaned up. She looks like the bearded lady from a solarpunk circus.

I pay, and we tumble into the Las Vegas night, where she points up to the High Roller Ferris wheel glowing bright blue against the sky. "Do you want to ride that?"

I want to do anything she wants to do, and that's the truth. "Why not?"

I think the disguises actually make more people recognize us than would have otherwise as we flag down a taxi and make our way to the Ferris wheel. When it's our turn, I slip the ride worker a hundred-dollar bill so we can get a private gondola. A moment later, we're in a blue-tinged bubble all our own. I pull off the nose and hat and set them aside. "No need for these in here."

Across from me, she tugs off her glasses and beard as we rocket upward. The Vegas skyline is the opposite of a sunset; the sky is as black as the ocean, and it's the world below that's all lit up.

"I'm sorry," Josie says, and I'm surprised to find her looking at me rather than the view.

"For what?"

"I never even asked about Seamus. How's he doing?"

I squirm and tug at my collar. "He's great. Losing himself in TV and unlimited alcohol. You know, living the black sheep dream."

"If you want to talk about it, I'm here to listen."

I don't. Our gondola crests the zenith of the ride. It's like we're floating in a *Lost Star* ship, hovering silent and watchful over alien lands. "I'd rather talk about you."

She focuses on the lights below. "Why would you want to do that? I'm not very interesting."

"I bet the real you is."

Her gaze jumps to mine, wary. This evening has been fun, but I'm tired of all the misdirection and sleight of hand. On the plane ride over, I looked Josie Days up—just a cursory Google search, nothing weird or intrusive—and no results came up from before 2010. No high school photos, no old Facebook accounts. No Mexican TV shows. Nothing.

"Why don't you start by telling me your real name? You changed it, didn't you?"

Her shoulders hunch in. "It changed itself. It had a midlife crisis and said, *Screw it all, I'm pivoting!*"

"I can hire a private detective, you know," I say, regretting the words before they even finish coming out of my mouth.

Her dark eyes flash with fear. "You wouldn't do that."

I scoff. "Of course I wouldn't do that." Shit, that was so stalkerish. What was I thinking? "But I would like to know who you really are. Please?"

I can almost see the circuits clicking in her head before she says, "I can't. Emmy doesn't even know."

I pull out my phone. "I bet I could figure it out. If I figure it out, will you admit it?" I thought about doing this on my own, but it felt icky and wrong. But if I had her permission...

"There's no way you can figure it out. You're not that smart."

"Is that a *yes*?"

She folds her arms across her chest with a smirk. "Fine. You have sixty seconds. Ready, set, go."

A clever and wholly unfair move, but I don't complain, instead diving right into my search. I swipe around, muttering my thought process out loud. "Let's see. You were an American actress in Mexico, worked at your stepdad's studio in Mexico City. His name was Juan Ernesto. You hate puppets, so you must have worked with one of those little assholes…"

Her eyes get big.

"Oh dear. Am I getting close?" I tease. "Also, I didn't see you set a timer."

"I'm counting in my head. And why do you swipe with your ring finger? That's so psychotic."

I stifle a chuckle. "Heckling won't stop the inevitable."

I find Castillo Studios, owned by one Juan Ernesto Castillo. A little more digging and I uncover a list of shows from the early 2010s. There's a teen variety show on the docket—*The Bilingual Club*. The list of actors includes a bunch of Spanish names and one English name: Savannah Bateman. That's got to be her.

"Time's up!" she cries.

"That wasn't even close to a minute," I argue, still digging. I'm looking for a photo. Proof.

"I said time's up!" She dives across the gondola to my side and grabs my forearm where I'm holding the phone. A picture is loading—the cast photo of *The Bilingual Club* with six smiling teens on a set. One of the two girls has long, shiny black hair and golden skin. The other one is tall and fair with blond waves cascading over her shoulders. Neither one of them looks like Josie.

Maybe I got it wrong.

Then I see Josie's horrified reaction, and I know I didn't get it wrong. And now that I look closer, the blond girl's eyes are deep-set. And it's hard to tell because she's smiling, but I do believe there's a full upper lip on that teeny-bopper mouth, with the slightest overbite.

Holy shit, I was right.

Josie Days is Savannah Bateman.

Chapter 27

I want to faint like a nineteenth-century
farmer's daughter.

Josie

"HELLO, SAVANNAH BATEMAN. Nice to meet you."

Hearing my real name come out of his mouth knocks me off-balance—like those moments in movies when the villain reveals his hand, and the heroine says, *Wait, I never told you that.*

Do I deny it? Own up? Make up some crazy explanation? I can't make a run for it since I'm trapped on a Ferris wheel.

"Blond, huh?" He doesn't wait for me to answer before turning back to his phone. "Now let's google your real name and see what comes up."

I watch in terrified suspense as Sean types my real name into the search bar. I've never done this. It feels like tempting fate, like some silent alarm might be triggered when he hits ENTER, and FBI paratroopers will swarm us, rip off the gondola door, and shout, *Aha! There she is!*

He scrolls through the results while I wait in agony. "Whoa, there's a lot! Except this isn't you. This Savannah Bateman is some kind of foodie influencer. She lives in Texas. She's got quite a following."

"What?" It's the first word I manage to get out. But, sure enough, when I study his screen, almost everything he's scrolling through is about a different Savannah Bateman. This lovely, spatula-happy woman has stolen my spotlight, God love her. And there are other Savannah Batemans, too. Lots of them, with way more recent history than me. Sean has to click through five pages of search results before he even gets to something I recognize.

"That one," I whisper, pointing to the article. "That's me."

It's a relief to say it. I haven't been to confession in a long time, but it feels like that—only without the scary priest box and the nine Hail Marys.

He clicks on the link, and the browser immediately translates. "Beloved Puppet Destroyed During Temper Tantrum by 'Yeehaw' Actress."

"Yeehaw actress?" he asks.

"My character said 'yeehaw' a lot. You know, like all us Americans do."

"How offensive," Sean says dryly.

"Not nearly as offensive as every Mexican on our TV shows being a drug dealer."

He nods. "Or every Irishman being a drunk. I get it."

The rest of the page is just a blown-up snapshot of the newspaper article, not translatable by the browser's software. Sean scrolls past the main image—a grainy black-and-white photo of the headshot my mom took me to get when I first auditioned for *Club Bilingüe*. The second image is one of Chuy with his sad eyes, lumpy nose, and spotted furry ears, perched on Lupe's knee. The third picture is a famous shot of Chuy in flames, sprawled across a Day of the Dead altar, his wide mouth open to the sky as if in mid-scream while I lose my shit in the background.

All my muscles contract at once. I can't move, and for a split second, I almost believe the stories about duendes and curses. Did Chuy have a fleck of ancient magic in him? Did I curse myself to turn to stone the moment I shared this secret?

"That girl in the meme is you." I give him credit for not laughing or, really, reacting at all. He squints at the text, trying to read the Spanish. "Let me get this straight. You murdered a puppet?"

"It was an accident."

He scrolls down some more, and there's a fourth picture of Lupe in tears. Not just crying—weeping and wailing.

"Who's this girl? Was it her puppet?"

I cover the screen with my hand. "She's my stepsister. And Chuy wasn't just her puppet. He was everybody's puppet. He was like Yoda or Elmo, with tons of people who loved him. I burned him and then hid the evidence, and I was canceled because of it, before canceling was even a thing. Not only did I lose my job, but the entire show tanked. All my friends lost their jobs. My stepfather's studio almost went under. Everyone suffered because of me."

"I thought you said it was an accident."

I stop myself there. I don't know how to explain it, how some things can be an accident and a person's fault at the same time.

When I don't reply, Sean turns his attention back to his phone and taps a video icon before I can stop him. My face heats as the live broadcast of Lupe and me improv-ing in the cemetery plays out. We'd been picking at each other all day, it was late, and we were both tired. Juan Ernesto could probably tell we were a tinderbox, ready to blow.

Your characters are best friends, he'd reminded us right before the cameras rolled. *You're examples to children everywhere—a bridge between cultures. Remember that.*

I watch myself ad-lib the scene in a bright voice. "Yeehaw! Halloween is such a fun holiday. What should I be for Halloween this year?"

Lupe mimes thinking hard for an answer. "A witch."

The flash of a frown on my face tells me there was some backstory there, though I can't remember exactly what. "I think I'll be an astronaut," Teenage Me says cheerfully, not taking the bait.

"No, you should definitely be a witch," Chuy replies from Lupe's lap.

"See?" Lupe says. "Chuy thinks you should be a witch, too."

"It suits you," Chuy adds.

I could have played along and agreed, made it about costumes and how much fun it would be to pretend to ride a broomstick while I collected candy from my neighbors. I could have used the segment to teach kids about Halloween—that was my job. But I didn't.

"Actually, *you* should be the witch," I retort. "You're much better at it than I am."

The gauntlet is thrown. Lupe's eyes flash. "No, you should definitely be the witch. Meanwhile, Chuy and I will eat candy skulls and make a beautiful altar dedicated to our ancestors for el Día de los Muertos." Chuy nods his head in agreement.

Yes, it was another dig, but it was followed by an out. All I had to do was take it. But I didn't.

"I bet your ancestors were witches," I blurt. Even now, watching this twelve years later, the contents of my stomach solidify into a block of concrete.

After a long, painful beat, Chuy is the one to respond. "Wow, she's disrespecting your ancestors, and on a day specifically meant to honor and pray for them." Lupe makes him shake his head in judgy disbelief before dropping his voice to a puppet stage whisper. "Maybe I got the English word wrong. What's that other word? The one that starts with 'b'?"

She's careful not to cross a line and outright call me a bitch on TV, but the message is loud and clear.

I'm not doing a very good job acting at this point in the clip. My lips move, but nothing comes out. In fact, it looks like my head might explode. I remember this moment vividly: Chuy's open, taunting mouth, Lupe's wicked grin, the fury and embarrassment spreading through me like poison. Juan Ernesto's horrified expression off camera as he waved his arms to signal us to stop. I remember reaching for the puppet. Hurling it.

"You're the bitch!" I blurt. "I hate you! And your stupid puppet, too!"

Chuy bursts into flame, and the video cuts out to the sound of our live audience crying out in dismay.

Humiliation and shame magnify the motion of the Ferris wheel, making my head swim. If this ride doesn't end soon, I might actually be sick. I think about nice smells—eucalyptus, mint—while I grip the bars inside the gondola and await Sean's reaction.

"Wow, you two got along like Siobhan and Seamus," he says, scrolling farther down the page. "Looks like your sister milked it, too." He clucks his tongue at the still shot of Lupe crying dramatically.

I'm so stunned it takes me a second to react.

Why isn't he more horrified, or even a little bit horrified? "Is that all you have to say?"

He waggles the phone at me. "Josie, this is kids' stuff."

"'Kids' stuff'?" I scoff. "I cussed out my costar on live TV during a children's show. I taught a bunch of Spanish-speaking kids the word *bitch*! We lost tens of thousands of dollars in contracts over this. I destroyed our brand. My stepfather's dream. We were supposed to teach kids how to respect other cultures, and I insulted hers. Did we not watch the same video?"

His eyes, dark as pine in the dim light, train on me. "I saw a video where two girls were shitty to each other. Not one. *Two*."

"But I was the one who crossed the line."

"Well," he scratches his chin, "first of all, your sister started it. And second of all, you didn't expect the puppet to catch fire. That part was an accident. You said so yourself."

"Well, yeah, but..." I trail off.

"I'm sure you apologized."

I don't respond.

Sean gives me a hard look. "You did apologize, didn't you?"

"Well, er," I stammer, averting my gaze from the swooping view.

Sean lifts the phone from his knee and aims the screen toward me. "In twelve years, you never apologized for this? Never made a statement? A tweet?"

That sick feeling rolls through my stomach again. "Everyone was so mad at me. And I was mad at myself...and ashamed."

He scrolls some more, tapping on a video of my family being interviewed. I flinch as the audio crackles to life. I hate this video, maybe even more than the one in the meme. I'll never forget the first time I saw the news footage of Juan Ernesto, flanked by my mom and a swollen-eyed Lupe, fielding questions from reporters, apologizing on my behalf, condemning my behavior, and assuring the world that I didn't represent what *Club Bilingüe* and Castillo Studios stood for.

When the video cuts out, Sean is frowning and shaking his head. Now he must be getting it. The gravity of it all. What an embarrassment I am. What a liability. Finally, he'll understand why we can't be together.

"Wow," he says, wiping his face with his hand. "That was harsh."

"Yeah," I agree, studying my lap. "I tried to tell you."

"No wonder you ran away."

My heart lurches, and my head snaps up. "What?"

He scrunches his face. "I don't want to disrespect your parents, but they really threw you under the bus. I mean I get it, brand safeguarding and reputation management, yada, yada, but you were their teenage daughter. Where's the part where they stick up for you? Where's the part where they say your safety is the most important thing? Where they tell you how much they want you to come home?"

My brain glitches, and I don't know how to respond. It's like he's speaking a language that I never learned.

"Your fans stuck up for you, though."

"They did?" I choke out.

He hands over the phone, and I see that he's right. There are people defending me in the comments, calling Lupe out for baiting me and stating that what happened to Chuy was clearly an accident. They're taking, or more accurately, they *took*, a lot of flak for me. I never realized that.

"What'd you do with the puppet?"

I have about eight lies that I've rehearsed to respond to this question, but they all seem to stick in my throat. I'm so tired of lying. And Sean seems to see this situation in a completely different light. Could he be even a little bit right? Can I trust him with the truth?

"I…" I hesitate. I'm not sure I know how to do this. Strip myself bare. Give it all away. If Josie Days doesn't have her secrets, does she have anything at all?

"Hey, you," he says in a soft voice, and even though they are two of the most bland and nondescript words he could have chosen, somehow, they tear me open. He reaches out to tuck a strand of hair behind my ear, his fingers lingering to lift my chin as his gaze captures mine. "It's okay. You can tell me anything."

Warmth spreads through my solar plexus. He's doing it again. Sean O'Sullivan is working his celebrity crush voodoo on me. Good thing I'm not entrusted with any state secrets.

"I buried it in the cemetery in Naolinco."

There. I've done it. All my secrets are out, loose, rampaging in the streets.

"Thanks for telling me." He smiles, and for a second, I think he's going to close the distance and reward my bravery with a kiss, but he pulls back instead and reaches for his disguise. Why? Is he judging me after all?

But, no. Our gondola is slowing to a stop. It's time to disembark. Numbly, I grab my beard and hook the elastic bands over my ears. My purple sunglasses go back on my face.

The same worker opens our door, eyes shining as he obviously spent the last twenty minutes figuring out who we are. He asks for a selfie, and I make sure my beard is well-affixed before obliging and then hurry out into the cool night, tugging my sweater around my shoulders. The air smells dry and raw. I feel the same way.

That was a stupid mistake, telling Sean as much as I did. *Another* stupid mistake. I've managed to stay hidden for so long. Why am I risking everything now?

And is he right about my family? Did they let me down? Was it not all on me?

"Hey, what's the matter?" Sean asks when I lurch to a halt near a Caesars Palace sign with its blinking, beckoning lights.

"I'm ready to go home," I say, stifling a shiver in the cool air.

He glances over my head across the crowd. "Look, I'm sorry I figured out who you are. I'll forget it instantly. As a matter of fact, it's gone. I have no idea who you used to be. To me, you are only Josie Days. How'd you come up with that name anyway?"

Since I've already told him everything else, it seems ridiculous to lie now. "It was the name on the tomb next to where I buried Chuy."

He freezes. "Is that a joke?"

"You'd think so, wouldn't you? Come on. Let's get out of here before more people recognize us."

"You want to leave, really?" he argues. "They'll talk about us anyway. They've been doing it for weeks now, and I'm the only one who's figured out who you are, and only because of the clues you gave me." Sean tilts his head. "Come on, let's control the narrative. *Josie and Sean spent a night on the town in Las Vegas. Boy, they look like they had fun.*"

"I don't know, Sean." I rub my arms, and he takes off his tuxedo jacket and puts it around my shoulders. He catches me eyeing the way his shirt fits him, the fabric pulling over his pecs, outlining the muscles of his arms.

"If I take off my shirt, too, will you come out with me?" With a straight face, he untucks and lifts his tuxedo shirt, showing off the chiseled abs underneath. "These guys are a lot of fun."

I want to faint like a nineteenth century farmer's daughter at the sight of that six-pack, but that'll only encourage him. Instead, I shoot out an arm and pinch him in the ribs, except he's got, like, zero body fat, so I don't even get a good one in.

"Geez, what are you, 3D printed?" I complain.

"Ach! That tickles!" He flinches and drops his shirt. "What do you say? Last chance. I'm not gonna beg."

Behind Sean, the Ferris wheel spins in slow motion as if stretching time itself. I feel like I'm being stretched, too. A rubber band holding on for as long as it can. My celebrity crush, Sean O'Sullivan, is right in front of me, within my reach, and we could spend the entire night in Vegas together, if I allow it.

It's risky. Out here we're exposed. The wrong person could recognize me, and it would all be over. But Sean's got a point. Savannah Bateman, puppet killer at large, is so far down on search lists that she practically doesn't exist. No one here is talking about her. No one's even thinking about her except me. And maybe I'm not the toxic screwup I thought I was.

It's a perfect October night in Las Vegas, and Sean O'Sullivan wants to spend it with me...in a tux, no less. Josie Days will never get a better offer in her life.

"All right," I mutter. "One buffet, two shows, and we play the poker machines until I at least get four of a kind."

He stifles a smile and laces his fingers in mine. "Yeehaw."

Chapter 28

I can salvage this with humor.

Sean

I STEAL A glimpse at Josie as we ride in the well-abused back-seat of our Uber on the way to the airstrip after five hours of nonstop Vegas nightlife. As promised, I took her to a buffet, a magic show, and even The Sphere Experience. It took an hour and three casinos to get four-of-a-kind on a poker machine, and she insisted on gambling with her own money, so it was touch and go at one point.

My gaze drifts from her profile against the window down the swell of her cleavage to the curve of her hips, and the white material hugging her thighs. She catches me checking her out and shifts to give me a better view, a tiny smile twitching on her lips.

Why do I like this woman so much? Maybe because she's not fawning all over me? Because she makes me work for every smile, every touch, every little spoken truth hidden under the layers of smart-assery and sarcasm?

I tip the driver well even though his car smelled like vomit forced into a medical coma by a burly team of air fresheners. Then we head across the tarmac to where my jet is parked. Jeff is already in the cockpit running his preflight check. The interior of my plane is always such a pleasure to step into with its tan leather seats and smell of luxury. It feels like home.

When Josie catches me watching her admire the plane, she straightens her shoulders. "What? No Austin Powers love nest? I expected more from the great Sean O'Sullivan."

Ah, Josie. I head for the onboard liquor cabinet as she lowers herself onto the love seat. She didn't choose one of the single seats. The implications aren't lost on me.

"Drink?" I ask her.

"Water would be good."

"We've got clearance," Jeff says over the intercom. "Prepare for takeoff."

Taking the other half of the love seat, I lean back against the leather upholstery and watch her as we take off: mysterious dark eyes, flushed cheeks, the hungry energy simmering just beneath the surface. Tantalizing—all of it.

"Thanks for a great date," she says, sipping her water.

"Oh, this wasn't a date," I say. "This was last-minute, thrown-together nonsense. I didn't even know you were coming."

"What would you have done differently?"

It's kind of stuffy in here. I take off my jacket and throw it onto the far seat, on top of our discarded disguises. "Well, first of all, I would've made dinner reservations somewhere with a Michelin rating." The bowtie goes next—I fling it as far as I can. "I would've scored tickets for a show that tends to sell out." I loosen the top buttons of my shirt. That's better. "And I would have ended it with a kiss."

She smirks. "Still desperate for that kiss, I see."

She wants it, too. I know she does, but if she wants to tease me first, I'll play. I start unbuttoning the rest of my shirt from the top down.

She bites her lip. "What are you doing?"

"As I recall, somebody stuffed a pastry into my mouth earlier tonight—I'm not naming names. That means I'm fifty push-ups short for the day. Think I'll get those in now."

I peel the shirt off and throw it on top of my jacket. Muscles bulge as I pull an arm across my body in a stretch. "Just gonna warm up a little here." I put on the serious captain's face as I flex for her, noting the way her hungry gaze flickers from my arms to my lats and pecs. Sometimes being a piece of meat is fun.

She traces my bulging bicep with a finger. "This isn't fair. Your muscles are seducing me."

I nod in sympathy. "They're shameless macho assholes."

"It won't be good for you, either, you know, if people find out who I really am. You could get canceled by association. Doesn't that worry you?"

I stop stretching. "Josie, we googled you, remember? There's nothing to worry about. And what happened in Mexico was like, what, ten years ago?"

"Twelve." The cabin lights dim on their timer, and her eyes go inky dark.

"You said your friends' careers all recovered," I continue. "That sci-fi show is great, by the way. It's given our producers all kinds of ideas for next season. They're even talking about sending us down there for some kind of collaboration. We're gonna get some new, diverse actors, add some salsa and merengue to the choreography. Some African dance. Bollywood…" I do a little come-hither dance with my hands.

"That sounds great, actually," she says, still looking unsure.

Alarm bells go off in my head. Suddenly, this doesn't feel fun anymore. It feels like a sales pitch. I drop my hands in my lap.

"Look, Josie, I told you, I don't chase. If you're not interested, say the word." I hate that answer, but whatever.

"You don't chase, huh?"

"Nope. Not my style."

"Well, you've been chasing me nonstop."

A zing of fear shoots through me. She's said this before. Could it be true? "Have not."

"Have, too."

I scoff to hide the sudden and dreadful suspicion that she knows everything—that I like her too much. That I think about her way too much. That when she showed up on that pool deck, I wondered, for the briefest and brightest of moments, if it was all my thinking about her and wanting her that had manifested her. That we'd somehow made magic together.

I'd really hoped she'd felt it, too.

But if she didn't, then this train is going off the rails big-time, and I've got to stop it.

"Li—listen," I stammer. "You've got it all wrong. It's not like I'm obsessed with you or anything." Oh shit. Did I really say that?

Her jaw falls open. "What did you say?"

"Nothing!" I lunge for my shirt to put it back on, but her hand shoots out with freakish speed and catches my wrist. I freeze and don the mask of nonchalance, but I'm not sure it's covering up the truth. "I—I didn't mean anything by that!" I sputter.

She lets go of my wrist, and I'm about to bolt out of the seat and, oh, I don't know, maybe throw open the emergency exit and leap out. Yes, it's dramatic, but it's not off the table.

Something changes in her expression. Her hands find their way to my bare chest, her touch firm and soft at the same time. Her dark eyes are lidded, and her mouth is suddenly very close to mine. My heart is a wartime drumbeat.

"That's too bad, Sean O'Sullivan," she whispers, "because I *want* you to be obsessed with me." She leans in, and her lips brush mine side to side with the feather-softest touch. It's not a kiss, really; it's a caress. A tease. A strike of flint. A spark.

"I want to be the only thing on your mind," she goes on. Her arms have snaked their way around my shoulders, and with a quick shift, she's gotten a knee across me and is straddling my lap. My spark jumps to flame.

It seems I don't have anything to be worried about. She wants the same thing I do. We're cleared for takeoff, at least inside the cabin.

"You want me to be obsessed with you?" I whisper into her mouth. It's taking everything in me to hold back, to not wrap my arms around her, crush her to me, cover her mouth with mine. But I do hold back. I let her drive because I'm loving this Josie ride, wherever it's going.

Her hands slide down the bare traps of my back, sending goose bumps down my torso. She scoots even closer on my lap, and I know she can feel what it does to me.

"Obsess over me, Sean O'Sullivan," she whispers into my mouth, and it's a delicious torture. She kisses me lightly, and I don't move. "And then obsess over me again." She kisses me again, this time deeper. "And again." I part my lips, inviting more. "And again."

I taste her tongue, and that's where I break, devouring her mouth with mine, an ocean of desire swamping me. The lead-up was perfection; all my parts are humming like a machine. This woman is something else. I want to peel her and take her apart like a mandarin orange. I want her skin against mine, every inch. I want—

My phone rings.

No, not rings. Blares. An alarm of some kind, and not the kind you set to remind yourself to take the turkey out of the oven.

"What's that?" Josie stiffens in my arms. "Is the plane going down?"

"The plane is not what's gonna be going down," I mutter into her mouth.

The phone blares a second time, and a terrible thought hits me: Seamus!

A freight train of curses pours from me. My phone has wormed its way out of my pants pocket and onto the floor. Holding onto Josie's hip with one hand, I reach down and pick it up.

"Just one second," I grumble, knowing it's going to take way more than a second to sort this out. I tap the notification, and the cameras at the front of my house show me the top of Seamus's head as well as the tops of the heads of two police officers. I check the clock in the corner of my phone. It's 4:20 AM.

Josie climbs off me. What a heartbreak. I tap the microphone.

"Hello! Hello! This is Sean O'Sullivan, the owner of that house. Is there something I can help you with?"

The police inform me that Seamus was found trying to break in. I explain the situation. He's my brother. He's staying with me. He's a friggin' idiot who lost his keys. In the background, Seamus is swaying on his feet, barely able to stand. Goddammit!

"I'll call my butler to come let him in," I tell the cops. "He can be there in fifteen minutes."

I open my texts, realizing that this is a terrible thing to ask of Rory. It's an ungodly hour, but my parents and Siobhan are still in Las Vegas, and I don't know who else to turn to.

"I bet Jason would go," Josie says, reading my mind.

"I don't want to drag Jason and Emmy into this mess."

"That's what friends are for."

A sigh escapes me like air from a balloon. Josie rests her cheek against my bare shoulder as I dial Jason's number. God, I feel so embarrassed. Why? It's not even my fault. It's my effed-up brother's fault!

Jason picks up almost immediately. "What do you need?"

My heart settles. God love Snack and his eternal desire to be useful. "I need a favor. A big one." I explain the situation, and Jason's on it.

I hang up, pressing the cool phone screen against my forehead. "That was not in the cards," I tell Josie, resting my head against hers.

She nips my bare shoulder with her teeth. "Well, you can still do the push-ups."

"Or bicep curls," I joke, scooping her into my arms.

She squeals as I curl her body up and down twice in my arms and then let her weight collapse us both down to the love seat cushions where we lay entangled, face-to-face. I study the long, smooth line of her neck, the sinewy muscle there. I nuzzle it, but by this point, it's pretty clear I'm not getting my mojo back anytime soon.

"I'm gonna have to take a raincheck on rocking your world. This whole Seamus thing is killing the vibe."

I plant a single kiss on her neck before I raise myself up and grab my shirt, shrugging it on unbuttoned.

She folds herself cross-legged on the love seat, so beautiful with her mussed hair and smeared mascara. "It's okay." She grabs her water bottle and guzzles it. "How long are you going to let him stay with you?"

I shrug. "I dunno. I can't just kick him out. Seamus was a good brother to me. He's not the monster everyone makes him out to be."

Josie offers her water bottle to me. "We're all just one wrong decision away from becoming the worst version of ourselves."

I take a drink. "Please tell me you're not talking about Señor Burney McBurnsalot." I mime the puppet's skyward grimace on the burning altar.

She swipes the bottle out of my hand. "That's not funny. If I'd burned up the Mona Lisa, you wouldn't think it was funny."

"If you burned up the Mona Lisa, I'd still think you were magnificent."

She opens her mouth but nothing comes out. She kind of pulls back.

Shit. I came on too strong again. "I mean, I don't think that in a weird, obsessive way or anything. Just in a normal, admiring sort of way."

"Wait a minute." She finishes the water and chucks the empty bottle across the cabin where it lands squarely in the garbage can. Impressive. "Are you afraid of being like your brother?"

Oh shit. "What? No! I'm nothing like him. He's a total weirdo. I'm super balanced." *Stop talking, Sean.* "Always have been." *Like, now. Stop talking* now. "Always will be." *Dammit! Why can't I stop talking?*

Her brow crinkles. "Yeah, you don't come across as obsessive. You're the opposite—like you don't care about anything. Like you're too big for your britches."

Okay, whew. I can salvage this with humor. "In my defense, my britches are pretty big. They have to house, you know, a space shuttle."

She ignores my lame joke. "I think it's really cool that you've been able to forgive Seamus even after everything he put your family through." She smiles—a wee, intimate thing.

"I'm the fixer, or so my sister claims."

"I wish my family had a fixer."

"It's a thankless job."

"I would thank them."

I brush a lock of purple hair away so I can see her face, so beautiful and haunted. It's not fair that she should have to feel this way, live this way, over something that wasn't entirely her fault. "You need to talk to your family about what happened. If you want to have meaningful relationships with people, you have to be honest with them about how you feel, even if it's hard."

She inhales a deep breath. "It's been so long. Too long."

"It's never too late for an apology."

"I can't risk it, Sean. If I come out of the woodwork now, and it goes badly, it could screw things up for Castillo Studios. And it would suck you in, too. And Emmy and Jason. With the baby coming, they don't need that kind of stress."

I frown. "Then it's up to you to find the right moment. In the meantime, don't let it ruin the one you're in."

Jeff's voice comes over the intercom, announcing that we're about to make our descent and to fasten our seat belts. We buckle in, and I find Josie's hand on the seat beside me, thread my fingers through hers, and give her an apologetic smile. "Sorry that my brother's shenanigans spoiled our night."

The corner of her mouth quirks. "That's it. Chivalry is officially dead."

"I don't know about chivalry." I raise her knuckles to my lips. "But I do know that I would've liked to wake up by your side."

She scoots my way until our foreheads touch. Then she lifts her chin and finds my mouth with hers. It's a gentle kiss, tentative even. For the first time, it doesn't feel like she's either pulling away from me or playing games.

"Okay," she whispers. "You win. You convinced me."

I squint at her. "Of what?"

"That maybe I don't need to cower in the shadows every time there's a camera around. That maybe we could..."

"We could what?"

"Try this."

I nod gravely in an attempt to hide the fireworks shooting off inside me. "That's great."

"Just tone down the intensity, if you can."

"Right."

"Hey, don't get me wrong. I like you for you. It's just...the less attention we get, the better."

Well, that's encouraging, somewhat. "So, you do like me, then?"

She rolls her eyes. "Listen, if your love language is words of affirmation, I can tell you right now this isn't going to go well."

All righty, then. She doesn't have to know how much I like her. I'll hide it, just like I do all the things I really care about. Roll it up into a tight little ball and stuff it somewhere deep down, where nobody can prove it exists.

I unclasp our hands and open my arms. "My love language is cuddles, actually."

She fake-groans. "God, that's even worse."

But she snuggles against me anyway. I close my arms around her and relish the feel of her relaxing into my embrace as the plane makes its gentle descent.

"What about you?" I whisper into her hair. "What's your love language?"

She plays with the buttons on my shirt. "I'm not sure," she whispers back.

"It's okay. You don't have to know." I tighten my arms around her, nuzzle her head with my chin, and hold back from kissing her. I don't want to scare her away, not when I've finally got her.

Stay blasé, Sean. You can do this.

Of course I can. For Josie, I can do anything.

Chapter 29

It's a biological imperative.

Josie

AT WORK THE following week, I'm applying Chelsea's makeup, but I can't stop looking at the door, waiting for Sean to pop in. It's been four days since our Vegas trip, and I know he's been busy with work, training, and Seamus, but the main cast is taping here today, and the whole studio is abuzz with rumors of contracts being signed and new cast members being introduced. Sean already told me they're sending him, Amanda, and Jason Ramirez to Mexico to do some taping there. (Jason Connor isn't going because Emmy is too close to her due date.) Miguel hinted at some news that he couldn't tell me. That must be it.

Speaking of Miguel, he's been pinging me all morning. I haven't had a moment to check our messaging app, but I'm guessing it's about how excited he is to get to meet the members of the *Lost Star* cast. They aren't going down there for another few weeks, but he probably just got the okay to share the news. I'll get back to him soon.

I hurry to apply the final airbrush layer on Chelsea. When I'm done, I might take a break and find Sean. Photos of us at his dad's party and flitting around Vegas are all over the internet. As a result, nobody has shut up about us, but, like Sean said, they're all focused on how good we look together and don't care where I come from or what puppet-related crimes I might have committed in my past. Apparently, "Josie Days, the ex-nun who stole Sean O'Sullivan's heart" is enough of a bio for them.

Have I stolen his heart? I think so. As for me, I've pretty much handed mine over.

"Good morning!"

Speak of the right sexy devil, and he'll appear. In the doorway. In his Captain Footwork uniform, one eyebrow raised.

"Josie, may I see you outside for a moment?"

My colleagues play it cool as I place the airbrush gun on my tray with forced nonchalance and saunter toward the door. On the way, my hip bangs into an empty chair, and I ricochet off it, sending a tray full of supplies flying. I can't bear to look at the stifled laughs on my friends' faces as I mutter, "I'll clean this up later" and lurch for the doorway.

"What the hell was that?" Sean asks, straight-faced.

"Shut up. I was running on adrenaline."

I follow him through the extra-busy hallways. Every room, every area of the set is crowded with people. Finally, he stops in front of the prop closet where I ambushed him with our first kiss. He pulls open the door and gestures for me to go in first.

"Wow, chivalry's not dead after all," I say, squeezing inside.

He steps in after me and pulls the door closed. "Chivalry missed you." He kisses me, and why, why, why am I never prepared? My whole body is like an electromagnetic roller coaster—one second sitting placidly in the loading area, the next careening off at breakneck speed. His cologne is triggering me in ways that are not appropriate for the workplace. Our thwarted interlude in the jet taunts me.

I break the kiss. "Did you bring me into the closet for a reason? Because I'm about to make my own reason."

"By all means."

God, his mouth. I just want to kiss it and kiss it and never stop, but we're at work.

"How's Seamus?" I ask, pulling myself together. "Any midnight police raids since I last saw you?"

"He won't go to the therapist I set up for him."

"I could talk to him," I offer. "I know a thing or two about making life-altering mistakes and then punishing yourself for them for the rest of your life."

"At least you're allowing yourself a big reward these days." He tugs me in closer.

"I'm guessing you're the big reward?"

"Yes, I'm the *ginormous* reward. Although, you know, I don't want to oversell it."

"You literally referred to it as a space shuttle the other day."

He glances sideways. "I was running on adrenaline."

A grin splits my face, and his mirrors it. "You don't really have a reason for dragging me into this closet, do you? Other than you're obsessed with me." I grab his face and start kissing him again.

"Not obsessed," he murmurs around my lips.

"Admit it. You want me so bad you can't even stand it." I nip at his bottom lip, dropping my voice to a husky whisper. "In fact, you need me. I'm a biological imperative. If you can't have me, you'll go crazy. You'll die."

The breath stutters out of him. My limbs go weak at the sound, and, for the second time in a month, I'm about to rip off all my clothes and have sex in a closet, which is impressive since I've managed to go the previous thirty years without being remotely tempted. Of course, that's not going to happen. We're keeping a low profile, and the door has little slats in it for ventilation so every sound we make will be broadcast to the entire building. But how can I be expected to care about such things when a guy who graced the cover of the Sexiest Men Alive magazine twice in the past five years is ready to let me climb him like a set of monkey bars?

A muffled shout from the hallway interrupts our tryst. "Meeting on the bridge! Everyone!"

"I wonder what that's all about," Sean says, his voice gravelly with desire.

"Who cares?" I reply, going for his mouth again.

"Maybe we should go."

I groan.

"Chain of command, babe." He cracks the closet door, and a blast of cool air from the hall makes it clear how steamy it was getting in there. We funnel into the crowd on the bridge where our lead director, Miles Gautier, stands in front of the captain's ready room door in his HEYDUDEs, dad jeans, and Andor T-shirt. When he sees Sean, he waves him over to stand at the front with the rest of the *Lost Star* cast. Sean throws me a wink and pats down his yellow lock of hair as he takes his place in the lineup between the two Jasons, while I hang back with the rest of the support team.

"Okay, have we got everybody here?" Miles looks around. There are about a hundred of us crammed onto the bridge. One of the marketing people sneaks behind Miles with his phone raised to take a shot of the room. I start to take a discreet step out of his line of sight but then stop. Sean is right. I've got to stop worrying so much.

"Next week, we're gonna start filming season seven," Miles begins, "and as you know, we've been talking about ways to freshen up the show. Make it more relevant. More diverse. More updated. We've got some great ideas, which I think you're all going to like, and we've got some new people coming on board. Are any of you familiar with a sci-fi TV show out of Mexico called *Beyond the Stars*?"

I hold up my hand along with several others.

"Great. Well, they've been doing some really exciting stuff with their plotlines and characters. They don't have the musical element that *Lost Star* does, but it got us thinking. Why don't we do a few crossover episodes between the two shows? They'll be bilingual. We'll tape parts here; they'll tape others down there. And we'll also use the episodes as a bridge to introduce some of our new characters."

So, they really did go with my idea! I add a whoop to the smattering of applause. I'm sure Kelly never mentioned me when she brought it to Miles, but it's probably better that way.

"I appreciate the vote of confidence," Miles says. "Anyway, no need to belabor this any longer. I just wanted you all to know where our heads are at, and I wanted to introduce two new people to you. These are a couple of the folks you'll be working with over the next week or so, and a couple more will be joining us tomorrow. Let's give them a warm welcome."

Miles starts clapping, and the rest of us follow suit as the ready room door slides open. We crane our necks to get a look at the actors who step out, costumed in white, squishy uniforms.

"Hola," the first guy says with a wave. I can barely see him through the people in front of me, but he's tall and lean, and kinda familiar. So is his costume, for that matter.

That's when it hits me. Miles said these were crossover episodes. These actors aren't new recruits—they're actual cast members from *Más Allá de las Estrellas*. I recognize this guy—his name is César Castaño Cortés, and he plays an engineer named Salvo. He wasn't on *Club Bilingüe* with me; I just know him from watching the show.

I struggle to get a glimpse of the second person through the swaying, applauding throng in front of me, and make out a shorter dude shooting jovial finger guns at everyone. My stomach drops out.

"¡Qué onda! How's everyone doing?"

His voice is the same. His energy is the same. Everything about him is the same. It's like I've been thrust backward through time.

Miguel, my childhood best friend, is here.

Chapter 30

I see an acute attack of incurable leprosy in
my near future.

Josie

I DUCK BEHIND a trio of hairdressers.

Did Miguel see me?

With what I hope is a discreet peek, I confirm that my child-hood friend is not craning his neck trying to get a look at me, so that's a good sign. Sean is right—I don't look like that skinny blond teenager on the show anymore. Plus, Miguel thinks I'm still in Florida. There's no way he'd expect to find me here. Cognitive dissonance alone may be enough to save me.

But what am I going to do? Get the heck out of here, for a start.

Miles dismisses us, thank God, and I bolt for the back door. I make a beeline down the curving hallway toward the makeup room, but the area is already clogging up with people exiting through the front door of the bridge. I whirl on a heel and am struck by a second deluge of people pouring from my exit. I shift and turn and flatten myself, working my way through the maze of bodies, but it's kind of like kayaking upstream. I peek over my shoulder, and Miguel is *right there*, literally three people away! He turns his head, and I whip my face around and zero in on the red EXIT sign at the end of the hallway. I've never used this back door before, but far be it for me to shy away from new experiences. I clear the crowd, legs pumping like a power walker, and heave the silver bar open.

I'm greeted by a smelly back lot alley housing a herd of rusty green dumpsters. Across the way, two men lean against another studio building, smoking cigarettes. I let the door fall shut with a bang and sag against the wall beside it.

How is Miguel here? Sean said the *Lost Star* cast was going to Mexico, not the other way around!

I pull out my phone and open the most recent message from my friend.

Miguel: Ok, Sheet, I can tell you my news now. They're sending me to the *Lost Star* studio to tape some crossover episodes! I'm going to Hollywood! Today!

The message is followed by a string of emojis as long as the Pandora line at Disney. Had I read it earlier, I might have avoided a nasty cortisol dump as well as an accidental run-in. I need to be better about checking my phone.

I rock my head against the concrete block wall to face the

door. Should I open it? I have no idea where Miguel is, so I can't be certain to avoid him. But my next client is probably sitting in my chair right now wondering where I am.

I take a deep breath of smoke-and-garbage-tinged air. It's hardly cleansing, but I won't be ruled by fear. I grab the handle and pull. It doesn't budge.

¡Maldita sea! I'm locked out.

I know how physics works, but there's something about today that makes anything seem possible, so I grab the handle with both hands and yank again. It's locked tight. Great, now I'll have to go around the front, which means even more exposure. The smokers across the way gesture at me and chuckle to one another.

"Lung cancer's not a conspiracy theory!" I shout in their direction just as the door in front of me explodes open. My heart launches into my throat, but it's just Chelsea.

"They're looking for you inside."

"Okay, I'll be right there."

I peer past her shoulder. No sign of Miguel. Everyone else is back to work. I should be, too. But I don't move.

It's not just that I don't want Miguel to discover my secret. It's more than that. We're supposed to be friends, and, just like with Emmy, I've been a terrible one. I've been using him to stay connected to my old life, but it hasn't been a fair trade because everything I've shared with Miguel has been hidden behind a firewall of lies. It seemed like a necessary precaution, but deep down, I knew it wasn't right.

How am I going to face him when he finds out?

"You coming?" Chelsea asks, her sneaker propping the door.

"Give her a minute."

The voice comes from behind me followed by a long exhale of smoke. I whirl, and there he is, hair longer than I remember, taller, more muscled—a man, even though his face hasn't changed: Miguel.

He puts the cigarette to his lips and takes another puff, leaving it pinched there. "Sábana. What the hell? How are you here?" He comes at me with arms wide.

My heart pinballs inside my body as I step into his embrace. We didn't hug a lot as teens, so this is doubly awkward. He holds on too long. It's going to make me cry. I pat his back, peering at the cigarette still pinched between his lips.

"Okay, okay. You're gonna set my hair on fire, wey." I swipe at my eyes before he can see them watering.

"¿Qué pasa?" he asks. "This is freaky. Did you come here to surprise me? I only told you about it this morning."

"It's a long story." I wave at the cigarette. "You still doing that?"

"It's the only way I can cope with living without you." He snort-chuckles, and it gets me laughing, too. Even though I'm all tied up inside, something else loosens. Miguel is here! I wasn't sure we'd ever see each other again.

"Listen, Migui, there are some things you should know. I don't go by Savannah Bateman anymore. You have to call me Josie."

He drops his cigarette and grinds it into the asphalt with the toe of his boot. "Why was that woman calling you back inside like you work here or something?"

I cringe. "I do work here."

Miguel was always that kid who could take a hit. A punch, an insult, a bad mood. He could let them all roll off, but the way his face twitches now, I can tell this one hurts. "For how long?"

"A couple of years."

"What do you do?"

"Makeup."

He nods at the ground. "You never told me you moved to Hollywood."

God, I feel like a bag of assholes. "Come here." I throw my arms around him again, this time meaning it. "I missed you! I'm so glad you're here! I'm so excited for you! I want to hear all about everything. And I'll tell you everything, too. I promise."

He pats my arm and pulls out of the hug. "I've gotta go back inside. They want to do a read-through for tomorrow." When he smiles, it's only a little forced. "But you can take me out tonight, no? Show me LA? Skybar?" He does a ridiculous hip-rotating dance move, at least I think that's what it is.

Good ol' Miguel, the human whack-a-mole, and I'm grateful for that. If I didn't have thick-skinned friends, I wouldn't have any friends at all.

But I can't take him out. We can't be seen together. I'll be recognized for sure. "Nobody cool goes to the Skybar anymore," I say.

"Then you can take me where they do go." He snaps his fingers, repeating that same slo-mo gyration.

"Or we can hang at my place. I can introduce you to Jason Connor and Emmy—"

"There's something else you should know," he cuts me off, hips ceasing in mid-roll.

Ice water sluices through my veins. "What?"

"Lupe's coming, too. She arrives tomorrow."

And, just like that, I see an acute attack of incurable leprosy in my near future. "Thanks for warning me."

"I gotta get back to work." Miguel reaches for the door handle. "And we're going out tonight. *Out*. Understood? This is Hollywood, baby. You owe me that."

"That's lock—" I start to say but shut up when the door opens outward for him. Miguel always was a lucky SOB.

Sean's head pops out. Okay, so maybe it wasn't luck, just timing.

"There you are." He's got his serious face on, and his gaze cycles between us before finally settling on Miguel. "Conference room's down that hall on the left."

Miguel holds up a hand to me. "Yeehaw!"

I give him an obligatory high five. He makes Sean do the same and then disappears into the building.

"Wait, is he one of your old castmates?" Sean asks.

I nod at the ground. "Yep."

"Sheeeyite."

"And my nemesis-slash-stepsister is arriving tomorrow. I might as well announce right now that I'm Savannah Bateman and let the world burn."

He props the door with his shoulder and gives me a pensive look. "It's an option." He sniffs the air. "Were you smoking?"

"Yes, when you're not looking, I'm a smokestack."

"C'mere to me, you." With a smile, he reaches for me, but I take a step backward.

"Sean, I don't think you realize how serious this is. If I go down, I'll take you with me."

He scoffs. "I'll chance it."

"Now that these two shows are partnering, a lot more people are going to be putting the pieces together." I wring my hands. "I think I'll have the flu while you guys are taping this crossover thing. Although, now that I think about it, I have enough vacation days saved up."

"Listen, Josie"—Sean looks behind himself down the hall—"I

have to go join that script reading, but my gut tells me you're overthinking this. It's all gonna be fine. You'll see."

I want to believe him. But I'll still be taking vacation days while Lupe's here.

He dips his chin. "Should we kiss before going back inside?"

I shuffle over to him, and we share a chaste little kiss. It's still enough to rev my engines. When I try to squeeze past him, he purposely doesn't move so our bodies are forced to slide against one another. I'm feeling better already.

"I love that you're so into me," I say over my shoulder as I head to the makeup room.

He catches my elbow right before I enter the room. "Want to see each other tonight?"

I wince. "I promised I'd hang with Miguel."

"Oh yeah? Doing what?"

Is Sean jealous? I kind of like that. "He wants to go out and meet some celebrities, but I can't risk us being seen together."

"Why don't I tag along? That way it looks like he's my guest, not yours."

"Actually, that's a good idea. We need to steer clear of the paparazzi, though. Any ideas?"

"Jimmy Fallon's in town. He's hosting a high ropes Halloween party tonight. Invitation only."

I hesitate. "I can't tell if you're joking."

"Alternatively, we could go to Clint Eastwood's shirtless gun show."

"High ropes it is." I pause and give him a real smile. "Thank you. You're a lifesaver. A smokin' hot, ripped, everything-flavored lifesaver. Oh, and there's a personality in there somewhere, too."

His jaw drops. "There is not. How dare you! I'm one-hundred-percent love machine."

I glance around to make sure no one is watching before going in for a kiss, this one not nearly as chaste. His response to it dissolves me, and I'm back in that closet again, ready to rip off all my clothes, but I hold it together because denying myself pleasure is one of my superpowers.

"*So* into me," I murmur over my shoulder as I head to my station.

"A matching amount!" he calls into the room, gaze ping-ponging around our small audience of Li Jing, their client, and mine. "Hello. Nice to see you," he says to all three of them before pointing a finger at me. "A perfectly normal amount of…what you said. One that matches yours."

I smirk. "Whatever you say, Captain."

Chapter 31

I told myself I wouldn't do this.

Sean

I COME HOME after work to find Seamus sitting at the kitchen bar, eating supper.

"How is it?" I ask my brother.

He forks up a mouthful of asparagus. "Grand, for a carbless wasteland."

I exchange a look with my chef, D'Andre, who is about twice my size. My face says, *It's okay, just ignore him.* His says, *I'll chop him into small bits and put him in a soup.*

"Mam would be happy you're eating, at least," I say.

"She doesn't care one way or the other. Neither does Da."

"That's not true." I accept a plate of food from D'Andre. "They just need a little time. Your homecoming was unexpected."

"Too unexpected to invite me to Da's party, huh? Not enough caviar for one more partygoer?"

Ouch. "How'd you find out?"

He holds his phone out to me, chewing loudly. "It's a video of your latest arm candy singing with Bono. How long have you been dating her?"

I force myself to bite into a piece of asparagus. "Couple of weeks."

"What? And you're already whipped?"

"I'm not whipped."

"Right." He sniggers. "Have you looked her up? Done a background check?"

I go cold inside. "That's not a normal thing people do."

"It's a normal thing for people like you. I looked her up for you, actually," Seamus says.

Shit. Josie would hate this. This is exactly why she didn't want to date me. "I didn't ask you to do that."

"Naw, brother. It's fine. There's hardly anything on her. But that's what makes it even stranger, because most people have a past. Josie Days doesn't."

The tone of his voice has gone dangerous. I don't like it one bit.

"D'Andre, you can go home. I'll finish up here." I turn on my stool toward Seamus, match his tone, and throw a little acid on it. "I don't need you spying on my girlfriend." When he starts to interrupt, I point a ringed finger at his face. "I don't want you anywhere near her, do you understand me?"

I know I shouldn't be confrontational like this. The family therapist we met with years ago called it "unhelpful." It's not that I think Seamus would hurt Josie, but even the tiniest crumb of an idea that he might boils my blood.

Seamus turns back to his food. "Oh, I see how it is."

I'm not sure what *it* is, but I do know that Seamus would never do something for me before doing something for himself. I narrow my eyes. "Josie wasn't the only person you researched, was it?"

He doesn't reply. Seamus's tell for lying has always been silence.

"Tell me you didn't look up Kokoro."

"So what if I did?"

"So, she's got a restraining order on you."

"I'm not gonna do anything. I just looked at her social media."

"She blocked you!"

"I used your computer."

Now I'm implicated. That's just effing great. Note to self to change my passwords. "Aren't you supposed to be focusing on your own life?"

A tumbler of whiskey appears in Seamus's hand, and I realize it's been present all along, just pushed to the side while he ate. "I will, yeah, Mr. High and Mighty. Why don't you keep on reminding me?" He takes a swig. "You and everybody else."

I pretend to look around the kitchen. "Who's everybody else, Seamus? I'm the only one here. Trying to help you."

He points the tumbler at me. "I don't need your help."

"You're literally living in my house. My staff is cooking your meals."

"It's the least you could do after stealing my role . . . Captain." His lip curls on the word, and his gaze flicks to my dyed-yellow lock of hair.

"I didn't steal anything from you," I say, but my voice cracks.

"But you took advantage of it, didn't you? Best thing that ever happened to you. Shy little Seanny Boy's now a fecking superhero."

His accent's gotten thick. It's even thicker now that he's angry.

"Yeah, well, if I were a real superhero, I would've stopped you from ruining Uncle's business!"

He doesn't take my bait. "You could've said no! Turned it down! I'm your brother for Christsakes!" The whiskey bottle clinks against the rim of his glass as he pours himself another.

"What, so if you can't have the opportunity of a lifetime, it means I can't, either?" This is the argument I tell myself over and over.

He mimes a dagger in his chest, and someone—me, apparently—twisting it. But I'm not going to apologize for taking the role. It's what launched me. And I'm a better Captain Footwork than Seamus could ever be. Strong, firm, able to make the tough decisions but gentlemanly and likable—that's what the showrunners said.

Besides, this isn't about me.

"You could've done great things with Uncle's business, you know. Instead, you trashed it. Is that my fault, too?"

"Ach, I was never cut out for business. I was a performer. You know that." His narrowed eyes flick to my yellow lock again— the red cape to his bull.

"Well, why don't you take this move as an opportunity to make a positive change in your life? Reinvent yourself. Find some meaningful work."

He gulps another shot. "Who's gonna hire me? The guy down at the 7-Eleven?"

I groan internally. I told myself I wouldn't do this, but… "I can ask around. See if there's anything at the studios. Backstage stuff. Extras. A foot in the door."

Not at my studio—I don't want Seamus there—but other studios, maybe.

Seamus reads my face. "But you're not gonna do that, Seanny Boy. Are you?"

"I said I would, didn't I? There's a party tonight. A lot of people will be there." I straighten up and make sure I'm eye to eye with him—the captain, the guy who's tasked with delivering the bad news as well as the good. "But there are no guarantees. Face it, Seamus. You blew up your life. I can't fix that for you. You're gonna have to figure this out for yourself. And yes, it may involve the 7-Eleven."

His face distorts into a look I recognize from, oh, my entire life: Seamus disgusted. "We're not all that different, Seanny Boy." He points the tumbler at me again. This time it feels like a weapon. "You and I both know that."

My stomach flip-flops.

"It's all a smokescreen, isn't it? The outfits you wear." He swipes at the sailor collar on my Givenchy jacquard overshirt. "The larger-than-life bullshit. You're over-the-top in public about the things that don't really matter. But the things that do matter, the things you're really over-the-top with…" He grins a slithery smile. "Those you keep hidden. Like your obsession with this woman. Deep down, you're still weird, shy little Seanny Boy playing dress-up backstage—"

"I'm not obsessed with her," I cut him off, but my brain is scrabbling for purchase on a slick wall. Did he manage to get into my cosplay room? I told Rory to keep it locked! Did he see the George Washington hat? Did he recognize it?

God, he was on my computer! He could've found the auction site. The purchase order. And what about Josie? If Seamus can see right through me, maybe everyone else can, too.

"Oh, you're not obsessed, right, of course not!" Seamus is loving this. I guess he's been waiting four years for a chance to come at me. "Like you weren't obsessed with Melody Winkman back in high school."

Of course he'd bring her up. "I was seventeen. I wrote some poems. I drew some pictures."

"They called it a *shrine* when I did it for Kokoro."

I start to feel sweaty. Clammy. Is my blood sugar low? My meal sits untouched on my plate. "I'm nothing like you." I stand up, shove my stool into its place under the bar, and ball my fists. "I'm normal."

"You're normal, huh?"

His laugh is ugly as he stands and kicks his own stool back into place. These are the results of childhoods lived with an Irishwoman who knew how to wield a broom. But I'm not afraid of Seamus. I could have an alien bursting out of my chest, and I'd still be able to take this rabbit turd down in a fight. When I take a step toward him, he backs up.

"Yeah, I'm normal! For one thing, if Josie told me to leave her alone, I'd leave her alone! I wouldn't hide in her car, for crying out loud. Follow her home. Destroy my career and embarrass my family. Over somebody who didn't even want me!"

The flicker of his upper lip is a small victory. That's it, brother, get mad. Lose control. Let's duke it out right here because at least I know that's a fight I'll win.

But instead of engaging, Seamus leans against the counter, a languid, self-serving piece of shit who learned how to play me a long time ago. "Sometimes you have to fight for the people you love, brother. You don't just give up."

"Yes, you do!" I bark into his shit-eating smirk. "When someone says *piss off*, you piss off!"

"And that's what you'd do if this Josie chick dumped you? You'd piss off?"

"Right into the sunset."

"Would you now, brother?" He lifts his tumbler between us and takes a sip, glaring at me over the rim. My face is so close to his that he has to lean back to do it. "And never look back?"

"And never look back. It's called respecting someone's wishes."

"Right. Okay." He slides out sideways from where I've got him pinned against the counter, grabs his bottle, and heads for the patio. "We'll see about that."

Chapter 32

DANGER: DO NOT RECOMMEND.

Josie

EMMY'S KNOCK ON the trailer door almost scares me out of my skin. Maybe it's all those damn Halloween movies I've been watching late at night or maybe it's because I'm staring into the mirror at a zombie makeup job. Jimmy Fallon's high ropes party is a Halloween party, after all, and I need a disguise.

When I open the door, Emmy gasps, and Mattie's eyes go wide. He raises Possessed Baby between himself and me, as if she might serve as some kind of protective barrier. Frankly, even if I were a real zombie, I'd still think twice about going after a kid with a doll that looked like that.

"It's just me, kiddo," I tell Mattie. To Emmy I say, "What's up?"

She swoops past me into the trailer with Mattie following

behind like a loyal little dog. "My midwife's on her way. The baby's breech, and we need to remedy that."

"How?"

"Moxibustion," Emmy says.

"Moxi-what?"

"It's, like, witchy acupuncture that makes babies turn head down."

"And we're doing it here, why?"

"Jason and Peyton went Halloween costume shopping." She plops down on the couch. "Jason's taking her to Jimmy Fallon's party tonight since I can't do high ropes. I was hoping you'd keep an eye on Mattie while Lukiana does her thing." She smiles. "Plus, you know, I thought it'd be something fun we could do together."

"Oh yes, women have been bonding over baby-flipping for centuries."

I glance at Mattie, who is staring up at me with his dad's hangdog look—the one that drives a thousand women a day mad. The kid is gonna be a heartbreaker.

"¿Qué quieres?" I ask him.

"Can he have a Coke?" Emmy cranes her neck on the couch. "I told him you have Coke out here."

Mattie's pleading look instantaneously converts into a Ralphie-from-*A-Christmas-Story* smile, and he starts to do a creepy little dance, shoulders bouncing, arms dangling.

"Oh my gosh, he's turning into a zombie! The cure for that is Coke. Go Coke it up, amigo. Ándale."

"¡Sólo uno!" Emmy shouts from the couch. "You look great, by the way," she says. "Zombie bride really suits you. Where'd you get the dress?"

"Bridal shop closeout sale and a pair of scissors."

"Are you going to add some bloodstains?"

I shake my head. "I prefer noir to gore."

"Good choice."

Another violent knock wracks the door. We all jump.

"That'll be her." Emmy starts to get up, but I intercept and open the door to a hunched, elderly woman in a pink velour tracksuit—Malibu Baba Yaga.

The midwife grunts a greeting and assesses the space like a cat deciding which pile of laundry to sit on. She clears the paintbrushes off my wicker coffee table to make room for her big bag o' pregnancy supplies and then plunks a box of acupuncture needles onto the table beside some kind of paper-wrapped stick the size of a kindergartner's pencil. "Take off your shoes and socks," she orders Emmy.

Emmy crunches to reach her feet, but at thirty-seven weeks pregnant can't quite reach.

"I've got you." I catch her foot and unlace her New Balance sneaker.

She settles back on the sofa with a sigh. "So, Jason told me there are a couple new actors on the show. Two guys from Mexico, and you know them."

Uh-oh.

"I know one of them. Miguel." I tug the shoe off and work on the laces of the second.

"How do you know him?"

"We lived in the same town."

It feels so wrong that Sean knows more about my time in Mexico than Emmy does. I did a decidedly thorough job of hiding my past when we were back in Florida. Yes, this stuff came up, but when I steered the conversation in another direction, Emmy just let me.

"We did some acting together, too," I add, feeling guilty.

"You were an actress?"

"I dabbled."

I yank off Emmy's socks and tuck them into her shoes. Her pedicure is perfect. Emmy lies down, and Lukiana immediately plunks two needles into the outsides of her pinkie toes. It's borderline barbaric.

I scuttle out of the way as the midwife pulls out a lighter, strikes it, and holds the end of the moxibustion stick to the flame. A sweet, herbal smell cuts the air, a little like marijuana.

"So, how are things going with Sean?" Emmy asks.

I perch a butt cheek on the arm of the couch. It feels weird to talk about this while the baby witch is burning weird herbs at my friend's toes, but here we are. "Things are good."

She does a silent cheer. "He really likes you. Jason and I agree, we've never seen him like this."

I want to believe what everyone's saying—that I'm good for Sean. That he's different with me. But it scares me, too. Sean's not just an actor—he's an A-lister. I could be the flavor of the week, just like all those other girls he's dated. People could be reading this all wrong.

And what if he really is falling for me? That might actually be worse. My celebrity dance card got stamped a long time ago—with black, angry letters that read DANGER: DO NOT RECOMMEND.

"And how do you feel about him?" Emmy asks.

I sigh and give her my bad news face. "I can't stand him. A *lot*."

"Yes! I knew it! Josie, I'm so happy for you!"

She speaks *me* too well. "No, it's not good," I reply. "I've still got the same . . . issues."

"Your pathological stage fright? What, did you have a traumatic thespian experience down in Mexico with what's-his-name? Miguel?"

I snicker because, wow, that is so ridiculously close to the truth that I might just use it as a euphemism from now on. "Something like that."

Lukiana blows out her smelly stick and retires to a far chair, plops some headphones on, and pulls out her knitting.

Emmy closes her eyes and folds her hands on top of her belly. This is our MO, Emmy's and mine. She pushes, I shut down, she stops pushing, and all my secrets get to stay happily buried. But I know it's not fair of me to keep doing this. I should tell her more. She's my best friend, and she deserves to know.

"Miguel and I were in a show together for a little while." Six seasons is a little while, right? It's all relative—*Guiding Light* ran for seventy-two years.

"A TV show? In Mexico?" Her eyes snap open, and she reaches for her phone on the coffee table. "How could you not have told me this? What was it called?"

Dammit, dammit, dammit! Not the phone. "It was a long time ago. And that's not what's impor—"

"What was it called?"

If she looks it up, she's going to find out everything, bit by bit, like hopping from one stepping stone to the next.

"What, was it a porno? Is that why you don't want to tell me?"

"Yes, it was the most popular teenage porno of the early 2000s."

"Never mind. I'll find it. I don't see anything under your name, but I can look him up. What's his last name? Never mind, I can find it in the entertainment news. Everybody's talking about the new *Lost Star* crossover."

Curse you, Information Age. But there's nothing I can do to stop this save ripping the phone out of Emmy's hands and throwing it across the room, which, let's face it, would only be a temporary solution anyway. I take a deep breath. Maybe her knowing will be a good thing. Maybe it's time.

"Oh my God!" Emmy cries, and I feel my eyes squeeze shut in shame. She starts to get up. Why? Can she not take my heinous puppet-torching past lying down? Is she mad that I lied to her? Is she going to slap me?

But no, she's just rolling onto her side. "Lukiana, the baby's moving! I think it's trying to flip!"

"Stop!" The midwife's roar is that of the goddess of fertility herself. She crosses the room like a Viking ship on a dark and dangerous sea. Then, plucking out the needles, she rotates Emmy like a pig on a spit.

"It flipped!" Emmy cries. "I felt it! It was like a loaf of bread just flopped inside of me."

Lukiana now has Emmy in a deep squat and is palpating her bump. "The baby has turned!" she confirms.

I exchange a baffled look with Mattie, who is lurking in the doorway of the spare room probably wondering if he should tell a trusted adult about what he's witnessing.

"Está bien. Todo está bien." I give him what I hope is a reassuring nod and add a thumbs-up for good measure. He backs into the room like Homer Simpson into the bushes.

Emmy grins from her squat. "This means I can still have my home birth."

Lukiana has whipped out an ear horn–looking thing from her bag o' pregnancy supplies and is bent over like a Cirque du Soleil performer, listening to Emmy's bump.

"Baby's heartbeat is good. You sit on the floor for a little while. I check again in fifteen minutes." She goes back to her knitting.

"I'm going to finish getting ready," I tell Emmy as she settles in a yoga pose on the floor. If I'm not in her sights, maybe she'll forget about looking up *Club Bilingüe.*

"Wait! Come here." She waves me over, her face giddy.

I take a deep breath and lower myself onto the couch near her. It appears I'm not getting off that easy. I steel myself to come clean. Tell her the whole thing. Should I start at the beginning? When my mom first met Juan Ernesto? Or should I jump right to the part where I blew it all up?

"I know what it is," she says, before I can start.

"You do?" How is that possible?

She nods, amber eyes shining. "It's a girl."

Oh! We're not talking about me. "But you asked Sean and me to do the gender reveal."

She wrinkles her nose. "I had the imaging center send the results to me instead. I had to know."

A little laugh bursts out of me. Suddenly this all seems more real, knowing it's a little girl in there and not just some shadowy mystery baby. "Are we still going to decorate the nursery with dinosaurs?"

"Yes, but I'm going to need you to paint bows and tutus on them. And the T. rex needs to be holding a cute little parasol."

"Pink rubber ducks floating in the tar pit?" I suggest.

"Shh! Lower your voice! I don't want Mattie to hear. Nobody can know that I know."

More secrets. I feel weighed down with them. At least this is a good one. I look up at the beach-themed clock on the wall, the same one that used to track the evenings back in our old trailer park in Florida.

I fold myself onto the floor with Emmy and drape my arms around her. Tears prick at my eyes. I don't know why. Maybe it's the mix of emotions: joy, excitement, gratitude. And guilt.

Yeah, guilt's in there, too. Emmy's just told me her biggest secret of the moment, as friends do. And I can't bring myself to tell her mine.

Plus, I can't help but wonder if I'll ever get to have a moment like this. Will there ever be a family that I can truly, one-hundred percent know I belong to, because I created it?

"I'm so happy for you and Jason," I whisper, giving her an extra squeeze. "And Peyton, too. She's going to be so excited about little Boba Tea!"

"Thanks for sharing this with me."

"Of course," I say, choking down the lump in my throat. "We're BFFs. Siempre y para toda la vida."

"Always and forever," she agrees.

Chapter 33

I didn't realize this was going to be
full-contact high ropes.

Sean

JOSIE MAKES HER way across the flagstones from her trailer to the driveway, a vision of the undead in a ripped bridal gown and blue-striped Adidas. To avoid messing up her makeup, I plant my kiss on the back of her hand. "I guess I should have known better than to expect a Disney princess."

She surveys my Han Solo outfit. "That's what all the nerf herders say."

I spin on a heel so she can admire the whole thing. "You like it?" I'm dying to tell her the vest is the real deal, but I'm not sure how she'll take it. I mean, all by itself, I imagine an original Han Solo vest worn by Harrison Ford himself is pretty dang cool, not obsessive at all, but better safe than sorry.

You're over-the-top in public about the things that don't really matter. But the things that do matter, the things you're really over-the-top with, those you keep hidden.

Maybe the fight with Seamus just has me all jittery.

We drive to the high ropes course where Miguel will meet us. I'm curious to see what this dude's all about and what manner of friends he and Josie are. Not that I'm the jealous type. The course is lit up with string lights—white, purple, and green. Halloween decorations dot the treed landscape. Big-shot guests and their families mill about, grabbing drinks from makeshift bars or coolers and fancy snacks from the myriad tables around the property. A stage has been set up with Jimmy Fallon at the mic. We spot Miguel waiting for us by security.

"Órale vato," Miguel says to me, holding out a hand—for a shake this time rather than a high five. His face is painted in a Day of the Dead skull, and he's wearing a mariachi outfit. "Wait a minute!" He stares at my chest. "Is that the real actual Han Solo vest? From the original movies?"

"Why, yes, it is." I shift to model it. "And thank you for noticing."

"That's crazy!" he says.

"Not crazy!" I smooth my hands down the front of it. "*Authentic.* Collectors like authentic things."

Miguel's black-ringed eyes are wide in amazement. "You're a collector? How many of these things do you have, man?"

I'm not sure what he means by "these things." Is he talking about authentic Han Solo vests? Because the answer would be one. Is he talking about authentic Star Wars memorabilia? Because the answer would be twenty-six. If he's talking about authentic *anything*, well, that's not a number I'm willing to publicly acknowledge.

"I have a few," I say.

"Hey, speaking of collectors, did you hear about the George Washington hat from *Hamilton* getting stolen?" he asks.

I swallow hard and look over his head, across the crowd, like I'm surveying the area with confidence because I'm in charge and not afraid of anything. "They haven't found that yet?"

"Naw, wey. Whoever stole it is still at large."

At the phrase *at large*, I decide I'm definitely turning the hat in after *Hamilton on the Roof* tomorrow. A saner person might head to the police station sooner rather than later, with two dozen donuts in tow for good measure, but I went through a lot of trouble to get that hat. I want to have it on my head when I belt out those songs. I want to feel like I was a part of that incredible show. Just for one night, I want to channel Christopher Jackson—look like his George Washington, feel like his George Washington, *be* his George Washington.

"You okay?" Josie whispers to me.

"Yeah, of course."

She hooks an arm in mine as we follow in Miguel's wake on the Tour du Celebrities. "Look over there! It's Ryan Gosling," he shouts. "And Scarlett Johansson! Margot Robbie!"

"Oh my God, what? There are famous people here?" Josie feigns shock.

"Cállate, Sábana." Even I recognize *shut up* in Spanish.

"Don't call me that, remember? I'm Josie, Sean's girlfriend. You and I have never met before today." Josie's gaze darts around, but everyone is busy eating and drinking and talking and traversing the wires above and around us.

It's not lost on me that she called herself my girlfriend. That's another first, and I like it.

Miguel's head is practically on a swivel. "Hey, do you think Robert Downey, Jr. is here, and if he is, will you introduce me?"

"Come on, Sean, let's get suited up," Josie says. "If we're lucky, Miguel will fanboy himself into a stupor, and then we can lose him."

"I heard that!" Miguel replies with a grin.

Jason and Peyton leave their place in line to join us. Peyton's dressed in a *Descendants* costume, purple extensions in her hair. Jason's got on shoulder pads and a Cincinnati Bengals jersey, black grease smeared under his eyes. Peyton squeals over our costumes, and I introduce Miguel to her as if he's my responsibility. Meanwhile, Josie's wired tight as a spring. I wonder briefly if we might be able to get out of here at some point. I mean, the whole idea was to take Miguel somewhere where he could rub elbows with celebrities. Check.

But when I think about bringing Josie home with me, I remember that I made my brother a sort-of promise. To try to find him work. I should at least make an attempt.

"How's Emmy?" I say to Jason as I thread my leg into a harness.

"She's ready to have this baby."

"I can be there in fifteen with my catcher's mitt."

"You're such a weirdo," he replies.

"What? It's the most natural thing in the world!"

The staff checks our harnesses, and Jason watches to make sure they do a thorough job with Peyton's. Josie's dress is all hiked up around her waist, and I can see her white bike shorts and long, shapely legs. She and Miguel are talking in Spanish. The conversation looks easy and congenial. Even her zombified smile is beautiful.

"You really like her, don't you?" Jason is grinning as we wait for the safety instructions to begin.

"Naw, man, what's not to like?" I realize I've just contradicted myself, but Jason takes it as confirmation.

"She's great. You two seem great together."

"Well, you know, we're just having fun." It's the truth. Neither Josie nor I have expressed that we want anything more than that.

"I think you two would be great for one another even when things weren't fun."

I don't say anything. I don't know what to say to that. It's almost like there's a disconnect in my brain. Like it doesn't compute: If you're not having fun, why even be with someone? I know where he's going with it—long-term relationship stuff—but I honestly don't know how to get my train to that station, or if I even have a connection to that line. To open yourself up to someone that much...it seems risky.

"Hey," I say, changing the subject. "You know of any studios that are looking to hire?"

"For what?"

"Something for Seamus."

"For Seamus..." he repeats, trailing off, and I feel the doors slamming shut, one by one.

"It's all right." I give his shoulder pads a no-hard-feelings pat. What did I expect?

The instructor explains all the things we have to do to not plummet to our deaths. Luckily, it's pretty foolproof, and Jason and I have been through all of this so many times we could probably outfit a family of chimpanzees for the course blind-folded and drunk—the chimps *and* us.

"How are you with heights?" I ask Josie as we climb the first ladder up into the starry sky.

"I eat them for breakfast and then punch their faces in."

"Of course you do."

There's a cooler of craft beers on the wooden platform. Miguel is halfway across when Josie calls his name and lobs a can to him. If he misses, it'll just fall into some bushes, but he doesn't miss. Instead, he balances on the zigzagging metal wires in his mariachi boots, pops the top, and chugs it.

"Zoe! Zoe Saldaña!" he shouts down into the crowd. I spot her in a Victorian dress, face tilting upward at her name. He presses his hands to his chest. "I love you! I love you so much!" Then he says a bunch of stuff in Spanish, and I'm sure it's just as cringey.

I sidle up to Josie on the platform. She's giggling.

"He's obsessed with her," she explains.

That word again. It drags me back to the conversation with Seamus about Melody Winkman, and then further back still, to how he mercilessly teased me when he found the notebook I'd dedicated to her. How he showed it to Melody, who told her mother, who reported it to the principal, who called my parents. They searched our room and found not only the notebook, but Seamus's binoculars, too, and immediately assumed they were mine. I didn't rat my brother out, and he didn't own up, either. In fact, he gave me shit for weeks about the fact that they'd been taken away.

I was forced to write an apology to Melody and her family, and the next day, the principal issued me a new schedule. The entire school knew why, too. It was humiliating. Of course, after I became the theater department's darling, all of that sort of…went away. Melody and I even became friends. Still, Seamus never let me forget it.

"Just because he's a fan doesn't mean he's obsessed," I say in Miguel's defense.

"Oh no, he's obsessed, trust me." She steps out onto the wires with nimble bounces. "You didn't see his childhood bedroom."

I don't wait for her to get all the way across before I step on, too. "And, um, what did you two do in that childhood bedroom?" I try to make the question light and teasing rather than jealous and stalker-y.

"Oh, you know, lots of teenage experimentation."

Of course she would say that. And the worst part is, I have no idea if it's a lie or the truth.

"I deserved that," I say. "And you deserve this." I clutch my safety line and bounce as hard as I can.

She cries out, laughing as she fights to keep her balance. My chest gets all warm inside.

"You'd better make a run for it!" I growl, lunging after her.

She emits a panicked squawk. The wires zigzag far apart, and Josie bounces across them, legs wide, like she's been riding a hippo all day and is now making a run for the safari hut. I spring after her, sticking to only the wire on the right, like a tightrope walker. Hand over hand, foot in front of foot, I catch up to her and take a leap, landing squarely behind her, my arm wrapping around her waist just in time to keep her from losing her balance when the wire dips violently from my extra weight and momentum.

"Gotcha!" I cry, nipping at her neck.

"If I go down, I'm taking you with me!" she laughs, trapping my hand around her middle.

"You can try," I say.

"¡Ándale, Sheet, I mean, Josie, I got you!" Miguel reaches out a hand from the platform.

Josie dives for it, and Miguel yanks her out of my grasp to safety. I almost lose my balance and manage to regain it just in time to feel the wires dance again and spot Jason over my shoulder, running at me like a linebacker. Shit! I hustle onto the platform before he plows into me. My heart is thumping. I didn't realize this was going to be full-contact high ropes. But it's fun.

After giving Snack some friendly heck, I glance over to where Josie chats with Miguel as they wait their turn for the next obstacle. She's practically hanging over the edge of the backed-up platform, confident in the security of her safety straps. Beautiful. Fearless. Everything.

Everything? I don't even know what that means, but my chest feels like a balloon. Maybe I have a deadly disease. Maybe someone spiked my water. Or maybe, like my brother claims, I'm obsessed.

"You know, it's okay to let yourself fall," Jason says from over my shoulder.

"Huh?"

"Just like that." He points to a zip line to the left of us, where our costar Kayla goes zipping by while her little sister and Peyton cheer her on.

"Oh, Kayla's here," I say flatly.

"You know what I'm talking about. It's okay to let yourself *fall*. For someone."

Of course I know what he's talking about, but I'm not about to admit it to Snack. I do another captain's move—looking past him instead of at him. "Whatever."

I manage to keep my hands off Josie as we traverse the next

few obstacles. I don't want to look like I'm too into her, and from Jason's comment, it's pretty clear I'm failing at that. Still, it's driving me crazy to be this close and not get to touch her. And she and Miguel spend most of their time speaking Spanish to each other. Is it a sign of jealousy to want to shove a mariachi fanboy off an obstacle so he winds up hanging by his safety line and has to be rescued by a worker? If so, I plead guilty.

"Hey, Miguel." I point vaguely into the crowd. "I just saw RDJ over there. Just now, I swear."

"Really? Where?"

Josie's eyebrows go up as Miguel hurries off, shoving his safety clip along the overhead wire. "You swear?" she asks.

I put a hand over my heart. "On Chuy's grave."

That earns me a smack and a smirk. Somehow, both feel like wins.

Right before the final zip line of our track, we run into Jason's ex, Margarita, and her husband, Rhett. Josie whips around and throws her arms around my neck.

"Kiss me," she demands, pulling me in close. "Make out with me. Hard."

She plasters her mouth onto mine. I love a slow-burn lead-up, but this onslaught is fantastic, too. My body lights up like a Geiger counter at Chernobyl.

I hear Jason chatting with Margarita. "What are they doing?" Margarita asks. I can only assume she's talking about us.

"What *are* we doing?" I mumble to Josie around our kisses. After all the agony of not touching her and having to share her with Miguel, it's a rush.

"Hiding from Margarita," Josie mumbles back. "She's seen *Club Bilingüe*, and she watches Hugo Valencia's show. She's onto me."

I peer over Josie's shoulder at Margarita, who is glaring at the two of us writhing in each other's arms. Frankly, I can't imagine that anyone with a line of sight *isn't* looking at us. I lift my hand from the middle of Josie's back and give Margarita a little wave.

I should've known better than to poke the bear. Margarita's blood-red lips set in a line of determination, and she marches our way in her Wonder Woman costume. She comes in close and perpendicular, her presence cutting right into our ravenous makeout session.

"Hello, Sean. Hello, Josie," she trumpets.

"Hi, Margarita," I mutter around Josie's unrelenting mouth. Josie doesn't say anything. Instead, she wraps a leg around mine. It's an even huger turn-on.

"You two look like you're having fun!" Margarita shouts, even though we're only inches away.

God, Margarita is fearless. "Kinda busy right now," I mutter as Josie continues to maul my mouth with hers. "Can you leave a message?"

She clears her throat. "I was just going to ask if you two needed any help planning Emmy and Jason's gender reveal."

Josie pulls back for a ragged breath. "We'll let you know." She dives back into devouring me.

"Great!" Margarita says and pushes her safety cord ahead of her as she marches back over to Rhett.

"Do we know what it is yet?" I murmur to Josie as her kisses slow down.

"A girl." She starts to pull away, but I tighten my grip.

"Wait," I whisper. Over her shoulder I call, "Hey Rhett, any chance you'd hire my brother?"

"Nope," he says before leaping off the platform on the zip line.

"Great. Thanks. Appreciate it," I say, mostly to myself.

Josie's fingers trail across my forehead, fixing my mussed-up Han Solo hair. "I guess the fixer can't always fix everything."

"Yeah, I'm starting to feel that. Some days I just want to punch him until he cries."

"I love that you're trying to help Seamus, but I'm worried about you. He needs professional help."

"He doesn't want it."

She cups my face and presses her forehead to mine. We stay that way for a moment, leaning into one another.

"If I'd had a brother like you, maybe things would've been different for me."

Out of my peripheral vision, I spot Miguel on the ground engaged in an animated conversation with Zoe Saldaña that has her chuckling. Go, Miguel.

"Wanna get out of here?" I whisper, gesturing to them. "Mission accomplished, right?"

Josie types a quick text into her phone, and we both watch as Miguel receives it and tilts his head back to give us a thumbs-up.

She pockets her phone and kisses my mouth. "Let's go."

Chapter 34

One leads to nirvana and the other to wonderland.

Sean

"WHERE ARE WE going?" Josie asks as I zoom out of the parking lot.

"We can go anywhere you want."

"How about your place?"

I press my lips together. "Seamus is there, remember?"

"I'd like to meet Seamus."

I shake my head. "You don't want to meet Seamus."

"I just said I did." She shifts sideways in the seat so she's facing me. "And then, after that, I'd like to do…other things."

I'd like to do other things, too, so I give her a sideways grin and start heading to my place. When we arrive, I glance around for Seamus while Josie admires the opulent marble foyer. Her gaze follows the length of first the left-hand spiral staircase then the right.

"One leads to nirvana and the other to wonderland," I joke.

"At least the backstage area of wonderland," Seamus says. "Have you not been here before, love?"

Shiteballs. Where did he come from? He leans against the doorjamb to the kitchen, clothes hanging loose on him, legs crossed at the ankle like the cartoon version of a lazy aristocrat. He shakes the Stanley in his hand the way a person does when they are checking liquid levels. I'm guessing that's not water in there.

"First time," Josie replies. "I'm Josie. You must be Seamus."

"Great!" I clap my hands in a bid to end this before it starts. "Introductions are done. Josie, let's go upstairs."

"Pardon my brother's disrespectfulness," Seamus interrupts in a slithery voice. "I'm sure he meant to give you a tour of this lovely estate before hurrying you off to bed."

I wince and point behind Seamus. "That's the kitchen and the west wing." I point ahead of us. "That's the patio area." I point to the right. "That's the living room. Upstairs are my rooms."

"Don't forget to show her *all* the rooms," Seamus says, sipping from his cup, "including the locked one."

Josie raises an eyebrow at me.

I'm going to beat my brother into a pulp. "It's for privacy."

"Privacy. Right." Seamus raises his cup with a smarmy grin, as if to toast my reply. "Josie, darling, whatever do you see in this oddball brother of mine?"

"I like how caring he is," Josie replies without hesitation, her gaze sharp. "Especially when it comes to his family."

That's sweet, but Seamus doesn't let it derail him. "He's not too much for you? Because he can be too much. Him and his secrets."

"Good night, Seamus!" I butt in, swooping Josie away and heading for the left-hand stairs.

"What's he talking about?" Josie asks as we climb. "What locked room? What secrets?"

"Nothing. I told you he was an arse."

Once upstairs, I head left, toward my bedroom ensuite, but Josie peels away from me and wanders right, down the long hallway, her gaze falling on each of the closed doors there.

Dammit, Seamus!

"This way, if you don't mind," I say, gesturing to my rooms with as much nonchalance as I can muster.

"I'd love that tour your brother mentioned." She gives me an unreadable look as she approaches the first door, her hand falling to the knob. When I don't protest, she throws open the door to my home gym and peers inside. "Wow, it looks like LA Fitness in here!"

My heart thuds. My cosplay room is two doors away.

"C'mere to me." I keep my voice playful. "All the best rooms are over here."

She ignores me and moves on to the second door. It's the library.

"We can read together later." I'm trying so hard to stay blasé, but I really don't want her to try door number three.

She walks backward, away from me, her expression wary, and places a hand on the third door handle. It's different from all the others—silver and industrial-strength with a keypad on it. A necessary precaution in a house that hosts a lot of parties.

When the door doesn't open, her jaw drops in faux surprise. "Locked."

Bloody hell.

"What's in here, Sean?" She presses her ear to the door. "I don't hear any unhappy kidnap victims or secret babies crying."

She's joking, but I can see the discomfort in her body language. This looks weird, I know it does. I scratch my nose. "It's… storage."

"I'd really love to see your storage." She steps away from the door and smiles at me. It's a weak smile. A test.

My heart is pounding. It feels like I've got snakes in my arteries. I have to open the door, don't I? I mean, it'll look even weirder if I don't.

"Sean?" she says.

"Josie," I reply.

She narrows her eyes. "Can you please open this door?"

I don't know how to answer that. I *can* open it. By that I mean, I'm physically capable of doing it. But if I do, Josie will see the side of me nobody but my family knows about—the infatuated, obsessive Seanny Boy, opposite of the larger-than-life Captain Footwork. I'll never be able to explain that hoard of costumes and accessories because that's what it is: a hoard. I'm a cosplay hoarder. A weirdo, off the rails, lowbrow, cosplay hoarder with an illegal hat to boot, and there's nothing attractive about that.

Then she'll see the rest of the truth—that weird doesn't usually stay in its lane. It usually spills over to other things.

"Josie," I say again, the word laden with pleading, with desperation, with The Force, although that's never actually worked for me.

Now her eyes flash with determination and a little bit of fear, which crushes me. "Sean, open it."

She's not backing down. What the hell am I going to do?

"Okay." I saunter her way as slowly as possible. Shit, shit, shit! How am I going to control this narrative? She steps aside as I position myself in front of the keypad. My brain is cycling so quickly that I'm having trouble remembering the code. I type the numbers in wrong, and the door chastises me with a red light and a warning buzz.

"Sorry." I shoot her a glance. "It's been a long time since I've gone in here to look at my...storage."

She presses her lips together. "Try again."

So, this is happening. Is the George Washington hat out where she can see it? Yes, it is. Will she recognize it? It's been all over the news. Or maybe she'll be so distracted and horrified by the towering mountains of shameless costumery and nerdiness that she won't even notice it. One thing's for sure, whatever we had, it's over now. She'll see the true weirdness hiding behind my eccentric persona. And then she'll wonder if my obsessions extend further than that. If they might extend to her, just like my brother's did with Kokoro. Like mine did with Melody Winkman.

Maybe it's better this way. If I really am as bad as my brother, she can get out now.

A second buzzing noise breaks the silence, and I flinch. I didn't even put any numbers in yet! But it's not the knob. The sound is different. A notification. Josie tugs her phone out of her purse and reads the text.

Her expression crumbles. "Oh no."

Chapter 35

It's game over!

Josie

Hugo: The jig is up, Savannah Bateman. Call me.

"I need some air." I lurch for the staircase, no longer interested in Sean's illegal white tiger or alien autopsy lab or whatever else it is he's hiding in that "storage" room. I have bigger problems.

"What's wrong?" Sean asks, chasing me down the stairs.

My shaking hands pass him the phone as I escape out the front door and pace the mansion's threshold while he reads.

"You've got this," Sean says in a voice so firm and assertive that it's never been clearer why they made him captain. He captures my shoulders to stop my pacing and presses the phone into my hand. "Call him."

"What? Like right now?"

"Call him," he repeats. "You control the narrative, remember?"

"I'm not very good at that!"

"Well, I'm here now. I'll help you."

I pull up the phone screen. It's too bright. It's burning my retinas. Hugo Valencia knows who I am! It's game over! It really is!

When it becomes clear that I'm trapped in a panic loop, Sean reaches over and taps the CALL icon for me and then SPEAKER. The phone rings once before Hugo picks up.

"Bueno."

English, Sean mouths at me, frowning and crossing his arms over his Han Solo vest.

"Hugo, hello," I say. Sean gives me a quick, encouraging nod, so I keep going. "I got your message."

"Ah, Josie." The Jabba-the-Hutt chuckle. "Or should I call you Savannah?"

I wince internally at the sound of my name. "How did you find out?"

"I thought you might ask that. It's easier to show than tell."

A download symbol appears on my phone. The image that loads is a screenshot of a social media post by the Ferris wheel worker in Vegas. The text reads: *Look who I ran into at work!!!* Our selfie is there. Our names are hashtagged. As far as I can tell, there's nothing incriminating about it at all.

"I don't understand."

"Look closer."

My face is almost totally obscured by the beard and glasses.

I'm not wearing a sign that says, Hey, everyone, I'm really Savannah Bateman. So, what is it?

Sean, who's been scanning the image over my shoulder, groans quietly and points to himself in the photo. I pinch the screen to zoom in, and sure enough, there's a newspaper article visible on the phone screen in his hand—the one about Chuy.

Oh no. "I knew there was something familiar about you!" Hugo's voice buzzes with excitement.

"Who else have you told?" I ask, teeth chattering even though it's a balmy sixty-nine degrees.

"No one."

Hope swells in my chest. "No one?"

"No one *yet*. I have to figure out how to roll this out. Luckily, with el Día de los Muertos around the corner, it's perfect timing!"

"What do you want, Hugo?" Sean cuts in, his tone laden. "Money?"

Hugo chuckles again. "That must be the dashing Mr. O'Sullivan. How are you, sir? And to answer your question, no, I don't want money. I'm not an extortionist. I'm a talk show host. I deal in information, especially exclusive information. And it seems your girlfriend has been holding out on me."

"She didn't hold out on you. The way I see it, you're the one breaking the deal. You promised you'd leave Josie's past alone, and here you are, ready to dox her without hesitation. I wonder how your future sources will feel about that." He points at me, forms a fist, and shakes it.

Control the narrative—right! "He's right, Hugo. I held up my end of the bargain. I expect you to hold up yours."

"I'm afraid that deal's off the table," Hugo replies in a somber tone. "I've been chasing this story for over a decade. And the people deserve answers. Where is the puppet, Savannah? What did you do with Chuy?"

Prickles break out all over my skin like I'm being bitten by some variety of California no-see-ums. I press the heels of my hands to my eyes to keep from crying. It's hard to do while holding a phone, but Sean ends that problem by taking it from me.

"Everyone's got a price, Hugo," he says. "Name yours."

"This story is going to get out whether I break it or not. I'm not the only one with access to that photo, so you might as well tell me."

My distress must be written all over my face because Sean pulls his shoulders back and uses his anything's-possible voice. "Look. We can make this a win-win. Keep this quiet, and we'll give you a story, Hugo—a story so big no one will care about Josie's past."

"What?" Hugo chuckles. "Are you going to propose to her?"

Some part of my digestive tract leaps into my throat, but Sean shrugs his shoulders at me like he's actually considering it. "What do you think? We don't have to go through with it."

"That's your advice?" I sputter. "That I don a wedding dress and take a lap?"

"I don't understand the big deal," Sean shoots back in exasperation. "Who cares that much about a stupid old puppet?"

"Eh, it's all in how you spin it," Hugo admits. "But I have a lot of years invested in the Bring Back Chuy movement, and I'm not going to quit now that the prize is right on my doorstep. I know you know where Chuy is, Savannah, and you're going to tell me."

Sean mutes the phone. "Why don't you just tell him? I'm sure it'll blow over in no time."

"I can't," I shoot back. "If this gets out, I'll get canceled again, and Castillo Studios will take the brunt of it. It might even sour this crossover opportunity with *Lost Star*. I mean, who wants to partner with a studio that's mired in bad press?"

"We'll control the narrative," Sean insists.

"We can't control everything, Sean."

"Sure, we can."

"No, we can't. Too many people are involved. Too much is at stake. This isn't something you can fix."

"If you don't want to answer, perhaps I should just go ahead and break this story right now," Hugo goes on, responding to our silence. "I may not have Chuy, but I have you, Savannah. With enough pressure, you will eventually cave."

He's right. If Hugo outs me, there'll be no point in hiding Chuy's whereabouts. But there is a way I can control the narrative that will protect the people I love. It's the only thing that will work. The only thing that ever works: I have to disappear. Again.

I take the phone from Sean's hand and unmute it. "Okay, Hugo, you win. I'll give you Chuy, but on one condition: You don't mention Savannah Bateman. You never saw me. I was never here. You found him on your own."

Sean's lips part in impressed surprise.

"But you're an essential part of the story," Hugo argues.

"I don't have to be. *Hugo Valencia solves decade-long mystery, locates beloved missing puppet* has a nice ring to it, no? Maybe you got an anonymous tip or had a revelation looking through some cold case files. Spin it however you want."

"Hmm," Hugo hems.

"And to sweeten the deal, I'll give you one last exclusive before you break the Chuy story. Josie Days's swan song. I'll tell you all about my whirlwind romance with Sean O'Sullivan.

How we fell madly in love, and then it ended just as abruptly. It was…"—I lock eyes with Sean as my insides wilt—"truly tragic."

Sean shakes his head *no*, eyes wide.

"And then you'll turn Chuy over to me?"

"I'll tell you where to find him," I promise, halting Sean's wordless protests with a raised palm. "But only after I'm out of the picture. No one needs to connect Josie Days with Chuy's comeback, and once she's out of the limelight, there's very little chance they ever will. In fact, it won't be long before everyone forgets about her entirely." A rogue tear tickles my cheek, and I swipe it away as Sean's expression transitions from despair to resignation. "It'll be like she never existed."

"I'll have to think about it," Hugo replies.

Not good enough. I have to control this narrative.

"Come on, Hugo," I press. "I know you don't want Castillo Studios to suffer any more than it already has. A win for *Más Allá de las Estrellas* is a win for Mexican television and Mexico itself, and you get that. I know you do." I pause and add one more thing, just in case, because although I don't know Hugo that well, I do know people. "Go on, Hugo, let yourself be the hero. Bring Chuy back to the world. You deserve nice things, too."

The line is quiet. The October wind tousles Sean's hair as he watches me, tight-jawed and grim in that Han Solo vest. Behind him, a sky full of stars glitters like the broken shards of all our possible futures. I swear it's a scene right out of a movie.

"All right, then," Hugo acquiesces. "It's a deal. You'll be the special guests on my show tomorrow evening."

"Friday," Sean interrupts. He clears his throat and finds his Captain Footwork voice. "Tomorrow, I'll be taking Josie on a real date, just the two of us, so we can say our goodbyes. Surely you won't begrudge us that?"

Hugo agrees, and when Sean hangs up, his small, pained smile threatens to snap me in two. I expect him to argue with me. To beg me not to end things between us. To tell me he's got a better plan.

Instead he says, "So, you said you liked *Hamilton*, right?"

Chapter 36

Why did I not predict this possible outcome?

Sean

WHEN I ARRIVE to collect Josie for our date, she texts me that she's inside Jason and Emmy's house and to pick her up there. I tell her okay, but to please meet me at the door. I don't want Snack or Emmy to see me like this.

I finished the coat, and it's glorious. The diet and exercise regimen for my upcoming audition has shaved off every last fat cell, so this George Washington is svelte. I added the powdery makeup and wig for camouflage—I don't want to be recognized. Of course, it makes me look weirder than if I'd just thrown on the jacket, boots, and hat like a lot of people do.

Yes, I'm wearing the hat. Of course I am.

Dangling from my finger is a hanger bearing my Thomas

Jefferson costume. It's not the one Daveed Diggs wore, but it's a decent likeness complete with a frilly white cravat, purple vest, short pants, stockings, and black tricorn hat. I tailored the slippery, shimmery suit to what I thought might fit Josie even though I didn't have her measurements.

I take a deep breath and consider turning around, getting into my car, and forgetting this whole thing. Bringing Josie to *Hamilton on the Roof* was the stupidest idea I've ever had, hands down. Why am I not taking her to P.F. Chang's and the opera? I'm courting disaster. No, actually, I'm marrying disaster. We've opened a gift registry.

She was right all along—she said I was too high-profile, that she'd be found out if she dated me, and that's exactly what happened. But at least this way, we can keep it contained. Hugo will keep his big fat mouth shut, and Josie can fade into the background, like she's been trying to do ever since I dragged her into the spotlight.

Maybe it's better this way. I like her too much, anyway. And tonight, like it or not, she's going to see the real me. She'll probably run for the Hollywood hills.

I ring the doorbell, and she opens it clad in jeans and a blouse. My heart rate jumps as she looks me up and down.

"Hello." I bounce on my toes and try to hold eye contact with her, but it's hard. This was a *terrible* idea.

She swallows. "If Paul Revere was supposed to give me a heads-up about this, you might want to fire the guy."

Ha ha, but I'm too nervous to laugh. I hold out the Thomas Jefferson costume. "I don't know if you want to…?" I trail off, looking at the ground. And then I wait with pulse thundering, collar dampening, jaw clenching. Snarky remarks and derisive laughter, come on in. I've pretty much thrown open the door.

Instead, I feel the hanger snatched from my finger.

"Come in."

"Actually, can we do this in your trail—"

"Come inside, Sean."

She's holding the door open. God almighty, why did I not predict this possible outcome? I take a couple hesitant steps into the foyer. "Is anyone else home?"

"Oh my," Emmy says, appearing from the kitchen in her pajamas. My cheeks are so hot under my powdered makeup that I can't even conjure up a greeting.

Jason turns around from where he's sitting on the couch in the sunken family room. "Whoaaaa…" He drags the word out like a fuse to a bomb.

"I'll be right back!" Josie bounds off with her costume.

"You look good, George," Jason says over the back of the couch, a shit-eating grin plastered to his face.

"That's General Washington to you, son," I manage to fire back, adding a pointing finger.

"It's not really much different from the kind of stuff he normally wears," Emmy tells Jason, her tone unconvincing. "Minus the *Esquire* stamp of approval."

God, I hate this.

"Hey, Peyton!" Jason yells, still grinning at me. "Come see who's here!"

"Aww, no, there's no need to bother h—" I start.

But Peyton bounces into the room anyway. "What's up—? Oh. Wow. Oh my…Is that? Shee—Ah…" She dissolves into some mumbled Gen Z slang I don't understand, but I think she throws "slay" in there just to make me feel good.

Mattie pops up from where he's sitting beside Jason. Grabbing a toy lightsaber, he runs over and begins slamming the thing into my thigh over and over.

"My name is Eego Montoy!" he yells.

"Wrong movie, buddy." I disarm him and lob the toy into the dining room. With a yell, he runs after it.

"Josie said you two were going to a *Hamilton* show," Emmy says, drying her hands on a kitchen towel.

"Yes."

"Are you starring in it?"

"It's complicated."

Peyton tilts her head at me. "I don't like the wig. It makes you look ugly."

Mattie is back now with the lightsaber. The onslaught renews, this time on the backs of both my thighs.

"Is this kid British?" I reach behind me to grab the flailing plastic blade again.

"Mattie, stop," Jason commands. "Come over here, or he's going to make you dress up like that, too."

Mattie shrieks and throws the lightsaber at me in one last Hail Mary attack before scampering back to his dad.

"It wouldn't be the worst thing in the world, you know!" I call after him.

"Are you going to sing the songs?" Peyton asks. "I mean, that's what you're doing, right?"

"Ohhh!" Jason wags a finger. "I know what this is! It's like *The Rocky Horror Picture Show* but with *Hamilton.* Lin-Manuel Miranda mentioned it in an interview."

"Okay." Emmy looks like a surprised puffer fish who can't quite figure out how to deflate.

"Josie, time to go!" I bellow.

"What'd I miss?" She pops into the room in the purple costume with jazz hands in full force. With her hair stuffed under the tricorn hat, she's rocking it, and the fit across her shoulders looks tailor-made, if I do say so myself. She's used eyeliner to draw a mustache on her lip, and her smile is radiant.

My heart thrills. I grab her hand and clear my throat, mustering my best George Washington accent.

"Farewell, good people. We're off!"

"Bye!" Josie calls over her shoulder, leading the way.

Part of me wants to get out of here as fast as possible, but it's a different part of me that halts on the threshold, pivots, and executes a sweeping Broadway bow on the way out.

Mattie actually cheers.

Chapter 37

I'm not sharing you with the hat.

Josie

SEAN HASN'T TOLD me much about this *Hamilton* event we're going to, and I haven't asked. The car ride is all adult alternative music and hand-holding. No rings, though. They would blow his cover. Our silence is complicated. This is going to be our one and only real, actual date. A beginning and an end. Bookends with nothing inside them. But if it's with Sean O'Sullivan, I know it's going to be unforgettable.

He pulls into a poorly lit open parking lot choked with cars. I don't see any other electric Fiats. There isn't even a charging station here. Are we still in California?

"What is this place?" I ask as we trickle into the river of

Revolutionary War–era costumed patrons headed for a stucco building lit by red and green colored bulbs. Music from above draws my eye to a rooftop bar adorned with colored paper lanterns and potted palms. Heat lamps cast an orange glow into the night. I'm pretty confident there are no Michelin stars associated with this venue.

Once inside, we clomp up the sleek mahogany stairs to the second-story rooftop. It's bigger than it looked from down below, with two bars, a bandstand, big dance floor, and plenty of low, modern-looking seating. The clash of eighteenth-century costumes against mid-century modern architecture delights my artist's eye. I'm having fun already.

"I think the air here is seventy-five percent pot smoke," I mumble to Sean.

"You get used to it." He's got a glass of champagne ready for me. It's like he conjured it with pure magic. The string lights shine in the dark green pools of his eyes as he holds up his can of LaCroix for a toast. "To Vera's faulty heart, without which we wouldn't be here tonight."

"To cheating a more deserving woman out of a charity date with Sean O'Sullivan. ¡Salud!"

We clink drinks and sip. He doesn't take his eyes off me. The band riffs in the background, warming up for the show, and I feel like Sean and I are warming up for something, too. It's the click of your seat belt on the roller coaster. The nervous shuffle you do in the wings as you await your cue. The electricity in the air before a lightning strike.

The mic crackles as someone grabs it. "Welcome! Welcome! You could've been anywhere tonight, but you're here with us for *Hamilton on the Roof!*"

"The roof! The roof! The roof is on fire!" everyone shouts, including Sean. They follow it up with a double stomp. He's right on cue.

"You've done this before," I say.

"Once or twice."

"Do I need a manual?"

"I'll be your manual. Every time they say *Hamilton on the Roof*, you do that."

"Got it. Anything else?"

"You drink every time we sing the word *shot*."

I nod. "Makes sense."

"When 'Right Hand Man' comes on, I'm gonna get a little… involved. And I'll have to share some of this with you." He sticks his hand in his pocket and pulls out a handful of something.

"Is that birdseed?"

"For the wedding scene. You're not weirded out, are you?"

I scoff. "Why would I be weirded out? What do you think I am, some rhododendron who can't pull off a Thomas Jefferson costume?"

He grins so wide it makes me grin, too. The opening song begins to play, and it's loud.

"There's more!" Sean shouts over the music. "Try to keep up!"

I pull out my phone and google the lyrics to the musical. I've seen the movie version a couple of times, and I'm familiar with the songs, but I'm no match for these people. It doesn't matter, though. We sing along, and Sean cues me in on all the extras. A couple of champagnes in, and I loosen up. There's no sign of paparazzi here, and everyone is in the moment, singing, danc- ing, stomping, clapping, throwing things, yelling at the band— whatever this motley sideshow calls for. Whenever we sing the name "Alexander Hamilton," on cue, we throw our arms in the air in the signature *Hamilton* salute.

"Get ready," Sean says, when "Right Hand Man" starts. I recognize the performer's twinkle in his eye because I get it, too. That itch. That spark. That fuse lit and sizzling inside you, reminding you what you were made for. I gave it up a long time ago, but that doesn't mean I've forgotten it. Or that I don't miss it.

Sean's cue arrives, and everyone sits down—except all the George Washingtons. They stay on their feet and sing his part. Act his part. Revel in it. Sean is an insanely good George Washington. At one point, he elbow cartwheels over an empty stool, hops up on the bar, and shoots up to standing, all the while maintaining a single note. The crowd cheers their heads off. So do I.

I don't think I've ever seen him so joyful. It's ironic…He plays roles all the time, but it's only now, when he gets to choose it, that he seems most like himself. Deep down inside, fancy pants Sean O'Sullivan is just a big theater kid.

"That was amazing!" I gush when he finally staggers, sweaty and smiling, into my arms.

"You liked it? You really liked it?"

"I have this, like, really intense George Washington fetish I've never told anyone about. It's the wig. And the wainscot."

"Waistcoat?"

"That's what I said."

He grins. "Well, your song is coming up, no pressure."

When Thomas Jefferson's song comes on, I'm ready for it. Because here's the thing I've *really* never told anyone—not Emmy, not Peyton, and definitely not Sean.

I can tap dance.

It was my big number in *Club Bilingüe*. My shoes aren't the right shoes, but the soles are stiff enough that when I part the Potomac River of people, take my place on the dance floor, and start stomping, it works. Wherever I fall short on the lyrics, my fellow Thomas Jeffersons pick up the slack. Besides, I'm too busy with my steps, stamps, and stomps. My shuffles and buffalo turns. I even throw an Alexander clunk in there because—well, you know, his name is *Alexander* Hamilton, after all. I'm sure nobody gets the joke but me.

Everyone does a chef's kiss when the words "France" or "Paris" come up, and even though I have no idea how this rooftop performance is normally done and, as a result, miss all the cues, no one seems to care. My dancing is met with wild applause, but the best part is seeing Sean's amazed face as he watches me perform. Oh yeah, and the very end, when he hikes me up on his shoulder and carries me off the stage for a muy theatrical exit during the very last line.

They do an actual break in the middle of the "Take a Break" song, and I'm still a little breathless from doing moves I haven't done in over a decade. But I feel alive and wild and like something is missing at the same time. The worry I've been carrying around seems absent for once. The bitterness, too. The regret.

I've missed this. And I'm going to miss *him*.

It's so unfair. I feel like I've just woken up from a coma, but the doctors are about to put me back under.

"I have a confession to make," Sean says as we retreat to a high top. "I was afraid you would think this was too weird. This place. These costumes." He looks down at himself. "How into all this I am."

I almost make a sarcastic remark but stop myself. Sean

O'Sullivan is being vulnerable. That doesn't happen very often. "Of course not. Why would you think that?"

"It's not a side of me I show to the world very often. Or ever."

I scoot forward so I can trail a finger down his cheek and jawline, all the way to his superhero chin. "I love this side of Sean O'Sullivan because this is the one that's happiest."

"Oh yeah?" His expression shifts to something shy and boyish, not captainly at all, and it feels like Christmas.

"You know what I love about you?" he asks.

"My rock-solid decision-making skills?"

He chuckles. "That, yes, absolutely. *And* the fact that you showed up to our date dressed as a Zentharian. That was bloody fearless. And you didn't hesitate to come here with me tonight." He pauses. "It makes me feel like I can tell you anything, and it won't scare you off. For example…" His eyes go wild, and his voice drops to a whisper. "This is the real, actual hat worn by Christopher Jackson on Broadway."

He can't be serious. "I thought that was stolen."

"It was," he whispers.

"You stole it?"

"No!" He shushes me, looking around for eavesdroppers, but no one is paying attention to us. "I bought it off the black market." He waits for my reaction. "Are you appalled?"

I'm a little concerned, but it'll take more than that to ruin this night. I throw back the last of my drink and slam the plastic cup down on the high-top table. "Actually, it's the sexiest thing I've ever heard. After this, you're going to take me back to your place, and I'm going to tear that ill-gotten George Washington costume off your sublime body, and I'm going to ravage you."

He nods, maintaining a straight face. "Can I keep the hat on?"

"No." I squeeze between his knees until his mouth is *right there*, just within reach, an instrument of tempting, teasing, tantalizing torture. "I'm not sharing you with the hat."

His muscles tighten in all the places our bodies touch. His fingers caress my ribcage. His inner thighs press against my hips, and I can't help but imagine all of these things happening again, somewhere else, with far fewer layers of clothing between us.

"Do you want to leave now?" His voice is hoarse.

"Yes," I say truthfully, and feel him shift to get up. "But we're not going to."

He stops. "We're not?"

"No." I bring my lips within a feather's brush of his. "We only get to have this one nice thing this once, so we're going to make it last as long as possible. We're going to drag this out until we can't stand it anymore. You're gonna make me beg for it. And I'm gonna make you beg for it. And only when we're literally dying of want for each other are we going to finally give in."

His serious Captain Footwork expression shifts to something more tender. "C'mere to me." He slides his hands around my ribcage to my back, pressing me against him, and his kiss is soft and slow and delicate, like one of those mournful guitar songs on his playlist. I melt into him, holding on tight. To him. To us. To this moment, which will soon be a memory. But I don't want to be sad. This time I have with Sean is a gift, and I need to treat it that way.

Suddenly, the whoop of a siren pierces the night. Our kiss breaks to flashing blue and red lights.

"Is it a raid?" I ask.

"Well, this is Van Nuys," Sean says, looking nervous.

"We should get out of here."

"We should do that, yes." He takes off his hat, tucking it against him like a small animal needing protection.

"Wait, you don't think they're here for that, do you?" I ask. When he shrugs, I laugh. "Well, leave it here."

He gives me a pained look. "I was going to turn it in!"

Three officers pour out of the elevator. I'm not laughing anymore. "It's just a hat, Sean. Let them find it. Come on, we have to go!"

He sets the hat on an abandoned stool. For a second, I think he's going to bid it farewell, but he only gives it a final, reluctant glance. "All right. Let's go."

We slip down the stairs, hand in hand, carried along with the crowd. It's thrilling, making me feel brave and wild. Sean O'Sullivan is mine! I kiss him the entire drive to Bel-Air. He manages to kiss me back, even while he's driving. God, that mouth. I'm going to let it destroy me. I'm giving it the key to the city. I'm putting it in my will—that's right, Sean O'Sullivan's mouth is getting *everything*.

By the time he pulls the Fiat into his enormous driveway, I'm not sure we're even going to make it inside. Somehow, we do, tangled up in each other's embrace. The front door slams behind us, sending an echo through the cavernous foyer with its cathedral ceilings and marble soul. Sean's keys fall to the floor with a clang. In our outrageous scuffle up the stairs, we lose my hat, our jacket, my shoes, his boots, and one of my tall white stockings. I'm fighting with the button on his fly when he finally drops me onto the shiny gold comforter of his cherry wood four-poster bed.

"Wait." He places a hand over mine to stop my furious unbuttoning. "Let me do it."

I prop myself up on my elbows, and my jaw actually drops as he peels the frilly white shirt over his head, throwing it to the side. Lord have all the mercies, he's got the body of a Greek statue. Every visually stimulated cell in my body wants to leap off this bed and take bites out of him. He finagles the stubborn button on his pants, and those go down, too. I'm not sure what Revolutionary War underwear looked like, but I'm pretty sure it's not the bulging black banana hammock I'm staring at.

He flexes his bicep and strikes a pose. Of course he does. I start to rise up off the bed, possessed by a visceral desire to do things to this man that will make him sell his soul to me. But he lays me back down with a gentle firmness and begins unbuttoning my own white shirt, parting the two halves of it with patience. I'm pretty sure Thomas Jefferson didn't wear a bra under his blouse, but mine is lacy and red. His fingers caress my shoulders as he slides the straps down. He's so slow. It's torture.

"Sean," I moan. "Please hurry."

"No," the captain says. "I don't want to rush this."

Oh God, I forgot. How could I forget? This is the one and done. Tomorrow, we'll be breaking up, publicly, and I'll never have him again.

Something splits inside me, but I ignore it and pull him down on top of me. That pouty, perfect mouth is ready for mine. His bare skin, unencumbered by costume or clothes, burns against me every place we touch. As he peppers kisses down my neck to my collarbone, I don't think about how I'm breaking the rules by doing this, how I forfeited a right to the Sean O'Sullivans and their world a long time ago and how the ghost of Chuy is probably documenting this transgression right now and calculating the price. Instead, I let the weight of this glorious man's body tear down all my walls, melt all my frozen parts.

"It's a good thing you're breaking up with me tomorrow," he whispers against my mouth.

"Oh?" I mumble. "Because you're about to use up all your good tricks?"

"I'll save one for the morning. But no, that's not it."

"What is it then?"

"Because otherwise, I might never let you leave this bed."

I twirl my finger in his lock of yellow hair. "So you *are* obsessed with me, Sean O'Sullivan?"

He doesn't smile, not even playfully. His kiss is soft, tender, melancholy. "Hopelessly."

Chapter 38

The sex was too good.

Transcript. *Hollywood, De Repente* with Hugo Valencia.
October 27. *[partially translated from Spanish]*

HUGO: Good afternoon, ladies and gentlemen. Please welcome back to the studio one of the most popular couples in Hollywood—Sean O'Sullivan and Josie Days.

JOSIE: Good afternoon, Hugo.

SEAN: Hello.

HUGO: So, you two are the couple of the hour. Everyone is talking about you. But today you have an announcement. A very sad announcement, isn't that right?

JOSIE: Yes, Hugo. We want to let the public know that we're breaking up.

HUGO: Oh my! Well, I think all of us are very surprised to hear that. And sad.

JOSIE: Not that it's anyone's business, but it just isn't working out.

HUGO: What happened?

JOSIE: It's really very simple. The sex was too good. That's it. The sex was too good, and when the sex is too good, you know the relationship isn't going to last.

HUGO: Oho!

SEAN: I agree. The sex was really, really good, and so we had to end it.

HUGO: This wasn't something you two could work around?

JOSIE: There's no working around sex like that, Hugo. But I do want to say to the next woman—you're very lucky. And buckle up.

SEAN: I appreciate that.

HUGO: So, you two are officially done?

JOSIE: Yes, sir. We even got the breakup notarized.

SEAN: Sealed with blood and wax.

JOSIE: A judge presided over our last kiss.

SEAN: A fat lady sang.

HUGO: Do you think you're still going to be friends?

SEAN: Absolut—

JOSIE: No! Sorry, Hugo, you won't be seeing us together anymore, even as friends. It wouldn't be fair since Sean's already dating someone else.

HUGO: He is?

SEAN: *[clears throat]* Tragically, yes.

HUGO: Who is it?

JOSIE: Oh, you know, some debutante.

HUGO: What's her name, Sean?

JOSIE: He doesn't need to know her name. They're all interchangeable.

HUGO: I guess once we see them together, we'll know who she is.

JOSIE: It might be awhile. She's having surgery.

HUGO: Oh. Is she ill?

JOSIE: It's elective. And facial. She's going to look like a pound of ground beef for weeks. And by then—

SEAN: By then, I'll have already dumped her.

JOSIE: Right! But that doesn't mean you shouldn't care about her. She's a person, and she's the one everyone should be focusing on right now. We can all refer to her as Susan for now. Healing vibes, Susan!

SEAN: Yeah. But before we replace Josie with my new, plastic-surgery-loving and very temporary girlfriend, Susan, I do want to say one last thing to her.

HUGO: Of course, Sean. Go ahead.

SEAN: I want Josie to know that, even though I apparently immediately ran into the arms of another woman the day after we broke up, it's not because I didn't care about her. I wish her the best. I truly do. I want her to be happy.

JOSIE: Thanks, Sean. I want you to be happy, too. And I'll miss the great sex.

SEAN: Me, too.

HUGO: So where did you two go on your last and final date
together?

JOSIE: Oh my God, we went to this amazing place
called *Ha—*

SEAN: Whale watching! We went whale watching!

JOSIE: That's what I meant to say.

CELEBRITY STRAIGHT TALK, OCTOBER 28

AMIL: Well, plug my blowhole and call me Moby Dick. Isla,
have you heard the news? Sean O'Sullivan and Josie Days
have broken up! Welcome, everyone, to another episode
of *Celebrity Straight Talk*. I'm Amil Nair, and this is my
cohost, Isla Wallace.

ISLA: Hi-la! I did hear that, Amil. The couple—well,
ex-couple now—gave an exclusive interview to
Hollywood, De Rep—Derrep— Dammit, I still can't
say it.

AMIL: *Hollywood, De Rrrrrepente!* God, my Spanish
is good. According to Josie, it was more physical than
anything else, so it was never going to last, and while I feel
that, deeply, I still need to ask: How, Isla? How does one

break up with Sean O'Sullivan, the Irish god of pectorals? I think Josie might need a cognitive test done. An MRI maybe. Something's wrong inside that girl's head.

ISLA: Agreed. People are losing their minds over this, Amil. There's wailing in the streets. Apparently, Sean-osie meant a lot to the masses, and they're not taking this breakup well.

AMIL: I cried. I did.

ISLA: But apparently there's another woman on the horizon for Sean already, and we'll be on the lookout for this mysterious Susan person who apparently has a terrible plastic surgeon.

AMIL: Probably not board certified. You always need to ask about board certification, Isla. Don't let any yahoo with letters behind their name cut on your face.

ISLA: Amen to that. I did hear some scuttlebutt that Josie and Sean are in charge of Emmy and Jason's gender reveal, so we'll be seeing Josie at least one more time.

AMIL: Ah, yes! On Halloween evening we'll be finding out the X and Y chromosome status of the Connor fetus. So very exciting.

ISLA: Speaking of exciting news, Amil, did you hear that the stolen George Washington hat from *Hamilton* was found?

AMIL: No!

ISLA: Yes! At a seedy bar in Van Nuys.

AMIL: Did they find the culprit?

ISLA: Not yet. But I'm sure it's just a matter of time. Anyway, I guess this is where we say goodbye to Josie Days.

AMIL: Alas, yes. Maybe we should see her off with a rhyming poem.

ISLA: Good idea! You start.

AMIL: Ahem. Josie Days. You're going aways. This is where we wave a handkerchief and sayz… *[mutters]* Help me out here, Isla.

ISLA: Olés?

AMIL: Damn, girl, give me a fist bump. You never cease to amaze me.

Chapter 39

I've got two fists and a lot of feelings to work through.

Sean

"SO, SHE BROKE up with you, eh? Ouch."

"It wasn't serious," I lie, launching into another round of reps on the leg machine in my home gym as I glare at Seamus and the dyed-blond lock of hair that appeared on his head yesterday. That lock of hair pisses me off more than I can express, but I won't give Seamus the satisfaction of letting him know.

He picks up a dumbbell and starts to do some curls—with terrible form, I might add. "You fancied her, and you know it."

I don't know why my brother suddenly cares about my love life, but my audition's tomorrow, and I need to stay focused. Thunderstrike is my dream role. I've been practicing my lines every day. That and watching the news to make sure no one's implicated me in the miraculous recovery of Christopher Jackson's hat.

Oh, and also nursing my broken heart.

"You gonna try to get her back?" he presses.

The suggestion throws me into a tailspin. I haven't been able to get Josie off my mind, but all of this is according to her plan: one and done, let her fade into the background while I run the spotlight off in a different direction. Yet it doesn't feel done. Not to me.

She's still in there, a piece of shrapnel in my heart.

I wipe my sweaty face with a towel. "I don't know. Maybe."

"Oh, really?" Seamus says in a pensive tone. "Wouldn't that make you a creep? A stalker?"

My stomach seizes up. It's like he's reading my mind. "No."

"But she broke up with you. She doesn't want to see you."

"It's different."

"How is it different?"

I launch into another round of reps, curling and uncurling my legs. It hurts so good and keeps me from boiling over. "Because she actually likes me, Seamus. She's just...got her own issues."

"Everyone has their own issues. She's not special. You're not special."

His goading is pushing me to the brink. If my brother wants to keep talking shite, I've got two fists and a lot of feelings to work through, but Josie's comments about Seamus while on the high ropes course come back to me. He needs professional help. Maybe it's time to have the hard conversation.

"I know you're mad at me, brother, but at some point you have to admit that you staying here at the house drinking yourself into oblivion every day isn't working out."

Now it's his turn to get angry. "Can you and everybody else back off me for a bloody second?"

"What's with this?" I grab the lock of yellow in my own hair. "Is that supposed to be a message to me?"

He drops the dumbbell and picks up an exercise band. "Maybe."

I rub a towel across the sweaty back of my neck. "Look. You're right. I could've said no to the role. Then what? Some other guy would've gotten it, and nothing would've changed for you."

"What would've changed is that my little brother wouldn't be a traitor!"

"A traitor like you when you let me take the fall for the binoculars back in high school?"

He snorts. "You still holding a grudge over that?"

"No, I'm not." I flick the towel so it wraps itself on the leg machine. "I never held a grudge against you, Seamus. I loved you, and I stood by you through everything. I still do. I want the best for you. I just don't know how to help you get it."

He plops down onto a machine and slumps his shoulders. His face is doing funny things, scrunching up like his nose itches, but I think he's just searching for words. "The dinner theater was a bore. Nobody there respected me. But the little old ladies at the bingo hall—they'd seen some of my old movies. They thought I was still a star. They treated me like one."

I nod in sympathy. "I can see the appeal."

"There were side bets, too, on the greyhounds and such. And poker. I didn't realize how much I was losing. And then I thought I could win it back. And then, after I was in too deep, it was the only thing keeping the sadness at bay. I knew Uncle would find out eventually. I just kept hoping that day was one day off."

"Right." I don't know what I'm doing here, but at least he's talking.

"I've ruined my life, Sean. I'm ready to give up. So, you know, maybe you could let your loser brother sit on your five-million-dollar porch and drown his sorrows, if it's not too much of a hardship." He's trying to sound tough, but his voice breaks.

"There are places you can go that'll help you get back on your feet again."

He scoffs.

"It's not anyone's first choice, but sometimes it's the best one."

He drops his face to his hands. "Mam and Da can hardly even look at me."

I was holding up pretty well until now, but this is crushing me. Now I get what Josie meant when she said she was the Seamus in her family. No wonder she'll do anything to avoid feeling like this: an outcast.

"They'll come around," I tell Seamus, choking down my emotion. "I'll speak to them."

"I don't need you to save me."

"You're right." I dig the phone out of my pocket, pull up Mam's number, and hold the phone out to him. "But maybe I can keep you company while you save yourself."

He stares at me, glassy-eyed and red-faced, like a boxer who took one too many hits. I wait. He'll either take the phone or he won't, but either way, I'm escalating this today.

Finally, he snatches the device from my hand and taps CALL.

Mam answers right away. "Seanny Bear?"

"Mam, it's me, Seamus." Seamus rubs his greasy forehead with the heel of his palm.

Mam is quiet at first. "Is everything all right?"

Seamus looks to me, and I give him the captain's nod.

"No, it's not," he says.

"Where are you? Are you with Sean?"

A sob breaks out of him, and I find myself standing behind him, hands on his shoulders. "We need a family meeting, Mam, tonight," I say loud enough so she can hear me through the speaker. "Let Da and Siobhan know. O'Donnell's Pub." It's Seamus's favorite restaurant, and we can all meet up there after the gender reveal party. "Half-past eight."

Mam's voice is small but determined. "I'll let them know."

When we hang up, I give Seamus's shoulders a final squeeze. "Nicely done, brother. We'll help you get through this, I promise. You won't have to do it alone."

Seamus makes a beeline for the door. I don't chase him. I let my brother have his privacy. I know this isn't the end of his problems, but it's the first step, and I feel good about taking it.

Unfortunately, I'm no longer in the mood for a workout. What I really want to do is talk to Josie, but my last text to her still lingers, unanswered. It's a punch in the gut every time I look at it.

I hate this whole breakup thing. It's so unfair. I've finally found someone whom I want to share everything with, and now I have to let her go.

Josie left so abruptly the morning after *Hamilton on the Roof*. It felt like I took a breath, and she was gone. I want to hear her voice, feel her body soft and pliant against mine. I want to coax out that elusive giggle that's like a skittish cat hiding under the bed. Hear her stories—the real ones—and tell her mine. When I showed her my real self, she didn't judge me. She joined in.

But I can't have what I want. She said it's over, and I'm not going to chase her. Seamus is right—if I chase her, I'm no different than him.

I won't do that. I won't *be* that. She deserves better.

I check my watch. It's time to get ready to leave for Jason and Emmy's. Time to set up for the gender reveal. My heart thrills at the chance to even spend these few hours with Josie. But I won't bug her. When we're together, I'll be cool. So cool. A veritable cryogenic freezing pod, even if it hurts like a son of a bitch.

Chapter 40

Braxton and Hicks walk into a bar.

Josie

I BALANCE ON a chair on Emmy and Jason's spacious patio on a cool, clear Halloween night, taping a cluster of pink and blue balloons to the gutter. It seems silly to be doing this reveal at all. This whole thing is really for Jason, and I'm sure he'd be just as happy if Emmy wrapped up a pink onesie and gave it to him over dinner.

But she's excited to surprise him, and I love my friend and her growing family. I glance over to the patio love seat where Sean is fiddling with the drone. I can barely even look at him. That Adonis body. That insane mouth. The straight man, unimpressed demeanor that transformed into something else entirely when we were together. The opposite of cool and detached. Plugged in. Tuned in—to me. He read all my body's signals and gave me what I wanted even when I didn't know I wanted it. It was like I was a gift, being carefully unwrapped by fingers that…

God, I need to stop.

I shouldn't have let myself fall so hard! What was I thinking?

I wasn't. I was being typical me—impulsive, chaotic. Letting my emotions take the wheel. Losing control. Over and over. Multiple times.

Lord, I need help.

The tape pulls free, and I find myself suddenly and viciously attacked by an enormous balloon entity.

"You okay over there?" Sean calls as I flail.

"I'll manage."

But I'm not sure I will.

What I can do is throw myself into my art. People are still demanding it like mad. That won't last, but for now I'll paint and package and sell and deposit the funds into my account. Maybe I can earn enough to get my own place. And Emmy will have the baby soon. She'll need my help, and that'll be a good distraction. Not to mention, when the crossover taping is finished and Miguel and Lupe and the rest of the cast from Castillo Studios leave, I can go back to work. I haven't even seen Miguel since Lupe arrived. According to him, it's been impossible to make plans with me without her finding out.

Of course, going back to work means potentially running into Sean, but maybe by then he'll have found someone to step into the void I've created. Even if he hasn't, our paths hardly crossed before, and they don't need to cross much afterward. He's the star. I'm the makeup person. Hardly the twain need to meet.

I trap the balloons against the gutter with a scandalous

amount of tape and hop down. Sean is hovering the drone over the pool now, our pink smoke bomb attached to the bottom. I can't tell what he's thinking. Since he arrived, he's hardly said a word to me. I shouldn't complain—he's doing what I asked him to do. We aren't supposed to be together, after all. But my heart doesn't know that.

"You okay?" I ask him.

"No," he says without hesitation. "Not at all."

"Me neither," I whisper, letting my gaze cleave onto the clover-green of his eyes. Neither one of us looks away. We owe each other that much.

Margarita and Rhett arrive with their daughter, Eva, and Peyton immediately dumps ice all over the kitchen floor and then short-circuits over whether to clean it up or greet them.

"Go, go, go," I tell her, bending down. "Your personal assistant will take care of it."

An ice emergency is the perfect excuse to avoid Margarita. Ever since she told me I looked familiar, being around her gives me a mini panic attack. As I'm finishing up, Emmy cracks the front door just enough to peer through. "Can we come in?"

"Stay off the patio," Sean warns.

"Yes, sir!" Jason salutes Sean in the *Lost Star* fashion, two taps of his fist against the left shoulder. He's grinning like a maniac.

"Someone's excited," I say.

Emmy bites her bottom lip and gives me a conspiratorial look that lasts all of a millisecond. It must be nice to be able to make someone that happy.

I enlist the kids to help Sean and me bring out the food, and Jason's in charge of greeting the guests who trickle in. We show the kids their pink T-shirts and run them through a brief verbal rehearsal of their parts. Pretty soon, the French doors open, and people spill out onto the balloon-filled Spanish revival patio, the same place where Emmy and Jason got married. The *Lost Star* cast is here, as well as Miles and a few more of our directors and ADs, plus a handful of people I recognize from Emmy's writer group. Amanda and Kayla both make their way over to me.

"Anything we can do to help?" Amanda asks.

I task her with photo and video duty and hand Kayla two pool towels. "You'll know what to do with these when the time comes."

She laughs. "I got you."

I see Sean snagging Jason Ramirez for pink balloon duty and take a deep breath. "Okay, kids, take your places."

Peyton ushers her stepbrother through another set of French doors into Emmy and Jason's room. It's showtime.

I join Sean at the mic stand he's set up. He gives me a tight smile that makes my chest hurt and brings the mic to his lips. "Welcome, everyone, and thank you for being here! Today, we get to find out if Emmy and Jason are having a boy or a girl!"

I take the mic from him. "Of course, Sean and I already know what it is, and we were debating how long to make the rest of you suffer." I pause. "We decided it should be a long time, so we're going to entertain you for a bit."

Warm chuckles ensue as I hand the mic back.

"Emmy is having a home birth. Did you all know that?" Sean gets a few claps. "You know, most medical professionals don't refer to home births as deliveries. That's because, if a baby is born at home, it's not delivery…it's DiGiorno."

Our audience groans, but there are a lot of grins and some clapping hands, too. This is going perfectly.

My turn. "Braxton and Hicks walk into a bar." I pause. "Nothing happens."

That one gets a few real laughs. Emmy is shaking her head and smiling. Jason's got his arm around her, beaming so brightly it's like he's got his own inner spotlight. A little ache throbs inside me. She's lucky. They're lucky. They have each other and all this.

"Why do you never see a pregnant Barbie?" Sean asks, voice low and serious. He gives the audience a beat to murmur among themselves. "Because Ken comes in a different box."

The laughs come harder now.

"That was a good one," I admit into the mic. "I don't know if I can top that, but I'll try. What did the drummer name his twin daughters?" I pause. "Anna One! Anna Two!"

Now that they're warmed up, our audience gives us a good, hearty reaction. Sean grins at me. It's time.

"All right, everyone," I say, "we're going to put you all out of your misery. Sean, will you hand the remote to Jason to do the honors?"

The sky is darkening. The solar lights on the patio have come alive. Sean tosses the drone remote in Jason's direction.

I give a thumbs-up to Peyton, who is peeking around the curtain in front of the French doors. Sean coaxes a lighter out of his pocket, picks up the drone, and lights the wick of the smoke bomb affixed to the bottom.

"Three, two, one…" he chants at Jason. "And liftoff!"

Jason works the controls, and the drone rises off Sean's palm into the air and over the pool.

The crowd falls quiet, all our eyes on the drone. The wick sputters, and then all at once, pink smoke plumes out of it. At the same time, Margarita executes her assigned job—switching on the pool lights, set to pink. Everyone cheers.

"It's a girl!" Jason cries, losing control of the drone in his excitement. People scream and duck as they're crop dusted with pink smoke. Meanwhile, Jason Ramirez has shaken open three huge garbage bags of pink balloons. They go bouncing across the patio. That's when the French doors scrape open, and Peyton and Mattie come screaming out in their pink Big Brother and Big Sister T-shirts, cannonballing into the pink pool.

Jason fights to gain control of the drone, but his attention is clearly all over the place, and his face is plastered with surprise and joy and something that might be diagnosed as clinical shock.

"Sean, get the drone!" I yell, as it dips toward the guests again like a killer robot insect.

But it's caught itself up in our decorations and is dragging streamers and clumps of balloons across the patio. I leap up to grab it and fail. Jason Ramirez tries, too, loses his balance, and staggers into the pool, swamping Mattie and Peyton—it's like an asteroid fell in there. Jason Connor wraps Emmy in a bear hug, abandoning the remote entirely. He kisses her a bunch of times and then runs off to cannonball into the pool, too, voice cracking as he shouts, "It's a girl! It's a girl! Woo-hoo!"

Ducking under the drone's onslaught, I hurry toward Emmy. "There's a return to home button!" I shout, and together, we find it and press it. The drone dutifully levels out and makes its way back.

"That's what you get when you put Sean and me in charge," I say to Emmy by way of an apology, but she's not paying attention to me. She's watching Jason splashing the kids in the pink pool, a huge grin on her face.

"It was perfect." She turns to me. "Thank you, Josie." She throws her arms around me and hugs me tight. "You and Sean did great. And now I don't have to pretend anymore. That was a hard secret to keep."

She has no idea.

The doorbell rings. Someone must have arrived late.

"I'll get it." I give her a squeeze before pulling away. "You stay here and enjoy the view."

Somehow, Sean has ended up in the pool, too, and a dripping-wet Jason Ramirez is chasing Kayla around the deck, trying to get her in. The gender reveal has turned into a full-on pool party.

I head to the front door and swing it open.

It's Miguel. And beside him, holding his hand—oh hell, no, how is this even possible?—is Lupe.

Chapter 41

Are you wearing anything under that towel?

Josie

I SLAM THE door in their faces.

What is Miguel doing here? What is Lupe doing here? What are *they* doing here *together*?

They were holding hands. How could he not tell me they were dating? What kind of a friend…? Shit. Never mind.

Did Lupe recognize me? I closed the door pretty fast. Maybe she didn't.

At that very moment, Rhett enters the house from the patio, and I seize his arm. "Can you get the door? Someone's there, and I…I need to go have a nervous breakdown." I dart for Emmy and Jason's room.

Amanda catches me on the way there. "I sent you all the

photos and video footage I took." She laughs her signature laugh, which turns into a kind of adorable snort at the end. "It's some good stuff." Then she gets a look at my face. "Are you okay?"

"Can you get Sean, please?" My voice is shaking.

"Sure thing, hon." Amanda touches my shoulder in a one-off pat of comfort before disappearing back out to the patio.

Meanwhile, I perch on the bed on the verge of not being able to breathe. Lupe's here! She saw me!

Sean arrives, shirtless, hair damp, one of the pool towels around his waist. When he sees me sitting on the bed, he closes the door behind him and crouches in front of me, taking my hands in his cold, damp ones. "What's wrong?"

"Miguel's here," I croak. "Did you invite him?" My gaze drops to his bare, dripping legs. "And are you wearing anything under that towel?"

"Barely anything. And no, I didn't invite him. But so what if he's here?"

"He brought Lupe with him!"

"Jason probably invited them." He squeezes my hands and smiles at me like a little boy. "Snack was so happy. We did good."

I yank my hands out of his. "Did you not hear me? My life is about to end!"

His towel falls to the floor. He does have something on under it—a pair of wet (this time red) men's bikini underwear.

"Oops." He stands up and tucks the towel back around his waist before heading for the exit. "Don't worry, I'll take care of it."

"What are you gonna do?" I jolt to my feet.

"I'll figure something out." He closes the door behind him.

I curse under my breath. I don't even know what that means. Maybe I can sneak back to my trailer. My work here is done—the gender of the Connor baby is officially revealed—but there's no way out of this room without potentially being seen. I'd have to go through either the house or the patio. But there's a fireplace in this room. I consider Ninja Warrior-ing my way up the chimney for the briefest of fever dreams. But no. I'll just have to wait for Sean.

I tug my phone out of my pocket and look at the photos and video Amanda sent me. She did a great job, and Sean's right; it's just what Jason and Emmy would have wanted. I forward the best ones to Emmy so she can be the first to post them. As I do, I notice my social media notifications have blown up more than usual. Curious, I click on one of them.

Sean and I are tagged in a news post. The stolen George Washington hat was identified at *Hamilton on the Roof*, and the police have pinpointed the patron who was wearing it: Sean.

Oh, crap!

My heart starts to race. Sean needs to know what's going on. The gossip columnists have been talking about the Connor baby gender reveal this week, and that means the cops know he's here. They could arrive any minute. I can't just sit here. I don't know if Lupe saw me, but I need a disguise just in case.

With some trepidation, I begin to rifle through the drawers of Emmy and Jason's dresser. "Don't look, don't look, don't look!" I mutter when I find myself elbow-deep in lingerie and novelty boxer briefs. The drawer next to it is crammed with adult toys. I slam that one shut immediately—I do not need to know my friends *that* intimately. Finally, I find an oversize *Lost Star* hoodie with a big picture of Orbit on the front. On any other day, I would rather stroll naked down the Pacific Coast Highway than wear this shameless piece of puppet porn, but over my head it goes. Nowhere in this room does a pair of sunglasses exist. How do these people even call themselves celebrities? I'm forced to tie a bandanna across my face. I tell myself that it's not regularly used in some kinky bondage scenario. Please, universe, let it just be an innocent bandanna. It's such a small ask.

I slink out on tiptoe and check every room in the house. No sign of Sean. Or Miguel and Lupe. I practically bump into one of the first ADs refilling her glass in the kitchen. She stares at the bandanna across my face.

"I have a cold sore," I tell her. "I'm very sensitive about it." Then I push my way through the French doors out to the patio. Sean's not here either.

What did he do? Teleport himself out?

A blue flickering light catches my eye. Emmy is casting from her phone to the patio flat-screen, the guests all turning to watch. She's uploading the photos and video from today, making their big announcement to the world over social media. I guess she couldn't wait until the party was over. Typical Emmy.

We all watch the page load. But my heart stops when I see what's on Emmy's feed. Someone's tagged her with a news story, asking, *Have you seen this?* And the preview picture being projected on the shameless eighty-five-inch TV is Sean in Revolutionary War garb, singing his heart out.

I hold my breath. It's just social media noise. Maybe she won't notice it.

But she does notice it. I watch her brow crinkle as she clicks on the link, launching a news article about the recovery of the stolen George Washington hat, complete with footage of the police raid on *Hamilton on the Roof*.

"What is this—?" Emmy android-scans the patio. I can almost hear the whirring of her eyepiece as she homes in on where I'm plastered against the wall next to the French doors, wearing Jason's Orbit sweatshirt, their sex bandanna around my neck.

Meanwhile, the story continues to play. Video clips from *Hamilton on the Roof* show Sean dancing and singing. Sean jumping up on the bar. The red and blue police lights flashing as the crowd scatters.

"Stop! Stop!"

Sean comes tearing across the patio deck, his face a mask of horror. One hand clutches the towel around his totally ripped waist while the other flaps in Emmy's direction. It's like watching the Sistine Chapel come to life and have a panic attack.

And then the Sistine Chapel drops its towel.

"Where did you get this? What did you—? Take it down!" he cries.

"I can't take it down. It's a news story," Emmy says.

"That's not—What the—? How?"

I've never seen Sean like this. He's sputtering and stammering and pattering around in his underwear like this is a comedy sketch. But he's not acting. The captain is a train wreck, and the way everyone is looking at him—it's not right. I'm embarrassed for him, and I can tell everyone else is, too.

I know exactly how this feels, and I can't let him go through it alone.

Striding over to the crowd, I hook Sean's arm in mine. "I don't know what all this drama is about a hat, but *Hamilton on the Roof* was the best date I've ever been on." Actually, that part's not even a lie.

Jason's voice is gentle. "It does look like fun."

"It looks like a *lot* of fun." Emmy chuckles, letting the rest of the video play. "And look at you, Josie! You're in the news clip, too."

Wait. Why am I in the news clip? I didn't steal any hats.

But I guess that doesn't matter because suddenly all 4000 x 2000 pixels of me are onscreen, tearing up the stage like a tap dancing mofo.

Emmy's lips part in amazement right before her face falls. "How come I never knew you could dance like that?" We stare each other down like two statues, her waiting for my explanation and me trying to come up with one, until…

"Oh my God," a woman's voice booms from a chair at the corner of the patio. "That's where I know you from!"

Margarita stands in her black sleeveless dress, pointing my way with a fingertip as red as a drop of blood. A wave of Shalimar comes off her like radiation.

"*Club Bilingüe*! You're the Yeehaw girl who tap danced and taught kids how to say things in English. You're Savannah Bateman!"

Every cell in my body seizes up. Then, as if I'd just pointed to my chest and shouted *Look at this!* the cartoon Orbit on my hoodie captures Margarita's attention. I watch the realization dawn on her like a sunrise on a mountain face. Her eyes widen. She opens her mouth, and…

"You're the puppet assassin!" she cries. "You're the girl who killed Chuy!"

"Margarita, don't be ridiculous!" Emmy jumps in. "This is Josie. You know her!" Her confused expression begs me to confirm it.

I apologize to her with my eyes and shift my attention to Margarita. "It was an accident."

"I knew it!" Margarita bursts into surprised laughter.

"Wait! What?" Emmy cries. "What's going on here?"

Panic surges through my veins. I stumble into the chair

behind me and almost fall over it. "I've got to get out of here," I mutter.

"I'll take you to my place," Sean says as I fumble with the stupid effing chair that has become my personal nemesis. The authority in his voice is clear even though he's standing in a crowd wearing nothing but a pair of underwear that is smaller than mine.

"No." I shove the chair out of the way and bolt for the screen door that leads to the side yard and my trailer. Sean misunderstood me. I didn't mean I needed to get out of here as in the patio. I need to get out of here, as in LA.

Behind me, Emmy is still demanding, "What the hell is happening here?" and Margarita is shouting, "Where is Chuy? You have him, don't you?"

I don't, and I don't think Hugo does yet, either. I told him I buried Chuy in the cemetery, but I didn't say exactly where. I was hoping that Castillo Studios might win that award before a certain zombie puppet was resurrected. Now, however, it's a moot point. Margarita knows who I am. Everything's going to come out.

I throw open the screen door and plow directly into Miguel and Lupe, barefoot and holding their shoes. Dammit! Sean must've convinced them to go take a walk on the beach, and now they're back, just in freaking time.

Lupe's mouth falls open, and a myriad of feelings swirl inside me as I stare into her big, dark eyes, her more grown-up features. "Savannah?"

Miguel just looks guilty.

I make a run for my trailer. I don't know what else to do. I can't face her. I can't face Emmy, either. All my deceitful, cowardly chickens have come home to roost, and it sucks just as much as I thought it would.

Margarita is going to leak my secret to the press, and then the judgment will come like a torrent, followed by the humiliation. It'll spill over to everyone else in my orbit. Juan Ernesto and Castillo Studios. Miguel and Lupe and the cast of *Más Allá de las Estrellas*. Knowing Sean and Emmy, they'll try to stand up for me and get sucked in, too.

I can't let that happen. I've got to get out of here. Disappear, and hope like hell that the scandal disappears with me.

What used to be Peyton's room has become storage for my art. I'll have to leave all that behind. I throw as many clothes and toiletries into my travel duffel as I can fit. I'm going to lose my home again and everyone I care about.

A gasping sob escapes me, but, no, Josie, there's no time for pity and self-loathing. Right now, you have to *get out*. Disappear. Go somewhere where people can't find you, where they won't recognize you. I'll get a new name. Start a new life, again. And this time, I won't be stupid enough to try to share it with a movie star.

There's a knock at the aluminum door, and I almost jump through the roof.

"Josie?" It's Sean.

"I can't right now, Sean! I just can't, okay?"

"The police have arrived. I have to go down to the station for questioning." His voice is muffled through the door. "But I'd really like to talk to you first."

I bury my face in my hands and gather my strength. How am I going to be able to do this—say goodbye to Sean forever? It was one thing to know that I'd still see him at work, that he'd still be a part of my life.

I swallow the burning ache in my chest, drag myself to the door, and open it, stopping just inside the doorway. Sean found his pants, but not his shirt, apparently. Behind him, a couple of early trick-or-treaters start to make their way toward Jason and Emmy's door, but their mom seizes their arms and steers them toward the next house—one without a half-naked man in the yard and a blinking police cruiser out front, probably.

Sean zeroes in on the overstuffed duffel bag behind me. "Are you leaving?"

"Yes."

"Please, don't."

The sheer fragility in his voice guts me. I stare at him. God, he's so perfect, everything about him, from the tousled, damp hair to that chiseled body to that matchless mouth and that gaze that is still captainly even in its vulnerability. I had that, for a minute. For a few short weeks, I had more than I could ever have imagined. More than I could ever deserve. I sear this moment into my brain so that I can paint it later: Sean O'Sullivan, my celebrity crush, bare-chested in my doorway, begging me to stay with him. In another moment, another universe, another lifetime, I'd give him what he was asking for. I'd stay. And I'd never say no to him again.

But this is the life I've created for myself, and I don't get to do that.

"My secret's out."

"Yes, and now you can face it. Look at this as an opportunity. Your sister is here. You could start by talking to her."

He's so good at this. So convincing. Talk to Lupe? Yeah, right. It's too late for that. It's been too late for that for a long time.

"My decision is made." There. I can play the captain, too.

"Josie, you can't just run and hide every time life gets hard."

"Yes, I can!" I blurt. "And it was working fine for me until you and Emmy forced me onto that show."

I expect him to argue. To "control the narrative," but he says nothing.

"Hugo's going to find Chuy. Margarita's going to dox me. And my family and friends are going to be humiliated all over again. Everyone's going to hate me even more than they already do!"

He's still quiet, and it's kind of scary.

"I did everything I could to make you choose somebody else in that contest. Why didn't you just let me? You were my celebrity crush. How was I supposed to say no to you?"

In this moment, I couldn't hate myself more. I hate my past self. I hate my present self. And I hate that I'm blaming him for something I would do again in a heartbeat if given the chance.

Sean's expression is broken, not a hint of nonchalance in sight. "Please tell me that's not how you really feel."

Well, would you look at that? It *is* possible to hate myself more.

"Please just let me go, Sean," I whisper.

His lips part, and I'm mesmerized again by that perfect, beautiful, sensual, unforgiving, ravenous, sublime mouth that will never be mine again. The police lights dance off his muscled torso as he stands there holding my gaze, saying nothing, respecting my wishes and destroying me at the same time. Letting me destroy him, too. Destroy us. Watching me burn it all down because that's what I do.

He's better off without me. They all are.

He turns to go, and I manage to hold in the tears until the aluminum door slams shut.

Chapter 42

Quote unquote.

CELEBRITY STRAIGHT TALK, NOVEMBER 1

AMIL: Hope your Halloween was a good one. I'm Amil Nair, and welcome to another action-packed episode of *Celebrity Straight Talk*. Boy, the *Lost Star* cast really keep our bills paid, don't they, Isla?

ISLA: Hi-la! It's Isla Wallace, and, yes, Amil, without the likes of Sean O'Sullivan and Jason Connor, you and I would probably be working at Pizza Guys.

AMIL: We have sooooo much to talk about today, but first things first. Jason and Emmy are having a baby girl! Yay!

Bring on the bows and those little elastic headbands that all babies hate!

ISLA: Yes, congratulations to them. However, the afternoon revealed more than Little Girl Connor's gender.

AMIL: That's right, Isla. It also revealed the seedy underbelly of Sean O'Sullivan's social life at a weirdo-fest called *Hamilton on the Roof.*

AMIL & ISLA: Oof!

AMIL: It's like *The Rocky Horror Picture Show* in petticoats and breeches.

ISLA: The American Revolution in a marijuana haze.

AMIL: It's odd for someone like Sean to hang out at a place like that, don't you think?

ISLA: It's definitely not the sort of thing celebrities tend to do.

AMIL: We also learned that Josie can tap. Did you see that? She was like Gene Kelly!

ISLA: Who?

AMIL: Oh, never mind. Some people never spent their childhood summers at their grandparents', and it shows.

ISLA: Don't forget that we also learned that Josie may have a secret, dark past as a puppet serial killer named Savannah Bateman!

AMIL: Technically, it was only one puppet, but who's counting, right?

ISLA: Apparently, in her youth, a tap dancing Savannah Bateman and her ventriloquist stepsister, Lupe Castillo, were paragons of multiculturalism. Until she torched her sister's puppet, called her the "b" word, and ran away.

AMIL: Wait a minute. I think I studied their stuff in my AP Spanish class. She murdered Chuy the Puppet? That's beyond wrong.

ISLA: It's not really about the puppet, Amil. It's more about the fact that her outburst got the show canceled and put all of her castmates out of a job.

AMIL: How can you say it's not about the puppet? What if it had been Baby Yoda? Or our dear Orbit? Or Lamb Chop!

ISLA: Who's Lamb Chop?

AMIL: Never mind.

ISLA: Lupe confirmed that Josie Days and Savannah Bateman are, indeed, the same person. *[aside]* She saw her at the Connor gender reveal.

AMIL: That poor baby. She'll have to spend her whole life overshadowed by this scandal. But do you think Josie Days is really Savannah Bateman?

ISLA: Yes, I do! Josie has been camera-shy from the beginning. We've seen her tap dancing skills firsthand in that video. Not to mention, in a fan-posted selfie of Sean and Josie in Las Vegas, Sean's phone screen is open to a browser showing a Mexican newspaper article about the very night Savannah went off the rails.

AMIL: ¡Ay, caramba!

ISLA: Which means he knew. Sean knew all along who she was. He lied to us.

AMIL: Okay, but I think we should cut him some slack, Isla. When you love someone, quote unquote, you do things for them. Like protect their secret identity.

ISLA: Do you think Sean loves Josie, quote unquote?

AMIL: I do, Isla. I think he loves Josie, quote unquote, more than anyone we've seen him with yet.

ISLA: But Sean may have lied to us about something else, too. A police raid on the very same *Hamilton on the Roof* event that Sean and Josie attended uncovered one stolen George Washington tricorn hat worn by Christopher Jackson on Broadway, and Sean may have been in possession of it.

AMIL: Oh dear. They didn't throw our sexy captain in the brig, did they? He'll be sullied!

ISLA: Relax, Amil. Sean hasn't been arrested. He's just being questioned, and he can't leave LA county until the investigation is closed.

AMIL: ¡Gracias a Dios!

ISLA: I'm a little worried about him, though. He's starting to remind me of another O'Sullivan, and not that rugged, sexy dad of his.

AMIL: His creepy brother, Seamus? Yeah, I got that vibe, too. *[shudders]*

ISLA: Dressing up like that. Hanging out in seedy joints. Stealing things. I mean, he's always been quirky, but this is something else.

AMIL: Sean, please don't do this to us! If you turn out to be a creepy weirdo like your brother, I just couldn't bear it!

ISLA: It's okay, Amil. We'll get through this.

HARPER'S HOT SEAT

HARPER: Welcome, fans, to *Harper's Hot Seat*, where your favorite celebs answer your most burning questions at top speed. Today we have Sean O'Sullivan, whom you know best as Captain Footwork from *Lost Star Dance Troupe Saves the Universe* but who, if he gets the part, may very soon also be known as Thunderstrike, Guardian of the Blaze Munchers.

SEAN: It's Guardian of the Blaze *Masters*, and yes, auditions are later today.

HARPER: You're looking good, I'll say that much.

SEAN: I haven't had a carb in over a month.

HARPER: I'm glad they didn't throw you in jail over the hat thing.

SEAN: I didn't steal the hat, but that's all I'm allowed to say as the investigation is ongoing.

HARPER: So, I have to ask it: how often do you go to those…events?

SEAN: It's important to get out of your comfort zone once in a while, Heather.

HARPER: Did you just call me Heather?

SEAN: Did I?

HARPER: Right. Okay, let's do this. Answer as fast as you can. Don't overthink it. Harper's Hot Seat commences…now! What was your nickname as a kid?

SEAN: Seanny Bear or Seanny Boy.

HARPER: Go-to breakfast?

SEAN: Whatever my chef makes me.

HARPER: What would a cologne called Sean O'Sullivan smell like?

SEAN: Push-ups and pomade.

HARPER: Cartoon crush?

SEAN: Rapunzel.

HARPER: How do you take your coffee?

SEAN: Organic, from the highlands of Guatemala. With six Splendas.

HARPER: How are you dealing with your breakup with Josie?

SEAN: I've moved on.

HARPER: I heard she quit the show and left LA.

SEAN: That she did.

HARPER: And how's Susan doing?

SEAN: Who?

HARPER: The woman you're currently dating.

SEAN: Oh, her. I really can't say. HIPAA.

HARPER: Have you ever made a shrine?

SEAN: Excuse me?

HARPER: A shrine, like with pictures and drawings and stuff, like your brother did with that stuntwoman a few years ago.

SEAN: Can we get the next question, Heather?

HARPER: It's Harper. You're doing that on purpose, aren't you?

SEAN: I would never do anything on purpose.

HARPER: Ha ha. Any plans tonight?

SEAN: Actually, yes. Vera, the lady whom Josie replaced on the show, has finally been discharged from the hospital, and we're going out on a date.

HARPER: Where will you take her? *The Rocky Horror Picture Show*?

SEAN: Er-

HARPER: Sorry, I couldn't resist.

Chapter 43

I hope you're not the jealous type.

Sean

THE DULCET TONES of a piano greet me in the foyer of the Shirley Brasserie. There are no TV cameras. No journalists. No paparazzi. No one knows I'm here except my date—one Vera Caladizzi. She raises a feeble hand and gives me the royal wave from a table by the window.

I lope over, take her hand, and kiss it. "How did I get so lucky to have dinner with the most beautiful woman in the room?"

She smiles around the oxygen tube in her nose. "After all I've been through these last few weeks, you're not getting away with just a kiss on the hand! Come here, you big hunk!"

She yanks me into her aura of baby powder and rosewater. For a woman who's just had heart surgery, she's surprisingly strong—and fast. I turn my face just in time for the kiss to land on my cheek rather than smack on my mouth.

Straightening the lapels of my tuxedo jacket—yes, I wore a tux for her—I slide into my chair and reach for the bottle of merlot that's already on the table, chilled to European standards.

"Did your doctor give me clearance to get you drunk, Vera?" I pour her a glass without waiting for an answer.

She picks it up by the stem. "If I can't die of pleasure drinking too much with Sean O'Sullivan, whatever was it all for?"

"Ah, a woman after my own heart."

I pour myself a glass, too. I got done with the audition less than two hours ago. It didn't go well. I was too distracted what with Josie's sudden departure and the police investigation. I admitted that I bought the hat online. I hope I convinced the LAPD that I didn't know it was the stolen one. If not, perhaps the very large check I sent to the NYC Theater Development Fund will keep them from pressing charges.

"I thought your heart was already taken," Vera replies, taking a prim sip of her wine.

"Propriety demands a gentleman only speak of the lady he's with."

"Well, propriety might want to step aside unless you want to talk about doctors and hospitals." She sets her glass down and smooths the napkin on her lap. "I'd rather talk about young love."

"Young love is a wily asshole." I take another swig. "Pardon the language."

"Or we can talk about *Hamilton*. I love that show."

I can't tell if she's teasing me. I gulp the rest of my wine and wince as I refill my glass. "It's a gem, all right."

"Will you sing me a piece?"

Okay, she's teasing me, there's no doubt about it. "What? Here?"

"Indulge a sick old lady, will you?"

"You're milking it, Vera. Shame on you." I wag a finger at her but sing a few lines of "One Last Time" anyway. It's worth it for the smile I get.

We order a selection from the raw bar and some salads. As we dive into the oysters and shrimp, I can't help thinking about Josie with her shellfish aversion or whatever love/hate thing she has with it. She's really gone, back to Florida, according to Emmy. Will I ever see her again? I don't know. Not that it matters. Regardless of our feelings for one another, she doesn't want anything to do with me. She made that clear. I'm her shellfish.

"I bet she's thinking about you, too," Vera says, peeling the scales off a shrimp.

"Oh, I'm not thinking about her." After abstaining from alcohol for so long, my face has a lovely numb feeling going on. Too bad it doesn't extend to my heart.

"This is a safe space, Sean."

I've heard that line before. I raise an eyebrow. "What did you used to do for a living, Vera?"

She sips her wine with a smile. "I was a therapist."

"Oh boy."

"The good news is, whatever we talk about is privileged, so you can stop pouring wine over all those feelings and get it out."

"I don't think so." Although maybe it's time. Maybe this woman can help me. "Okay, fine, I *am* thinking about her. I can't stop thinking about her." I pause. "Does that make me weird?"

"Why would that make you weird?"

A shrimp cartwheels across my fingers as I fumble with it.

"It's just that she told me to leave her alone. She doesn't want to be with me, and I should respect that, right?"

"Of course."

"But I'm worried about her. Not even Emmy has heard from her since she left. And the press are having a field day with her." My stomach clenches. Maybe this wasn't such a good idea. I feel so exposed. "I just want to know that she's okay."

"What's so weird about wanting to know that she's okay?"

"Because I'm doing it all the time. Constantly. Like, I can't relax. Unless I'm jumping out of the way of a bomb—literally, on set—I'm thinking about her. I'm worrying about her. I'm missing her. I'm talking myself out of calling her. I'm…" I take a deep breath. I hate this, everything about it, but if I don't do this now, it's never going to happen. I glance around and lower my voice to a whisper. "I think I might be obsessed with her."

"What?" Vera leans in. "I didn't quite catch that."

I lean forward, too. "I might be obsessed with her."

"What?" Vera cups her ear.

"Obsessed! Obsessed! I might be obsessed!" My shoulder bumps the wine bottle, and I grab it with a yelp. The couples near us glance our way. Our server looks like she's about to call for backup. Meanwhile, Vera is chuckling to herself. She's messing with me! I can't believe it.

"That was mean, Vera," I growl. "I don't like you anymore."

"I'm sorry." She pats her lips with the corner of her napkin. "I was just having a little fun. But in all seriousness, you're not the first person to come to me with this concern."

My heart jolts. "Really?"

"Really." She pauses as our salads are served. "But I think we need to talk definitions for a moment. Obsession is something very specific and unhealthy. It's not just thinking too much about someone or something. It's about being unable to separate yourself from them. Hoarding their love or their attention. Not caring about their happiness, only your own. It's a selfish, jealous feeling. Does that sound like what you feel for Josie?"

My fork hovers over my salad as I ponder it. "I don't think so."

"How *do* you feel about her?"

I gulp air. "I want her to be happy. I'd love for us to be happy together."

Vera narrows her eyes at me. "What a monster you are." She titters and stabs a tomato.

I'm not sure what's happening. I expected a different reaction. Horror. Or sympathy. Maybe a twelve-step program. "You don't…see a problem here?"

Vera's eyebrows lift as she swallows. "I don't think you're obsessed with this woman, Sean. I think you just really like her and don't want to lose her."

I take a huge lungful of air, like I'm facing an incoming tidal wave because, if I want to trust what Vera is telling me, she has to have all the information. "When I was a teenager, I filled this notebook with poems and drawings of this one girl I liked."

"How sweet."

"No, not sweet. Excessive."

She gives me a pointed look. "I cut off a lock of Luke Appleby's hair when he was having a sleepover with my brother and kept it in my jewelry box for eleven years."

I cough a little. "You—Are you messing with me again?"

She pops a bite into her mouth. "No. That's a true story."

"That's insane." Although it does make me feel better. Maybe we're all obsessive weirdos sometimes. My fork hangs in midair. "What about—" I start to ask but then chicken out. There's no need to go there.

"Go on, Sean. No use being a quitter now."

"What about the cosplay?" I whisper. "Am I obsessed with that? Because I really like it. I really, *really* like it. Like, I'm so happy doing it. And I have way too many costumes."

"Liking something a lot isn't bad, Sean. In fact, this cosplay hobby of yours doesn't sound all that different from what you do for a living, and no one would accuse you of being obsessed with your work, would they?"

"It's different," I say. "It's embarrassing."

She sets down her fork. "Who did that to you?"

"Who did what?"

"Who took your passions and made you ashamed of them?"

I stutter. "I—I'm not sure."

"What was something you loved to do as a child? Something that lit you up?"

I don't even have to think about it. "Working in the costume room with Mam."

"Hmm." She nods. "And who made fun of you for it?"

I feel my lip twitch. "My da, a little. But more my brother."

"Did your brother do it to you with other things, too? Maybe that notebook you told me about?"

I feel my jaw tighten. "As a matter of fact, he did."

"I wonder why he would do that?" Vera nudges her wineglass at me.

I refill it, memories of Seamus with his binoculars filling my mind's eye. I think I'm starting to get what's going on. "Because he was ashamed of himself, and picking on me made him feel better."

Vera taps her nose and points to me. "You got it, Seanny Bear."

It's like a map has been unfolded in front of me, one that leads to new and exciting places in my brain where I'm not an incurable weirdo.

"Buying a stolen hat is a little over the top, though," she admits. "You did know it was stolen, didn't you?"

Emboldened, I try to explain. "I like authentic things. There's history behind them. When I wear them, it's more than a costume—it's like I get to be part of something I couldn't be a part of when it was happening. Maybe I was too young when it filmed, maybe I wasn't the right person for the part, maybe someone I really respect wore it. And somehow that energy"—I use my hands to mime this magical, invisible energy that comes from these things. I'm sure I look like a loony doing it, but Vera's convinced me she's my safe person—"that energy comes through the costume. I feed off it. It invigorates me. Plus, the auctions are really thrilling, too, especially when a lot of people are bidding for the same item and there's a lot of money involved."

She smiles gently. "Well, here's the thing, Sean. It's not the hobby itself that's problematic. It's how you go about it. If you're pouring your love and attention into the hobby as a replacement for pouring your love and attention into the people in your life, that's not healthy." Her gaze goes sharp. "Have you been doing that?"

I think about all of my past relationships, how I kept those women at arm's length. How I was never able to get close to anyone. And how the only place I felt I could really let go, really *feel*, was when I was dressed up. Hidden.

I shake my head. "I don't know."

"Did your costumes ever love you back?" Vera prods.

I chuckle. "All right, you've made your point, Dr. Heartbreak."

"Don't be afraid to feel deeply, Sean. Passion is not perversion. The people who feel most deeply are the ones who get the most out of life and who give the most to others, if they're brave enough." She puts down her fork. "That was delicious. Now what shall we share for dessert?"

We split the profiteroles and a lime sorbet. All my tightness has loosened up, and I find myself telling Vera more stories about my cosplay adventures and even about Josie and me. She tells me about her kids and grandkids, about her first husband, George, and how awful that marriage was, and then her second husband, Frank, who was the exact opposite.

"Is Frank still with you?" I ask. "Or did you dump him for me?"

She smiles. "He died six years ago."

I place my hand over hers on the table. "I'm sorry. You must miss him terribly."

"I do, but at least I had him to miss." She squeezes my hand. "So, did you and my stand-in do anything after you ate? Don't you dare hold out on me! I want everything she got!"

I chuckle, thinking it's a good thing I don't have to base this date off of our *Hamilton on the Roof* adventure. "Well, we didn't go anywhere afterward, although now that you mention it, we did get a dance in."

"Lovely!" She pats her oxygen tank. "But I'll have to bring Harold with me."

I hop up and grab the machine's handle. "Hello, Harold," I say. "I hope you're not the jealous type."

The piano player sees us coming and gives a nod and a smile—it's the same dude from before. Vera and I dance to an easy three-step, careful to go only as far as the oxygen tubing allows. Her hand is as light and fragile as a bird in mine. I can feel the bones of her spine. What must it be like to have most of your life behind you? More adventures in your past than in your future? And how would it feel to dance like this with Josie fifty years in the future? Would she feel like this in my arms?

I've never caught myself thinking this far ahead before. It makes me wonder if my train has added some stops to it, after all. Like, maybe it doesn't just run between Good Time Guy and Obsessive Weirdo. Maybe there's some nuance to Sean O'Sullivan, after all.

And, maybe, like Snack suggested, Josie and I could be good for one another even when it's not fun. It's a little late for that, perhaps, but maybe not. A trip to Florida isn't completely out of the range of possibilities.

When we're done, I thank Vera for the pleasure of her company and, with an unexplainable skip in my step, accompany her to the parking lot where her son is waiting with the car.

"Now be honest, Vera," I tease. "Are you going to try to kiss me on the mouth again when we say our goodbyes?"

"No!" She titters.

"Vera," I warn. "Tell the truth."

"Well, maybe. Actually, yes."

Chapter 44

From everything I've heard, smoking sounds like a great idea.

Sean

"CUT! SEAN, PRACTICE those lines again. Your accent's almost there. We'll try again in twenty." Miles turns to the AD. "How's the coffee situation?"

I rub my forehead and squint at my Spanish language coach, who is already making a beeline toward me, script in hand. I grab the papers and wave him off. "I got this."

We're in the green screen studio, where, supposedly, the crew of the *Noche de Fuego* is searching for a lost passenger with help from Orbit and me. Kai props my little furry blue crewmate on a fake boulder and heads out for a break. I wander over to Jason, who is checking his phone. He's bouncing like a bowl of eggplant-colored Jell-O.

"What's up, Hard-On?"

"Emmy called. Maybe it's time!"

He rings her back on speaker. When she picks up, she sounds upset—all snotty and sniffly, like she's been crying.

"Honey? What's wrong? Is everything okay?"

"No! Everything is terrible!"

Jason and I exchange worried looks. "What happened?"

She blows her nose right into the phone. "It's not me. It's Josie!"

My pulse jumps, and I can't help butting in. "What about Josie?"

"We had a big fight before she left. I pleaded with her not to go, but she was completely unreasonable, talking about this puppet and how it was going to ruin our lives. I figured, let her go home to Florida for a little while, cool off, come back to her senses. But this morning, I woke up to her video!"

"What video?" Jason and I ask at the same time.

"It's terrible!" Emmy wails. "It's awful."

I wrangle my emotions. I don't want to lose my cool here in front of everyone, but Emmy is terrifying me.

"Emmy, send us the video," I say in my Captain Footwork voice. I can feel my face doing twitchy things. "Right now."

When it comes through, Jason holds up the phone so we can both see it. Josie's face is in the frame. It's dark, and she's outdoors. It must have been filmed last night.

JOSIE: Hey, Emmy. I just wanted to let you know that I'm okay, but I'm not in Florida. I'm not going to Florida.

There's the sound of crunching leaves. She's walking as she's recording. In the background I see … tombstones?

JOSIE: I've found a place to stay for now, and there's a little
    cemetery here, and since it's almost Day of the Dead,
    I thought I'd come out here and make a little altar for
    my dad.

The camera shifts as she sits down. I didn't know her dad had passed away. What other important pieces of her life don't I know? There's a canvas drawstring bag beside her from which she begins to pull things. A framed photo. Tea light candles. A couple of bottles of AmberBock beer. A box of cookies. She holds up the photo to the camera so we can see it. It's a faded snapshot of a man with a crew cut and a slight overbite holding a chubby baby in a blue dress.

JOSIE: This is my dad and me.

She pans across the other items.

JOSIE: These were all the things he liked.

She sets everything up under a tree, balancing the phone against the trunk. An owl hoots in the background. Something about it sends ice through my veins. She shouldn't be all alone, at night, in a strange place. What if it's dangerous? She uses a pocket knife to pop the top from one of the beer bottles and clinks it against the other.

JOSIE: To you, Dad.

She takes a swig. Her eyes are glassy as she focuses back on the camera.

JOSIE: The reason I'm telling you these details about my dad is because it's what friends do. They tell each other about their lives and about what's important to them and about their fears and their failures and their hopes and their dreams, and I haven't done any of that with you.

A match sizzles, and she lights the tea lights one by one, cursing once as she burns her fingers. She proceeds to tell Emmy what I already know, about her mom meeting and marrying Juan Ernesto, about the TV studio and her role in *The Bilingual Club*. About Savannah Bateman. About Lupe and Chuy the Puppet.

Her face squints. I think she's trying not to cry. An ache swells in my throat.

JOSIE: After my dad died, I lived alone for six years. I felt miserable, and lonely, and basically invisible…And then I met you, Emmy. And Peyton. And my life took a huge turn. You and Peyton were the best thing to happen to me in a long time. You've been such a good friend to me, and I've been a terrible one to you. Oh no! The candles are going out. It's this wind.

She pauses to relight and adjust them while Jason and I wait in rapt silence. I can see the flames of the candles burning in the dark pools of her eyes.

JOSIE: If it makes you feel any better, I lied to Miguel, too. So, there you go—I'm an equal opportunity asshole. But it would truly devastate me if you thought for a moment that I didn't consider you my truest, closest friend. And I want you to know that I will miss you tremendously. And Peyton, too. And Jason and Mattie. As for that sweet new baby that you're gonna give birth to and then dress in sauce-colored clothing… tell her her Tía Josie loves her. And I'm sorry I never got to meet her.

Her hand reaches forward, and the video cuts out.

"I'm worried about her," Emmy admits, blowing her nose again. "She can be dark sometimes, but I've never seen her like this."

I dig my own phone out of my pocket. Josie's being way too hard on herself, and it's got to stop. I don't care that she told me to bugger off. Vera said I shouldn't hide my feelings. I'm calling her. Right now.

My call goes immediately to voicemail. I try again. She has to pick up eventually, right?

"Emmy's been trying for an hour," Jason tells me.

Right. Of course. I dial Josie a third time. Still, she doesn't pick up. Dammit, Josie. But I'll keep calling. I have to. This isn't stalking. This is friendship, maybe more, I don't know. All I know is that, like Emmy, I'm worried about her. And seeing her hurting hurts me, too.

I should be studying my lines, but my feelings won't shut up. As we shoot the next take, the little buggers are busy concocting a plan, and it's a doozy. It will make me miss work, putting me in breach of my contract. It'll also violate the LAPD's mandate for me to stay in the county for the remainder of the hat investigation. But my fretting may have kept me from overthinking my lines because my accent doesn't suck and the AD calls a wrap.

I glance at Orbit, perched next to me on a fake rock. The puppet itself seems to be saying, *Don't do it, Captain. You'll regret it.*

I stare into its huge, shiny eyes. *It's not really that bad of an idea, is it?*

You'll look as crazy as Seamus, the Orbit in my head says. *Maybe crazier.*

What if I said I don't care about that?

You care, Orbit says.

He's right. I do care.

But I care about Josie more.

I shuffle into my street clothes and search out Miguel. When I find him, I throw an arm around his shoulders and steer him toward the back exit. "¡Amigo! Fumar, por favor." I'm sure my grammar's wrong, but it's good to practice.

He digs the pack out of his pocket. "I didn't know you smoked."

"I don't, but I'm thinking of starting." I glance around, making sure no one is watching us as I shove the door open. "From everything I've heard, smoking sounds like a great idea."

Chapter 45

I really wish I hadn't thrown away my phone.

Josie

IT'S MORNING IN my new life. I wake up on an inflatable mattress in a one-window rented room with a shared bathroom down the hall. I hold my pee while I get dressed and rescue a barely cool milk carton out of the ancient mini fridge. I fill my one bowl with Cheerios and sniff the milk before adding it. I'm seventy-percent convinced it's not going to kill me.

I have to hold my breath while I use the communal bathroom because I know from prior experience that it smells like I'm sharing it with a family of raccoons. In the three days I've been here, I've learned that the best time to take a shower is either 2:00 in the morning or never. Luckily, I have a washcloth, soap, and dry shampoo so I can sponge bath it with the best of them. Life is good.

No, it isn't.

Life is definitely not good. Life is a shit show, warmed up.

Outside, I step around the bodies (they're alive but homeless) on my way to the nail salon in downtown San Francisco where Li Jing hooked me up with a job. Their cousin owns it, and the salon employees were "excited to have an FX makeup artist on staff." Now that they've met me, they seem less excited. They speak Chinese to me, and my brain immediately goes to Spanish. I don't think I have the will to learn another language. I barely have the will to get up in the morning. The upside is they've never heard of Chuy the Puppet or Savannah Bateman.

I do nails all day. The first set is therapeutic. The second set is fun. The third set and my back is already hurting. The fourth set—is it lunchtime yet? Hurry up and eat because it's time for the fifth set and a second wind. More like a second breeze. A second slight movement of air? I wish the TV was working. Why isn't the TV working?

I really wish I hadn't thrown away my phone.

They said there was a hot plate in my apartment. My rent included a hot plate. But there's no hot plate, so after work, I head to the noodle place down the street. Mucho slurping ensues. I don't want to cry. Actually, every part of me wants to cry, but I won't let it. I brought this on myself, so crying is useless and stupid.

Besides, I don't have to stay here forever. On my day off, I'll go down to the courthouse and fill out the paperwork to change my name. I've got a few picked out. What I want to do is go with something wild and flamboyant and improper. Persephone Molotov Cocktail of the Nine Fingers. What I'll probably do is go with Addison Wade. Then my initials can spell out the pity party I can have for myself whenever I feel like it. AW.

After dinner, it's back to my room and reinflating my air mattress by mouth. It's like sleeping on a pool raft. I fall back on it and hear the moment it pops.

Universe, I swear I will cut you.

But, of course, I have no power here. I am mortal, and I am alone, and I have ruined my life. Again.

I'm pretty sure I've pinpointed the moment when it all fell apart. It was when Sean asked me to do the *Date Your Celebrity Crush!* show. Because when he asked me, when my freaking celebrity crush trained those laser-green eyes on me and opened that glorious mouth of his and asked me to please, please be Vera's replacement, what the hell was I supposed to do? Be strong? I'm not strong.

I miss Sean. I miss Emmy. I miss Peyton. I miss Jason handing me an alcoholic beverage every day at 5:00 in the evening. I miss believing that I deserve to be happy. I miss daydreaming that I could spend that happiness in Sean's arms.

Did Castillo Studios win the award? Or did the resurgence of this scandal steal it from them? Do they hate me? Did the crossover get canceled? I wish I knew. Or maybe I don't. Ignorance is bliss. Or at least it's better than knowledge that makes you feel like crap.

I fall asleep somehow. The next morning it's the same. Breakfast. Bathroom. Walk. Work. And the next. And the next. Except today, Sunday, the TV in the salon is fixed (yay!), and they turn it on.

It's Chinese TV, but the news is local, and when I see Sean and Miguel's faces plastered up behind the anchors, I leap up from the set of acrylics in front of me.

"What are they saying?" I shout. "Someone! Please!"

Everyone in the salon looks at me like I've just invited them to join my exciting new cult. Finally, Xiang, a twentysomething nail tech, takes pity on me and translates.

"They went missing three days ago," she says. "They think the captain guy kidnapped the other."

"Kidnapped?" Something must have been lost in translation. "Are you sure that's what they said?"

"Yeah, kidnapped," she confirms. "Like, when you take someone against their will."

No, that can't be true. Sean kidnapping Miguel? Although he does have that locked room in his house.

"Can I look for another channel?"

Xiang hands me the remote, and I click around until I find the entertainment news in English. Unfortunately, it's about me. Like a train wreck I can't look away from, I watch the reporter on the *Lost Star* set interviewing Lupe. "She hasn't spoken to me or my dad in twelve years," Lupe says with a wry frown. "And, no, we have no idea what she did with Chuy. The last thing I saw was her running off with him into the night."

It's not a lie, but it feels like she's throwing me under the bus, again. The noodles in my stomach feel like they've come to life.

Also, Hugo hasn't found Chuy yet? Why not?

Thankfully, the next segment is about Sean and Miguel.

NEWS ANCHOR: The whereabouts of actors Sean O'Sullivan and Miguel Angel Aguilar Porras are still unknown. Police say both men disappeared after a taping at the *Lost Star* studio in Hollywood on November 2 and haven't been seen since. Foul play is suspected based on a security camera that captured footage of Sean urging

Miguel into the trunk of his car. Officials haven't ruled out kidnapping, especially since Miguel's phone was found crushed and in a dumpster on the property. These findings, coupled with the fact that Sean O'Sullivan is still under investigation for the theft of a wardrobe piece from a Broadway warehouse in New York City, are disconcerting. More news as it unfolds.

Stunned doesn't begin to describe how I feel. This can't be right. Sean would never do something like this! Dammit, why did I get rid of my phone? I'm completely cut off.

"Xiang, can I borrow your phone?" I don't have Sean's number memorized, but I do know Emmy's. She picks up on the first ring. "Emmy, it's Josie."

"Josie!" she squeals with joy and relief. "Thank God! Where are you? Is this your new number? Are you coming home?"

"It's a friend's phone. Listen. I can't come home." My stomach clenches at the thought of going back to LA, of being swarmed by cameras and people.

"I miss you," she says. "Peyton misses you."

"I miss you, too." Desperately. "Please just tell me what you know about Sean and Miguel."

"I showed Sean your video, and later that day, this happened. No one's seen them since."

My boss comes over and starts reprimanding me in Mandarin. My client isn't looking too happy, either, sitting at my station with her half-done nails.

I tell Emmy I'll call her again as soon as I can. "Thanks," I say, handing Xiang back her phone. But I feel anything but thankful. A witch hunt is on, and Sean is in their sights.

Sean didn't kidnap Miguel—there's a perfectly reasonable

explanation for that locked room and the trunk thing. Sean is nothing like his brother. He's warm and caring and responsible, and all of this is a huge misunderstanding. It has to be. Either that or they're both in danger.

My heart stutters.

What if they're in danger? What if someone blackmailed Sean to do what he did? Or what if there was an accident and they're both injured, or worse? And what if it's my fault?

I glance up at the TV. My boss has changed the channel back, and the programming has moved on to a documentary on Chinese shadow puppets.

Puppets?

Seriously?

You've got to be kidding me. It feels like a throwdown from the universe.

The kettle on the backroom burner starts to whistle, and I feel a similar hot fury pressing against my insides. Fine, universe. You want a fight? You got one. I told you I'd cut you, and now that you're going after the man I love, I will.

That's right, bitches. I'm going back to LA.

Chapter 46

I can get a composting toilet and
embrace a simple life.

Josie

THE BUS RIDE from San Francisco to Hollywood is eight hours and twenty-six minutes overnight, and I sleep on the way. I use the word *sleep* lightly. It's more accurate to say I lose consciousness repeatedly over the course of the trip, waking long enough to acknowledge the pain in my lower back and wipe the slobber from my headrest.

I arrive at the house, and after Emmy finishes hugging me for, like, a full three minutes, she brings me up to speed. There's still no sign of Sean or Miguel. Sean's private jet did log a flight to San Antonio, and the pilot said Sean and someone matching

Miguel's description were on it, but no one has any idea where they went from there.

"San Antonio?" I ask. "What's in San Antonio?"

"I was hoping you might know."

While we're talking, Peyton comes out of her room, ready for school. She shrieks when she sees me and throws her arms around my neck. "Tía!" she cries.

I squeeze her tight. "Hey, munchkin." It feels good to be home, even if it's just for a little while.

Once Peyton's on her way to school, I turn to Emmy. "I feel like we should check Sean's house for clues."

Emmy rubs her swollen abdomen, which has gotten even bigger in the six days I've been gone. "The police have already looked."

I've never felt so helpless. "We've got to do something!"

Emmy's arms come around me. "It's okay. It's going to be okay."

After how I treated her, she still comforts me. I squeeze her back. "I can't believe you don't hate me."

She pinches the fleshy part of my arm, hard.

"Ouch!"

"There. That's for keeping secrets from me for our entire friendship. Now forget about it. We need to be sharp. We need to think!"

"You said this happened after Sean saw my video." I grit my teeth. It took a lot out of me to make that video for Emmy. Being open about who I really am and all the ways I've screwed up wasn't easy. "If this is my fault…If they thought maybe I was in San Antonio, and something happened to them while they were looking for me—I couldn't handle that."

"No!" she shouts at me in the same Tony Robbins-esque way I've been known to do to her. The shock does keep me from breaking down completely. "This isn't your fault, Josie. And they're gonna be so happy when they hear you're safe."

"But they've been gone for days!"

Emmy's phone rings. "It's Jason! Hey, hon! What's up?"

I wring my hands as she listens and then reports to me. "Sean and Miguel are both at the studio!"

I gasp. "Are they okay? What happened?"

"He didn't say. Just that they're back."

Emmy grabs her keys from the hook in the kitchen, and I follow her to the car. My old trailer is still there in the side yard, glaring at me like it's judging me for leaving it. We'll have to talk about that later, trailer. But all my regular worries evaporate when we arrive at the lot. A throng of news crews has gathered just outside the main door of Studio 11.

My heart takes a dive, and I turn a quick one-eighty. San Francisco is looking better and better. Who needs a hot plate or a bed? I can get a composting toilet and embrace a simple life.

"Emmy, let's get out of here! We can find out what happened over the phone."

"Oh, no you don't!" Emmy grabs my arm. "We are *not* leaving until we have answers."

"I can't face them," I tell her, indicating the media.

Emmy takes a deep breath and bends forward, hands on her knees. Alarm bells go off in my head.

"What are you doing?"

"It's just Braxton-Hicks contractions. It's been happening a lot. Don't worry about me. Let's just figure out a way to get us inside without the news crews seeing you."

I spot Yesenia with her roller bag, headed for the side door. "Come on! I've got a plan."

I tow Emmy by the elbow while she sashays to try to go

faster. But before reaching Yesenia, I stop short behind a building. What if I ask for her help and she won't help me? What if she's angry about Chuy or upset that I never told her who I really was?

But Sean and Miguel are inside, and they've been missing for four days. I need to know what happened. I need to make sure they're okay.

I take a deep breath. "Yesenia!" I stage-whisper.

She stops and gives me a funny look rather than her usual happy greeting. That doesn't bode well. She approaches, and I brace myself for whatever it is she has to say.

"¿Es cierto?" she asks in Spanish.

Heat spreads across my face and neck. Every cell in my body wants to flee the scene, jump in a runaway car, and get the hell out of Dodge, but I anchor myself and reply in Spanish, "Yes, it's true." I wince, and my next words come out hesitant. "Were you a Chuy fan?"

"I watched the show a few times with my niece." She tilts her head, studying my features. "I never would have recognized you."

Relief overwhelms me. She's not mad. We're still friends, at least I hope we are. "Will you get us in?"

"Claro que sí."

I duck down and try to use Yesenia and her roller bag to block me from the view of the news crews as we scurry toward the side door, but, at five foot three, there's only so much blocking she can do. Not to mention, a pregnant woman about to pop draws a lot of attention. A camerawoman looks our way just as I poke my head out. Her arm comes up, finger pointing straight at me. Even if I couldn't hear her, I'd know what she was saying just by reading her lips.

"Josie Days! It's her!"

Shit.

The throng stirs and then flows toward us. Cameras and microphones bombard me. Questions echo in my ears.

"Josie Days, is it true Sean and Miguel are back?"

"Do you know anything about their disappearance?"

"Why would Sean kidnap Miguel?"

"Did he exhibit any other criminal behavior?"

I grit my teeth against the onslaught. It feels like the scene in that Alfred Hitchcock movie except I'm being pecked to death by reporters instead of birds. But I find myself more angry than terrified. They're going after Sean, not me.

Hells, no. Not on my watch.

I grab a mic. "I don't know anything about their disappearance, but Sean would never kidnap anyone. As for criminal behavior, that's ridiculous! He's the most kind and caring person I know. If I had to bet, I'd say Sean was going out of his way to help someone. That's the kind of person he is." I glare right into the camera lens. "And anyone who says anything different will have to deal with me."

Someone shouts from the back of the pack. "What are you going to do? Burn them up like you did with that puppet?"

Oh, so we have a heckler. "Why don't you come find out?"

He doesn't reply, and he doesn't come find out, thank goodness, because I have no follow-through.

"Anybody else have questions about the kind of person Sean O'Sullivan is?" I growl into the mic.

No one answers. I may be high on adrenaline and righteous indignation right now, but apparently no one wants to press their luck with the unhinged puppet assassin. Thank you, Savannah Bateman. I'm not sure Josie Days could've pulled that off without you.

"Oye! What's going on here?" The voice comes from behind me, and Miguel winds his way through the crowd.

"Miguel! Are you all right?" I seize his shoulders and study him, searching for signs of injury. "What happened? Where's Sean?"

"He's fine. He's inside."

"Thank God."

The back door bursts open. My heart leaps, and I whirl, expecting to see Sean emerge, safe and gorgeous and blasé as a men's underwear ad.

But it's not Sean. It's Lupe, a cigarette balanced between her fingers in that elegant way of women who actually learned how to smoke.

We lock eyes, and this time, there's nowhere for me to run to. She looks so different, and still the same. Beautiful and confident and in charge in her *Beyond the Stars* captain's uniform. My old insecurities rise up and shake off the dust of the years. New ones emerge as well. What will she say after all this time? What will she do? Did my reappearance ruin things for Castillo Studios again? If so, how badly?

A hush falls over the media. I'm not sure if it's one of awe and reverence because here is the person who was hurt most by my actions come to exact her revenge or if they're just admiring her astonishing, four-inch platform boots. She saunters up to me, hips swinging. Her jaw is still square and challenging. Her hard gaze still misses nothing. Lupe was always the smarter one.

"Sábana." A smile plays on her black-lipsticked lips, which may or may not have received some professional help over the years, along with her cleavage.

"Loopy," I reply, my nickname for her.

She pulls me into a hug, and I almost don't believe it's

happening. Like, even as she embraces me, I expect her to slide a hidden knife between my ribs, Shakespeare-style.

But her hug is real, if short. She ruffles my short purple locks. "Your hair!"

"Your boobs!"

She laughs out loud. "I can refer you to the doctor. She's amazing!"

The newspeople murmur around Miguel and Lupe, jockeying for their attention. But one reporter's voice cuts through the chatter.

"Lupe Castillo, are you really going to let your sister off the hook just like that? After she derailed your career?"

Lupe appears to ponder the question as she lights her cigarette. "My career is doing just fine. Besides, I was pretty mean to her back then. And jealous."

What? "You were jealous of me?"

"Papi indulged you so much. *Poor little Savannah. Be nice to her. Help her fit in.*" She rolls her perfectly made-up eyes.

"But those interviews and that photo of you crying." I'm not sure how to say this without sounding like a jerk. "You played it up. You didn't take any of the blame."

She chuckles dryly. "I mean, what did you expect? I was seventeen, and I'm an actress. But I did feel bad. And Papi grounded me for a long time. You weren't there, so I was the only one around to punish." I recognize the sly glint in her eye from all the times we faced Juan Ernesto's fatherly wrath together. "I suppose I deserved it."

I can't believe this is happening. "Are you...apologizing?"

She blows a plume of smoke at me. "Pues, sí. I guess so."

"Well, I'm sorry, too. Really sorry." This feels so weird, so anticlimactic. "By the way, I'm really happy for you with this *Lost Star* crossover thing and that award you were nominated for."

"Actually, we won. La Patria's Pick for best new sci-fi series."

My heart stutters. That's amazing news, but… "They gave it to you? Even after all this? Even after… me?"

Lupe scoffs. "Not everything's about you, brat."

I gasp with relief, with disbelief, with joy. "Congratulations!"

"I mean, don't get me wrong, having all this come out again sucks." She takes another drag and tosses a bored look to the press, who have crowded around Miguel. "But it is what it is."

I have to ask her something. I can't help myself. I lower my voice. "So, you and Miguel, huh? You used to say he was so pesado."

She scrunches her nose. "He's still annoying, and I think he likes boys more, but, you know…" She trails off.

I *don't* know, and, frankly, I'm dying to. But before I can ask, a reporter peels off and comes toward us. "Savannah Bateman, where is Chuy? Are you going to tell us?"

"Who cares?" Lupe drops her cigarette and grinds it out with the platform sole of her boot. "It's a stupid puppet from forever ago." She turns to me. "Come on, let's go inside."

I motion to Emmy and Yesenia, and we start to make our way to the studio door, but something doesn't feel right. I stop, and my companions halt along with me.

"What's wrong?" Emmy asks.

Her hazel eyes search mine. Normally, this is where I'd give her some sarcastic remark to hide my real feelings, but she's my best friend. It's time to change that.

"It feels like running again," I whisper.

She nods and looks pensive. "And you don't want to run anymore?"

I ponder that. "Sean says I can't run and hide every time things get hard. He says the only way to have meaningful relationships is to be honest."

She smiles. "Sounds like good advice from the captain."

Yes, it does. And even though my heart is pounding and my mouth is dry, I turn back to the throng and announce, "I have a statement to make."

Microphones materialize around me. Cameras zoom in on me with their dreaded little movements. I try to ignore the writhing snake nest in my stomach as the crowd falls silent.

I'm terrified beyond belief, not gonna lie. But I'm going to be honest with the world right now. And then, when I see him again, I'm going to be honest with the man I love. No more games, no more running, no more excuses.

In my mind's eye, I see Sean giving me that encouraging captainly nod. I open my mouth.

Here we go.

"I'm Josie Days, or Savannah Bateman, as some of you know me. I'm the girl from *Club Bilingüe* who called my sister a bitch on live TV, burned up Chuy the Puppet, and then hid his body. Remains. Whatever. I still haven't figured out what to call it. I know this has been a long time coming, but someone recently told me that it's never too late to apologize, so I'd like to do that now."

I sweep my gaze over the sea of cameras. "To the fans of *Club Bilingüe* and Chuy lovers everywhere, I'm sorry I lost my temper and destroyed our mascot. I didn't mean for any of that to happen. I was young, and Lupe and I were grumpy that night, and while I really did believe in what the show stood for, building bridges with my sister was easier some days than others." I take a breath. "I should've stuck around and faced the consequences, but I was embarrassed, and running away seemed easier. I regret that choice, and I'm sorry for any pain I caused."

"I'm sorry, too." Lupe appears at my shoulder, leaning into the mic. "I provoked her, and that wasn't very nice of me."

We exchange a smile, and my arm surprises me by wrapping around her shoulders. Suddenly I'm side-hugging my stepsister, an act which is definitely on the top ten list of things I didn't see happening today. Our theme song, "Friends Para Siempre," pops into my brain, and before I know what's happening, I'm overcome with warm fuzzies and launch into the first line.

"Don't do that." Lupe cuts me off from the side of her mouth.

I stop singing. "Too soon?"

We exchange a clandestine grin, and the nostalgia threatens to overwhelm me, but in the best way.

"Do you think Papi will ever forgive me?" I ask her, ignoring the barrage of follow-up questions coming our way.

"Why don't you ask him yourself? They flew in this morning to watch the taping."

I track her gaze to stage left where, on the edge of the crowd, my mother and stepfather stand together, watching us. Once they see that I've noticed them, they make their way forward, and before I know it, I'm wrapped in my mother's strong embrace.

"Savannah!" She pushes my hair back from my face and then steps back to toggle a smile between Lupe and me, the same way she used to do when we'd track her down in the courtyard of our house, begging for a snack.

From behind her, Juan Ernesto takes a hesitant step forward and stops. I don't move, either. The years of guilt and fear and dread are like cement in my veins. But this time, I don't let that stop me.

"Papi, I'm really sorry," I say.

At the same time, he says, "Savannah, lo siento tanto, hija."

We wind up in an awkward hug. When it ends, we all stand around looking at one another. A familiar sickening feeling washes over me. I've just reunited with my family, so why do I still feel like crap? Then I remember Sean's reaction to the video of my parents' interview.

Where's the part where they stick up for you? Where's the part where they say your safety is the most important thing? Where's the part where they tell you how much they want you to come home?

"I have something hard to tell you," I say, and I see Lupe's eyebrows jump. I step backward, giving myself space, and take a deep breath. "I know I screwed up, and I understand that the business was important. But it really hurt that you two, as my parents, didn't stick up for me." I'm shaking, my whole body— but on the inside. "I was eighteen years old. I'd made a huge mistake. I was embarrassed and scared and overwhelmed, and I needed someone to be on my side. To make me feel like I wasn't a total screw-up. To at least try to understand where I was coming from and to help me come back from it."

My gaze flicks to Lupe, who looks like she might like to have a big bag of popcorn to stuff in her face right about now as I confront our parents. That's okay. I'm doing this for her, too.

"You went to your father," Mom argues. "I thought that's what you wanted. You were an adult."

"I was an adult on paper," I concede. "But I was still a teenager. And I don't regret the time I spent with Dad, but it would have been nice for it to have felt like a choice rather than a necessity."

Mom starts to reply, but Juan Ernesto touches her arm, stopping her. "Let her speak, Lydia."

"All these years I've blamed myself. And, yes, I bear a lot of the responsibility. But I can't help but think that you could have found a way to manage the studio's reputation while still being there for me. Instead, you just…let me go."

As scary as that was, I feel a sense of relief. Whatever happens next, at least I was honest.

"You're right, Savannah," Juan Ernesto says in his gruff voice. "I prioritized the studio. There were a lot of people counting on me, and I took my responsibilities to them seriously. But it was wrong of me to let you take the fall. At the same time, I knew that you were struggling in Mexico. When you went to live with your father, I didn't feel it was my place to get in between the two of you."

"We didn't know you had changed your name," my mom adds, tearing up. "We didn't know you felt you had to go into hiding over it."

"I should have reached out," Juan Ernesto continues. "I chose to let sleeping dogs lie, and clearly that was the wrong choice."

It makes sense, now that I think about it, that Juan Ernesto didn't want to overstep when it came to my dad and me. I'd never thought about that. But…

"What about after my dad died?" I ask. "Why didn't you reach out then?"

He gives me a sad look. "So much time had passed. I didn't know what to do."

Wow. He was struggling in the same way I was.

"Sean is the fixer in his family," I tell my parents with a smile. "We don't have one in ours. That means we all have to do our part to fix things when they get broken."

There's a long pause, and the familiar anxiety grips me. Did I go too far? Will they reject me again?

Finally, Lupe steps up beside me. "I'm in."

Mom wipes her eyes and smiles. "Me, too."

Juan Ernesto opens his arms wide. "Yo también."

And before I realize it, we're in a four-way hug, and it feels really nice, even though I've never been that big of a hugger.

"Savannah Bateman!" the same reporter from before interrupts, "Where's Chuy the Puppet? Can you tell us?"

I stiffen. I promised Hugo the exclusive, and he should have found Chuy by now. Maybe his charred wooden body broke down in the soil. Maybe erosion got him, and he was washed away. Or maybe that one psychic was right and what's left of him somehow made its way to a flat in England.

"He's gone," I tell her sadly. "Chuy the Puppet is gone."

Just then, the door behind us *thunks* open, and my heart leaps. Sean struts out in his Captain Footwork costume. His green eyes are as serious as a leprechaun's heart attack. His pompadour is pristine. His lock of yellow hair catches the sun, glowing like spun gold. He's the captain, the main character, safe and sound, always escaping peril. He's carrying something in his arms. It looks like—

No.

It can't be.

My breath catches in my lungs. My knees buckle. My brain starts to short circuit because what I'm seeing isn't possible, physically speaking. I buried that thing twelve years ago in a graveyard, burned to a crisp. But Sean's holding it in his hands like none of that ever happened. Like my starship captain boyfriend went back in time and changed history. Like he's rescued Chuy from the jaws of ruin, perfectly intact, ugly as sin, and…wearing a space suit.

Chapter 47

Híjole is like wow, right?

**Transcript. *Hollywood, De Repente* with Hugo
  Valencia.**
November 6. *[translated from Spanish]*

HUGO: Ladies and gentlemen, *Hollywood, De Repente*
  comes before you today with news of great joy! Today, we
  have in the studio Sean O'Sullivan, along with a translator,
  and Miguel Angel Aguilar Porras. They've both had a bit
  of an adventure. I'll let them tell it.

MIGUEL: Good afternoon. It's a pleasure to be here.

SEAN: Hello.

HUGO: Let's get right to the point. You two were gone for over one hundred hours. And you came back with the beloved puppet Chuy, who has been missing for twelve years, in your arms. What happened? Start at the beginning.

MIGUEL: It all started the afternoon of Day of the Dead. We were done taping, and Sean invited me outside for a cigarette. Little did I know, he was going to force me into his car and make me help him drive to Mexico.

HUGO: Wow, that sounds harrowing. Sean, is that accurate?

SEAN: It's accurate, Hugo. And, fortunately, Miguel has decided not to press charges.

HUGO: And, Miguel, you're not upset with Sean?

MIGUEL: I was at first, but then he told me it was to protect me from being in breach of my contract. Plus, when he promised to introduce me to Robert Downey, Jr. at his next party, I forgave everything.

HUGO: And your phone that was found in the dumpster?

MIGUEL: That was so they couldn't track us. He got me a new one. The latest iPhone! With a really cute Orbit case.

SEAN: I got you, bro. Put 'er there.

[Sean holds out a fist, and Miguel bumps it.]

HUGO: What happened next?

MIGUEL: So, we stopped at his house to pick up his passport. The traffic was a nightmare. Probably the worst part of the trip.

SEAN: The 405 was terrible. But we made it through, didn't we, man?

[Sean and Miguel fist bump again.]

MIGUEL: We sure did. And we flew to San Antonio in his supercool private jet and rented a car to drive down. I'd never ridden in a private jet before. That thing had a fridge. And it had a bathroom. And it had leather seats. And it had—

HUGO: *[interrupts]* Let's fast-forward to how you recovered Chuy.

SEAN: What, Hugo? You mean you don't want to hear about all the beef jerky and Takis and chili-flavored candy involved in this trip? Or how hard it is to find an electric vehicle charging station in Mexico?

HUGO: You rented an electric vehicle to drive down to Mexico?

SEAN: I always drive electric. It offsets the carbon footprint of my jet. Go on, Miguel. Get to the good part.

MIGUEL: We drove all night and finally got down to Naolinco. But it was the day after the Fiesta de la Cantada, and the place was packed. People were everywhere. Some were still partying. And what happened with Chuy happened a long time ago, so I wasn't confident that we'd find him.

HUGO: Let me stop you there, Miguel, because I, too, was in Naolinco during La Cantada. I had been searching for Chuy for days using information Savannah Bateman gave me, with no luck. You mean to tell us that you've known where Chuy was all this time?

SEAN: *[interrupts]* No, he didn't. But *I* did! Josie told me she'd buried it in a cemetery near a tombstone with her name on it. In fact, she said that's how she picked her new name.

HUGO: *[grumbles]* She neglected to tell me that part. So, you're saying she buried Chuy near a tombstone with the name Josie Days?

SEAN: *[chuckles]* Yeah, that was the tricky part, see. I was looking for that, and I wasn't finding it, but then my buddy here, Miguel. God, I love you, man. We're such good friends now.

MIGUEL: Yeah. We are.

[Sean and Miguel fist bump a third time.]

SEAN: My bruh here, my second, my Number One, he says, "Maybe we should be looking for the Mexican version of her name." And I said, "What would that be?" And he points to a tombstone with the name José Díaz.

MIGUEL: José Díaz. Josie Days.

HUGO: Astounding!

SEAN: I saw this little bit of red cloth poking out from the dirt. And whaddaya know. It was Chuy's sleeve.

HUGO: Oh my, I'm getting emotional here.

SEAN: He was in bad shape, but salvageable. I just needed to get him back to my cosplay room where I could—

HUGO: Excuse me, your what?

SEAN: My workshop! Which has a sewing machine in it. When we got back, I cleaned him up, made him a new outfit.

HUGO: You sew?

SEAN: Yes, Hugo, I sew. My mother taught me.

HUGO: Did you witness this, Miguel?

MIGUEL: I was taking a nap on a raft in the pool, so I didn't see anything. All I know is, whatever he did, it took all the soot off Chuy's face. And he fixed his ears and made new clothes for him. I couldn't believe it!

SEAN: I was quite pleased with the outcome.

HUGO: Wow. I don't know what to say. And all this time you didn't tell anyone you were back?

SEAN: Well, I knew the length of time we'd been gone was going to be a problem. In my defense, I didn't realize it was going to take that long. As I mentioned before, there aren't a lot of charging stations on the route, and when you find one, sometimes there's a queue.

MIGUEL: I told him the electric car was a bad idea.

SEAN: Robert Downey, Jr. doesn't like gloaters, Miguel. Anyway, I felt like the best course of action was to come back with a big splashy opportunity that would detract from the fact that we'd held taping up for almost a week.

HUGO: And your big splashy opportunity was…

SEAN: To introduce Chuy into *Beyond the Stars*! I mean, after we let you break the story, of course. Chuy was always meant to be a symbol of friendship across cultures. I thought the crossover would be the perfect way to help him find his way back where he belongs, with Castillo Studios, representing friendship across galaxies.

HUGO: So, Chuy now has a role in the *Lost Star/Beyond the Stars* crossover thread?

SEAN: Well, we have to clear it with the producers first, but that's our hope.

HUGO: That's quite a story. I think we might all need a moment to process it. And I think many of us who love Chuy have to thank you both for recovering him, although, you know, some of us were very close and would have found him in the next day or so.

SEAN: Of course.

HUGO: But I have to ask you a question, Sean, on a more personal level.

SEAN: Okay, sure.

HUGO: Clearly, this was a big risk. Actors have lost their jobs over less. Not to mention the rumors that have been flying around about that stolen hat. Which raises the question…did you do this all for Savannah? Were you hoping it would act as a recompense for her past, bring her out of hiding, and, hopefully, help you win her back?

SEAN: That's a great question, Hugo. Did I jeopardize my job, kidnap a dude, and let the world think I'm an unhinged, desperate weirdo—not to mention risk jail time—all for Josie? *[pauses]* Yes. Yes, I did. And I'd do it again.

HUGO: Híjole.

SEAN: That's right. Híjole.

MIGUEL: Órale.

SEAN: *[to Miguel]* Órale? I thought it was híjole. *Híjole* is like *wow*, right?

MIGUEL: Yeah. And *órale* is like *right on*. And *órale wey* is like, *right on, man*!

SEAN: ¡Órale wey!

MIGUEL: ¡Ándale!

SEAN: Wait, what's *ándale*?

Chapter 48

Why aren't you listening, feet?

Josie

THE CROWD OF newspeople swarms him, and Sean hands off the puppet and announces in his Captain Footwork voice, "Tune in to Hugo Valencia's show. You'll get all your answers there!"

Then he heads straight to me, stopping about a foot away. "Hi."

I throw my arms around him, burying my face in his neck. "I was so worried about you! I'm glad you're not dead or ruined!"

"I am ruined. I ate street tacos, and they might have had brains in them." He holds me tightly, like he never wants to let go. "I was worried about you, too," he whispers into my hair. "I thought you were going back to Florida. I didn't realize you were disappearing."

"Well, you know, that's part of the whole disappearing thing. It doesn't work if you see it coming."

Around us, everyone is jockeying for a closer look at the resurrected (refurbished?) Chuy. Everyone except Emmy, who looks peaked and unhappy.

I frown. "Sean, I can't wait to hear all about what just happened here, but I think we need to get Emmy home."

Sean takes one look at her and raises an eyebrow. "Agreed. I'll text Snack to catch up with us."

I say goodbye to Yesenia and tell Miguel and my family that I'll meet up with them later. Jason joins us, and we head for the parking lot. Emmy is quiet. Too quiet—not at all like her. Halfway through zigzagging our way through the studio lot grid, she says, "Guys, I need to sit down." We walk her over to a shaded outdoor garden set with a tinkling fountain and a stone bench upon which she gingerly balances one butt cheek.

"Honey, are you okay?" Jason asks.

"I don't think Braxton and Hicks are going to the bar today." She meets his worried gaze with one of her own as her nostrils flare with a deep intake of breath.

"Okay! All right! We've got this!" Jason bounces on his toes. "We'll call the midwife and meet her at the house."

Emmy makes a noise I've never heard come out of a human before. It sounds like a siren for an incoming airstrike.

"Call the midwife," Sean says with zero humor. "Call her now, Snack!"

Emmy's not a big cusser, but she's opened up the f-bomb water main. Jason's flailing to find the right number in his phone. While I stand paralyzed with no idea how to help, Sean kneels next to Emmy.

"Do you feel pressure?" he asks, voice calm as he takes off his jacket and lays it on the fake grass at her feet.

"Midwife's on her way!" Jason announces, eyes wild.

"To the house or to here?" Emmy asks.

Jason's face falls. "Oh, crap!"

"Call her back, Snack," Sean says in the captain's voice. "Josie, see if you can find something to give us some privacy."

I don't do well with emergencies. I tell myself to go and grab the trellises leaning against the building next to us, but my feet don't listen. Why aren't you listening, feet?

"Josie, go!" Sean gives me a nudge. It short-circuits whatever loop I was in, and I lurch into action.

By the time I get a privacy area set up, Sean's got Jason's Hadron jacket off and draped over Emmy's lap as she perches on the edge of the bench. Jason looks like a bouncy ball, the good-looking boy-next-door version. Now Emmy's f-bomb main line has ruptured. It's a profanity tsunami up in here. I take a seat next to her on the bench. "What can I do?"

Emmy stops cussing long enough to whine in misery, "I can't believe Sean O'Sullivan is catching my baby! He's never going to shut up about it."

"I'm not catching your baby," Sean says. "Your husband is. Snack, you're needed down in engineering—stat!"

Jason drops to his knees on the faux grass. "What do I do?"

"Check and see if there's a head."

"How do I do that?"

"Use your imagination."

"There's a head!" Emmy shouts, writhing on the bench. "I can confirm it!"

Jason confirms it, too. Now he's got his own profanity leak underway.

"You're going to catch it when it comes out, just like a little medicine ball."

"How do you know how to do all this?" I ask Sean. Meanwhile, Emmy grabs my hand and squeezes it so hard, I'm afraid that she might break some bones.

Sean hesitates. "Siobhan would kill me if she finds out I ever told anyone, but…I actually had to catch my second nephew when he was born."

"What?"

"Yeah, we don't talk about it."

"Oh my God, it's coming, it's coming!" Jason yells.

"Hello!" someone calls from behind the barrier. "I'm a set medic. Can I help?"

"It's all under control. We'll shout if we need you," Sean says. When I give him a baffled look, he grins. "Snack's got this. Let him have his moment."

The two of them do seem to have everything under control. Jason is murmuring encouragement to Emmy, who has gone quiet and purple-faced during pushes but clearly knows what she's doing. She even manages to smile at him in the lull between contractions.

I wince at another bone-crunching squeeze of my hand and mutter, "If I ever have to go through this, I get to dress it in stripes. Nothing but stripes. That's a deal-breaker."

"I like stripes."

I shoot Sean a sideways look. "Tell me you did not just offer to sire my striped baby."

"I mean, it could happen. If you plan on sticking around long enough." His eyes flicker with hope before shifting to his go-to nonchalance. "I owe Miguel a party, and I could use some help getting Robert Downey, Jr. there. He might feel a little sheepish after beating me out for the Thunderstrike role."

"You didn't get the part? I'm sorry," I say, matching his blasé tone. "For what it's worth, I'm sure he'll do a much better job."

He breaks character, finally, shaking his head in amused disbelief.

"Too soon?"

I smirk at his struggle to maintain his straight-man facade. His hand rises to his mouth to hide a chuckle à la Ryan Gosling in *Crazy, Stupid, Love*, and then he straight-up bursts into laughter. He keeps laughing. He can't stop.

It's contagious. I try to hold back because my best friend is literally pushing out seven-to-ten pounds of human being right next to me, but I fail. Hard. I don't think Sean and I have ever laughed together like this. Actually, I'm sure we haven't.

"It's not your fault," I go on, fighting the giggles. "After that *Hamilton* performance, you've probably been typecast. Try auditioning for *Bridgerton*. Or *Outlander*. By the way, whatever happened with the hat?"

"I'm off the hook," he sputters. "The police found the real hat thief."

"Sounds like something the real hat thief would say."

At this point, our outbursts have become completely inappropriate, but I'm having too much fun to care. Laughing like this feels amazing. It's like all my pent-up feelings have finally found the escape hatch. Laughing with Sean feels even better.

"Oh my God, she's here! She's here!"

Emmy slumps against me, and I look down to see Jason holding a wet and slippery-looking baby of dubious coloring. He's beaming like it's an Oscar.

Híjole, it's like magic. One minute there's nothing, and the next—a whole new person.

Tears well up, and I try to hide them by looking over Emmy's shoulder as I fold her into a hug. "Look what you did," I whisper. "You're a freaking superhero. You're my idol."

"Congratulations!" Sean announces, the edges of his mouth still quirking up with unspent laughter. "Well done, Snack. Give her to Mom. She did all the work."

Jason carefully passes the baby to Emmy. She's mewling and already looking more pink than gray. She's tiny and perfect and beautiful, and I can't believe I got to be here for her grand entrance into the world. I also can't believe I almost missed it.

What a fool I would've been to let myself miss this.

Sean moves the barrier aside so the medic can come in with one of those silver blankets and a stethoscope. We step away to give them space, and Sean's arms find their place around me, easy, confident, comfortable.

"That was amazing!" I gush, the sarcasm temporarily ripped from me. "Wasn't that amazing?"

"It was pretty amazing," Sean agrees.

"And you almost ended up catching Emmy's baby after all!"

"Trust me, I never wanted to. I just said all that stuff to give Snack the confidence in case he had to do it. Second babies come fast."

"Siobhan would know, huh?"

"I told you, we don't talk about that." He kisses my temple and whispers into my hair, "I'm so glad you're back. I mean, I don't know if you're, like, *back* back." He pauses. "But I hope you are."

I hesitate. It feels surreal, this moment, like it shouldn't be happening, like the laws of physics shouldn't allow it. I'm in LA with Sean, I'm jobless, my cover is blown, and, to top it all off, my family is here.

The sky has fallen, and yet, when I look up, the sun is still there.

"Well, you know, *back* back is a strong way of putting it," I tell him, watching Emmy and Jason marvel over their new daughter, both of them grinning like maniacs. "But Emmy's going to need some help, and the slums of San Francisco are surprisingly overrated…plus, I'd really like to see where things go with this amazing guy I've been dating."

Sean cups my face and touches his forehead to mine. "I'm glad to hear that."

I trace the ringed fingers caressing the line of my jaw. "If I'd said *no*, were you going to kidnap me and put me in that locked room of yours?"

"Yes, I was. And I'm so relieved because now I don't have to remodel it. I was really struggling with the color palette."

"I hope you weren't going to go with yellow. Being a kidnap victim is stressful enough."

"For what it's worth, I was gonna put a hot tub in it for you."

"Nice. We can soak in it together—you, me, and Seamus."

"Seamus is gone. I called a family meeting, and together we convinced him to go into rehab. He needs more help than any of us can give him."

"Did you punch him until he cried first?" I joke.

He chuckles. "I tried, but he's a fast little bugger."

I study his face. Something's changed in Sean. His smile is wider and more genuine, radiant and relaxed. It dawns on me that all this time he's been holding back, putting on a mask, controlling the narrative with me, maybe even with himself. It doesn't feel like he's doing that anymore. Being with him now, like this, feels real. Authentic. Wonderful. Limitless.

I give him a brazen, uninhibited kiss, even though there are cameras everywhere and this place is literally crawling with paparazzi. Let them take their pictures. Let them talk. Let them judge, for good or bad. I'm never hiding again.

I guess something's changed in me, too.

"I can't believe you drove to Mexico and dug up Chuy from a graveyard for me," I murmur against his lips. "What kind of a weirdo does that?"

He pulls me in tight. "The kind who's completely and totally obsessed with you."

"Good." I don't suppress my smile. "Because I'm completely and totally obsessed with you, too."

He kisses me slowly, deeply, and the world disappears. My neurons all self-destruct, my blood boils off, and I start to wonder if this is what all those losers out there mean when they talk about being quote unquote *happy*. I'm not just talking about the kiss, either, although if kissing Sean O'Sullivan for eternity were my fate, I assure you, there would be zero complaints. I'm talking about my Schrödinger's life. I've opened the box, and yet it still feels like anything is possible. I've got these people in my life—Sean, Emmy, Peyton, Jason, and my family and friends in Mexico. Their love is the brand of love I need. Our narrative is the one that matters, whether I'm canceled or not.

I break our kiss, much as it pains me to do so. His mouth really is a portal to sexy Narnia. "So, uh, the next time we're at your place, would you put the Han Solo costume back on for me?"

"Sure thing." He kisses me some more, and I try not to fall completely apart. "You like it, huh?"

"I do. I'd like to dress you in it and then undress you, over and over again, like a Ken doll."

He smiles against my lips, and it's sexy as hell. "In that case, I can't wait to show you what's really behind that locked door."

Epilogue

HARPER: Hey, everyone, we're back with another round of *Harper's Hot Seat* with cast members from the *Lost Star* and *Beyond the Stars* crossover. Welcome, Sean O'Sullivan, Amanda Trett, Jason Connor, Miguel Aguilar, Josie Days, and Lupe Castillo with special guest Chuy the Puppet. Let's get right to it. Sean, you're up first. What's your favorite character to cosplay?

SEAN: Cosplay? What? That's for losers. Just kidding. Lately, I've had fun being a Hobbit. I got a pair of those big hairy feet. Elevensies!

HARPER: Josie, what's a typical date like with Sean?

JOSIE: Singing show tunes in his palace chiseled from emeralds.

SEAN: They aren't real emeralds.

HARPER: Jason, coolest thing you've ever done?

JASON: Catching Boba Tea, I mean, Chloe, when she was born.

HARPER: Aw, that's sweet. Miguel, your favorite Avenger?

MIGUEL: Iron Man! I love you three thousand, RDJ! Congratulations on landing the role of Thunderstrike! Can't wait to meet you at Sean's party!

SEAN: Dude, we need to talk about subtlety.

HARPER: Chuy, what's your favorite part of being on TV again?

CHUY: Being with all my amigos.

HARPER: Aren't you adorable?

CHUY: Except her.

HARPER: Who? You mean Josie?

CHUY: Yes, her. My murderer.

JOSIE: *[to Lupe]* I know where your hotel room is.

HARPER: Amanda, what is something you suck at?

AMANDA: Nothing! I'm good at everything. Wait… swimming.

SEAN: You can't swim?

AMANDA: I didn't say I can't swim, I said I suck at it.

HARPER: Jason, what's the craziest thing a fan ever gave you?

JASON: A daughter.

HARPER: Rrrright. Josie, how do you take your coffee?

JOSIE: Like my men, hot and Irish.

SEAN: *[leans over to kiss Josie]* And with sugar.

AMANDA: Irish coffee includes sugar. It's in the definition.

SEAN: *[kisses Josie again]* With extra sugar.

JOSIE: *[kisses him back]* And first thing in the morning.

AMANDA: You two are weirdos.

SEAN: *[smiles]* Yes. Yes, we are.

Acknowledgments

First of all, this book would not exist if I had not had the opportunity to travel and experience life in different countries and cultures. Thank you to all of my friends and colleagues in Spain and Mexico, as well as their families, who opened their homes and their hearts to a twentysomething American girl with wanderlust and passable Spanish. I appreciate your friendship and all of the wonderful cultural and culinary experiences you shared with me. (Specifically, to my ex-boyfriend and his brother in Veracruz: I'm sorry for that time I cussed in front of your mom and she blamed you. You guys used that word *all the time*, and I sincerely did not know it was considered profanity.) For the inquiring minds, yes, the Mexican bus story did happen to me. Luckily, there was a piece of plexiglass in between me and the rest of the coach, so no one saw. And, yes, it was a long time ago, but I do also want to thank a particular group of Latinx boys at the University of South Florida who took me under their wing and brought me along to salsa night in downtown Tampa on Tuesdays. Those were some fun times. At the end of the day, I hope this book helps to build some bridges and maybe even inspires a few people to learn a new language. At the very least, I hope it is a reminder that across every language and culture, we are all on the same human journey, and the desire for true human connection is universal.

As for book stuff, I cannot thank my agent Cathie Hedrick-Armstrong enough for bringing me in and championing me. Also, Alex Logan, my editor, who pointed out all of the parts of this book that were "not sexy" (I fixed them) and encouraged my *Hamilton* obsession. Thank you to my daughters, Kira, Ocean, Shea, and Megan, my son-in-law, Taylor, and my grandsons, Ashur, Ezra, and Malachi for providing happy distraction and cheering me along the way. And to my parents, Jim and Lucia, who not only shouted my praises from the rooftops but also helped me through an extremely difficult time personally as I was finishing this book. I couldn't have made it through without your support.

I owe a huge debt of gratitude to my Sprinters, especially Lisa Amowitz, Emily Colin, and Angela Sierra, who took the time to read early versions of this and give invaluable feedback. Also, Sara Anderson, Rachael Peery, and John Klekamp for all the times they read excerpts and kept my spirits high. My Write Squad peeps will always get a mention for being my first critique partners and online writer friends: Shannon Balloon, Joel Brigham, Audrey Burges, Kelly Kates, and Kelly Ohlert. Love you guys. Also, thanks to the Florida STAR Fiction Writers and my Thursday night Barnes & Noble crew, Heather Montgomery, Keiti Pierce, Naomi Bellina, and Ann McIntosh.

A big shout-out goes to Tina Purcell and Bonnie Swanson. I also want to thank the entire team at Grand Central/Forever, including my amazing publicist, Caroline Green, as well as art director Daniela Medina, production editor Jeff Holt, interior designer Taylor Navis, assistant editor Grace Fischetti, and early reader Sofia Erreguerena. Thank you to all of the booksellers, librarians, Bookstagrammers (especially Corrine Minshall—you are a star!), BookTokers, bloggers, reviewers, journalists, book clubs (thank you, Aunt Kim and Azil Malan), festival and event organizers, and podcasters. A special thank-you to Stephanie Carr, the Literary Hypewoman, for your enthusiastic hyping of *Celebrity Crush* as well as scoring me an invite to the Tampa Bay Comic Con and a slot on Daytime TV. I would not have gotten that hug and peck on the cheek from Gimli, son of Gloin, without you!

To my BFF, Minna, the inspiration for Josie, thank you for your love and support over these past forty years that we've known each other and for much of the fodder for these books. Also, can you believe the day has come when I get to dedicate a book to you???

Lastly, I feel like I would be remiss if I did not give a little shout-out to some of the celebrities who inspired this book. Robert Downey, Jr., I dipped into the confidence of Tony Stark to help with Sean's captainly demeanor, so thank you for that. I hope you don't mind the homage. Lin-Manuel Miranda, I have never been a musical theater person, but my daughters started obsessing over *Hamilton*, and once I watched it, I was hooked. Christopher Jackson, yes, I have a crush on your George Washington. (Is it that obvious?) And if anyone, anywhere, is ever tempted to make *Hamilton on the Roof* a reality, please, please, please drop me a line.

About the Author

Christy Swift writes nerdy romcoms and is a sci-fi fangirl who loves it all, from Star Trek to *Firefly* to the MCU. She has lived in many places including Spain, Mexico, Canada, and all over Florida. She loves the ocean, geeky board games, and watching her four daughters and three grandsons grow into the people they're meant to be. In her spare time, you can find her watching rockets launch or kayaking through bioluminescent waterways, dreaming up new stories.

RAISING READERS
Books Build Bright Futures

Thank you for reading this book and for being a reader of books in general. We are so grateful to share being part of a community of readers with you, and we hope you will join us in passing our love of books on to the next generation of readers.

Did you know that reading for enjoyment is the single biggest predictor of a child's future happiness and success?

More than family circumstances, parents' educational background, or income, reading impacts a child's future academic performance, emotional well-being, communication skills, economic security, ambition, and happiness.

Studies show that kids reading for enjoyment in the US is in rapid decline:

- In 2012, 53% of 9-year-olds read almost every day. Just 10 years later, in 2022, the number had fallen to 39%.
- In 2012, 27% of 13-year-olds read for fun daily. By 2023, that number was just 14%.

Together, we can commit to **Raising Readers** and change this trend. How?

- Read to children in your life daily.
- Model reading as a fun activity.
- Reduce screen time.
- Start a family, school, or community book club.
- Visit bookstores and libraries regularly.
- Listen to audiobooks.
- Read the book before you see the movie.
- Encourage your child to read aloud to a pet or stuffed animal.
- Give books as gifts.
- Donate books to families and communities in need.

BOB1217

Books build bright futures, and **Raising Readers** is our shared responsibility.

For more information, visit **JoinRaisingReaders.com**

Sources: National Endowment for the Arts, National Assessment of Educational Progress, WorldBookDay.com, Nielsen BookData's 2023 "Understanding the Children's Book Consumer"